THE ATOPIA CHRONICLES

by Matthew Mather

47NORTH

Text copyright © 2013 by Matthew Mather
Originally published in 2012 by Matthew Mather

Published by 47North, Seattle
www.apub.com

ISBN-13: 9781477849286
ISBN-10: 1477849289
Library of Congress Control Number: 2013944438

Cover illustrated by Paul Youll
Cover designed by Jason Gurley

In memory of my uncle, Michael Knuckey.
Thanks for helping put the stars in my eyes.

Prologue

"ARE YOU SURE?"

Atopia wasn't only about perfecting synthetic reality. As senior researcher, my own pet project was the deep neutrino array. We'd seeded the Pacific Ocean basin with a vast carpet of sensor-mote networks of photoreceptors, searching out the blackness of the depths for flashes of Cherenkov radiation that signaled the passing of neutrinos. The POND—Pacific Ocean Neutrino Detector—was our part of the quest to verify predictions of neutrinos from parallel universes passing through our own.

"The signal is there, Dr. Killiam," replied my researcher.

"Don't release any results. Not yet. Run all the tests again and see if it stays. Not a word to anyone, you understand?"

Neutrinos were maddeningly difficult to work with. Even with a planetary-scale telescope like the POND, it wouldn't have been the first time an experiment with them had gone wrong.

My researcher nodded earnestly, keeping her eyes on me. I'd better keep an agent watching her. The slightest leak to the press of something of this magnitude would be sure to destabilize the timeline we were trying to follow.

"Are you sure this isn't coming from a terrestrial source?"

"We're sure, Dr. Killiam."

"Don't tell anyone," I repeated. "Keep this absolutely secret to us three."

"Not even Kesselring?"

"Especially not Kesselring."

How is it possible this is happening now? I cringed thinking of what Cognix might do if they heard of this. "Once you've run the tests again, shut it all down."

"Yes, Dr. Killiam."

I was about to let my primary subjective leave this space when the researcher grabbed my arm.

"One more thing," she said.

I waited, watching fear creep into her eyes.

"We applied the full battery of communication memes to the signal to see if we could decipher anything."

"And?"

"It's not really clear...."

"Out with it," I encouraged.

She took a deep breath. "It seems to be some kind of a warning."

◆◆◆ BLUE SKIES

Part I:

Olympia Onassis

1

Identity: Olympia Onassis

"NO! NO! YOUR other left!" I barked, gesturing toward the pack of cigarettes I wanted. My heart was still pounding after the screaming fight I'd had with Alex in the street outside. He'd wanted us to move in together—or rather, he'd wanted to move in with me. I wasn't ready, and frankly I wasn't sure I'd *ever* be. We'd just broken up, and this time for the *last* time.

It wasn't helping that I hadn't slept properly in weeks.

The pharmacist behind the counter stared at me and began speaking in something foreign. Even with languages going extinct faster than frogs, I'd read that the city still had nearly a thousand spoken throughout its many boroughs. What a mess.

He shrugged as if to say, "Now what?"

The rumbling impatience of the line behind me almost overcame my need for nicotine. Almost, but not quite. Buying one stupid pack of cigarettes required a pharmacist to personally verify my nano-cleaning certification, and I wasn't about to go through this hassle all over again.

"Wait a minute!" I held up one hand and rummaged around in my purse for my mobile with the other. Squeamish of surgical implants, I still used an old-fashioned earbud. Acutely aware of the eyes on me, I popped it into my ear.

"Camel Lights!" I repeated, jabbing my finger at the display case.

Whatever language he was speaking was instantly translated. "Like I said, lady, those aren't Camels. The package looks the same, but you'll have to go across the street to find those." He pointed hopefully out the door.

I sighed. "Whatever, that's fine, whatever those are."

Reaching into the display, he handed them over, and I grabbed them and began pushing my way back through the crowd toward the entrance, credits for the transaction automatically charged to me as I opened the pack. I banged open the door to the street as I stormed out, startling the incoming customers.

Smoking was a bad habit I'd picked up from my mother. We hadn't spoken in years, but then she'd barely ever shown any interest in me when we had. She'd shown about as much interest in my father, eventually driving him away to some kind of Luddite commune back in Montana with the rest of his family. I hadn't been able to reach him in almost as long as I hadn't spoken to my mother, and it wasn't something I was going to forgive her for anytime soon.

I stopped just outside the door of the pharmacy to light up, closing my eyes and taking a deep drag.

Midtown blazed away before me in an orgy of advertising. Almost every square inch of space, from lamppost to sidewalk, was full of commercials heralding a new Broadway show or multiverse world. A holographic head danced above me, sparkling and wobbling as the smoke from my cigarette drifted up into it. "Come to Titan, experience the methane rain."

Taking another drag, I glanced up at the grinning head. "Experience the methane rain?" *Not exactly sexy.* They should have been pitching something like, "Take her to new heights—make love in the hydrocarbon desert." I laughed grimly to myself—"make love," now there was something alien, never- mind Titan.

Without warning, the metallic robotic surrogate I'd noticed lining up behind me in the shop came barreling into me, pinning me hard against the wall. It fumbled at me. Blood drained from my face in shock, but my confusion and fear were quickly replaced by a bolt of fury, and I lashed back, yelling and flailing.

"Get off me!"

It bounced back much more easily than I'd anticipated. We stood staring at each other for a moment, my angry gaze meeting its dead, gunmetal-grey orbs. With what I could only interpret as a furtive glance, it shifted its shoulders in an oddly mechanical shrug before turning to disappear into the stream of pedestrian traffic. I lurched forward to give chase but gave up almost instantly.

I was shaking.

Breathing raggedly, I wiped spittle from the side of my mouth. Looking down, I noticed that he had stolen my cigarette pack. The tremble in my hands matched the wobble of the hologram touting Titan above me. In my right hand, the cigarette continued to burn away, unconcerned.

Nobody walking by seemed to have noticed anything, or at least, nobody had wanted to notice anything. I guess it was just after the cigarettes, although why a robot would want cigarettes was beyond me.

This goddamn city.

I had half a mind to call Alex, but remembered the fight we just had, and I was already late for my presentation. Still shaking, I dropped my smoke and ground it out underfoot before venturing out from under the awning to merge into the sea of pedestrians flowing down West Fifty-Seventh Street.

Surging with the crowd, I watched for a current that could carry me toward the curb. Up ahead, someone swore out loud and then stopped. His arrested momentum forced a wave of people to flow outward and around him.

This was my chance.

Sailing up beside him, I ducked in behind and was caught perfectly in the opposite flow going in the direction I needed. Then

I ran straight smack into a ridiculous-looking woman in sparkling red body paint and peacock feathers.

"Out of my way!" I growled. Shoving her aside, I rotated toward the edge of the street and elbowed my way to the curb, where I stretched out my arm to join with the forest of other outstretched limbs.

"Ten! Ten!" I yelled at the top of my lungs, offering ten times the going rate. I was tired and frightened and wanted to get out of there.

A cab slipped from traffic to pull up beside me, my generosity earning me dirty looks from the people around me trying to snag their own ride. In return, I offered them my finger as the tiny gull-wing door of the cab opened.

I stepped inside and sat down. Cool, recycled air swept around me as the door clicked shut. I took a moment to collect myself, closing my eyes, exhaling softly, trying to relieve the pressure.

"Where to, lady?" chimed a metallic voice. It was a self-driving electric, one of those Hondasoft ones with the motors in the wheels—barely more than a plastic tub on roller skates, if you asked me, but a cab nonetheless.

I took a deep breath. "Ah . . . ." What the hell was my office address? I sat upright in a panic. What was wrong with me? I'd worked there for over ten years.

"Lady, where to?"

"One second," I snapped. Remembering I still had the mobile bud in place, I called up my tech assistant. "Kenny, what's our office address?"

"555 Fifth Avenue," a perplexed Kenny responded almost instantly, which I relayed to the cabbie.

My face flushed. How could I have forgotten my own office address? I needed a drink. The cab immediately accelerated and merged into traffic. Sitting back I took some deep breaths, trying to loosen up the tightness in my chest while we sped off.

2

Carefully taking one bright paper napkin from the black conference room table, I wiped the sweat from the nape of my neck. I was nervous. Patricia Killiam, the famous godmother of synthetic reality, had decided to personally attend the marketing meeting we had planned today, or at least her bio-simulation *proxxi* had.

This was much the same thing to Atopians.

The new Cognix account was the biggest to ever come through our office, and I'd been named as the lead for closing the deal. By winning it, I could finally step out from the shadows and take center stage. The pressure was intense.

I'd had to rush to get there, sprinting the last yards from the elevators, but I'd made it just in time. They'd immediately jumped me into my presentation to the Cognix people. My pitch was a mess—the incident with the robot and my blank-out in the cab had really thrown me—and my timing was off.

Well, at least my part was done. I sat back and watched my colleague Bertram finish the presentation.

I was thinking of my fight with Alex. It wasn't just about living together. He was always on me to spend more time with his family, his brothers and sisters, but they always seemed to ready to critique me. It was a constant source of friction between us, made worse when he kept insisting that it was just my own insecurities. Raised in a big family, he wanted kids, but I had no idea how anyone could want to bring a child into this world. It was falling apart.

Out of the corner of my eye, I saw an incoming email from the Washington Heights orphanage I was working with. Maybe I didn't want to have a kid with Alex, but that didn't mean I didn't care. I understood what it was like to be left alone. But that was my business. I erased the message before anyone else could see it.

I looked back up at Bertram. After the endless overtime I'd put into this account, I couldn't believe my boss had almost given Bertram the lead on closing it. Floppy mop of brown hair, pantomiming away in that ridiculous multi-phasic suit, laughing at his own jokes. Judging from the way everyone was reacting to his end of the pitch, however, whatever he was doing was working. I could almost feel my career slipping away.

I needed a smoke.

Maybe I was getting too old for this. Kids nowadays had AIs running around doing most of their jobs for them. I had a hard time keeping up with it all. Thinking about kids made me think about Alex again. Had I made a terrible mistake? My stomach lurched.

"Cognix, making tomorrow your today!" gushed Bertram as he finished up, sweeping his hand into the distance with a flourish.

There was a smattering of applause.

Wait a minute. That's my tagline. What was he doing presenting that today? I was supposed to be using it tomorrow. I thought we'd agreed.

My boss glanced at me. "Something wrong, Olympia?" The epitome of middle-management, Roger always had a coffee cup in hand and a seemingly unending supply of ill-fitting suits and cheap ties. "Do you have anything to add?" He lifted his coffee to take a sip. Everyone turned to look at me.

My God, it's stuffy in here.

"I, uh, I…," I stammered, but I couldn't get anything out.

It seemed as if all the air in the room evacuated, and a crushing pain tightened my chest like a vise. Wrenching myself up from the table I fled through the door in search of air.

"Someone call a doctor!" I heard Roger yelling behind me. My vision faded and blackness descended.

3

"Nothing more than a simple panic attack." The doctor's bald pate reflected the overhead panel lighting like a shimmering, sweaty halo above his radiantly clean lab coat. A stethoscope hung uselessly around his neck. He leaned forward over his desk and clasped his hands, bringing them up to support his chin in what I assumed was his thoughtful pose. "Are you still smoking?"

A stupid question. Of course he knew.

"Yes, but I stay fit."

He nodded and looked at his notes, sensing this was a fight he didn't want to get into. "This could be fixable via medication—"

"I'm trying to keep on an organic farmaceutical diet," I interrupted. "I need to limit the medications."

Something about him reminded me of the endless string of men my mother had dated after my father left. My parents' relationship had been doomed from the start—trying to mix a Greek and a Scot was a surefire recipe for disaster.

The doctor stared at me, considering what to say next. "Stress and anxiety are the big killers these days. You really need to take care of this."

They'd had me as an excuse to try to justify their angry entanglement, a glue that hadn't worked despite their best attempts to argue and fight their way through it. In the process, neither of them had paid much attention to me. I'd taken my mother's name, Onassis, as an adult. It was the only thing I wanted from her anymore.

"Olympia, are you all right?" The doctor had noticed my attention wandering.

"Yes, yes." I just wanted to get out of there. "But there must be something else. What about more nanobots?"

"Those still use medications," he explained. "Mostly they're just delivery systems."

"So I have to figure this out myself." I rolled my eyes. "Meditation, relaxation. . . ." *What a load of bullshit*, I didn't need to add.

"That would probably work best in the long term, but I'm not so sure in your case."

"So what are you suggesting?" Why couldn't he get to the point already?

He took a deep breath. "I think we have something perfect for you, but I've been weighing the options."

"And?" I waited for his revelation. He struck another irritatingly thoughtful pose.

"Stress and anxiety are deeply rooted problems in society," he replied calmly. "While they respond to drugs, these don't correct the underlying issues. Medical science has found ways to fix most major diseases, but the mind is a tricky thing. . . ."

He adjusted himself in his seat. "There's a new synthetic reality system that we've been testing with select clients," he began, raising his hands to fend off my objections. "Before you say anything, there are no implants, nothing surgical anyway. You've already used the delivery nanobots, and this is just one step further."

I wagged my head. "Okay. . . ."

"All you do is swallow a pill with a glass of water. Nanoscale devices in the pill called 'smarticles' diffuse through your body and attach themselves to your neural system. They're able to modify signals flowing through your neurons—"

My attention began to wander again and the doctor could see it. I hated technical mumbo-jumbo.

He stopped and looked at me before continuing, "If you ever decide you don't like or want it anymore, a simple verbal command deactivates the whole thing and it washes back out of your system and is excreted. It's as simple as that."

He smiled, but now I smiled back. I'd realized what it was that he was describing.

"And it's been tested?" I asked.

This must be the new Atopian Cognix system we were pitching at the office. It wasn't on the market yet, but I knew they were doing restricted trials. I brightened up. It looked like someone on top had given me the nod. Maybe I would win the account after all.

"The system has been in clinical trials for years already and is fairly well understood. I can't give you the brand name, but that shouldn't make any difference. Does it?"

I was sure he knew I knew what he was talking about, but he had to go through the motions anyway. I played along, knowing that all this would be reviewed by someone at Cognix as soon as I gave my consent.

"No, not really, but if you say it'll help," I replied, trying to conceal my glee. I wondered if he would be feeding me any of my own marketing spiel.

"One of the major causes of stress and anxiety is advertising." He paused, knowing I was an advertising executive. "My recommendation is that you should use this system to remove advertising from your environment for a time; see how you feel."

"Sure, that sounds like a good idea."

He seemed unsure whether I was being sarcastic or not, but he could sense my mood lightening. "Should I write you a prescription?"

I nodded. "So I'll have complete control over it?"

"Of course."

A pause while we looked at each other.

"Are you ready?"

"What, now?"

"If you're ready...."

Another pause, and then I nodded again. The mobile, still in my ear, chimed softly as it received the electronic prescription from the doctor's automated assistant.

The doctor filled a small paper cup from a bottle of water in the cabinet behind his desk and handed it to me along with a small white tablet.

"Just swallow this. It includes a sedative to help keep you immobile during the initial data-gathering session."

I took the pill and cup from him. He looked me in the eye.

"Olympia, do you give your consent to give your personal data to the program?"

I nodded once more.

"This includes background personal data, you understand?"

"Yes," I replied.

"We won't be able to activate it today. You'll have to come back later in the week, but we can install it now."

I studied the pill briefly, popped it into my mouth and washed it down, then handed the empty cup back to him.

"Follow me." He stood up and led me out of his office and into a smaller room containing a human-shaped pod. It looked like one of those old tanning beds. "You'll need to completely undress."

I lazily complied. The sedative was already taking hold and my brain had started swimming peacefully. I lay down in the pod, and the gooey gel inside it conformed around my body.

"Now just relax." He lowered the top of the enclosure.

It suctioned onto me, completely enveloping my body. In a dream-like state I felt tiny fingers probing and tickling me, lights and patterns flashing in my eyes, and sounds like some kind of hearing test. My muscles twitched as small electric shocks raced back and forth across my body. Sweet and salty liquids washed through my mouth as my nostrils filled with acrid smoke, and the whole thing cycled from hot to cold and back again.

I fell asleep and dreamt of flying above fields of golden daisies with sunshine filling a perfect golden sky. I dreamt of babies with blue eyes, alive but never living, their blue eyes filling blue seas with blue pain.

4

"Olympia...."

"Olympia," came the voice again.

I was floating, peacefully alone, and some pestering thing had broken the tranquility. My brain tried to ignore it, but....

"Olympia?"

I reluctantly opened my eyes to find an angel hovering above me, an angel that somehow reminded me of my cat, Mr. Tweedles. No wait, not an angel, it was a nurse. That's right. A few days ago I'd installed that system, and I was back at the doctor's office getting it activated. They'd sedated me again. Closing my eyes, I brought up a hand to rub my face, and then opened them and sighed irritably. "Yes?"

"Seems like someone needs a little more sleepy time," laughed the nurse. "Come on, I'll get you up and dressed."

I propped myself up on my elbows and frowned at her. "How long was I out?"

"Hmm...," she considered. "About two hours, I'd say. Everything seems to be working perfectly. We just activated the system. Your proxxi will explain everything to you once you get home. I would have woken you sooner, but you seemed so peaceful."

Shaking my head, I swung my legs off the side of the pod as I sat up, pushing off her attempts to help me. "I can take it from here, thank you very much."

She looked at me and narrowed her eyes, but then her smile returned and she turned to go. "I'm going to bring you in to speak to the doctor before you leave—he needs to have a final word," she said on her way out and closed the door behind her.

After a minute or two I finished getting dressed and opened the door to walk into the hallway. The nurse watched me from a distance, studying me. I stopped at the doctor's office and half-hung my head inside.

"How do you feel?" he asked immediately, looking up from some paperwork. "Please, come in."

"No, no, I'm fine. I mean, I just want to get going. I've got things to do. So just tell me quick, what do I need to know?"

He paused. "You have a very powerful new tool at your disposal. Be careful with it, and don't activate any of the distributed consciousness features yet."

"Distributed consciousness," I snorted, looking back toward the nurse who'd positioned herself behind me in the hallway. "Where do they get these ideas?"

"If you want to talk with me," the doctor continued patiently, "just say my name anytime of the day or night and you will be instantly patched through to me."

"Great," I replied. "Got it."

"When you get home today, just say 'pssi instructions' and you will get all the information you need from your new proxxi."

"Perfect." I felt almost cheerful, sensing an imminent exit. "I'll be in touch."

With the tiniest of waves I bid him good-bye and marched off down the hallway and out the door, purposely ignoring the nurse who watched me the whole way out.

The air outside was crisp and fresh, and for the first time in ages I felt a surge of optimism. *I should walk home—I could use a breath of fresh air.*

I stopped to light a cigarette.

I'd decided that I hadn't made a mistake with Alex. I needed to be alone for a while.

The heat of late summer was just winding down, and the air had a refreshing edge. I strode energetically along the sidewalks, enjoying myself, looking at everything around me.

I didn't feel any different, and a part of me doubted that whatever they had done would work as well as it was billed—despite that I was marketing it. The crowds on the Upper East Side were dense but navigable, with billboards and holograms cluttering the view, but it still made for a nice walk. Eventually, I arrived at the personal oasis of my brownstone walk-up.

Mr. Tweedles sprang at me the moment I opened the door and began purring loudly as he rubbed himself against my pant leg. I closed the door and emptied my pockets. The cat had been my friend Mary's idea. *To provide some companionship*, she'd said. I shooed him away, hating the thought of all the hair he was depositing on me with each purring caress.

Immediately, I made for the bottle of wine on my kitchen counter and poured myself a glass. Collapsing onto my couch, I drank a big mouthful, savoring it. Rummaging around in my purse, I found the last cigarette in my pack. With all this technological wizardry, you'd think they could invent a realistic endless cigarette—those e-cigarettes were just so unsatisfying. I crumpled up the empty cardboard packaging and threw it onto the table.

Might as well get it over with. "Pssi instructions," I called out, lighting up my smoke.

"System activated," I heard from a voice that seemed to be inside my head. "I will now appear on the chair beside you. Please do not be alarmed."

With that, something materialized beside me sitting on my matching armchair, something that looked sort of like me. In fact, it looked *exactly* like me.

"I am your new polysynthetic sensory interface—or pssi— proxxi," it said. "I will now explain the system features to you. You can stop me at any time."

"Wait, wait, wait," I objected, waving my smoke in front of me, "hold on a sec."

I wanted to get Kenny from work in on this. I fumbled around in my purse for my mobile.

"You don't need your mobile anymore," suggested my new proxxi, seeming to know what I was thinking. That stopped me in my tracks.

"Kenny?" I called out tentatively, and his projection instantly appeared floating in the middle of my living room. Always dressed in a T-shirt and jeans, with eternally messy hair, Kenny constantly frustrated my requests for more formal office attire. He was dedicated, however, and a consummate nerd when it came to technology, so I put up with him.

"Yes, boss?" he asked from behind his square-rimmed glasses. "Whoa, you got some kind of fancy lens display system going on?"

I'd tripped his geek-chic alarm, and I waited for him to collect himself.

"Please listen to what, this, ah, woman is saying," I said, pointing toward my new proxxi. "Pssi interface, or proxxi, or whatever, please continue."

Kenny's eyes grew wide as the proxxi began describing the system controls. I just sat back and enjoyed one glass of wine and then another.

Presently, the proxxi faded away and I turned to Kenny to finish up. "Can I give you root access to my system and you handle the settings and dealing with this proxxi? I don't want to have any-thing to do with it, and quite frankly I find it, or her, or whatever, disturbing."

"Not sure, boss. From what I understood, you can't hand off all the root functions, but give me a day or two to look into it."

His geek love was sparking hard.

"Just don't waste too much time, right?" He'd just use this as an excuse to duck out of other work if I let him.

He nodded. "Right."

"Any problem I have, I just call your name and you pop up, right?"

"Exactly. Anytime, anywhere."

"Perfect."

I was about to dismiss him, but he was staring at me intently. "What?"

"You were you paying attention to the safety stuff, right?" he asked. "If you need to reset the system there's this hardwired gesture recognition." He began motioning in the air, reaching toward his chest and twisting and pulling. It looked ridiculous.

"Look, Kenny, I've got you, right? Or Dr. Simmons, or failing that, I just call this proxxi thing, correct?"

He stopped what he was doing in mid-motion. "Sure, yeah."

"Just take care of it for me, okay?"

"Okay, boss."

"Now, please, set it so it removes all advertising as my doctor prescribed."

There was a short pause while he spoke to my new proxxi on his end.

"All done," he replied quickly. He smiled and raised his eyebrows.

That was fast. I had to admit I liked not needing the mobile bud anymore, and the technology looked amazing, even from just the proxxi session.

Waving Kenny away, I settled back into the couch and let Mr. Tweedles cuddle up into me. I scratched his ears and felt him purring, and then felt a sudden twinge of realization that Alex wouldn't be coming by anymore. *It's just and me and you, Mr. Tweedles.*

5

The next morning I awoke early, feeling unusually refreshed. At this time of year, the rising sun just managed to sneak into the alleyway between the buildings next to me and cast cheerful rays in through my bedroom window. I dreamily watched motes of dust settle and spin in the sunlight streaming through the blinds. My mind was at ease for the first time in longer than I could remember. Something was different, but what?

Then slowly, very slowly, the noise of the world outside rose in volume, growing until it filled the same space in my consciousness that it usually did. I realized then that the pssi interface had been keeping it quiet while I was asleep.

Energized, I pulled back the sheets. Time to face the day! Swinging my legs off the bed, I called out to Mr. Tweedles, who trotted in to rub up against me. I leaned down to pet him, then stretched and yawned, sitting for a moment on the edge of the bed as I collected myself and put on my slippers and robe. Picking up Mr. Tweedles, I got up and walked into the kitchen, grabbing my waiting morning cup of coffee.

As I rooted around for the holographic remote in the bowl of junk in the middle of the kitchen counter, my morning Phuture News Network sprang into life by itself, dissolving the opposite wall of my living room. Surprised, I blinked and realized this must be another feature of my new pssi system.

A message flashed up on the display. Mary had called again. I didn't make friends easily, but we'd met a few months ago at a coffee shop nearby and hit it off. We'd struck up an immediate friendship, but lately she was beginning to annoy me as we got to know each other better. I was finding her to be a bit of a hypocrite. I ignored the message.

Sitting down on a stool at my breakfast countertop, I passed my bowl of instant oats under the tap and a short jet of boiling water filled it to the prescribed level. I stirred it absentmindedly while I watched predictions of the day's news to come on Phuture News.

This new pssi display is amazing. It looked so realistic that I felt as if I could get up and walk right from my living room into whatever I was looking it. At that moment it was a swirling storm system out in the Atlantic, grinding its way toward some unfortunate Caribbean island. The image was far superior to my old holographic display, and much better than the contact lens systems I found so irritating and headache-inducing.

"By the end of the week," predicted the Phuture News weather anchor who floated to one side of the display, "tropical storm Ignacia will reach hurricane status and progress into the third major storm of the season." They were projecting it would wash all the way up the coast and threaten New York.

An almost regular occurrence these days.

In an overlaid display, Phuture News described soon-to-be-emerging conflicts in the Weather Wars, along with a list of predicted famines and disasters. It was all they ever talked about. No wonder everyone was anxious and depressed, never mind the advertising. I spooned my oatmeal absentmindedly into my mouth as they detailed the death and destruction.

"Good morning. I hope you didn't mind, but I filtered out the street noise last night. I thought it would help you sleep better."

I looked up from my oatmeal. My proxxi was sitting across the counter from me, strikingly composed in a tight, fashionable business suit with her hair done up in a severe bun. *She looks amazing.* Oatmeal dripped off my spoon as I took her in, uncomfortably aware that my own hair was a frizzy mess.

"I also took the liberty of preparing a relevant summary of world events that happened while you were sleeping," she said brightly.

I stared at her. I just wanted to have my oatmeal in peace.

"I think that these may be most relevant regarding your work today," she continued, and a blur of images hung in an augmented display space in front of me. I put my spoon down. "Instead of talking, it would be easier if we could commingle my subjective reality with yours—"

"Look," I cut her off, "I just wanted to try this for the advertising block. I realize you are the main system interface, but please deal through Kenny, okay?" Anyway, my doctor had said to avoid the distributed consciousness features, which was what her commingling of realities sounded like.

She smiled. "Of course, Olympia. My apologies. I will interface with Kenny from now on until I hear otherwise from you."

With that, she faded away. This proxxi thing was unnerving, but at least she hadn't given me any attitude. I returned my gaze to Phuture News and my oatmeal.

"News off!" I announced, wondering how the pssi system would respond.

Magically, the display faded and my wall returned, but the system left behind a persistent visual overlay that was both visible and somehow invisible at the same time—information about some war that was about to start in Africa hung in my new overlaid display.

"Maybe I shouldn't start my days with Phuture News," I muttered aloud, and immediately a Phuture News feed at the bottom of my display said there was a 90 percent chance I would anyway. I laughed. The system was a comedian as well.

Picking up the new edition of *Marketing Miracles* from the counter, a rare print magazine, I leafed through it. *That's odd.* Something wasn't right.

And then I figured it out.

"Kenny," I announced into thin air, "could you switch the advertisement blocking system off?"

Before my eyes, the pages of the magazine began to morph, shifting and dissolving until the same page appeared before me, but this time with the advertisements on it.

"Kenny, put the advertisement block back on, please."

The images and text on the page quickly shape-shifted back and the adverts dissolved away.

Amazing.

As I considered this, I realized that the news broadcast hadn't had any ads floating across it either, nor had it been interrupted by any advertising breaks. Sitting bolt upright, I listened hard to the noise from outside. I could still hear the traffic and bustle of people, but the baseline clatter of the street hawkers and holo-ads was absent.

Really amazing.

6

"Congratulations on the win, Olympia."

"Thank you, Ms. Mitchell," I replied quietly. We'd won the first phase of the Cognix account, and I was sitting next to one of the firm's senior partners, Antonia Mitchell.

It was the biggest contract our company had ever been awarded, and I was something of a hero around the office. Bertram had even been tolerable lately.

Antonia smiled back at me. "Sorry, I didn't mean to interrupt, please continue."

The day's main event was helping run an online press conference with Patricia Killiam, Cognix's most famous scientist and primary press presence. The meeting was being held in one of the Atopian conference rooms. Many of the reporters were actually on Atopia with Patricia in the room, but most people, like Antonia and I, were attending remotely.

Atopia was one of the floating city-states, physically located somewhere in the thousands of miles of open ocean in the Pacific off California. The technology they were developing, and we were marketing for them, enabled perfect simulated reality. That meant place and distance ceased to have any real meaning for them. Antonia was participating in the meeting using an older, lens-based virtual reality technology, but I used my new pssi system.

I started up the holographic promo-world for the reporters to get the show started.

"Imagine," said an attractive young woman, or man, depending on your preference, "have you ever thought of hiking the Himalayas in the morning and finishing off the day on a beach in the Bahamas?"

As she walked along an exotic anonymous beach, she smiled confidently, conveying to us that not only was it possible, but it was something we needed, and needed right away. "Pssionics enables limitless travel with no environmental impact. You'll be having the most fun, with the lowest combined footprint, of anyone in your social cloud!"

"And you'll never forget anything again," she laughed, reminding us of all the things we'd ever thought we'd forgotten. "You'll never again have to argue about who said what!"

While we all contemplated the things our mates had gotten wrong over the years, her face became more serious.

"Imagine performing more at work while being there less. Want to get in shape? Your new proxxi can take you for a run while you relax by the pool!" she exclaimed, stopping her walk to look directly into each viewer's eyes. "Look how you want, when you want, where you want, and live longer doing it. Create the reality you need right now with Atopian pssionics. Sign up soon for zero cost!"

The woman faded into the slowly rotating Atopian logo, a pyramid with a sphere balanced at its apex. A short silence settled while Patricia let it sink in. She was the master at this, and she should be after the lifetime she'd spent working on it.

"So how exactly is pssionics going to make the world a better place?" asked an attractive blond reporter from one of the entertainment outlets.

I watched Patricia roll her eyes. She didn't like the term "pssionics," too much baggage. The blond reporter's name floated into view in one of my display spaces: Ginny.

"Well, Ginny, I prefer to use the term 'polysynthetic sensory interface,' or just pssi," Patricia replied, detaching from her body.

A computerized image of Patricia floated up above her body and continued to talk with the reporters while her proxxi walked her body along beneath the projection. Nobody batted an eye. They weren't easily impressed anymore.

"We've been able to demonstrate here on Atopia that people are just as happy with virtual goods as material ones. You just need to make the simulation good enough, real enough."

Everyone nodded. They'd heard this before—as had I, at least a dozen times, and my mind wandered off to thinking about how pssi had already changed my life. I certainly felt more rested, and I started to consider calling Alex, perhaps just to chat.

"Now, if you'll allow me," continued Patricia, "I'd like to take whoever is coming up to watch the slingshot's test firing."

Her asking was a formality as they'd all signed off already, but they all nodded just the same. Patricia took control of our collective visual points-of-view and pulled us up through the ceiling of the conference room and out above Atopia with dizzying speed. We shot upward into the sky, while the green dot of Atopia receded into the endless blue of the Pacific below us.

"To answer Ginny's original question, pssi will change the world by moving it from the destructive downward spiral of material consumption and into the clean world of synthetic consumption."

Our viewpoint began to slow as we neared the edge of space. The Earth's curved horizon spread out in the distance, above the oceans far below. The sun was just rising.

"Ten billion people all fighting for their piece of the material dream is destroying the planet, and pssi is the solution that will bring us back from the brink!"

Her finale was punctuated by a growling roar as the slingshot filled the air around us with a fiery inferno. The reporters clapped loudly in the background.

They couldn't get enough of this stuff.

7

It had been a long day, and a creeping headache was reaching its roaring finale by the time I finished late that night. After a few weeks of smooth sailing on the Cognix account, we'd hit our first major speed bump with the disasterous launch of a Cognix-related project called Infinixx.

We were in damage-control mode, and the spectacle of Bertram in another one of his ridiculous outfits had just topped it all off. While I was slaving away, he'd spent most of the day trolling around the office assistant pool, looking for some ditzy new romance victim.

Bertram and I had a big argument about whether to use Patricia or a young pssi-kid named Jimmy as the main media presence for marketing. I was adamant about sticking with Patricia, but Bertram was just as convinced we should switch to someone newer and younger. Antonia was on my side, but Bertram had allies against us in some of the other senior partners.

Everything and everyone at the office was getting on my nerves, and I'd escaped outside for a cigarette nearly every hour just to get away.

Alex had started dating my sort-of-friend Mary. *Is this what friends do?* I was having a hard time getting it out of my mind, and I'd blocked all of their incoming messages and removed them from my social clouds. Grabbing a handful of anti-inflammatories from my desk drawer, I got up to leave for the night. Downing the pills dry, I exited the giant brass-and-glass doors of our building and walked out onto Fifth Avenue.

I was lost deep in thought about how to spin the Infinixx mess when I stopped in my tracks to marvel again at my new city. Blinking, I looked out above the sea of people jostling past me. It was as if a layer of noisy fluorescent dirt had been scraped off the City by the hand of God—all the advertisements were gone, as if they had never been there.

I could actually see the buildings around me.

Stepping into the flow of pedestrian traffic, I looked up above me in wonderment, admiring all the views I'd never been able to see before because they'd been blocked by billboards and holograms. The flow carried me up Fifth and into Central Park, and in a dreamy state, I continued to walk around the edge of the park, staring at my city with new eyes.

I'd been using my pssi for some time already, but New York without advertising still felt special. It was relaxing, and as my head-ache subsided, I decided to get some exercise and finish my return home by foot.

The gathering darkness was something else I still wasn't accustomed to. Normally, the advertisements lit up the streets and sidewalks. As I neared home, staring up and around, I was nearly tripped by a bum splayed out on the street. The stench of his body odor should have been forewarning enough, but the darkness and my wandering eyes betrayed me.

"Lady! Lady! Watch it!"

Looking down just in time, I danced awkwardly over the grubby man at my feet, knocking over his collection bowl. Nobody around me even glanced at the commotion as they swept past.

He cowered for an instant with me jittering over him, then shot outward on all fours to collect the bills I'd scattered, darting this way and that beneath the feet of human traffic.

The frustration of the day and my lingering headache got the better of me. *I bet he's not even legal.* What was he doing there, dirtying up my neighborhood?

"Get out of the way!"

He looked up at me. I'd expected to see a scowl, but he simply stared at me. "You think you're important, lady? I used to be a stockbroker."

People streamed past us as we stared at each other. Still the blank stare. Was he about to cry? My sympathy and frustration fought with each other, and I fumbled around in my pockets but had no change. *Who carried money these days?* Wanting to escape, I turned away, merging back into the pedestrian flow.

"You should be more careful. Life can throw you funny curveballs, lady," I heard him shout, his voice fading away.

I shivered. At that moment, an incoming ping arrived from Kenny.

"Yes?" I asked aloud, happy to move onto a new topic.

Kenny materialized, walking in step beside me. "That was close."

"What was close?" Was he spying on me?

"That bum that almost kneecapped you just now."

"How do *you* know what just happened?" The encounter had hit a nerve, exposing some unreasonable fear that I couldn't identify.

"Your pssi has automated threat detection, and since I'm the root user, a security alert popped up on my display," he replied defensively. "You know, there's an automated collision avoidance system you could activate."

"You're not watching me with that thing are you?"

"It's just an alarm," protested Kenny, his projection ducking and weaving around the foot traffic as he kept pace with me. "As root user, I get security alerts fed to me and thought you might need help."

I looked at him. "So you managed to get root access? I thought you said it didn't allow it?"

That was good news. I didn't need any more responsibilities on my plate.

"Someone authorized it as part of the testing and gave us a workaround."

Probably because we had a close working relationship with them. "Good."

At least something was going my way. Kenny stared at me as I squinted into the darkness. I could see he had something more to say.

"What?"

"Want me to make it easier for you to see things?" he asked. "I could set the pssi to adjust your perceptual brightness, even optimize contrast."

I wasn't too keen on the thing controlling my body, but this seemed reasonable. "Sure."

Immediately, the scene around me brightened and the edges grew sharper. I knew it was dark out, but I could see everything clearly and in even sharper detail than full daylight.

"Kenny, that is actually…great," I said after a moment. "Good work."

He brightened up like a puppy at my praise.

"Believe it or not, but we could filter out street people, too," he added. "I could also set it so that garbage and dirt is cleaned off the street or remove graffiti. There are all kinds of reality skins you can set in this thing. We'd need to initiate some of the kinesthetic features, though."

We turned onto Seventy-Fifth, my street, and I could see a few homeless people hanging around on the corner up ahead, begging for money. An image of the bum I'd nearly tripped over floated into my mind, and my chest tightened up.

"Sure, let's try it."

Nearly the instant I said it, the panhandlers up ahead melted away and the walls of the buildings washed free of graffiti. The sidewalk beneath me began to glisten as if it was newly poured.

"How's that?" Kenny asked.

I stopped walking. "Amazing."

It *was* amazing. It was my neighborhood, just a better version. Scrubbed clean.

But if I couldn't see them... "What happens if I run into them?"

"The kinesthetic function is turned on now, so it won't let you run into them," explained Kenny. "You're *guiding* your body, but the system takes over your foot placements, even modifies what you see so that you don't notice your body making the detours your kinesthetic system makes for you."

I nodded. Of course I'd read all about it, but experiencing it was different.

In the distance, a robot walked by.

"Could you also set it to remove all robotics, I mean, unless they directly address me?" They still made me nervous. This gave me another idea. "And remove all couples holding hands as well."

Perhaps this was too much to share with Kenny, but I said it without thinking. Kenny nodded, and I realized then that he was perhaps the closest thing that I had to a friend.

"All done," he replied after a few seconds. "So this is the new pssi system that Cognix is going to release, huh?"

I had been busy enjoying myself, admiring my new neighborhood—Kenny's innocent mention of Cognix brought me roughly back down to Earth. My nerves were frayed. "I don't know, Kenny, but they're going to be giving it away soon, so you'll be able to play with it to your heart's content. I'll make sure you're first in line."

"Cool." In an overlaid display space I could see him tuning into a media broadcast from Patricia Killiam.

8

New York could make you crazy, but if I'd ever had a bad day at work, this was the worst. I'd spent the past week almost sleeping at the office, preparing reams of new material for the Cognix launch. It was a simultaneous worldwide release, the biggest media campaign in the history of the world, and we were in a fever pitch trying to get everything ready.

Storms were sweeping up the eastern Pacific toward Atopia. Hurricanes by themselves were nothing unusual these days, and they weren't really threatening the island-city, but Atopia had inexplicably begun moving itself much closer toward America. Too close, some were saying, and the Atopians weren't offering any explanations for why.

We had to somehow spin it positively in addition to everything else going on.

Kenny had installed filters in my pssi so that Bertram and the floozies in the assistant pool were filtered out of my visual input unless they directly addressed me in some way. That was great to begin with, but as the days went by, the stress was piling on, and I'd been growing more and more frustrated with almost everyone.

The showstopper came at the end of the week.

"Olympia," came the call from Roger, "could you come in here, please?"

It was the final decision on the last stage of the Cognix account and I was nervous. The old school and new school were facing down in the battle brewing between Bertram and me, and I felt my career hanging in the balance.

Flicking off a gossip-girl channel on Phuture News, I collected my Cognix materials and sent them over to the conference room, closing down my workspaces as I got up to leave. I ran a hand through my hair to straighten it out and absently brushed some lint off my shoulder as I looked out at the wall of the building facing my window, hardly ten feet away.

My reflected image hung thinly over the cold, chipped brick beyond. *My God, is that me?* I looked so old. My long blond hair, the pride of my youth, hung in a frazzled mess around my shoulders. Even from here, I could see the lines in my face. I'd always been slender, but my reflection looked gaunt. My heart thumped loudly in my chest, each contraction forcing the blood through my arteries, straining it into the smallest of vessels as the pressure built up.

I tried taking a deep breath, but there was nowhere for the air to go as my chest tightened. Sweat beaded on my forehead.

Shake it off, take the fight to them. A vision of that bum on the street crowded my mind and I looked down.

My heart began racing.

You're a high-powered executive, a queen of New York. You have savings, you have important friends, you own your home, and you've even got Mr. Tweedles. I smiled at that. The doctor was right—the stress was getting to me.

Letting out a big sigh, I collected myself and made for the door. Everything would be fine.

I entered the conference room down the hallway and was surprised to find that projections of our Cognix customers—Patricia Killiam and the others—weren't filling the holographic wall. Roger and Bertram were sitting down on the other side of the long table, looking at me.

Pulling up a chair opposite them, I leaned into the table, feeling my old friend anger begin to make an appearance.

"What's up, guys?" I half-asked, half-challenged.

"Olympia, we're glad you're here," Roger began, opening clasped hands that had been supporting his chin.

I let go an audible groan. "What's up? Cut the bullshit. Did we lose the final phase?"

"No," he announced with pronounced lack of enthusiasm. "Actually, we won."

"So what's the problem?"

"No problem at all. In fact, we want to use all of the materials you created. Great work!"

"Well, good then," I replied carefully, relaxing my shoulders.

"But...."

"But what?"

"We've made, ah, our client wants...." Roger coughed and wiped a hand across his face. "We want Bertram to head the account. You'll be working under him on this. But I'd like you to show him the ropes, you know, you're the expert."

He smiled at me weakly while Bertram beamed. The simmering pot inside me exploded.

"Are you out of your mind?" I barked back at them both.

Bertram shifted back in his chair, enjoying the spectacle, his grin floating disconnectedly in my red-shifted vision. My chest tightened. Gripping the table with white knuckles, my vision swam. "Does this have anything to do with me not wanting to use that kid Jimmy instead of Patricia?"

"Nothing like that," said Bertram, smiling. I didn't believe him.

"Olympia, look, I understand how you feel," pleaded my boss, "but you could learn a lot from Bertram, too. Look how calm and collected he is." He looked back at Bertram. "There is no rush on this. Why don't you take next week off, paid leave, and think about everything?"

I stared down at the table, trying to get a grip.

"Fine," I grumbled under my breath. This wasn't a fight I could win right now. "Glad we won the contract, sir. I could actually use a little time off."

"See," said Roger, brightening, "now that's the spirit. Take as much time as you need, Olympia, we need you here in top shape. This will be a big job."

Yes, I thought, *this* will *be a big job.*

Taking off early, I got home quickly and was just into a second bottle of wine and curled up on my couch with Mr. Tweedles when night began to fall. It started raining outside, and through my large bay window I watched the wind drive the sudden downpour in the streets outside.

After polishing off the wine, I was having a hard time concentrating on a new romance novel I'd started. My mind was constantly shifting back to plotting the downfall of Bertram.

Mr. Tweedles started purring and rubbing up against me. I'd been enjoying cuddling with him, but he'd rolled over onto his back, inviting me to scratch his tummy. I'd obliged, and been rewarded with a nip for my efforts. I kicked the ungrateful little fuzz-ball off the couch.

Sighing, I washed a sleeping pill down with a mouthful of wine. Lighting up my last cigarette for the night, I called Kenny.

"Yes, ma'am," he replied instantly, appearing with a careful smile in my primary display space. I was sure he'd heard about my little incident with Roger and Bertram. I bet I'd been the talk of the office.

I'd show them.

"Kenny, look, could you set my pssi to filter out anything that I find annoying until you hear different from me?" If I have some time off, I reasoned, I might as well make the most of the tools at my disposal.

"Sure," he replied. "I guess I could do that."

"I'll just ping you if I need anything, okay?"

"Sounds good, no problem," he said, then added, "And hey, enjoy the time off."

Was that sarcasm?

Without another word, I clicked him out of my sensory spaces and got up off the couch—*whoa, drunker than I thought*—and wandered into my bedroom to collapse.

9

Oouf, my head hurt.

I groggily lifted it off the sheets and waited while my blurry vision adjusted to the semidarkness of my bedroom. It was still early. *Wait a minute, it's Saturday.* I didn't need to go to work. Memories seeped into my brain, and I realized I had a pass from work the whole next week, perhaps longer. Flopping my head back onto my pillow, I called out weakly for Mr. Tweedles.

"Hey, kitty kitty."

He didn't appear. *That's odd. Ah, well.* I conked back out.

What seemed like moments later, bright light was streaming in through the window. I flopped out of bed and made for the kitchen to get a glass of water.

Mr. Tweedles was still nowhere to be seen. In a sudden panicked thought I tried to remember if I'd let him out the night before. I usually didn't, but I had been a little drunk. I looked out the front door and the windows, but he was nowhere to be seen. Perhaps he was hiding, I thought guiltily, remembering shoving him off the couch.

Maybe I should go for a run.

That'd get the gears going. There was nothing like a good run to fire up the imagination, and my mind was already cycling with ways to get back at Bertram. If Mr. Tweedles was out, he'd be back by the time I returned, and if he was hiding, maybe he'd have forgiven me by then.

Walking into my bedroom, I pulled on some sports gear. Moments later, I was bounding down my front steps. I drank in the cool morning air, enjoying the crisp bite of the rain of the night before as it burned off in the early sunshine.

I admired the scenery, which was completely devoid of any ads, the streets sparkling and walls scrubbed clean, with no vagrants to spoil the view or inspire guilt. It was perfect. I jogged along Seventy-Fifth toward Central Park.

Gradually, I began to get the feeling something was wrong.

There was a complete lack of other people on the streets, or even in cars. It was early morning on the weekend, but even so. As I made it to the corner of the park, I decided I'd better check in with Kenny to make sure my pssi was working properly.

"Kenny, could you check the pssi system for me?"

No response. I slowed up my jog. Maybe he was hungover, too.

"Kenny!" I called out again, stopping and waiting for him to appear.

"Kenny!" I yelled, and then screamed, "*Kenny!*"

My voice echoed back from the empty space of the park.

There were no sounds at all except for seagulls squawking in the distance. I turned around and began to sprint back to my apartment, calling out people's names.

"Pssi interface!" I screeched as I ran.

No response.

"Dr. Simmons!" I pleaded, but there was no answer.

Maybe the pssi is broken—I'll try my mobile. I burst through my front door, grabbed my purse, and rummaged around in it for my earbud. I popped it in and began pinging people. Still nothing.

Alarm settled into my gut and I fled back outside in a panic, purse in hand.

Cars lined the street, but no one drove them—there were no people anywhere, and no Mr. Tweedles. How was it possible I could be walking right down the middle of Seventy-Fifth Street and not see anyone, anywhere?

My mind raced. Last night I'd told Kenny to set the system to erase anything I found annoying. I'd given him root executive control—and I certainly found Kenny annoying lately, as well as my doctor.

My God, what have I done?

I ran down the street, my eyes watering and my chest burning. *My office*, I thought. *Someone will be there even on the weekend.* They would see me, they could fix this. My legs tired, and I slowed to a walk. *This is ridiculous. Don't panic. Stay calm,* I told myself.

Eventually, I rounded the last block before my building, and turning the corner, I tried to tell myself how I'd soon be laughing this off with everyone. Then my heart fell through my stomach. My office tower was gone, replaced by some other morphed amalgamation that looked similar but dissimilar at the same time.

I began to weep. Of course I'd found work annoying. In fact, I found almost everything and everyone annoying.

"Please, someone help me! I'm stuck in the pssi! Please someone help me!" I cried out into the empty streets, utterly alone in one of the world's most densely populated cities.

10

At first I'd wandered through the empty streets of New York. In desperation, I took the New York Passenger Cannon, operating perfectly to timetable but empty of passengers, to San Francisco. But that foggy city was as empty as New York.

For the first few days, I'd tried to remember the deactivation gesture that Kenny had attempted to show me—the hardwired fail-safe—but I hadn't been paying enough attention. What was the sequence; what was the motion?

Wandering around, I pulled and scraped at my chest, twisting and turning and muttering random words, hoping that something would deactivate it. But nothing changed. With a mounting sense of horror, I slowly realized that perhaps I was the only person left— the last person on Earth, or at least the last person on whatever version of the Earth I'd led myself onto.

I stopped at the end of the pier at Fisherman's Wharf. This place was usually packed with tourists, but, of course, it too was desolate.

Opening my purse, I stared at the pack of cigarettes inside. It had become endless. No matter how many cigarettes I took from it, the next time I opened my purse, it was full once more. I'd even tried throwing it away in a fit of frustration, but there it was again the next time I felt an urge coming on. With shaking hands, I pulled out a cigarette and lit it, realizing I was smoking some kind of virtual cigarette but not able to stop.

I'd explored everywhere, tried everything. I didn't need to bring any luggage with me for traveling, as I could just pick up clothes, any clothes I wanted, right off the racks in empty department stores. Everwhere I went, the stores and restaurants were always open, but totally empty of people. At first, when I got hungry I just grabbed things off shelves in corner stores. After a while, I'd discovered that if I had an urge for anything, I could just enter a restaurant, and magically, the meal I wanted would be there, ready for me to sit down and eat alone.

All of the mediaworlds were still broadcasting, but the news was filled with stories about families, about happy reunions and lost children who had been found. I often spent my afternoons sitting alone in cinemas, watching endless reruns of old romance films.

Weren't the smarticles supposed to wash out of my system by themselves eventually? Somebody out there would figure it out, somebody would save me, and then just as suddenly as it had started—it would be over.

Wouldn't it?

Something had to be wrong with the pssi system; it wasn't working as it was supposed to. I'd gone to the orphanage in New York where I'd helped out, but it was gone too. I hadn't been annoyed with them, had I? I wasn't sure. Perhaps I'd been upset with everyone, angry at the world, but certainly I wasn't anymore, so shouldn't people be appearing back in my sensory spaces? Beyond terrified of being alone, I just desperately wanted to see someone, *anyone.*

11

Was it weeks or months?

It was hard to tell. My psyche was ungluing itself.

How long could this last? My thoughts kept returning to my own marketing campaigns, to pssi's main selling feature of dramatically stretching the human lifespan. Was it possible that I could be left wandering alone for years or decades? *Or even longer?*

My mind frantically circled around and around this thought, unable to fathom it, clawing desperately at the edges of this prison without walls. I suspected that the system wouldn't even let me kill myself. There was no escape.

My wanderings had taken me to Madrid, and I walked around Beun Retiro Park. It was as empty of people as everywhere else my lonely travels had taken me. I walked between rows of skeleton trees, across carpets of golden leaves that they were shedding like tears just for me. It was a beautiful day under a perfect sky as fall settled in.

At least, it *would* have been beautiful if there'd been anybody else there to share it with.

I thought a lot about Mr. Tweedles. Everywhere I went, I kept imagining I saw him, just up ahead, just passing a lamppost. I'd feel him brushing up against my leg, and then wake up, realizing I was still stuck in this nightmare. I think he'd been about the only creature who'd ever loved me. I hoped someone was taking care of him.

My life hadn't ended, but without anyone else in it, it had ceased to have any meaning.

Stopping next to the Crystal Palace in the middle of the park, I opened my purse to take out another of the endless cigarettes. I lit up, and then bent down to pick up one of the leaves from the gravel path. I studied it carefully and began to laugh, and then to cry.

It was so peaceful. It was what I'd always wanted, just to be left alone, and I only had myself to blame, or to thank. My sobs of laughter rang out through the empty morning sunshine, under a faultless, empty blue sky.

◆◆◆ CHILDPLAY

Part 2:

Commander Rick Strong

1

Identity: Commander Rick Strong

From this altitude, the stars just began to poke their pinpricks of light through the dark blue-violet sky. As the sun rose and morning broke fully, the hazy film of the Earth's atmosphere painted a milky edge onto the curved horizon.

Looking down, I could just make out Atopia flashing like a distant green gem beneath wisps of stratospheric clouds, almost swallowed in the endless seas below. Zooming in to view it from here, Atopia appeared as a forested island about a mile across fringed by white-sand beaches. The only visible structures on its surface were the ring of the mass driver circling it and the four gleaming farm towers that rose up out of its center.

Returning my focus to the job at hand, I did another sweep of the area. *Still nothing.* I zeroed in on one of our UAVs, a giant, gossamer-winged creature whose photovoltaics glittered and reflected the morning sunshine back into the emptiness. In my telepresence point-of-view I followed it, watching its massive transparent propeller swing slowly around and around, urging it onward into the edge of space.

"Good enough?" I asked.

"Yeah, I think that's far enough," responded Echo, my proxxi.

"No hurry. Let's make sure nothing is out here."

I was enjoying the lazy crawl across the top of the world with the UAV. I took a deep breath, watching the sun reflect off the seas. The silence was serene. *I should come up more often.*

Just then, the new metasense I'd had installed prickled the back of my neck.

Turning my viewpoint around, I could see Patricia Killiam and her gaggle of reporters from the marketing presentation rising up from Atopia. In this augmented display space, each of their points-of-presence blinked and then brightened to a steady glow as they assembled around the test range. They appeared as a halo of tiny stars hanging ninety thousand feet up here with me.

They were waiting for the show to begin.

"Okay, Adriana, let's light this thing up," I said to one of my system operators, pushing my focus back to the dot of Atopia below and leaving the UAV to spin off into the distance.

Immediately, the speck of Atopia began pulsing with intense flickers of light, and I waited for the show to begin. I counted—one...two...three...four—and then the first flashes began to glitter in the near distance.

Tiny concentric shockwaves flashed outward and away. The empty space began to shimmer, filling with hundreds, and then thousands, and then tens of thousands of white-hot streaks that pancaked and mushroomed into a wall of flame. The inferno spread and engulfed me in a booming roar. Backpedaling down and away, I watched the sheet of flame envelope the sky.

"Very nice," I declared, snapping into my body at Atopia Defense Force Command.

Everyone was watching a three-dimensional display of the firestorm hovering over the center of the room, surrounded by the floating control systems of the slingshot battery.

"Would have been nice on that mission back in Nanda Devi, huh?" suggested Echo, standing with folded arms beside me, admiring the show with the rest of the ADF Command team.

I took a deep breath. "That's just what I was thinking."

Jimmy, my up-and-coming protégé, laughed, pointing toward his temple. "The wars of the future are going to be fought in here."

"Wars have always been fought in there," I chuckled back. "But even so, these babies sure make me feel better."

The slingshot batteries were rotating platforms that could sling tens of thousands of tiny explosive pellets into the sky at speeds of up to seven miles per second. The pellets were set to disintegrate and spread their incendiary contents at preset distances, creating a shield-effect weapon that could put up an almost impenetrable wall of superheated plasma at ranges of a hundred or more miles away. It could take out incoming ballistic missiles, cruise weapons, aircraft, pretty much anything coming our way.

Heck, if I feel like it, I thought, *I could even take out a mean-looking flock of seagulls from two hundred clicks.*

And so far, seagulls were all that dared come near us.

Atopia bristled with an array of fearsome weapons, of which the slingshots were just one part. Some of my other toys included the mass driver and the aerial and submarine UAV defense systems, not to mention the offensive and defensive cyberweapons. Everything was dusted down so heavy with smarticle sensor motes that even a flea couldn't hop out there without me getting a bead on it. We were locked down tighter than a nun's thighs, and that's just how I liked it.

All that neo-hippie stuff that Atopia floated on in the waters of the world media didn't mean that a lot of nasty people out there weren't eyeing this little piece of heaven with very bad things in mind. Atopia was in international waters, and as one of the first floating sovereign city-states, it had to be able to protect itself from all comers. At some point, the Atopian masters of synthetic reality had to bow to where the rubber met the road in the dirty, physical world, and that was where I came in.

We were closely allied with America, of course, but the United States had enough trouble taking care of its shrinking sphere of influence. I should know—I spent my earlier career in the thick of the first Weather War battles.

What had begun with China diverting water from rivers flowing out of the Himalayas had quickly turned the roof of the world into a global hot spot. After damming nearly all of the water flowing out of the mountains, China's double-punch of seeding clouds to drop their rain before reaching India was what had really tipped the bucket. The combination had driven crop failures, mass starvations, and a nasty confrontation between the newly muscular superpowers.

While the initial conflict was long over, regional wars over a growing variety of resource depletions had continued to expand and engulf most of Asia and Africa. Of course, the world teetering on the brink of destruction was nothing new.

And now I was in the center of the cyber-universe.

Proudly, I looked around at the Command staff. They were really starting to come together as a team. Just then, I received a ping from Patricia Killiam asking for a quick chat.

The air began to shimmer in an empty space beside me, and her image slowly materialized. She was lighting up a cigarette and smiling at me, dressed in a dark business suit, old-school style, her hair done up in a tight gray bun. Relaxed, but never slouching.

I liked Patricia.

"Finished playtime yet, Rick?" she asked, shifting her hips from one side to the other and taking a drag from her smoke. She took a quick glance at the dissipating blaze on the main display, raising her eyebrows.

It was the first time we'd tested the slingshots, and they'd more than lived up to expectations.

I checked some last-second details. "That about does it."

"Good, because you scared the heck out of what wildlife I've managed to nurture on this tin can," she admonished cheerfully and took a puff from her smoke. "And the tourists want to go back in the water—not that you didn't put on a good show. That was quite the shock-and-awe campaign."

"You gotta wake up the neighbors from time to time," I laughed.

We'd purposely decided not to pssi-block anything in order to measure emotional responses during the test. I'd talked to Dr. Granger about getting the best bang for the buck out of our weapons exercises to impress upon the rest of the world how they'd better not mess with us.

"That's your job, Rick, to help scare the world into respecting us. My job is to help scare the world into saving itself," she said without a trace of humor. "Good work."

"Did you see that thunderstorm coming in? We've been tracking that depression for weeks, but we can't avoid them all. Anyway, it'll water your plants up top."

She smiled. "Why don't you take the rest of the day off?"

I'd returned to fiddling with the slingshot control systems, but this got my attention. I looked up at her.

"Actually," I said slowly, "that would be great. You wouldn't mind?" Cindy, my wife, was having a hard time adjusting to us coming to Atopia. We could use the time together to re-connect. "So you really think that whole sim kid thing might be a good idea?"

Patricia hesitated. "Yes, if you're careful."

"Maybe I'll speak to her about it then. I'll see you later." I smiled at her as she thanked me again and walked off, fading away without another word.

Patricia was one of the founding fathers, so to speak, of Atopia. After the mess the rest of the world had become, the best and brightest of the world had emigrated to build the *new* New World, the Bensalem group of seasteads in the Pacific Ocean, of which Atopia was the crown jewel. Atopia was supposed to be—was marketed as—this shining beacon of libertarian ideals. She was, by far, the largest in a collection of platforms in the oceans off California, a kind of new Silicon Valley that would solve the world's problems with technological wizardry.

Come to the offshore colonies, they said, for the security, fresh air, good food, the sun, the sea, and first dibs on the latest and greatest in cyber-gadgets. Come to escape the crowding, the pollution, the strife and conflict—and that, brother, was the truth. So the rich came here and to other places like this while the rest of humanity watched us needily and greedily.

It was my job to protect them—the rich folks of Atopia, of course, not the rest of humanity.

I laughed to myself. Tough guy, huh? Who was I kidding? I was a washed-up basket case who could barely manage a night of sleep without waking up in a terrified sweat half of the time. The only reason I was here was to try to revive my relationship with my wife. Without Cindy, I would be off in some seedy corner of the world acting out a kind of "heart of darkness" finale to my life in a psychotic blaze of glory.

Maybe that was a little dramatic.

I'd probably be off soaking my sorrows in a bottle while desk jockeying in Washington. That sounded a little more likely. I smiled and began to run through the slingshot shutdown checklist, but then paused, feeling that old guilt begin to bleed out around the edges of my life.

"Want me to pick up some flowers for her from Vince?" asked Echo.

He always knew what I was thinking, especially when I was thinking about her.

"Please," I responded without looking away from what I was doing. Noticing a breach report from Jimmy, I added, "And could you look into what made that UAV malfunction? The damn thing circled back and burned up in the blaze."

Echo nodded and silently walked off to fetch the flowers. He was good at taking orders.

The excitement of the slingshot test hadn't yet faded, and I walked briskly home. The flowers Echo had gotten from Vince were perfect.

"Hi, sweetie! I'm home!"

I proudly held the bouquet in front of me as I walked through the door. I'd snuck along the corridors with them, trying to avoid the prying eyes and bad graces of our neighbors. They would see *real* flowers as wasteful.

Cindy looked at the flowers less than enthusiastically.

She hadn't even bothered to shower today and sat in a dreary heap on the couch, bags under her eyes, watching a dimstim projection. A large head floated in the middle of our living room, contorting itself in the middle of a joke while a laugh track droned in the background. Cindy wasn't smiling, though, her face dully reflecting the light from the display.

It was going to be another one of those nights.

"You didn't need to buy flowers," she complained. "What are the neighbors going to think?"

"Sorry, sweetie." I was always sorry.

Walking in, I saw it was Dr. Hal Granger's *EmoShow* floating in the display space in the middle of the room.

"Could we turn off Dr. Emo, please?" I asked more edgily than I intended. "I get enough of him during the day."

I felt stupid standing there with the flowers.

"Sure. He's all that gets me through the days here, but no problem." Hal's head disappeared from the middle of the room and cast the place into a sullen silence.

With a great sigh, she glanced at me and declared, "I guess I'll get a vase or something," before swinging herself laboriously off the couch to walk into the kitchen.

"How was your day?" I said brightly, trying to restart the conversation.

She rummaged around in some drawers in the kitchen. "It was fine," she replied, lightening up a bit. "But this place is so depressing. I feel like I can't get any air. This apartment is so . . . subterranean."

By Atopian standards, we lived in a palace. Our place was near the edge of the underwater shelf, not more than eighty feet down. A large curved window looked out into the kelp forests, and rays of sunlight danced through from the waves above, illuminating the brightly colored fish swimming past.

Most people didn't even have an exterior window, never mind all this space and furnishings. But then that was the entire point of Atopia: everyone had unlimited access to perfect synthetic reality, so you didn't need much in the way of space or material things in the physical world.

"Sub-marine," I corrected her pointlessly. "You mean sub-marine."

"Whatever. It's dark and claustrophobic." She found a vase and filled it with water, then walked toward me with it in hand, reaching for the flowers.

"Sweetheart . . . ," I started to say, then stopped, searching for the right words. "Just try to use the pssi system. You can be anywhere, do anything you want."

But that was the wrong thing to say.

"I hate the *pssi system!*" she spat at me, but then she took a deep breath and closed her eyes. Backing up a little, her shoulders relaxed and she opened her eyes.

I said nothing.

"Sorry, I had a bad day." She paused. "Pssi is great for watching programs and surfing the 'net, but I don't like all this... this..." she stuttered, waving her hands around in the air, "all this flittering and stimswitching. It's weird."

"I know," I acknowledged. I'd been subjected to enough of Dr. Hal's *EmoShow* to know that acknowledging your partner's feelings was important. "I know this isn't working out the way we hoped, but I took on a commitment. I can't crawl back to Washington with my tail between my legs. Can't you give it a chance?"

"You're right." She sighed once again and put the flowers down on our coffee table, stepping back to admire them. "I'll try. I will."

My heart filled with small hope. "Thank you, sweetheart. You might like it, if you give it a chance."

"It is nice being able to use pssi to spend time with my sister back home," she admitted. "Her kids are great."

I knew what was coming next, and my heart sank.

"Have you thought about what we talked about? The reason I thought we came here?"

Now it was my turn to sigh. "I've thought about it, but I'm not sure that either of us is ready for it. Maybe soon, okay?"

"Okay," she replied, her voice small.

Maybe it was time to talk about Patricia's idea.

2

There was still nothing like a hot cup of jamoke to get me kick-started in the morning. I was back in Command, getting a bright and early start to the day. Patricia had given me some homework assignments, and I was reading about the synthetic reality system that everything on Atopia depended upon.

The pssi—polysynthetic sensory interface—system had originally grown out of research to move artificial limbs, using nanoscale smarticles embedded in the nervous system to control signals passing through it. Fairly quickly, they'd learned the trick of modifying the signals going to our eyes, ears, and other sensory channels, making it possible to perfectly simulate our senses. Creating completely synthetic worlds had followed in short order. In this they'd more than succeeded—to most Atopians, synthetic reality was more real than the real world.

You didn't need to understand how it worked to use it, though. The proxxi program, a kind of digital alter ego designed to help users navigate pssi space, was almost as amazing as the platform itself. After only a year of using my own proxxi, Echo felt as much a part of me as I was myself. It was hard to imagine how I'd gotten along before.

I clicked over to watch Patricia Killiam in another of her press conferences, promoting the upcoming launch of pssi to the world.

"Describe a proxxi again?" asked a reporter.

"Proxxies are like biological-digital symbiotes that attach to your neural system. They share all your memories and sensory data as well as control your motor system. You could think of them as your digital twin."

"And why would I need one?"

"That is a very good question," replied Patricia, smiling approvingly. "Did you know that more people are injured today while they're off in virtual worlds and games than in auto and air accidents combined? Proxxies help solve this problem by controlling and protecting your body while you're away, so to speak...."

My mind wandered as the press conference continued. Despite the endless list of projects to get through, my thoughts couldn't help circling back to Cindy. Clicking off the visual overlay of Patricia's press conference, I returned my attention to my Command task list as the rest of my staff arrived for the day. The first task of the day, of every day, was to look at the weather systems coming our way.

Patricia had just uploaded some of her latest weather forecasts, and we'd been surprised by her upgrading of tropical storm Ignacia in the North Atlantic. Our own weather systems hadn't predicted this, but as we reviewed her datasets, it all suddenly fit. It worried me that, despite all the technology we had, we could miss something like this—even if it was in another ocean and off our radar screens.

Mother Nature was a far more tangible danger to Atopia than a foreign attack, and we needed to do our best to steer clear of her. Record global temperatures predicted an intense hurricane season this year, putting us well into the seasonal dance of avoiding disturbances coming our way.

This usually wasn't much of a problem out here in the east Pacific off the Baja Peninsula. Most of the intense hurricanes and cyclones tended to keep to the North Atlantic and Western Pacific basins. Still, Atopia had a draft of more than five hundred feet below the waterline, and the thought of the fusion reactor core down there grinding into a seamount made me sweaty.

A simulation graphic occupied almost the entire volume of the room, and a pssi-kid grunt from Solomon House was driving our point-of-view around it with dizzying speed. It was a month-ahead projection of winds, storms, currents, and temperatures, so we could plot an optimal course through it all.

"Looks good to me," I offered.

Atopia wasn't really a ship—she was a platform—but we could drive her around comfortably at a few miles per hour. More, if we really needed to. Staying away from bad weather also meant that the beaches were usually sunny, which was a plus even in a place where everyone was off in synthetic space most of the time. Long-range predictions indicated a gathering string of depressions coming our way, so we'd begun backing away north and eastward toward the distant coast of America.

"Great! Well, that's it then," said the grunt, a pssi-kid named Eddy.

He floated in a lotus position in the middle of the display, toying with it. The Command ops team needed my sign off, and I gave it almost right away, but they could see my mind was elsewhere. They were just humoring me with their detailed explanations. Eddy rode the disappearing projection like a magic carpet, receding into an infinitesimal point in the middle of the room.

I rolled my eyes, taking a sip from my coffee.

"So you think I should bring on Jimmy, huh?" I asked, looking at a note from Patricia Killiam in the report. Her proxxi, a young-looking woman named Marie, materialized in front of me, leaning on a railing and stretching her long legs between us.

"Yes, we do, absolutely," Marie responded. "You need all the help you can get, and it's his area of expertise."

"I don't disagree, but he's just a kid."

Patricia had taken Jimmy under her wing like her own child when his parents had abruptly left Atopia, so beyond his doubtless qualifications there were other factors involved. His situation struck a very personal chord for me.

"He's a kid that knows more about conscious security systems than the whole rest of your team," she argued, adding, "and pretty much more than anyone else for that matter. We have to stay on top of the threat posed by Terra Nova."

Personally, I didn't go for all that stuff about Terra Nova. They didn't pose any tactical threat, but that didn't stop Atopians from getting worked up. In the outside world, Atopia and Terra Nova were seen as two sides to the same coin, but the rivalry between these competing colonies was being whipped into a fervor. I wasn't sure it was for the best.

"You're right," was all I could think to say at that point. "This tub is your party. If you want a kid with peach fuzz for whiskers on the Security Council, it's all good with me."

"Jimmy is a special kid," said Marie quietly. "Anyway, he's our pick."

I registered the finality in her tone. "Good enough for me."

"Good." She smiled winningly at me and disappeared.

It was a long day, and I'd been worrying about Cindy the whole time. Standing alone in the featureless corridor outside our apartment, I hesitated. *Is it really what I want?* Our door slid open and I strode in.

"Hey honey, I'm home!" I yelled out then stopped as I tried to make sense of what greeted me.

Our apartment was gone—not exactly gone, but replaced by a pssi projection.

Marbled columns rose up around a sunken living area in the middle of the room, surrounded by a raised terrace. A feast awaited on a low table, with red and gold pillows littered around it. Incense filled the room, and two handservants quietly and quickly moved toward me and bowed. A gentle wind blew in through billowing silk curtains, revealing the jumbled and exotic skyline of Mumbai framed in the distance.

Cindy swept through one of the doorways to the side, filmy skirt of shimmering red swirling about her legs, and jumped into my arms.

"Isn't it just dreamy?" Draping her arms around me, she kissed me wetly. "Thanks for those flowers yesterday. That was really sweet."

"Looks fantastic," I said from beneath her kiss. Cindy sometimes swung from depression into manic episodes. I smiled cautiously.

"Come on, let's eat!" She took me by the hand and led me down the stairs to a low table where she had bunched up some throw pillows and blankets. She kissed me again, and sat us both down. Reaching onto the table, she grabbed a bunch of grapes and began feeding them to me, one at a time.

"How was work today?" she asked, popping a grape into my mouth.

"Long," I replied, laughing. "We've nominated Jimmy to the Security Council as our specialist in conscious security. He'll be a big help."

"Jimmy—Bob's adopted brother Jimmy?"

"Yeah, that's right, I guess." For brothers, adopted or not, Jimmy and Bob sure didn't seem to talk much. Of course, I hardly spoke to my own brother either.

We pulled some more pillows around ourselves, and the sun began setting while we chatted and began eating. She'd planned a feast for evening, all my favorites—fried shrimp, filet steak, even profiteroles for desert. It was the first time I felt totally at ease with

Cindy in longer than I could remember. When I was about stuffed, she surprised me again.

"So, Mr. Rick Strong, who would you like me to be tonight?" she asked as all of the serving and cleaning staff retreated into the antechambers.

"What do you mean?"

"You know what I mean." She cast her eyes down, then looked back at me, smiling.

"Really?"

She nodded bashfully.

"Would you like me to skin-up, too?"

"Sure...," she giggled. "You first." We hadn't made love in months. Unbuttoning my shirt, she began rubbing my chest.

She nudged me with a phantom for a stimshare. Surprised that she used a phantom, I looked into her eyes, and she winked at me. I quickly accepted and watched her shiver as my sensory input filled her senses.

I hadn't expected *this* when I walked in the door. I didn't really go for this stuff, but I was happy to experiment a little, especially when it was me that had asked her to try and get into it.

"No, you go first. Who would you like me to be?" I asked.

She looked at me shyly. "That Spanish guy in the crime dramas, you know, Julio...."

I laughed. "Are you sure?"

She nodded.

Echo sent me the licensing agreement in an overlay-display the moment she uttered the words. Skin-time in this Julio guy was expensive. He must be popular.

What the heck.

I punched the "buy" and "skin" buttons with a phantom hand and detached out of myself to look down at some Spanish guy sitting on the pillows, cuddling with my wife. It was hard getting used to this stuff. I snapped back into my body.

"What do you think?" I sat up and put myself on display, raising my eyebrows and winking at her.

"Very sexy, Mr. Commander," she laughed. "Now it's your turn."

"Ahh...how about that Phuture News Network celebrity girl?"

"What!?" she exclaimed, laughing and punching me gently in the shoulder.

"Yeah, yeah, that girl...you know, the one with the...." I laughed awkwardly. The Phuture News girl's large breasts were about all that came to mind on such short notice.

"Okay," she agreed, grinning. "If that's what you'd like."

As I held her, she morphed into the Phuture News announcer. With particular fascination, I watched her breasts swell under the transparent fabric of her kurta. She looked up at me bashfully.

I could get used to this.

A rush of animal desire coursed through me. Lifting her top, I scooped her into my arms.

I could definitely get used to this.

Afterward, back in our own skins, we rested in a jumble of pillows beside the table. Cindy was curled up beside me with one of my arms wrapped around her. My brain was lazily tingling. She was trying—maybe it was time for me to try, too.

Baby steps, baby steps. I smiled.

Cindy gently twitched against me, dropping off to sleep. Then she twitched harder, and then again. *Wait, is that a sob?*

"Cindy...," I said gently, my brain fighting back from the fog it had drifted into. Her body shook again. "Are you okay?"

She slowly turned to me, her eyes wet above cheeks streaked with tears. Wiping them away with the back of one hand, she looked away.

"What's wrong?"

"I don't know," she said quietly.

"Come on, baby, what's wrong?"

She hunched inward. "I didn't like that. That way you looked at me. You were happy I was someone else."

Sensing imminent danger, the fog around my brain evaporated.

"Honey, that's not true at all." I raised myself up on one elbow to look down at her. "I was only doing it because you wanted to."

That was true enough.

"And I was only doing it because I thought that's what you wanted." She wiped away new tears. "I know I haven't been great to be around lately."

"Aw, honey," I replied, searching for the right way out of this. "I love you. You're the only person I want to be with." That was absolutely the truth. "If anything, it's me that wants to make you happy. I want to make us work again. It's my fault, all this, I mean...you know what I mean."

"I love you, too," she replied. "I'm not comfortable with all this pssi stuff. But I am trying."

This seemed like the right time. "Look, I've been thinking."

"Uh huh," she sniffled.

I took a deep breath. "I'm not sure if we're ready for kids yet, but maybe we could find out. Maybe we could take a half-step and get you more into the pssi system at the same time."

"I'm listening." She reached up to stroke my chin with one hand.

"What would you think about proxxids?"

She crinkled her nose. "Fake kids?"

"I've been talking to Jimmy and Patricia. I think it could be perfect for us."

Silence settled, then: "I'm still listening."

"They're not just 'fake kids.' They take our actual DNA code, mix it together as if it were a real fertilization, and then simulate the developmental process to generate what our real little baby would be like."

I took a breath, watching her carefully before continuing.

"You can pick traits, of course, like eye color, or more subtle stuff if you want, but that's sort of the point," I explained. "It's like trying out a trial version of how our kids will look and behave."

"Uh huh," she replied skeptically. "Why don't you just get them to send a bunch of mock-ups, and we can stick them up on the wall and pick a model we like?"

A hint of the wit I remembered from when we first met. Maybe the clouds were clearing.

"It's not just that," I added. "These things, you have to take care of them, just like they were real babies—feed them, burp them, put them to sleep. You get the full treatment, and that's the point. You can see how your kid might behave at different ages before you have them, to make sure you'll be comfortable with what you're getting."

"And why would I want to do this?"

"I thought that if we took care of a proxxid for a few weeks or months," I answered, looking straight into her eyes, "we could see if we liked having a screaming kid around."

"And then?"

"And then, if it felt right, we could have a real child. What do you think?"

She cuddled into me and looked up into my face. "Okay, Mr. Rick Strong, I'm willing to give it a try."

A weight lifted from my chest.

3

Baby shower—I never really understood the term. Why did they call it a shower? Because they showered the mother with gifts? Weren't they supposed to have these parties before the baby arrived? Anyway, I guess it didn't matter, and I had to admit, he sure was a cute little sucker.

Our little Ricky had bright blue eyes—his daddy's eyes.

The baby shower turned into a coming-out party for the Strong family on Atopia. The place was packed, and everyone was milling about our apartment with drinks in hand, chatting amiably in the entertainment space I had Echo create for us. The star of the evening, of course, was Ricky, our bouncing baby proxxid, who burbled and gurgled away in his mother's arms.

Cindy positively glowed.

From the corner of one eye, I could see the blond dreadlocks of Bobby Baxter, Jimmy's brother, through the crowd. Even in a pssi projection, he emanated a laid-back surfer vibe that seemed to warm up the room. He was making his way toward us with an attractive brunette in tow.

"Congratulations, Commander Strong!" he blurted out, extending his hand.

Smiling, I gripped his hand and shook it. "Thanks, Bob." I wasn't quite sure if everyone's well-wishes were genuine, or if they were gently poking fun at our simulated life, our imaginary baby.

"Is Jimmy coming?" I asked.

Bob shook his head. "You'd know more than me, Commander."

There was an awkward pause.

"And, of course, congratulations to the lovely new proxxid mother," Bob laughed as he let go of my hand and leaned over to kiss my wife on the cheek.

I glanced past him to have a look at his date, who shifted uncomfortably, waiting to be introduced. The rumor mill was constantly circulating with stories about how Bob was wasting his life away, but he sure could pick his women.

"And this lovely lady is?" I asked, smiling at his date. She smiled back.

"Oh, ah," mumbled Bob, "this is Nicky."

"Pleased to meet you," I said as I reached out to shake her hand.

"A pleasure," replied Nicky, smiling radiantly.

Bob wandered off for a drink while my wife and I exchanged some pleasantries with his girlfriend. A few more women arrived and began mobbing Cindy to have a look at the proxxid.

She lifted him to me. "Here, could you hold him for a second, honey?"

"Sure."

The group of woman all smiled, watching me awkwardly take hold of Ricky. Such a tiny package, so warm and soft. It was disarming to look down into his little face and see part of myself staring back up at me. I couldn't help but smile.

"I'll be back in a sec," said Cindy as she released him. "I just need to get some juice."

The baby let out a loud squeal as she left and wriggled in my arms. The overhead lights reflected brightly in his wet little eyes. He smiled a toothless, gummy grin at me.

When we'd ordered the proxxid, it had come with some warnings, but I had a hard time seeing how an imaginary baby could be dangerous. It certainly seemed to be doing Cindy a world of good.

Adriana, my slingshot lead at Command, stood beside me and poked Ricky gently in the tummy, tickling him to generate more squeals and giggles. "Just so sweet," she whispered.

I couldn't resist. "He sure is, just like his daddy."

Adriana was the one with the sensorgy artist boyfriend. To me, it all seemed like pornography, but to them, well, I was just old.

"Look at those bright blue eyes. I hope you'll get those same blue eyes when you have your real kid. So beautiful. He'll be a lady killer!" she exclaimed, tickling his ribs again for more squeals. "What a happy boy!"

I laughed and began bouncing Ricky up and down a bit, thinking that this was what one did with babies. Perhaps it really was best to have a proxxid before attempting the real thing.

Cindy returned and tapped me on the shoulder, taking a sidelong glance at Adriana. "I'll take him back now, tiger." She nodded toward the door, where Vince Indigo, the famous founder of the Phuture News Network, had just appeared. He'd gone out of his way to welcome us here when we first arrived.

He looked awful, as if he hadn't slept in days, but smiled at me as I looked his way.

I gave him a small wave, then cooed at Ricky one more time before handing him back to my wife. I walked over to say hello to Vince and grab a drink. I could use one, and I knew from experience that he enjoyed a drink or two himself.

"Congrats, Rick!" he exclaimed as I neared, reaching out to shake my hand.

I took his hand firmly and motioned him over to the bar. Again, I felt slightly foolish. "Thanks, Vince. Oh, and thanks for those flowers the other day. Cindy really loved them."

"No problem at all."

We'd reached the bar.

"So what'll it be?" I asked.

Vince surveyed the bottles but shook his head. "Nothing for me, thanks."

That's odd.

"You sure?" I dropped some ice cubes into a cut-glass tumbler and topped it off with some whiskey.

"I'm kind of busy...." His voice trailed off and he stared at the floor.

Definitely not the Vince I knew. *What's going on?* Maybe he was trying his best not to offend me, thinking this whole thing ridiculous.

"This is just a little game," I laughed, looking toward my wife and simulated baby. "I'm only doing it to keep her happy; you know how it is."

At that, Vince's attention sharpened. "No, no, this is the best thing," he replied warmly. "You need to do this. It's the way of the future!"

He slapped me enthusiastically on the back. I snorted and took a sip of my drink, feeling less self-conscious.

"I mean it," he continued. "You should have as many proxxids as you can before going on to the real thing."

He seemed genuine about it.

"You really think so?"

"I do, my friend." He put his hand on my shoulder and squeezed it. "I have to get going, though. Sorry. Give Cindy a kiss for me, okay?"

"I will." I nodded, smiling. "Go on, get going!"

Vince nodded, smiled, and with a wave good-bye, he faded away from this reality.

I took a long pull of my drink and looked around.

69

Bob was sulking on a couch in a corner, flicking little fireballs at what looked like tiny rabbits. I guess he didn't understand baby showers either. I poured myself another celebratory cocktail. My heart was bursting with pride.

This proxxid thing is the best idea I ever had.

4

Maybe these proxxids were a bad idea. Everything had started off great a few weeks ago, but Cindy continued to insist on the full treatment, diapers and screams and all. She liked to remind me that it had been my idea.

I hadn't slept properly in weeks.

It had been a long and difficult day of trying to stay on top of the blended threats that were testing our defenses. Cyberattacks were constantly probing our perimeter, searching for vulnerabilities and weaknesses. They'd also upgraded a large storm moving up the coast of Central America in the Eastern Pacific to tropical storm Newton, and another depression was following quickly behind.

I had a pile of more work to try to get done, but at the same time, I wanted to spend quality time with Cindy and the boys. In the end, I came home as early as I could, but regretted it the moment I stepped across the threshold.

My home was a pigsty of toys. But then "my home" hadn't resembled our old apartment in weeks. Cindy had turned it into a kind of suburban estate somewhere in Connecticut, complete with an enormous backyard with a trampoline and swimming pool. I guessed it reminded her of where she'd grown up.

Half a dozen sim-kids were over to play with little Ricky, and they were all screaming and running past me as I came in the door.

"Hey, Dad!" Ricky squealed as he flew past, chasing the others into the living room.

It was amazing how fast they grew up. I mean, *really* amazing. Proxxids were designed to give you the full spectrum of how your kids would look and act, and we had them aging at an exponential pace. So while Ricky had aged one year during the first month that we had him, during the next three weeks he had aged five more.

It was hard to keep in mind they were just simulations, and they didn't seem to notice because of the built-in cognitive blind spots. Most people only stepped them through a few target ages to get the general idea, but Cindy was enjoying the whole, painful process—if at warp speed.

"Hey, Ricky," I called back.

Despite my grumpiness, I couldn't help smiling at the glee on his face. At that point, a big black Labrador appeared. It scuttled around the same corner the kids had come from, the last in the chase pack. Shooting by behind my legs and into the living room, it set off another round of excited screams. I raised my eyebrows.

"Biffy is the newest addition to the family," declared Cindy.

She was sitting at the dining room table feeding Derek, our second proxxid. She'd seen me eyeing the dog.

"Biffy, huh? I thought Derek was the newest addition to the family."

"That was last week, honey."

She hardly looked up at me. I thought she was joking, but she didn't crack a smile.

Derek dribbled carrot down his chin as Cindy tried to spoon it in. He looked up at me, letting go a big squeak, and pounded his rattle on the tray, sending thick orange splatters up around the room and onto Cindy. She patiently smiled in a motherly way and leaned forward with the spoon.

"It's nice to see how their personalities would react with animals, no?" She wiped the carrot puree from her hair with the back of one hand. "Isn't this what we're trying to do, to try out different things?"

"You're right." I had to admit, my plan was working.

Since we had the proxxids in our lives, Cindy was using her pssi more and more. To begin with, she tried adding some rooms to our place, and then she'd begun changing the configuration of our home and location ever more elaborately to suit her needs. Now it was something new almost every day, and it wasn't grudgingly like before. She was taking to it as a part of her day-to-day life.

Not only that, but she was great at it.

She was sticking with the whole nine yards of the mothering experience, feeding and changing the proxxids, bringing simulated kids over for playtime, everything. It really did seem to suit her.

She picked up Derek and sat him on her lap, looking into his face. "What do you think of brown eyes?"

I walked over to the both of them. "I like brown," I replied. I still found how real these kids seemed disconcerting, and maybe that was part of the reason for my frayed nerves.

While Cindy had taken to the full-blown experience like a duck to water, I was having a hard time balancing it with my other responsibilities. Cindy was interrupting me a dozen times a day to tell me about something one of them did, explaining how great it was and how it related to this or that genetic expression.

"You seem to 'like' everything," she replied after a pause, then gently put Derek down. "Go on and play with your brother," she told him, and he squeaked and began wriggling across the floor into the living room. She turned back to me. "You're the one who wanted to do this. It would be nice if you could participate a little more."

Tired and irritated, I began to stammer, "I am...I mean, I'm trying—" but I was cut short by a cacophony of shrieks.

The boys appeared from the living room and began running around the table we were sitting at, laughing and chasing a flock of tiny flying dragons. I stopped, scratching the stubble on my neck, waiting for them to go away.

"Do we really need to have half a dozen simulated brats running around?" I said more loudly than I intended. I'd done a lot of thinking on the walk home, and I'd decided to tell Cindy that I was ready to have real kids. But I couldn't find the words with these kids running around me screaming their heads off.

Her eyes flashed angrily at me, and she turned to the kids. "Boys, boys, we're trying to talk here," she said softly, shooing the flock of dragons back toward the living room. "Please."

When I wasn't looking, they'd all skinned themselves up as miniature purple tyrannosaurs and were effecting puzzled little dinosaur expressions. Ricky, though, could take a hint, and he turned to lead the squealing pack back into the other room.

Cindy smiled and turned back to me.

"Did you see that? How he took the lead? We need to see how Ricky socializes, don't we? I mean, we picked a specific set of genes regarding his personality, and I for one want to see what this really means. Expression markers on a piece of paper are one thing, but—"

The noise level in the next room exploded in screeches again, cutting her off.

"Can't we just turn the simulation off for a minute?" I was getting a headache.

"You can't just turn kids off, can you, Rick?"

"No, but we can sure as heck turn these ones off."

Echo materialized in my display space beside her, sensing something imminent. Cindy turned to him angrily.

"You mind your own business, mister!" she spat at him, wagging a finger in his direction. If a proxxi could be taken aback, he was, and he rapidly dematerialized.

She turned back to me. "This is just what I was talking about. If you find Ricky too rambunctious, maybe we should select for more introverted character traits. Part of this process is understanding how our children would affect us and our relationship."

I could see her point, but I already had a head of steam brewing. "I don't *want* to have an introvert as a son. I had something important to tell you this evening—"

"And I had something important, too," she gushed out breathlessly before I could continue. "I want another proxxid."

I was stunned. In another week, Ricky would be ten years old, Derek would be heading into the terrible twos, and now she wanted another one?

"We're getting rid of these ones, though, right?" I asked incredulously.

"Getting rid of them?" The whites of her eyes grew as she worked into a panic. "We haven't even gotten started with them. You want to stop halfway through and call this whole thing a waste of time? Call *my* effort a waste of time?"

"Waste of time? I'll tell you what a waste of time is! I'm trying to make sure this tin can we're floating in isn't sabotaged or wrecked by some storm, and I can't think straight because I'm strung out on Sleep-Overs from waking up to rock these stupid *simulated* babies to sleep every night!"

I didn't notice that I was yelling, and suddenly everything was very quiet. The boys had circled back into the dining room, and the tiny dinosaurs were staring at me, tears welling in their little carnivorous eyes. Derek started crying.

Cindy looked up at me and said quietly, "I just wanted to try having a little girl proxxid to see what that was like."

I pinched the bridge of my nose between my index and forefinger, my eyes tightly closed. "I'm going to go back to work for a while, okay? I really have some stuff I need to get done. We'll talk later. I'm sorry."

Cindy tried to reach for me, but I shrugged her off and walked quickly back out the door.

It was almost pitch black under the dense tropical canopy as I worked myself up into a full sprint, dodging and weaving between the tree trunks. At first I'd gone back to the office to burrow into a pile of work, and Echo had said nothing, just working with me on the files, but after an hour I'd decided to come up top to go for a run through the jungles that covered the surface of Atopia. Most people couldn't get easy access to the topside—there were advantages to being Commander.

Pssi was many things, but it was something else at night. What to my unaided eyes was pitch darkness was now overlaid with infra-red and enhanced color images, so I could make my way easily even in the blackness.

While I was primarily in charge of the run, Echo was subtly shifting my foot placements and balance here and there and duck-ing my head slightly every now and then to adjust my trajectory through the jungle maze as I shot through it.

Echo also networked in a few wild horses to stampede through the underbrush with us. Even a few monkeys swung hooting overhead. The whole result was a mad, euphoric rush through the undergrowth.

It was the best way I knew to burn off steam.

The argument with Cindy reminded me of how my parents had fought, of how my father had treated us, and memories of child-hood jumped back into my mind. I just wanted to tell her that I was ready to take the next step, but it had turned into another well-worn fight. It felt like a sign, and I'd fought that, too.

My cheekbone bounced off something as I ricocheted off to one side and spun into a thicket of palmettos. Wetness spread across my face. The horde around me stopped, dousing the rampage with sudden stillness.

"Maybe you should let me do more of the night driving," said Echo.

He waited for me to pick myself up. I must have hit a tree branch. *Ouch.* The animals quietly dispersed, sensing an end to our fun.

"I like to keep myself as in touch with my body as I can, you know that." The more you used a proxxi to guide your body, the more you stood to lose neural cohesion, and that led down a slippery slope.

When we used pssi prototypes in combat in the Weather Wars, I'd always made it a point to keep my team and myself in perfect neural coherence between our simulated and real bodies. Pssi was great for adjusting your aim or getting through trauma, but for the day-to-day stuff, I still believed in plain old wetware as much as possible.

"For a guy who likes to keep in touch with his body, you sure can't feel a thing," commented Echo, standing beside me. "That's going to leave a mark in the morning."

I had my neural pain network tuned down so low I had almost no sensation, at least none of the pain coming from my nervous system. My heart ached something terrible, but there wasn't much I could do about that. The perception of emotional pain was a funny thing. The more you tried to push it out, the more it seemed to dig itself in.

"Just combat training," I tried to tell him, but he knew me better than I knew myself.

I tuned my pain filters back up and felt a flood of hurt from my face and ankle. It wasn't smart to try to walk on a sprained ankle without your pain receptors fired up, not unless you had to.

"We're not in combat training, soldier," laughed Echo.

I limped toward the edge of the woods with Echo walking beside me. Just past the tree line, I could see waves breaking along the shore.

"You can't turn off the pain, and you can't beat yourself up either," my proxxi continued as we reached the sand and walked out onto the empty beach. "You're not your parents, Rick."

"I know."

"I'm not sure that you do, actually."

A silence settled.

"Nice out here tonight, huh?" I said after a bit, changing the topic.

Echo looked at me and nodded. "Sure is."

We lay down in the sand, side by side, and looked up at the bright stars hanging silently above us. I tuned my visual system into the ultraviolet and x-ray spectra and watched the night sky begin to glow in neon blues and ghostly whites above us.

"Beautiful to be alive, isn't it?"

I hardly noticed that Echo didn't respond.

I stayed out the rest of that evening, not wanting to fight with Cindy again or explain a bloody and bruised face in the middle of the night. Feeling like a coward, I had Echo leave her a message that I was sorry but everything was fine, and that I'd be staying at the office overnight.

After nearly not sleeping again, the next day was a blur. I gobbled Sleep-Over tabs like candy and tried to pull myself together.

My Command staffers were sympathetically amused at my swollen, purpled face. Even though I'd tried to secure a reality filter over the top of it, most of them overrode it for a laugh. I was mostly just waiting 'til the end of the day to speak with Cindy.

"You look the worse for wear," said Jimmy as we started going over the daily threat reports after lunch. He was smiling.

"Yeah, yeah," I replied with a grin. "I am supposed to be the fighting part of this unit, remember?"

"Of course." He grinned ever so slightly. "Hey, want me to finish up with this stuff?" he offered. "I can see you have a lot on your mind."

The reports and diagrams floating in the shared display space between us seemed to stretch off into infinity. Looking at them made my headache worse.

"Actually, Jimmy, that'd be great."

"No problem."

"Why don't you just take the rest of the day off? I think Jimmy is right," Echo added. "And I just checked with Cindy, she has the afternoon free."

I looked up at him. "You talked to Cindy?"

"She was just checking in on you while you were busy with Jimmy."

"Thanks guys," I said, looking at the two of them. "I really appreciate it."

"Oh, Rick, by the way," said Jimmy as I began to get up to go. "Your wife asked me to help her with some stuff with your proxxids. You're okay with all that?"

"Yeah, yeah, sure," I said, waving him on, "whatever she needs."

I forwarded him my proxxid credentials and flitted off.

◆◆◆

Echo walked my body most of the way home while I finished some paperwork. Reaching the door, I stowed the paperwork in my virtual office and took control back. I paused, thinking about what I wanted to say to Cindy. With a deep breath, I opened the door to our apartment, expecting a wave of screaming kids. It was completely quiet, however, and right away, I was worried.

Tentatively, I looked around inside.

Cindy was sitting by herself on a small couch in the center. Our place was pristine white, a nearly featureless projection—calm and quiet.

It felt creepy.

"Oh, Rick," she exclaimed, getting up off the couch and coming to me as I entered. "What did you do to yourself?"

"It's not your fault. It was my fault." I held up my hands. "I'm okay, it's just a scratch. I was out doing some night drills for work."

She looked unconvinced. "About last night, Rick, I know you had something important to say—"

"And I still do," I interrupted. "Look, I know it's been a long time getting here, but I'm ready now, and I know you are."

She smiled and wrapped her arms around me, kissing me. "That's wonderful news, baby."

I'd expected a little more. I repeated myself. "I want to have a real baby with you, you understand?"

She nodded. "Of course I do, and that's wonderful news. Let's get it just right then."

I took a deep breath, feeling relief wash through my body. "Where are the boys?"

"Oh, they're gone now," she replied casually, surprising me.

As long as she was happy, which she seemed to be, it was fine with me. Still, I had to admit I felt some sudden pangs of regret.

"But," she continued, "I do have someone I'd like you to meet."

A crack appeared in the smooth white wall behind the couch. She led me by the hand toward it as the wall slid open to reveal a room beyond. I heard a soft gurgling sound. We walked up to the edge of a cradle, and Cindy bent over to pick up a baby girl who lay inside it.

She held her up to me, and I took the baby in my arms.

"Rick, please meet Brianna," Cindy announced softly.

I looked down into my new daughter's face. She was beautiful.

Maybe I'd always wanted a baby girl.

5

Cindy had transported our family into a Norman Rockwell–like setting. We were outside, sitting together at an old weather-beaten table at the edge of an apple orchard behind a gray-shingled cottage complete with peeling paint and a musty interior full of yellowing family photographs on mantelpieces.

It was warm, hot even, as the sun lazily set under a cloudless blue sky. We were on Martha's Vineyard in a circa-1940s wikiworld. The fading day had a languid, easygoing feel to it, which was nice after a hectic day of chasing down cyberthreats. Sea air rustled in through tall, unkempt grasses atop the nearby dunes.

Like getting a fresh fix, our first baby girl proxxid had injected new life into our relationship, and the days and weeks had passed with a sense of rejuvenated expectations. Jimmy and Echo sensed what was going on, and the pair of them had volunteered to take on a lot of my Command functions, giving me the time to work things out with Cindy.

The highlight of each day became a ritualized homecoming to explore a new metaworld that Cindy would create for us, and, of course, to play with the latest proxxid. As time went on, we progressed, one by one, through Brianna, our first girl proxxid, and then Georgina, Paul, Pauli, and eventually to our new favorite, Ricky-Two.

"Adriana was right," said Cindy, looking down into Ricky-Two's face. "Blue eyes are the best. Just like little Ricky's."

"Huh?"

I was deep into a Phuture News report predicting a flare-up in the Weather Wars. I flicked away tabloid splinters that tried to correlate this to some paranormal reports. Of course, a lot of people were tracking events in the Weather Wars, and with so many people getting advance notice of events on this scale, there was a good chance the event wouldn't happen.

As I was thinking this, the *new* news reported that the offensive was delayed and then quickly canceled. Suddenly, a report came in that a tactical nuclear weapon would be launched against a target in Kashmir, but this was aborted at the last instant. All sides were already at the negotiating table.

Accurate futuring technology was bringing out random behavior—phuturecasting meant everyone could see you coming, so being unpredictable and random had its advantages, usually at the expense of lacking strategic intent. The irony that "knowing the future" seemed to make things even less predictable didn't escape me, but the serious strategists on the topic said that this perception was just the result of our primary subjectives being stuck in a single timeline.

I sighed.

The ops teams were reporting that Hurricane Ignacia had shifted directions entirely and now looked like it would slam into Costa Rica and cross over from the Caribbean into the Eastern Pacific. It had grown into a monster Category 4.

We were already backpedaling away from Hurricane Newton, a steady Category 2, as it wound its way up the coast of Mexico, and so were suddenly faced with two major hurricanes in our oceanic basin, with several other depressions spinning up in the background. Not unprecedented, but certainly unusual.

A mosquito hovered uncertainly before me, and I swatted it away, shaking my head.

"Remember our first Ricky's eyes?" repeated Cindy. "I replayed them in Ricky-Two's features. I just love them."

She choked up as she said this, even though it had been six weeks since we'd discontinued the original Ricky proxxid. Sensing tears coming, I snapped out of Phuture News and focused my attention on Cindy.

"Yes, I love them, too," I replied.

One of our favorite activities was to discuss and compare features of each proxxid. I thought I'd try launching into this to avert whatever was happening.

"I really like the face structure of Ricky-Two," I suggested helpfully.

Cindy went completely still. In the sudden silence, I could hear the wooden grandfather clock in the cottage's main hallway ticking through the seconds. Cindy stared down into Ricky-Two's face. She seemed about to cry.

"Me too," replied Cindy, catching herself. With a deep breath, she recovered from whatever it was.

"Who's my cute little baby boy?" she whispered to the baby, jiggling him softly and then squeezing him against her body. He burbled with delight and cuddled his head into her.

Something definitely wasn't right. "Are you okay?"

"I'm fine." She held the synthetic baby ever tighter.

A cicada's whine played high in the distance. I squinted into the sunlight slanting through the apple trees and watched my wife doting over the proxxid. This was all very nice, but my uneasiness was wearing my patience thin. I'd been more than ready to move onto the real thing for some time.

I held up one hand to shield my eyes. "How about we step this one quickly through his age profiles, maybe see what he'd be like at five years old tomorrow?"

She didn't say anything.

"Then maybe as a twenty-something the day after?"

Cindy shot me a hateful look and tightly cradled Ricky-Two. "We don't need to do that. I already have a pretty good idea."

Irritated, I looked down to inspect some crabgrass sprouting desperately out from under one of the feet of the table. A breeze rippled the struggling blades of grass as I watched, bringing with it the moldering decay of spoiled apples out in the yard.

"What do you mean, you have a good idea?" I asked. "We only let the first Ricky develop to about five, and Derek was just a baby when we terminated. Don't you want to see what they'll be like when they're older?"

"You just know these things when you're a mother," she said firmly. "You can look at the older simulations if you like, but I don't need to."

She held the baby in front of her and began cooing softly at him.

The discussion was apparently over. I felt both uncomfortable and annoyed. "Isn't that what the proxxids are for?"

"Honey," she answered, staring at our proxxid. "I don't want to argue with you, okay? It's just not something I want to do."

I sat for a moment, quietly putting my emotions in order before responding. "Cindy, please, put Ricky down for a second."

"Okay, Mr. Big Ricky," she replied finally. She turned and sat the baby on her lap, cradling him defensively. Looking up at me, she was about to say something but I cut her off.

"Can we turn this simulation off for a minute?" I asked. "I'm not comfortable here anymore."

Hurt blossomed in her eyes, and she resisted for a moment, glancing back and forth at the cottage and then at me. Sensing my aggravation, though, she let the apple orchard and cottage fade away.

She still held Ricky-Two, but we were sitting back at our own dining room table in real-space. Behind her, light danced down from the kelp forests, illuminating a school of angelfish that swam past the window-walls of our apartment.

I leaned forward and put one hand on her knee. "I love you, honey."

"And I love you, too." She took my cue and held my hand with one of hers but still held tightly onto the proxxid with her other arm.

"I know this was all my idea," I explained, "and I've enjoyed it, but I think this is enough. It's time to get onto the real thing, don't you think?"

I waited, expecting the worst.

She just smiled. "I think you're right. This is enough."

"Really?" I was surprised. "So we can move onto the real thing?"

She bounced Ricky-Two on her knee. "Well, give me a little time to myself, no?"

As suddenly as it had started, it was over.

The next day I came home from work and there were no more proxxids. We were childfree for the first time in months, like proxxid empty nesters. It was a shock to my system to begin with—coming home to find only Cindy waiting for me, with no new proxxid to play with—but I was happy it was over. In retrospect, I'd enjoyed the process of picking out the perfect baby for us, but putting it all behind us felt like we'd crossed an important threshold.

I was finally ready for the real thing.

The experience seemed to have brought Cindy back to life, the clouds of her chronic depression lifting. I figured it was the prospect of finally having a child together, the whole process we'd been through together. Each day I would return from work and she was energized and refreshed, and we would enjoy long lovemaking sessions more often than not.

It was after one of those sessions, as we lay amid a mess of pillows, that I asked if she might not want to go off her birth control. "I mean, we could be making our baby right now."

"Silly," she replied, poking my nose playfully with one finger, "just give me some time. I'm really enjoying myself."

I couldn't argue with that. She was being terrific.

"I don't want to do it artificially," I continued dreamily. "I'd prefer that we inseminate ourselves, or rather, I inseminate you." And, of course, have the labs tweak its genetics afterward to match the Ricky proxxid, by far our favorite.

She giggled and I scooped her up into my arms.

"Is that good enough for you?" I teased.

"Sure is, Commander."

"Let's stay in bed and splinter into the Infinixx launch party tonight," I said, smiling at her. "No fixing your hair, no nothing. We can just stay here and cuddle and project ourselves there, all spiffed up. What do you think?"

She giggled again. "Whatever you say, Sir."

6

"There is something very unnatural going on here."

With that statement, our mandroid guest reached down with one slender metallic arm to adjust the snug jumpsuit along her thin, gleaming legs. I couldn't help feeling some revulsion watching her standing there, despite many friends who'd come back from the Wars in bits and pieces to be rebuilt robotically.

It was early Saturday morning, but we'd all been called into Command to review scenarios around the threat of the storms that were pinching Atopia toward the coast. Although we couldn't figure out how yet, it seemed these storms weren't natural, and our mandroid guest was presenting some possible explanations of what was going on.

On top of it, Patricia Killiam had suffered some kind of medical emergency after the disaster of the Infinixx launch a few weeks back. She said she was fine, but she'd been acting strangely since.

"Do you think the Terra Novans are involved?" I asked it, or her, or whatever. All the theorizing on how this could be made to happen was academically interesting, but I needed to know who, and more importantly, why.

"We're not sure," it responded.

Neither was I. Something wasn't right about this mandroid; nothing I could put my finger on, but she'd been rushed in by Patricia as an outside expert. Whatever had happened to her, it must have been incredibly traumatic. She was barely more than a stump of flesh suspended between spindly robotic appendages.

"Do you have any idea where this is coming from?" I demanded.

"We can't say for certain yet, but there's something too perfect about these storms."

Too perfect? Too perfect for whom? This is a waste of time. I looked toward Jimmy to see if he had anything to add. He didn't. *Great.* I rubbed my eyes, trying to wipe away my headache.

Cindy had begun to fall back into depression, and I was having a hard time focusing at work. Having a few drinks last night hadn't helped anything. Cindy's moods had become even worse than before, where just a short time ago she'd been doing so well. She didn't even want to speak about having children anymore.

"Jimmy, could look into this more? I need to take care of things at home." Honestly, I needed to go and lie down.

"No problem," he replied immediately.

I nodded my thanks and was about to flit off when Jimmy added something. "Oh, wait. I have that date tonight, remember."

I looked up toward the ceiling. "Susie, right?" I laughed. "So that's going well?"

"I can cancel," Jimmy offered.

"No, no, keep the date. I know you'll keep a few splinters around if I need you. I'll be back."

As I entered our apartment, a foreboding gloom enveloped me. It was dark inside, with the glimmering reflections of a holo-projection playing off the walls.

"Honey?" I cautiously peered around the door as I entered.

Cindy was in a heap on the couch, the same as when I'd left several hours ago, and our home was a mess. The room was almost pitch black, with Hal's *EmoShow* playing endlessly in the center. My unease growing, I walked over to the couch and sat down with her.

I put my hand on Cindy's knee. "You okay?"

She put her hand on mine and sat up a bit. Hal's head disappeared as she turned off the *EmoShow*, and the lights in the room came up. At least she was trying.

"I'm okay," she replied, sounding less than okay. "How are you?"

"Seriously, baby, what's up? Talk to me."

"I'm just a little down. It's hard, you know."

"What's hard?"

She didn't reply, just looked at me sadly.

"Do you want to speak to someone, maybe someone other than me, have you tried that?"

Maybe it was something to do with me.

"I have someone to talk to," she said. "It's okay sweetheart, but thanks."

"What about our plans?" I asked gently. "I thought having a child was what you wanted, what would make you happy. You were so great with the proxxids. Don't you want to try to have our own? We're ready now."

Cindy looked at me and smiled her eyes looking a thousand miles away. "I know you are, honey."

7

The call came the next day, on Sunday morning.

We were all back at Command again, running through the storm predictions for the millionth time as they swung around in perfectly the wrong way, trapping Atopia against the coast. We'd just decided that we needed to take some emergency action, and we were about to begin the escalation process when the doctor called.

Echo patched the communication straight through, immediately requesting to take over all of my Command functions. I glanced at him but took the call without asking.

"Something is wrong with your wife, Commander Strong," the doctor announced, his image floating in a display space while I sat in my workspace.

"What do you mean, *something is wrong?*"

"I think you'd better come down here."

I immediately punched down, and in the next instant I was standing beside him in the infirmary and looking at Cindy, who lay on a raised bed in front of us. The infirmary had an otherworldly look and feel to it, with glowing, pinkish-hued walls and ceilings that were there, but not there, in a soothingly anesthetic sort of way. The doctor was the only one in attendance, and he looked at me with detached concern. I looked at Cindy. She appeared to be in a deep sleep.

"It seems to be something we're calling reality suicide," explained the doctor.

"What does that mean?"

"It's a condition where the subject—in this case, your wife—withdraw completely from reality to permanently lock their mind in some fantasy metaworld that they've created."

"Can't you stop it? Can I talk to her?"

"I'm sorry, but we can't reach her," explained the doctor. "Her pssi and inVerse are completely contained within her own body, a kind of extension of her own mind. We have control over the technology, but not over her mind, and she's chosen to do this to herself."

"Chosen to do what to herself?" I demanded.

Apparently, he wasn't sure. "We could physiologically remove the pssi network by flushing out all the smarticles, but this could trigger an unstable feedback loop that could destroy her psyche in the process."

I stared at him.

"So what *can* you do?"

"Commander Strong, it would help if we understood why. Is there anything that happened recently? I noted that you'd been experimenting with proxxids."

"Yes," I responded, feeling mounting dread, "sure we did. That's what this place is for, right?"

"Commander Strong," the doctor continued slowly, "proxxids can have very powerful emotional side effects if not handled properly. Did you read the warning labels before acquiring so many of them? Tell me, Commander Strong, what did you do with the proxxids when you were done?"

8

An investigation uncovered that Cindy hadn't been terminating our proxxids. Instead, she'd been secreting them away, one by one, in her own private metaworlds. As she'd become more pssi aware, she started constructing ever more elaborate worlds. She hid them deeper and deeper away from me, using private networks and security blankets to cover her tracks and protect her ever-growing family.

It wasn't all that hard, and I hadn't really been paying attention. Her mood had been so great at the time that I hadn't dug too deeply into what she was up to when I was away.

All the questions she had been asking about the lifespan of the proxxids floated into sharp detail in my mind. She'd begun demanding more and more flexibility for each of them as we'd spawned them. I'd always refused, wanting to keep their terms as short as possible to try and move the process along.

Since they used a recombination of our DNA, using our individual legal copyrights, both of us had to agree on the format of the proxxid before spawning. Once their processes had been started, they could only be changed by resetting the system, effectively terminating that instance. So she hadn't been able to modify them without destroying them.

Despite the mounting emergency facing Atopia, I could hardly muster the energy to spend any time at Command, especially after

Jimmy had cracked into her private worlds and delivered copies to me.

Jimmy and Echo could handle what was going on as well as I could. Atopia would push through the storms, and even if it didn't, what would it matter to me? I was busy fighting for my own peace of mind amid the wreckage of what had once been my life.

There were security controls in place to protect against certain psychological dangers involved in using proxxids, but Cindy had overridden the controls using my own security clearance. A desperate mother could find a way around any obstacle that threatened her children.

As I accessed the copies of the worlds she'd created, I began a bizarre journey, watching them all grow up together in that little white-washed cottage on Martha's Vineyard I had once visited with her. It was like watching an ancient rerun of a television show about country living, complete with sheets flapping like white flags surrendering yesteryear on the clothesline out back.

I spent my days sitting and watching little Ricky, Derek, Brianna, Georgina, Paul, Pauli, and Ricky-Two playing together, growing up together, and living out their lives. I smiled as I watched them, remembering them all as babies in my arms.

The simulation mechanics of the proxxids, which I'd forced upon Cindy, created surreally accelerated lifespans where they'd aged from babies into old men and women in varying spans of up to three months—a crazy, nonlinear time warp.

They didn't seem to notice anything odd was happening due to the cognitive blind spot built into them; or maybe because, as children living the only lives they ever knew, they couldn't have imagined anything different. It was impossible to know.

She had only brought me there that one time. As it turned out, it was just after they'd had the first Ricky's funeral. The illicit gang of proxxid children, my children, were all hiding upstairs when I'd arrived that afternoon at the cottage. They were on the strictest of instructions to remain quiet. Most of them were still small children at that point.

I replayed that scene over and over again, standing with them in the darkened upstairs room as they giggled and hid, looking down at Cindy and me talking in the yard. I think she'd been on the verge of telling me and was planning on bringing them all out as a big surprise.

Ricky's funeral had been an emotional tidal wave for her, and she'd been trying her best to reach out to me, but I hadn't let her. She'd wanted my help to somehow extend their lives, but I had shut her down before she'd even been able to ask.

My anger had cut her short, as it always had.

I found myself going back and replaying, over and over again, one scene in particular, just before the first Ricky's death. He'd been a wizened old man at that point, bent over and leaning on his cane as he came out onto the back porch of the cottage, the door squeaking on its hinges as he exited. Two of the girls came running past him as he closed the door, Georgina squealing as she was chased by Brianna.

Ricky wobbled unsteadily as they flew past, but he smiled at them. I smiled at them, too.

"Come sit down, Ricky," said Cindy, getting up from the great old oak table we had sat at together not so very long ago.

Time was a funny thing—even as I traveled through it freely back and forth to view what had happened, it was frozen now, my life as immobile as an insect caught in amber.

As I replayed the scene, sitting with them at the table, a wasp buzzed by angrily on its way to a nest under the eaves. Cindy took Ricky by the arm, carefully easing him into his seat and sitting down across from him, her hands on his hands across the table, looking into his eyes.

"I don't know how much longer this old body is going to last, mother," Ricky said, matter-of-factly. Tears spilled down Cindy's face.

"Don't cry, mother. What's there to be sad about? It's a beautiful day." He rocked his old head back to look up at the perfect blue sky and smiled. "What a beautiful day to be alive."

9

I learned that we'd acquired Ricky-Two right after the first Ricky had died. I guessed it was an attempt to fill the gap that had appeared in her life. The rest of them soon passed as well, and it had all just become too much for her.

Watching reruns of this family that I had, but never had, I was filled with an indescribable sadness. But maybe, just maybe, Cindy had gotten what she'd wanted. Did living a full life, in a few short months, make it any less? Did I feel any less sense of meaning in my life, having watched my children grow up and grow old and pass before my eyes so quickly?

It was all very hard to say.

What I could say with certainty was that Cindy's family flatly refused to allow me to have access to her DNA for the purposes of having children, which I'd petitioned for in case anything else went wrong.

"Rick," her father told me, "I know Cindy loved you, more than we could understand after you kept leaving her alone for each new tour of duty. You nearly killed her each time you went back out."

"I know, sir—"

"She begged you for children, and now you've...." He tried to stay calm, but his voice trembled. "This is an abomination, man! What in the world are you people doing out there?"

They didn't ask to move Cindy from Atopia, as this remained the one place where they could still hold out hope. The future was approaching fast out here, and maybe there was a way we could fix what had happened.

"So you have no ideas left, doc?"

"Commander Strong, we're going to have to refuse any further meeting requests until we have something new," said the doc's proxxi. "It's one thing to play with the inputs and outputs to the brain, but the actual place where the mind comes together . . . it's a tricky thing."

Jimmy was with me, trying to help out. "Why don't you just take it easy, Commander? I'll keep you posted if we can figure anything out."

So I left it in their hands. Apart from watching reruns of my family, I spent a lot of my time floating back up on the edge of space, following the UAVs in their lazy orbits high in the stratosphere around Atopia, looking down at the storms that threatened to crush and destroy it.

They could figure it out without me. I had other things to do.

Sitting near the top of the bleachers, the drama of the Little League game was spread out before me. Tensions were running high at the bottom of the ninth inning, and everyone held their breath as the final hitter came to the plate.

Nervously shifting silhouettes far in the outfield cast long shadows in the last rays of a late summer sunset. I squinted into the sun, trying to make out which kid was which, then turned my attention back to the hitter.

Strike went the first pitch. Then *strike* again went the second. Hushed silence as the pitcher went into his windup.

"Strike three!" thundered the umpire, and the field erupted in pandemonium.

"What a great game!" said the man standing beside me. "You got a kid playing?"

"I sure do," I replied as my boy scampered up the stairs through the departing crowd. Leaping into my arms, he squealed in excitement. "We won, Dad!" He looked up at me. "Why are you crying, Dad? We won!"

I wiped my face. "You sure have your mother's eyes, you know that?"

Ricky smiled without understanding. Drying my eyes I took his hand, and we walked down off the bleachers, across the infield, and into the dying sunshine.

◆◆◆ TIMEDROPS

Part 3:

Vince Indigo

1

Identity: Vince Indigo

In the thin air at the edge of space, I could feel more than hear the steady beat of the UAV's massive propeller dragging me onward toward my death.

I'd been able to see this moment coming for a long time. The tight compartment I was in had never been meant to fit a human. I shifted uncomfortably, feeling the cold metal pressing against me through the thin pressure suit of the improvised life support system I'd rigged up.

I shouldn't have tried to escape.

Alarms signaling the start of the slingshot weapon's test fire rang out across the multiverse spectrum. They would have canceled the test if they knew I was hidden up here in this thing, but in my desperate bid to erase my tracks, I'd cut myself off entirely from the communications networks—concealing what I was doing, and even why I was doing it.

It was a gamble that hadn't paid off, as the UAV's control system signaled the start of a system malfunction that I always knew was coming. It lurched sickeningly off to the left, cutting and sliding through empty space, turning inexorably back toward my doom.

In the near distance, the boom of the slingshot began, thundering as it demonstrated its fearsome power to the world. My heart was racing, my breathing ragged and shallow. For days, weeks even, I had been able to see this exact moment arriving, yet here I was, unable to prevent it.

The awful growl of the slingshot grew and began rattling the delicate cage of the UAV's body. The cold metal pressing against me warmed, and then turned hot as the acrid stench of molten plastic burned into my lungs. I gagged, shrinking up into myself, terrified.

Engulfed in roaring flames, the UAV pitched over, its metal and plastic skin coming apart in great fiery gobs as it disintegrated, offering me up into the emptiness—spinning, falling, and burning as my wings fell away. In my last instants of life, I caught a distant glimpse of Atopia, a cool green speck between the flames, her siren song calling me back toward the endless seas below.

2

The last dregs of the night drained sleeplessly away, and despite the world's best efforts, my life filled with yet another new day. More dreams of death—but then, they weren't just dreams.

Or were they?

I felt nauseated.

It was still early morning. From beneath the sheets, I could just glimpse the dawning sky regaining its composure as the roar and flame of the slingshot test began to die down. Dread filled me as I watched stiletto-tipped, fishnet-clad legs stalking toward me from the living area.

The lights flipped on as Hotstuff tore the sheets off me.

"Aw, come on!" I whimpered, weakly fumbling for the covers.

Hotstuff was done up in a bad-schoolgirl outfit today, complete with a checked miniskirt and a starched men's dress shirt. The shirt was knotted at the bottom to expose her belly ring, and unbuttoned far enough to reveal hints of something naughty underneath. She knew I was depressed and was doing her part to keep me alert and in the game.

What I didn't immediately notice was the riding crop in her hand.

"Ouch!"

She giggled and wound back up to smack me again.

"Hey!" I screeched, grabbing some sheets to protect myself and jumping out of bed to chase her across the room.

She squealed, running away from me, and my bedroom morphed into the battle room we'd created to track my looming future death threats. Hotstuff had already transitioned into wearing tight-fitting army fatigues. She menaced me with the riding crop as I stood, rubbing my stubble with one hand and defending myself with the other.

Spinning my point-of-view into Hotstuff's, I took a look at myself. Disheveled and still cowering from the riding crop, I looked ridiculous. I straightened up and dropped the sheets. With all the gene therapy, I looked barely forty, though we both knew it wouldn't be long before I was twice that. A thick shock of graying hair still hung playfully, if listlessly, over the bleary eyes that stared back at me. I clicked back into my own point-of-view.

"Two things before we get started, sir," announced Hotstuff, snapping smartly to attention and giving me a salute with her riding crop. "Commander Strong's proxxi asked for some flowers for his wife—which I provided from our private gardens—and Bob just pinged you to go surfing." She raised her eyebrows.

"Patch Bob through," I replied groggily. Sensing Hotstuff hesitating, I added, "Now, Hotstuff!"

Bob immediately materialized before me, holding his yellow longboard, smirking. He looked stoned already.

What a great kid; it was just too bad.

"So...surfing today?" asked Bob lazily. Sizing up Hotstuff's outfit, he grinned.

Yep, he's high. "Sorry, Bob. Can't make it. Something's popped up."

"Popped up, huh?" he laughed, looking at Hotstuff again. He'd begun projecting some nicely curling waves into my display spaces. "Come on, dude! It's going to be monster out there today!"

"I really can't."

Jealously, I watched the waves. My nerves were frazzled, and I hadn't been out surfing in weeks.

"What could you possibly have to do? I thought you were, like, the richest guy in the world?"

"I wish I could...."

I looked pleadingly toward Hotstuff. She rolled her eyes and wagged the riding crop at me.

"It's your life, mister," she scolded, sensing I was going to do what I wanted anyway. "I suppose an hour couldn't hurt. We don't have anything imminent I can't handle. But only one hour, right? After that it could get dangerous."

I was already halfway out the door, getting my wetsuit, by the time she finished the sentence. Bob gave me a goofy thumbs-up before flitting away to rejoin his body in the hunt for killer waves. I'd catch up with him in a minute.

Bob and I sat on our boards and waited for a decent set of waves just inside the edge of the kelp forest near the Western Inlet, not far from my habitat.

Atopian kelp, the base of our ecological chain, had been bioengineered to grow inverted, with its holdfast becoming a gas-filled bladder floating on the surface and the kelp blades spreading hundreds of feet down into the depths. It sprouted outward at a fantastic rate like a watery mangrove, beginning near the edge of the underwater extremity of Atopia and stretching from there to about two miles out across the water.

From here I could just see my personal habitat bobbing in the distance. My wealth afforded me the luxury of my own private living space, a household attached to one of the passenger cannon supports, sprouting up out of the water and into the sunshine. Most of the million-plus inhabitants lived below decks in the seascrapers stretching into the depths. Atopia was the ultimate in dense, urban planning.

I'd been one of the earliest converts to the Atopia marketing program, pulling up stakes from my wandering existence around the Bay Area to move onto the original Atopian platform nearly thirty years ago. Of course, some of my closest friends were founders of the Atopian program, so it hadn't really surprised anyone.

America just wasn't what it used to be anymore, with constant cyberattacks pushing it into an insular downward spiral and the Midwest returning to the dustbowl of more than a hundred years earlier. No good end was in sight, and entanglements in the Weather Wars were squeezing the last drops of blood from a country already gone dry.

For me, the kicker had been the surfing. Floating free in the Pacific, Atopia was exposed to huge, open-ocean swells. When they caught just right, these would break and curl into pipes that broke for miles as they swept around its perfectly circular edge. Atopia was a magnet for the best surfers in the world, but it was hard for them to compete with residents who used pssi. Outsiders thought that with pssi we were cheating the gods, but really the gods were jealous.

These days, those gods seemed to be having a particular issue with me.

Bob was waiting for the ultimate wave, and while I'd managed to catch one good one, I didn't have his attuned water-sense and was having a hard time relaxing into it. Time was pressing down heavily.

"Bob!" I yelled out across the water, interrupting a conversation I could see he was having with his brother-of-sorts, Martin. "I need to get going!"

"Already?"

"Yeah, I need to get back to that thing. Hotstuff is on my back. "

My promised hour wasn't up, yet Hotstuff was flooding me with things we needed to get done. It was impossible to enjoy the surfing, perhaps even dangerous.

I'd better get on with it.

"I have a hard time imagining anyone telling you what to do," declared Bob. "Anyway, ping me if you change your mind."

With a wave good-bye I flitted off back to my habitat, leaving Hotstuff to guide my body home.

3

I checked out some news Bob sent me as I returned to the top deck of my habitat. There'd been a rash of UFO sightings in the Midwest the night before, and he knew I was a paranormal fan-boy. On this day, though, more important things were on the agenda.

I strode back and forth like a caged animal, my mind racing, and then made my decision. I looked out toward the breaking waves. There was really no option.

"Ready for business?" Hotstuff was waiting for me on a stool at the deck bar, drinking a latte and going over the morning's news, tapping her high heels against the polished blue-marble floor. Behind her, my carefully curated collection of some of the world's rarest whiskeys and cognacs sparkled in the midmorning sunshine. It was about the time I'd usually be waking up, but I'd already been up since dawn.

"Do we have to?" I asked uselessly. A little taste of that Aberlour would be nice.

"Some kind of action is required," Hotstuff observed. "Even in-action is an action. Perhaps the only kind of action you seem to enjoy lately." She raised her eyebrows in disdain while she scanned the European financial reports.

"Summon the Council." I sighed, scratching my stubble.

Portals to my homeworld opened up off the deck, and I walked into our main conference room, shifting my attire into a navy sport coat with a stiff-collared white shirt. Hotstuff strode in behind me, her tidy chignon and crisp suit radiating efficiency and purpose.

One by one, my councilors materialized around the long cherry-wood conference table that glistened under the bioluminescent ceiling. About half of them appeared dull-eyed, having just woken to patch in from whatever time zone they were in for this surprise meeting. The other half weren't human, but our trusted synthetics, and they appeared bright and cheerful, their smiles following me around the room toward the head of the table.

Then again, perhaps I had them mixed up. Maybe the dull-eyed ones were my synthetics. I had a hard time telling the difference anymore.

These weren't just your run-of-the-mill women and sims, but, like Hotstuff, more like a twelve-year-old boy's fantasy. They posed casually around the room as if a fashion shoot could be announced at any instant, with the long conference table springing into action as a catwalk.

My calling a sudden meeting like this was unusual, to say the least, and they watched me cautiously. Information packets were dispersed, appearing on the table in front of them as I sat down.

"No need for pleasantries." This wasn't a social call. "Look at your instructions. We're going to be liquidating everything."

A pause while they assimilated the data downloads.

"Questions?"

"No questions regarding the details, sir," chimed one of them, Alessandria. "But it may help to understand your motivation. Some of the assets you are seeking to liquidate, are, um, well, they're not what you want people to know you're in a hurry to sell."

My motivation, now *that* was a good question.

There were only two things I really knew. First, that I had no idea what I was trying to escape from, just that, whatever it was, it was trying to kill me. And second, just sharing the idea that something was trying to hunt me down made my situation even more dangerous. To minimize risk, I had to pretend nothing was happening.

"No reason," I replied as casually as I could. "Just the whim of a bored trillionaire. I don't want to raise suspicion, so keep this on the down-low, right?"

Perhaps that was the wrong choice of words.

"On the *down-low*?" Roxanne, my resource manager for the Asia Pacific region raised her eyebrows. "You want me to just dump all the yachts, the islands, the racetracks...?"

"Yes."

At this I felt a twinge of remorse. The baubles of Indigo Entertainment, my latest and ill-fated attempt at a new foray into the business world, still held some sparkle in my eye.

While I could lay claim to being super-wealthy, I had to admit I couldn't say the same about being super-intelligent. My success in the business world was more about luck, and luck was hard to replicate. My original luck, the good fortune that had made me *my* fortune, had been helped along by my friend and long-time mentor, Patricia Killiam, and a team of incredibly smart people. It had also been born from a single-minded obsession with the future, or perhaps, just one future in particular.

"Don't go out and just dump it," explained Hotstuff. "Don't attract attention. Be subtle. Go out there and do what we pay you for. Anyway, most of the Indigo Entertainment stuff is a waste of time." Hotstuff looked toward me. "I don't think we'll need to explain ourselves very much."

Roxanne considered this, shifting around in her chair. "I may have someone who could be interested."

The paranoia set in. Perhaps these assets were what whoever was messing with me wanted. *Is Roxanne in on the fix?* I looked carefully at her. Hotstuff sensed what I was thinking and headed me off before I could say anything.

"Very good," Hotstuff replied to Roxanne. "If there are no more questions, please everyone, get to work."

Nobody objected, and, one by one, just as they'd appeared, my councilors faded from the conference room.

When they'd all gone, Hotstuff looked at me sympathetically. "You're going to need to trust your team," she said slowly. After a pause she added, "And you're going to need to trust me."

Visions of Kurt Gödel, the famous Austrian mathematician, sprang to mind. Suffering from deep paranoia, he'd only accepted food prepared by his wife to eat. When she fell ill one day and was sent to hospital, he refused to eat food given to him by anyone else. He died of starvation just shortly before his wife had returned.

"I just hope nothing happens to you," I replied. "I'm not sure I could starve myself."

While proxxi had full access to our memories and sensory systems and could usually guess what we were thinking, they couldn't read our minds. Not yet, anyway.

Hotstuff gave me a funny look.

I shrugged. It wasn't worth explaining.

4

I was up at sunrise the next day as well, my sleep again filled with nightmares, but nightmares that were spilling from dreamland into reality. The darkness was smearing into light, unconsciousness into consciousness, dream life into waking life, all becoming barely distinguishable from each other. Hotstuff was waiting patiently in our war room while I dragged myself into the bathroom for a shower to wake up.

I stared into the depths of my bloodshot eyes in the mirror. Condensation from the hot shower fogged my image while I inspected the angry blood vessels ringing my irises.

"Can we take a short surf break again this morning?" I asked Hotstuff, reaching into a drawer below the sink to get my eye drops.

"I don't think that's a good idea," she replied, shouting over the noise of the shower. "We have a lot to do. It's getting more dangerous."

I sighed, unscrewing the bottle cap and holding it between my teeth. Leaning back, I pulled back the lid of my left eye and deposited a drop into it. Rubbing that eye, I switched to the other.

"Come on," I grunted from between clenched teeth, holding the bottle cap in place as I lined up the dropper above my right eye. "A half an hour out on the...."

I gagged. The bottle cap had popped like a cork from between my teeth to lodge itself into my windpipe. My body convulsed as

I tried to pull air into my lungs. Hotstuff was immediately beside me and already alerting the emergency services. Panic exploded in my veins. I clawed at the bathroom walls, doubling over onto the floor, my chest heaving....

"See what I mean?"

I was standing back at the sink, staring into my bloodshot eyes, but Hotstuff was there with me, holding out her hand to take the bottle cap.

That was close.

I'd barely escaped that event, less than five seconds away in the future on an alternate timeline. I handed Hotstuff the cap and then, after a split second of contemplation, handed over the whole bottle. My eyes weren't that bloodshot.

"I guess surfing can wait."

Whatever it was that was hunting me down, it had infected the very personal and immediate realities surrounding me.

"Forget the shower," I added. "Let's just get to work."

While my physical body remained in the shower, and Hotstuff controlled it to clean me up, my point-of-view switched into a virtual body. From my perspective, the bathroom immediately morphed into my battle room. Hotstuff splintered a hyperdimensional graphic into my display spaces that plotted several thousand alternate future-worlds of my life. Many of the lifelines terminated abruptly, and therein laid the problem with going surfing—I had to save my own life today, and not once, but many dozens of times over.

The day before, there had been over a hundred ways I could have died in the millions of future simulations that we had running for me as we tried to pick a safe path forward for my primary lifeline.

My plan of trying to escape in the UAV, the one that was destroyed in the slingshot test the morning before, was one future that I'd barely avoided.

I picked out and watched one of the day's more gruesomely predicted terminations. It played in a three-dimensional projection that hung in the middle of the room before me, starting with me being cut in half, then being burned to a crisp in some freak accident outside the passenger cannon. I watched with a morbid curiosity. My planned trip on the passenger cannon was definitely off the list of things to do.

The problem had originally surfaced some months ago, and it was accelerating at a worrying pace.

One morning, Hotstuff had mentioned to me that there was a high probability of my being killed in a scheduled stratospheric HALO jump. My future prediction system that morning had calculated that due to inclement weather and the likelihood of my skydiving partner being intoxicated the evening before thanks to a probable incident with his wife, there was a very large chance of an accident occurring. No problem, I'd happily announced over my morning coffee, just cancel the jump.

A few days later, I received another prediction informing me that there were a half a dozen likely scenarios involving my death. It was a fairly simple task to engineer a path through them all, but from that point, the solution to my "non-death" had started to become increasingly complicated. On top of it, I couldn't tell anyone what was happening—the solution sets became unstable unless I kept it to myself.

So I found myself running around Atopia, asking people to do odd jobs for me, and flittering off to the four corners of the multiverse on inane assignments just to keep myself alive. Things began spinning out of control like a surreal joke, the punchline far out of reach.

We managed to rout the incoming threats the day before by sending out bots and synthetics—and in critical cases, myself personally—to nudge the advancing future timeline of my world this way or that.

Lately, however, some of the future death events were beginning to creep into the hours and minutes just ahead. What started out a few months ago as the odd warning of some low-probability events to be carefully avoided had progressed into a constant stream of events that signaled my impending death. We had no idea how or why it was happening.

"Most of the bases are covered for today," Hotstuff explained, summoning up a probability scatter grid that sprouted outward from some critical nexus points. "There are just a few events that you need to handle personally, starting with this one in New York."

She pointed to the nexus closest to me, and the future reality of that event spun out around us. I nodded, trying to take it in.

Someone with lesser resources than I had would've just died, without fanfare, and that would have been that. In my unique position as owner of Phuture News, and with my almost limitless finances, however, I could literally see the future coming and dodge and weave my way through it. Anyone else edging up on seventy might have accepted their mortality with a little more grace, but here on Atopia, I was still a spring chicken. I wasn't ready to accept a trip on the ultimate voyage just yet.

Sensing my mind wandering, Hotstuff decided to summon up another gruesome termination. She growled playfully, swatting at me with her riding crop while I watched myself being liquefied in the bio-sludge facilities. I felt like I was being stalked by the army of darkness with Betty Boop as my sidekick.

How many ways can a person die?

Her tactic was successful, however, and I refocused on the New York project.

"You just need to steal a pack of cigarettes," she explained while I watched the simulation play through.

"Sounds good," I sighed. "Time to get ready for work."

Sitting on the rooftop deck of my habitat, I took one longing look toward the breaking surf and then grumpily got up from my chair to begin the day's activity list to keep me alive. How exactly stealing a pack of cigarettes from some woman in New York would help me out was impossible to understand, but there it was.

Resisting the almost uncontrollable urge to procrastinate, I heard myself say, "Okay, Hotstuff, let's get this show on the road."

The deck of my habitat faded away to reveal the grimy walls of a convenience store in New York. My consciousness had been implanted into a robotic surrogate that Hotstuff had set into position. The pristine lines of Atopia disappeared from my sensory frames, and even through the thin sensory input, the overpowering odor and seediness of the place hit me like a wave of virtual sewage.

I felt dirty, despite being remote from the robotic body, and had to fight back an urge to go and wash myself. I'd had a very bad time in New York as a young man, and memories of it still haunted me. This was the first time I'd gone back in forty years.

The target in question was yelling at the cashier behind the counter in front of me. In fact, she looked like she was about to hit him.

"Lady!" I shouted above her, raising my spindly metal arms in the cashier's defense. "Lady, take it easy!"

She didn't notice me as she fumbled around in her purse, entirely engrossed in whatever it was she was trying to do. Her face registered disgust, and she looked like she was having a worse day than even I was.

Eventually, after more theatrics, she negotiated her purchase. I hung back and followed her out the door, but at a distance.

She stopped outside to light up, standing under a wobbly holographic advertisement. After a few moments, I saw my chance. I moved, taking her by surprise, and pinned her against the wall. Terrified, she froze, and I fumbled at her, trying to grab the pack of cigarettes. Quickly, I pried it out of her hands.

"Get off me!" she screamed.

Jumping back with my prize in hand, I felt like I wanted to apologize, and I stared for a moment into her green eyes. She looked like someone standing on the edge of a cliff. Explaining myself wasn't an option, however, and instead I melted backward into the pedestrian flow, leaving her there, shaking. It seemed absurd, but stealing this pack of cigarettes would collapse a whole stream of dangerous alternate futures for me.

5

Time—Einstein famously said that it was purely an illusion, just a construct of the conscious mind. A nice idea, but try having this conversation with someone who sensed their ending. Time was something we all desperately wanted more of when it ran short, yet we wasted it frivolously when we thought we had enough.

I was in a bad mood after a long day of saving my own life dozens of times. Midnight was rolling around, and I'd just finished with the last of it. The air was calm and a full moon was out as I sat out on the top deck of my habitat, watching glittering waves swell over the kelp. I leaned back in my chair and considered my problem for a moment.

I could use a walk to clear my mind.

"Hotstuff, could you drop me into Retiro Park, near the Crystal Palace?"

The surging ocean and the outlines of my deck faded from view, replaced with afternoon sunshine and the greens and golds of Madrid's Buen Retiro Park. I was standing on a gravel path beside the Crystal Palace as requested. It was one of my favorite places to take a walk when I was having a hard time with something.

I looked down at my hands, admiring their apparent solidity, and took a moment to gaze around the park. It never ceased to amaze me how well this technology worked. I could smell grass that was being noisily cut by a mower in the distance. A woman pushing a baby carriage passed by and glanced at me, smiling. I heard the gravel crunching under the carriage wheels and the soft burble of the baby inside.

Most people took the wikiworld—the collected audiovisual and sensor inputs of all people and networks and cameras spanning the world—for granted. But for those of us who had slaved away to make it a reality, it still evoked a certain sense of awe.

I took a deep breath, straightened up, and began walking down the path.

The wikiworld was great, but the thing that had made me really famous was the future—literally.

Science was, at its root, just a hodgepodge of rules for predicting the future. How to achieve the same sort of success science had in the physical domain, and replicate this to predict daily human life, had seemed beyond grasping, until I lit upon a place to start.

Slumbering one morning, my great idea came to me suddenly, as great ideas tended to do, and that idea was celebrity gossip. As social animals, gossip was something humans couldn't do without.

A student of history, I'd noticed that as civilizations advanced, they tended to become more and more interested in the tiny details of famous peoples' lives. The Romans were the great innovators, but it was modern America that had really taken it to new heights.

When you started with any new technology, you needed to establish a foothold, a niche you could call your own, and I'd been struggling to find a niche for synthetic future world predictions, or phuturing—a term I had coined. A "phuture" was an alternate future reality that sprouted off from the present moment of time. The future, with an "f," was the actual, single future that you ended up sliding along your timeline into; but *the* future was only one of many possible phutures.

Weather forecasting and stock markets were well covered with established brands and pundits, but this wasn't the kind of future I had been interested in. I wanted to know the future of individual people, on the most detailed possible levels.

A problem with making predictions, especially the ones involving people, was that as soon as they knew about a prediction, they would tend to confound it, and the more people that knew, the more confounding these effects became. My insight was that celebrities acted as a foil to this. Even when they were presented with a prediction concerning them, most enjoyed the attention enough that they would go along with whatever the prediction was.

We soon began to make a name for ourselves by scooping major news outlets to break stories that hadn't even happened yet, beating entertainment and gossip media to the punch by featuring the celebrity headlines of the future before they even happened.

Celebrity gossip set the sails of the Phuture News Network to become a commercial success, and we gradually expanded our predictive systems to encompass nearly every aspect of daily life. Advertising revenue had skyrocketed as we began selling ad space for things we could predict people would want tomorrow, but it was nothing compared to the money people were willing to pay for the service itself. Almost overnight, we became one of the world's most valuable companies, rising to the top of the tech industry in earnings and sales.

Kicking gravel down the path, I sent up a cloud of dust and overlaid a visual phuturecast onto it. I watched it as it was carried away by the wind, flowing into its future self as it dissipated and eventually disappeared.

On Atopia, we'd taken Phuture News to the next level and begun constructing perfect, sensory realistic phutureworlds. Some scientists began claiming that these weren't just predictions, but portals into alternate parallel universes further forward along our timeline, and had started to use this as the technical definition of a "phuture."

Not quite what I'd had in mind when I began the whole enterprise into divining tomorrow's cocktail-dress-du-jour, but in all cases, people had begun to live ever more progressively in the worlds of tomorrow.

While the personalized future predictions we generated for people were private to them, as the owner of Phuture News, I built in one proviso: I could confidentially gain access to any and all phutures generated in order to build my own personal, and highly detailed, phutureworlds.

It had been fascinating to tie everything together, to peer into the collective future of the world. At least, it had been fascinating to begin with, until I could see far enough forward. Then it became depressing.

In all cases, it turned out that the biggest killer app of the future was the future itself, and sitting atop the greatest computing installation the world had ever known, I became the only person on the planet who could literally see into the world of tomorrow.

With great powers, they said, came strange responsibilities, and therein was the problem—for while I could see the future, it seemed that the future now refused to see me.

At least, it refused to see me in it.

Hotstuff had already snuggled my body comfortably into bed as I collapsed my subjective away from Retiro Park and back home. I sighed and pulled the sheets closer around me. It was time to get some sleep.

I had a feeling I'd need it.

6

"A great evil will consume you all!" The man's filthy, mottled face barely restrained a threatened apoplectic fit as he balanced precariously atop an upturned four-gallon paint can.

Wheezing asthmatically, his eyes rolled up toward the damp skies before returning to earth to hunt through the crowd. His gaze swung around to lock onto me and I stared back. Trembling slightly, his already distended pupils widened as he peered at me.

"A great evil is already consuming you, sir," he whispered, directly addressing me as I passed. And then he screeched to the crowd, pointing at me, "A GREAT EVIL is upon us!"

Shivering, I looked away, but nobody paid much attention.

I was off on another one of my walks to try and clear my mind, this time through Hyde Park in London, and I was just passing Speakers' Corner near Marble Arch. The steady thrum of the automated passenger traffic hummed in the background while the electric crackle of London's city center hung just past the peripheries of my senses.

It was morning for me, but already well past midday here, halfway around the world from Atopia. The usual collection of crackpots and doomsayers had already installed themselves for the afternoon tourist crowds. I usually enjoyed standing and watching, listening to the passionate ramblings of the desperate men and women on their soapboxes, exhorting us to save ourselves. But today it felt wrong, or perhaps worse, it felt right.

Hunching over, I kept my eyes to the ground and wound my way through the crowd, making my escape into the sanctuary of the park.

Even here in my virtual presence, I had to keep up my guard, a point-of-presence being a potential point of entry into my networks. I had a whole sentry system of future-selves walking through the park in the immediate future ahead of me.

Threading my way through the periphery of the crowd, my splintered ghosts walked seconds and minutes ahead of me, testing the informational flow through this path and that, dropping data honey pots here and there to pick up straggling invaders, testing for the safest narrow corridor into my future. Salvation for me was threading the eye of a needle, and without being able to see a clear future, it felt as if my hands were tied behind my back or my limbs amputated.

Taking some slow, deep breaths, I tried to relax.

The sun was bravely fighting its way through the wet skies, and small collections of people had begun to install themselves on the low-slung green-and-white striped loungers scattered across the grassy expanse at this end of the park. I was heading directly toward the constabulary near the eastern end of the Serpentine. On my rambles through Hyde Park, I always ran a historical skin so that I could enjoy the Crystal Palace of the Great Exhibition of 1851, and I could see its roof gleaming past a copse of trees in the distance.

I'd developed a thing for Crystal Palaces.

Right at that moment, however, that same reality overlay was projecting the Tyburn gallows next to a gaggle of old ladies who'd slumped into their loungers in the middle of the field. An execution was in progress, or at least a hanging. The ashen corpse of Oliver Cromwell spun slowly in the breeze, much to the delight of the crowd collected for the spectacle that had ushered London into 1661.

"Old Crommie is dancing the Tyburn jig!" leered the ghost of a sharp-jawed woman in sodden rags.

No matter which way I turned, death seemed to surround me. Quickly I cropped the reality skin into a narrow window of time around the present and 1851, and the crowd and execution dropped away.

Visions of the trail around the Serpentine pond floated into my consciousness as my splinters walked ahead of me. I collapsed my probable paths to head toward Kensington Road and the entrance of the Crystal Palace and the cool of the ancient oaks that stood there, quietly marking their own way through time.

Patricia Killiam had asked to speak with me today. Walking across the edge of the park, I summoned a splinter into a media feed of her in another of her endless string of press conferences, and an image of the live event popped into my mind. She'd been an early supporter of much of the deep technology behind the Phuture News Network and was one of my oldest and dearest friends.

In an overlaid visual display, a reporter was just asking her a question. "Isn't the world population stable now, even declining? Shouldn't that help calm the resource shortages?"

"The core problem isn't population," explained Patricia, "but that everyone wants to live lives of material luxury. Supporting ten billion middle-class citizens on planet Earth was never going to work, and the only solution is to create a simulated reality that is good enough to satisfy our material cravings."

It was probably the millionth time that Patricia had gone through this.

"And why is this proxxi thing such a key part of all this?" asked the same reporter.

"Your proxxi controls a dynamic image of your neural wetware so it can control your physical body when you're away," she continued. "This enables you to seamlessly drop off into any virtual space, any time you like—even in the middle of a conversation, since your proxxi can finish it for you. It's like an airbag for your body and mind, except that this airbag can act as your official representative."

The crowd nodded. They loved this stuff.

"If you don't want to go to that meeting or work cocktail tonight," she finished, "just send your proxxi! Why not? It's your life!"

This earned a big round of applause.

As the press conference split up, Patricia's main point-of-presence shifted into my reality, and she materialized walking in step beside me in the park. Her eyes watched me all the way through her transition. I could almost feel her weariness.

"So what's all this on Phuture News about you dying today?"

Now I understood why she'd wanted to chat in person. I tensed up.

"The reports of my death have been greatly exaggerated, old friend," I replied, shaking my head and smiling.

She raised her eyebrows. "At least you seem to have a sense of humor about it."

Phuture News had begun publishing stories about the death of its founder. The mounting density of my termination events had pushed my death into reality for everyone living in the world of tomorrow.

"I wanted to check up on you in person," she continued, "to see if you needed anything."

"Don't worry about me. I'm just fooling around."

A lie, but I had no choice. In my situation, admitting anyone into the circle of trust was extremely dangerous. Expanding the network of people who knew what was happening would spread the probability matrices, and I needed razor-sharp phutures to effectively head off my threats.

She watched me curiously, almost sadly. "Playing? You sure? This seems a funny way to have a laugh."

"Don't worry," I reassured her.

She cocked her eyebrows at me.

"Really, don't worry," I repeated. "And thanks for taking the time to drop in."

By now we'd reached the edge of the Serpentine. It was filled with small blue paddleboats being driven around by enthusiastic tourists. Views of Kensington Palace crept over the weeping willows in the distance, and despite the brave advances of the sun, a light rain had begun to fall again.

"Is there anything I can help with?" she asked. "You can trust me, Vince. Tell me what's happening...."

The walls of my future squeezed ever tighter around me.

"Everything's fine," I reiterated. "And I do trust you, Pat. I just still have a hard time believing you work for Kesselring now."

Kesselring had tried to engineer a hostile takeover of Phuture News many years ago, back when it was barely a start-up, with plans to strip it down and profiteer from the future. He'd used some aggressive and illegal tactics to try and get what he wanted. Patricia had been on our board back then, and we'd fought off Kesselring together.

"A necessary evil," replied Patricia. She looked into the distance. "You promise to ping me if you need anything. I mean it, if you need anything...."

"I will."

She stared at me silently. We'd known each other a long time.

"I promise, I will," I laughed. "Now go on, I know how busy you are."

Patricia nodded and smiled.

"You take care, Vince."

With that, she faded away to leave me alone to finish my walk, or at least, alone with my crowd of future-selves arrayed around me.

"It does seem to be getting worse, though," I said to myself glumly after she was gone. I was covering up the issue of my increasingly probable death as some kind of prank. Most people didn't seem to think it was very funny. Neither did I.

I scuffed my foot in the dirt again as I passed in front of the Crystal Palace. Looking up, I watched some leaves falling from the trees in the distance, wondering if they felt any regret as they came to rest against the earth.

7

"Are you sure that's right?"

I laughed and pulled the girl closer. "Everything is right when I'm with you."

She wriggled away, giggling. "Quit it. Is that the right time?"

I looked up at the curved clock face. "Yeah, I think so, nearly eight."

"Come on then, we're going to be late!"

She pulled me along, and I looked up from the clock at the high vaulted ceiling of New York's Grand Central Station. This place always inspired a sense of awe in me, or, if not exactly awe, then a deep feeling of history. I felt a certain sense of nostalgia for all the human stories that had passed through this place, or, like me, were dragged through.

Looking up and around as we wound our way through the hustle and bustle across the white marble floors, my eyes came to rest on the news display at one end. She was looking at it as well.

"Carrier groups set to high alert," read the rolling display. "NSA warnings of cyberattacks."

She let go of me and stared at the news display, then looked back at me. Her blue eyes shone, twinkling in the station's lighting. She was so beautiful.

"Are you sure it's safe?"

I looked briefly up at the news before looking back into her eyes.

"These things always blow over," I reassured her.

"Seriously, Vince, you're the expert. You're sure, right?" She stood stock still, looking into my face.

"Yes, I'm sure. If we don't take this one, they'll probably cancel everything later."

A huge snowstorm was descending on New York and Boston. We had to hurry if we were going to make it on time to catch the last train out.

She shrugged. "Okay."

We began running again, hand in hand, and soon we were on the Metronorth, cuddled up together for the ride to New Haven to visit her parents, the soft *ka-chunk-ka-chunk* of the tracks lulling us into a peaceful slumber as the miles rolled away.

What seemed like moments later, I awoke with a start, my heart racing. Somebody was yelling. Sitting upright, I looked out the window into a swirling whiteout.

Then the screams and the terrible squeal of metal tearing and gnashing into itself as the train car pitched back and forth. I jammed my feet into the seat into front of me, bracing myself for what was to come, holding onto the girl who clutched desperately back onto me.

The world exploded.

Sucking in air, I sat bolt upright in bed, looking around, but she was gone. I hadn't died in that reality, but then, that one was in the past, now an unchangeable part of my timeline. I didn't die in the train crash, but she had—Sophie, the love of my young life, back when I was an engineering student at MIT. I calmed my breathing, telling myself that everything was all right, but even now, over forty years later, I knew that it wasn't—that it never would be.

It was a perpetually recurring dream, dulled only slightly with time, of the day when I'd lost her. I'd promised her there was nothing to worry about, and it had cost her life. I'd been in the middle of my master's degree at the MIT Media Lab, an expert in the cyber realm, with Patricia Killiam as my thesis professor. I'd been studying the use of predictive systems in social networks, a pursuit that became a passion after the accident. If I'd just been able to see the future a little more clearly, been able to know a little more, I could have saved her. That's what I could never forgive myself for.

I wiped the sweat off my forehead, rubbing my eyes. Why had she returned to my dreams now? I sighed. It must be the baby shower I was going to later in the day. Family events always made me think of her and a life I'd lost so long ago, a life I'd filled with senseless fluff but was now defending with everything I had.

Perhaps it's not worth it. Why am I even trying?

I could save my own life, but the future of the world? I knew the future, and it wasn't something I wished I did know. It was something I'd been doing my best to forget.

I laid down in bed, put my heart back away, and closed my eyes.

8

Wasn't a baby shower supposed to come *before* a baby was born?

I'd just materialized in the entertainment metaworld that Commander Strong had created for his family's coming out party. Well, his sort-of family. Rick waved at me and I smiled and waved back, watching him hand his new simulated baby back to his wife.

Despite being a big believer in Patricia's synthetic reality program, I couldn't help feeling that these "proxxid" babies were creepy, and I'd been hearing dark rumors hinting at the things that Dr. Granger had been using them for.

I would have avoided coming entirely, but this event had sprung up on my threat radar today. Convincing Rick that this proxxid, and having many more besides, was a good idea would somehow collapse a whole subset of threat vectors coming my way.

I didn't like the idea of being so disingenuous, and I'd argued and tried to plan other contingencies all night with Hotstuff, but the alternatives were a lot more dangerous. After a little reflection, it didn't seem like *too* much of a bad thing, and the happy couple looked like they were enjoying it.

"Congrats, Rick!" I exclaimed as the commander neared, extending my hand. He shook it firmly, looking a little sheepish, and motioned toward the bar.

"Thanks, Vince. Oh, and thanks for those flowers the other day, Cindy really loved them."

"No problem at all."

We'd reached the bar. "So what'll it be?" he asked.

I surveyed the bottles. "Nothing for me, thanks."

Now wasn't the time for a drink. It would have only been a synthetic drink, so I could choose to feel intoxicated or not, but the real issue was the interpersonal engagement. Taking a drink would necessitate having a chat, and I was uncomfortable about having to lie to my friend.

I shrugged weakly.

"You sure?" he asked, giving himself a generous dose of whiskey in a tumbler.

"I'm kind of busy...." I struggled with what came next. Rick fidgeted in front of me, taking a gulp from his drink, smiling awkwardly.

"This thing, it's just a little game," he laughed, misinterpreting my discomfort. Knocking back another big swig from his drink he shook his head, looking toward his wife holding their proxxid. "I'm just doing it to keep her happy, you know how it is."

The time had come.

"No, no, this is the best thing," I said enthusiastically. "You need to do this. It's the way of the future!" I slapped him on the back to emphasize the point.

He snorted and took another drink, his face brightening.

"I mean it. You should have as many proxxids as you can before going on to the real thing."

"You really think so?"

"I do my friend." I put a hand on his shoulder and squeezed it. I felt terrible. I had to get out of there as quickly as possible if I wasn't going to blow it. "I have to get going, though. Sorry. Give Cindy a kiss for me, okay?"

"I will." He nodded, smiling.

I hesitated. *I shouldn't do this.* I should just come clean, see if maybe he could help me.

"Go on," laughed Rick. "Get going!"

Nodding good-bye, I decided to say nothing and faded away from the sensory space of his party.

I needed a break to think, so I decided on yet another walk in one of my private spaces. I materialized on a dusty path next to the Crystal Mountain in the middle of the Sahara Desert in Egypt, near the border of Libya.

This place held a mystical, almost magnetic, attraction to me, a massive single quartzite crystal that rose up hundreds of feet out of the barren limestone landscape surrounding it. I'd recently installed my own private sensor network here, in secret, as the open wikiworld version lacked the resolution to really experience it, to enjoy the nuances and stark beauty of the place. It allowed me a place to wander truly alone, to enjoy some peace for short stretches in my newly frightening personal reality.

Night was falling, spreading its inky carpet across the sky to reveal the cathedral of stars that shone only in the deepest of deserts. The perpetual Sirocco wind whistled softly, carrying with it the sand that over the eons had etched the limestone bedrock into fantastical forms that sprang up out of the desert floor like mysterious blooms, lending the lifeless place an interior life of its own.

Massive sand dunes sat hunched in the distance, slowly sailing their lonely courses across the bare bedrock, their hulks propelled by the same unrelenting wind that shaped this place. As they moved, they swallowed everything in their paths, but just as inevitably as they consumed, they would eventually surrender as they moved on. You just had to stand still long enough, exist long enough, to be released.

I stepped slowly between the ghostly sandstone figures that towered above me, frozen in time in their mad dance together. The Crystal Mountain glowed in an ethereal purple above it all, its interior lit by a million tiny points of starlight.

It was strange not being able to see my future hanging in front of me. I mean, I could see my phutures, sense the nearness of their realities spreading out ahead of me, but now they all terminated abruptly. The fingers of time I'd carefully nurtured over the years had been painfully amputated.

Where before the future had flowed straight ahead of me, like a train running to known destinations, now all its tracks ahead ended in flames. A suffocating fire enveloped me, the future choking the lifeblood out of my present. I felt trapped in the moment.

"Hotstuff, could you pop in for a sec?"

She obediently materialized walking next to me. In sharp contrast to the dreamlike landscape I had lost myself in, her vitality and energy sizzled into this space. She was looking extremely sharp in tight striped riding pants, boots, and a high-necked red jacket. Her long blond hair fell in waves down her back and across her shoulders.

Some people liked to create some sort of alter ego as their proxxi, which was fine for them. I preferred to have an attractive woman as my personal assistant. Plus, I liked the idea of a woman driving my body around when I wasn't in it.

I felt better with Hotstuff near, but I was still nervously fidgeting my phantoms' limbs.

"Stop that," she commanded.

She stopped walking, looking up to consider one of the limestone figures.

"Stop it," she repeated softly.

"Stop what?"

I'd begun a nervous drumbeat with the phantom limb that controlled my future social connectivity.

"Stop playing with your phantoms," laughed Hotstuff, continuing to walk on. "You're going to grow hair on them. Seriously, stop it. You're jiggling your phutures back and forth, muddying up your timeline. Stay focused."

I stopped and relaxed my phantoms, releasing them back to her. We'd reached a natural stone archway at the end of the limestone menagerie, on an outcropping above a steep drop to the plateau below. Sitting down together on the edge of the cliff, we looked down at the sand dunes spreading out into the distance, disappearing into the gathering gloom.

"Do you think someone is phuture-spoofing me?"

Phuture-spoofing was growing into a major business as hacking spilled into the worlds of tomorrow and phuture crackers began engineering their own timelines.

"Boss, we've been over this a hundred times, and I don't see how someone could be phuture-spoofing you," Hotstuff replied. "In all cases, I've had specialized agents rooting through the Phuture News system and sniffers floating at choke points throughout the open multiverse with nothing suspicious to report. To manage it on this scale, they'd need almost the same computing infrastructure as the Phuture News Network itself."

Which would be impossible to hide, she didn't need to add.

"So summarize the situation?" I leaned back and looked up at the stars.

"The good news is that we've made some progress," she said brightly. "We've plotted a path to extricate your physical body from Atopia, giving us a much larger playing field to work with."

"That sounds good," I replied. "So what's the bad news?"

"The *bad* news is that the system is predicting about seven thousand possible outcomes for your, ah, demise in the next few days."

"So that's it, I'm dead?" The stars shone like steely pins, puncturing the night sky around me.

"Don't be so defeatist. You only have a dozen things to get done personally today, so we can head this thing off. Tomorrow is another day. Just focus, be in the moment."

"That's what you said yesterday," I complained.

I was being petulant. It was the last redoubt of the rich and aimless when faced with hard work. After I'd gotten over the initial shock of almost dying day after day, I'd found the urge to beg off and go surfing almost irresistible, and it was annoying me that I had to save my own life. This was the sort of stuff I was supposed to pay people for. Secretly, though, I was beginning to settle into it, even enjoying some of the new activity forced onto me, but I wouldn't ever admit it.

Hotstuff gave me a sidelong glance and raised one eyebrow. "Hey tough guy, it's your life. The probability is only nine in ten you'll kick the celestial bucket today if you wing it. Go ahead, go surfing."

I nodded, digging my fingers into the sand.

"You know, boss, this may not be an entirely bad thing...."

That stopped me in my tracks.

"What the hell do you mean by that?" I almost spat the words out, nearly deciding to point out that proxxies terminated when their owners did, but held my tongue.

Hotstuff took a moment to choose her words. "I mean, before, well...."

"What?"

"Before, you were kind of aimless—you'd lost any interest in the future."

"You think this is better?"

"At least you're up in the mornings."

I snorted. "Yeah, to live another day, to fight to stay alive."

She let me consider what I'd just said. "See what I mean?"

I sighed. I was frustrated, but not as scared anymore. As perverse at it sounded, maybe she was right. I was certainly savoring the little moments of time that I could get to myself.

"Whatever. Anyway, it's getting better, right?"

"We're managing the best we can."

"The best that you can, huh?" I replied dejectedly, looking up at my task list for the day as it appeared in one of my display spaces. Something popped out. "So I need to short Cognix stock?"

"Nobody will know it's you. Look, I'm setting up defensive perimeters," explained Hotstuff, "and we'll drop some intelligent agents into them to look for any cross-phuture scripting. We'll figure this out, boss, don't worry."

"Don't worry?" *Is she serious?*

"I don't want to get your hopes up, but I think we're starting to see a pattern, hidden deep in the probability matrices that connect together whatever is chasing you. A pattern in the future, but one that points somewhere far in the past."

Finally, some progress.

"Can you explain a little more?"

"It would be easier to show you."

9

Dappled sunlight streamed down through the jungle canopy high above, illuminating the hard-packed earth below. It cast a patchwork of light and dark that stitched together scenes of smoke rising from cooking fires, laughing children darting between thatched huts, and women sitting and gossiping together as they stripped the white skins off sweet potatoes, carefully wrapping each one in banana leaves and depositing them into a stone-lined pit.

The men were hunting today, chasing pigs that escaped from neighboring villages in the thunderstorms of the night before. Monkeys barked through the underbrush, their catcalls joining the symphonies of songbirds whose feathers lit up the steaming forest like splashes of flickering paint against a knotted green canvas.

Picking up a smooth stone sitting on the earth, I casually ducked my head as a dart snipped past, barely missing me. One of the children cried out to my right. A mother picked the child up by his arm and spanked him. He'd been playing with his father's blowgun, not knowing what he was doing, probably imitating his dad. Even as I inhabited someone else, whatever was hunting me down was trying to kill this body as well.

The mother looked toward me and shrugged, apologizing. I smiled back, returning my attention to the witch doctor. Dodging death was nothing new anymore.

"In da roond," explained the tribal elder, speaking in variant of Tok Pisin, an English pidgin that was the lingua franca of the Papua New Guinea highlands.

The two most linguistically diverse places left on Earth were also the most culturally and technologically polarized: this place, barely out of the Stone Age, and New York City, the bustling megalopolis tipping the world into the twenty-second century. Each retained over a thousand languages, but where almost all in New York were machine translatable, and thus part of the new global lingua franca, almost none of the New Guinea languages were. I was struggling to understand what this elder was struggling just as hard to explain to me.

"Round, like, like in a circle?" I stuttered in my best attempt at native Yupno, the tribe here. Speaking through this body was difficult.

A giant tree frog watched me lazily from its perch in the branches nearby. I couldn't remember the last time I'd seen a frog in the wild. Of course, I couldn't remember the last time I'd been in the wild either.

To get to this remote and rugged place, we'd had a portable communication base station dropped in, and then we convinced a nun running a nearby mission to persuade one of the villagers to drink a glass of water laden with smarticles, allowing my subjective to enter and control his body through the communication link.

It was the only way I could speak with this particular elder, the Yupno witch doctor and keeper of holy secrets. The smarticles hadn't fully suffused into this body, so I felt numb and disconnected, and they would be soon flushed out, so I had to hurry.

The witch doctor shrugged and smiled, revealing a mouthful of blackened teeth. His eyes sparkled at me. I smiled back, my pssi filtering his body language into a form that made sense to me. My gaze shifted to a break in the jungle that revealed the glacier-capped mountain ranges beyond stretching upward into the bright sky. He was trying to explain his perception of the shape of time, or rather, its lack of shape.

"Here and now," "back in the twenties," "going forward"...the modern world was fixated on spatial metaphors for time, the idea of the past being behind us and the future ahead. Not the Yupno, though. In this remote valley, time seemed to have no linear form to its inhabitants.

To them, it flowed uphill, backward, in forms and in shapes. They laughed at our conception of its forward flow. This Stone Age culture directly experienced something Einstein had only glimpsed through his equations.

The pattern Hotstuff detected had led us here, and she was sitting on a log across the cooking fire from the elder and me, fetchingly dressed in safari shorts with her hair done up in a long single braid that she was playing with, twirling between her fingers. Of course, since she was simply an augmented reality projection in the pssi system, I was the only one who could see her.

"He means time runs forward and backward, but not like a stream—more like currents in a lake," she suggested. "No, like a reservoir, that's more what he means."

"Like a reservoir?" I asked the elder.

He nodded. With long arms, he reached up and circled his hands around slowly, finally coming to rest, ending at me. The Yupno had a way of pointing toward doorways when speaking about time, a curiosity I was beginning to understand.

Inhabiting the body of this tribal member, I was trying to see if time felt any different for me. It didn't, but something felt odd.

Amazingly, the elders hadn't batted an eye at the idea of one of their own being magically inhabited by an alien spirit, nor the idea that I was conversing with an invisible ghost, Hotstuff, in their midst. It seemed perfectly natural to them.

The witch doctor pointed to where Hotstuff was sitting, almost as if he could see her.

"The spirit name?" he asked.

Hotstuff raised her eyebrows.

"Hotstuff," I replied, shrugging at her.

"HOT stuff," he repeated, "hot STUFF?"

I nodded, and his smiled widened.

"And your name?" I asked—I hadn't thought to inquire before.

He pointed to his chest. "Nicky," he said proudly, and then added, "Nicky Nixons."

I laughed—Nicky Nixons the witch doctor.

"It is a pleasure to meet you, Dr. Nicky Nixons. My name," I said, pointing to myself, "is Vince Indigo."

"Yes, in—dee—go...," he replied, nodding sagely, as if he'd always known.

"This is all very touching," interjected Hotstuff, "but we have to get going. We're out of time here."

She splintered some upcoming death events into my display spaces, one of them a bio-electronic Ebola-based retrovirus that ended with my internal organs liquefying while I brushed my teeth the following morning. She firewalled off the data tunnel from the jungle we were sitting in, just in case.

"It's getting dangerous just being here."

I nodded. "Okay, let's get me going," I replied. "But you stay awhile, see what you can learn from him."

It was time to get to work again. The sensory frames of the jungle and Nicky Nixons quickly faded away to reveal the confines of a small, sparse apartment somewhere in the lower levels of the Atopian seascraper complex. In augmented space, an endless array of workspace cubicles radiated outward in the New London financial metaworld. The cubicles were busily oc-cupied by thousands of copies of Willy McIntyre, one of my surfer friend Bob's best friends and my newly appointed stock trader.

"So I assume business is good?" I asked Willy, sensing the arrival of his primary subjective.

Hotstuff was feeding me a report on Willy's activities, and I could see that these weren't just bots and synthetics he had working—these were full-blown splinters, hundreds of them. I didn't care what he was up to. I just needed to get in and out.

Time was, as ever, against me.

"Business is very, very good," replied Willy, now standing beside me, watching me watching his financial army at work below.

He looked like the cat that had eaten the canary: about to burst with some secret. In the report from Hotstuff, I could see that Willy had fully paid off the multi-generational mortgage for his family. He was well on his way to amassing a sizeable fortune, but I didn't have the time or energy to talk.

Death was calling.

"I noticed you amped up your Phuture News services," I said carefully, "but that's not why I'm here. I'm sending the details of what I need, right now."

I uploaded the transaction into one of his splinters.

"You want me to what?!" he exclaimed. "You know this is going to look suspicious, especially with me working for Infinixx."

"From what I've heard, you don't work for them anymore."

Willy stopped fidgeting and stared at me. "Sure, but it'll still look odd."

"I know it seems crazy, but if you could do this for me, and keep it quiet, I can pay you an awful lot of money. I need you to dump all that stock and chalk up a huge loss, and I need you to do it from New York."

I looked at his face. He was aware of the way I was watching him.

"And be careful," I said after a moment, feeling he was in over his head.

"It doesn't look like there will be any problems with this transaction—"

"Not with that," I interrupted. He wasn't catching my meaning. "I mean with whatever you have going on here."

"There's nothing going on here."

We stared at each other.

I needed to get going. "Just be careful, okay?"

He hesitated, but then smiled. "No problem, Mr. Indigo."

This kid was going to get himself in trouble. He offered his hand and I shook it, but my mind was already elsewhere.

I quickly flitted off to the roof of the Cognix towers.

10

A deep, haunting wail reverberated through the morning air, carrying me upward, beyond the highest of the Himalayan peaks, but also inward and backward, deep into my mother's womb. A million deaths surrounded me, all threaded outward from my moment of creation, a cosmic embryo of existence secured by the thin timeline threading through it all that kept me alive.

My body was drenched in sweat under the hot sun that beat down from the Columbian sky. Making my way across the Plaza de Bolivar, I wiped the sweat off the nape of my neck with a T-shirt I'd pulled out of my backpack. Tourists stood around in small groups, looking at the grand framed-portico walls, perspiring together under the same sun that was baking me.

Pigeons scattered at my feet, but I had to keep moving. A small security contingent was shadowing me from a distance, but I was trying to stay incognito. Out of the corner of my eye, a Coca-Cola sign called out from under the shade of an awning, and I shifted my path toward it and the small convenience shop beneath it at the corner of the plaza.

"*Hola!*" I announced as I entered, feeling the relief of air-conditioning sweeping over me. I slid open the door to a refrigerator at the side of the register, pulling out a can of soda, and, parched, opened it and began gulping it down. The shopkeeper appeared from the back, just as I was about finished with it.

"*Señor!*" he exclaimed with eyes wide, staring at me.

"What?"

I put the can down. *Was he that upset I didn't pay for it first?*

Reaching into my pockets, I felt energized and awake. I fumbled around excitedly for some pesos. A small group of people had appeared in the shop, staring at me, which I knew could only mean one thing.

My heart banged in my chest. I couldn't breathe. I looked at the shopkeeper, who stared in horror at the can of soda in my hand. My vision began to swim as I made for the door, my knees giving way in a euphoric rush. At the edges of my senses, I could hear applause. I waved to my fans as blackness descended.

The *dungchen* horns sounded again, their low, baleful moans awakening my mind from its semilucid dream state. I blinked and looked out the window of the room I'd been sleeping in. The rising sun was announcing the start of a new day, though Lhasa was still enveloped in shade as the sun fought its way over the towering peaks surrounding the valley.

Still half-asleep, I let my mind wander back to the death event in Columbia we'd just averted. They'd been smuggling narcotics in the soda cans, and I would have unwittingly downed one before anyone could warn me off. We shifted the path of my walk later in the day through Bogota, away from the Plaza de Bolivar entirely, just in case.

The FDMs were a troubling development. The same way that people would mob around an accident on a street corner to gawk, with future prediction technology and the wikiworld, people could now flit to nearly any spot on the planet to witness accidents taking place. They called them FDMs—flash death mobs.

With so many predicted future deaths, I'd now attracted my own FDM fan club, and my future deaths became celebrations, with people flitting in to witness the endless sequences of clever deaths that I would narrowly avert. They figured this was a future installation art project of some kind, and I couldn't afford to tell the world the truth, so I was just rolling with it.

The patterns Hostuff had detected had led us to Lhasa, to study the Tibetan Book of the Dead, a text dedicated to experiences that lay between life and death. It was maddeningly difficult to understand since most of it was coded in ancient symbols. We'd gone there to participate in the Monk Debates, to talk directly with those who really understood it.

A familiar tapping echoed through the slightly ajar wooden door of the shared room I was sleeping in. I was inhabiting the body of a Buddhist monk from the Sera Monastery on the outskirts of Lhasa. In return for borrowing his corporal form, I'd offered the monk a chance for some truly out-of-body meditation sessions using the pssi network, something they didn't normally have access to here.

Smarticles were an internationally controlled substance. My transport of them outside of Atopia, and especially with what I was doing here, was highly illegal.

"Don't even try it," I warned Hotstuff.

She stood pouting in the doorway, done up in a French maid outfit, but, of course, still with her riding crop in hand. I pulled the bed sheets off before she could get to me. I stood and pulled my maroon *dhonka* robe around me.

Weeks had passed, and I was still here, but barely. The day before there'd been fifty thousand ways I could have died in the millions of phutures we were tracking, and I'd had to fight off two sequences in real time and real space—an incredibly close call.

While we'd slowed down the contagion, we hadn't been able to stop it spreading. We tried simulations of locking my body in a vault, but this made things worse. The death events piled up, making even the slightest of exposures of my body to the outside disastrously threatening, eventually ending in some kind of terrorist strike against my hiding place.

Hundreds of thousands of bots and synthetics were running around doing large and small things to sweep the death events back, but I was still the key to many of them. This was going to be a big day. We would be fighting death off more fiercely than ever.

"So what's the bad news?" I sighed.

The rest of the sleeping mats in my room were empty, the other monks apparently much earlier risers than me, but then again, they were real Buddhist monks. I stretched, yawning, and rubbed my neck, expecting the worst. I needed to get some hot tea into this body before the morning meditation session.

"Good news!" exclaimed Madame Hotstuff, snapping the riding crop across my ass, urging me awake. She swished the air in front of her with the crop, ending by pointing toward the door. We began to walk. "The threats are receding, or at least, they've stabilized."

"Really?"

My constricted future eased ever so slightly. *Finally.*

We walked out the door and into the hallway, passing a group of monks busily on their way somewhere. Hotstuff sashayed her way past them in her stilettos and knee-high stockings, smiling at them.

"Really," she stated, looking back at me and stopping to lean against the rough-hewn rock wall of the corridor. "It looks like the new ring fencing of a perimeter around your phutures has begun to pay off. *That,* combined with this new meditation and awareness stuff."

"So what was it then?" If we'd found a way to contain it, then there must be a path to the root source, some forensic process we could use to follow it backward.

Hotstuff lowered the riding crop. "Vince, honey, remember what Nicky Nixons said, what Yongdzin, your Buddhist master, is saying. You need to stop thinking in deterministic terms. Live in the moment."

"Right. Live in the moment, effortless action."

"Exactly."

"Hotstuff…Hotstuff…," I intoned solemnly, pressing my monk's hands together in a prayer while we walked.

"I wish you'd chosen a different word for your mantra than my name."

I opened my eyes and winked at her. "Works for me."

She rolled her eyes. "The patterns are solidifying. Whoever did this left a trail of Easter eggs, we think leading to a back door."

"Remind me to thank him personally." I was eager to have a look at today's agenda.

We arrived in the cafeteria, if one could call it that, in the center of Sera Jey. I grabbed a cup of tea and sat down with Hotstuff at a wooden table in the corner. A list of activities floated into view over the bench.

"Not so bad for today, mister, not as bad as yesterday."

By now, we'd built up an espionage, and counterespionage, network that outstripped any but the wealthiest of corporations and nation-states, all with the specific directive of bending the future timeline to my will to keep me alive. We funneled all the money we could from Phuture News and had sold off all my assets to fund the program.

One particular item floated up through the threat matrices.

"So there's no way around it?" In the long list of things I'd had to do, this one hit closest to home. I was struggling with it.

"Sorry, boss. You'd better take care of it before the morning meditation."

I felt terrible about sabotaging the launch of the Infinixx distributed consciousness project, but there wasn't any way around it. A Triad gangster network in Hong Kong would have used it to pinpoint some of my other activities, and disabling the launch was a key vector in keeping my lifeline intact.

I shrugged. *Progress is progress.* I'd better stick with the program. Using a communication phantom, I punched up Patricia's networks, requesting an urgent, private meeting with her primary subjective.

A large Chenrezig statue, the Buddha of Compassion, sat at the head of the long chamber I was in. Its dozens of arms stretched out around it like star fire, its many faces gazing down at me benevolently. Its array of outstretched arms seemed eerily like phantom pssi limbs made visible in real-space. Unnerved, I turned my gaze to the window and the majestic peaks around us.

The plains surrounding Lhasa were filled with permanent, makeshift encampments of international troops that stood as a buffer between the Chinese and Indian bases lining the opposite sides of the valley. The Americans were there as part of the UN mission, as were NATO forces, but the largest contingent was the African Union.

Many thought hope for the future could be found in Africa—where the engine of a new economic powerhouse was already growling, and the last place left on Earth that still had a growing population. Lagos, the capital of the African Union, was closely linked with Terra Nova, the offshore colony in the South Atlantic. Terra Nova had their own synthetic reality product that was set to compete with pssi.

"You want me to what?" asked Patricia, materializing in the seat across from me.

I pulled my gaze back from looking out the window. A glittering security blanket settled around us with her arrival. Patricia paused for a moment while the blanket sealed.

"Do you have everything you need? What's this about?"

She'd helped me smuggle the smarticles out of Atopia, even helped me create my covert communications network, and all without even asking what it was for. Thank God for old friends.

"I'm fine," I replied quietly. "I don't need any more materials, but I do need you to come help me, right now, in your physical form." This sounded odd even before it came out, especially coming from the slight frame of my monk, diminutive in front of this world-famous scientist. "I can't say more, except that it's critical and needs to be kept secret."

Patricia eyed me. "You realize the launch of Infinixx is less than an hour away?"

"I'm not saying you can't go. Go virtually. Isn't that what your whole project is about? What's the difference?"

This was weird, but I'd gotten over my squeamishness about these sorts of requests.

She hesitated.

"You said I could rely on you if I ever needed anything, right?"

"Yes, I suppose...."

"So I'm asking."

She sighed. "Okay."

"Perfect," I replied, sensing this mission accomplished. "I appreciate it, Pat."

An awkward silence descended.

"So what's going on with these storm systems?" I asked casually, changing the topic. I was curious to see if Patricia had anything more to say than what I got through the mediaworlds. I'd been so caught up in my own disasters that I'd hardly paid attention to the storm systems that were threatening Atopia. With a little more breathing space, I'd started to let my mind assimilate more of what was happening on the outside.

These storms were the big news.

"We don't know," she replied, shrugging, "but they're definitely not natural."

Not natural? I hadn't heard that before.

"Something is going on, and we're not sure what."

No kidding, I thought to myself.

11

Finally, after longer than I could remember, I was really enjoying my walk through Buen Retiro Park in Madrid. Summer was turning fully towards fall, and the leaves were starting to come off the trees, creating a beautiful golden carpet underfoot. A perfectly faultless blue sky hung overhead.

In my mind's eye, I saw myself stepping gracefully to the side as a helicopter crashed down from the heavens, nearly crushing me on a walk through Stanley Park in Vancouver the next day. In another splinter, I watched a car swerve, bouncing into my beach buggy as I turned into a parking lot in Malibu a few days later. The car clipped the surfboard I'd tied to the back of the beach buggy, sending it spinning around. I ducked just before the board would have knocked my head off.

It was all effortless action, like a ballet with death.

We'd found a solution to my problem. Since we'd stabilized them a few weeks back when I was in Tibet, the density of death events had quickly fallen. There were still nearly twenty thousand future fatalities we had to avoid to maintain my healthy timeline, but what had been terrifying a few weeks ago was now just a walk in the park.

Literally.

I strode purposefully as I walked around Retiro Park, on each step picking out another yellow leaf underfoot to grind into the gravel, imagining them to be tiny harbingers of doom I was snuffing out. Looking up from my work, I found myself standing in front of the Crystal Palace.

Down the path a little way, a woman leaned over to pick up one of the leaves and began laughing then crying, completely oblivious to everyone around her. Not wanting to disturb her, I shifted my walk onto another trail. I glanced back over my shoulder, but she was already gone.

She'd looked awfully familiar.

To protect myself, I'd developed a kind of temporal immune system, stretching out into the alternate universes connected to me. An army of killer-tomorrow-bots spun through the probabilistic spaces surrounding me, neutralizing threats, clotting dangerous portals and pathways both into the future and through the past. This immune system had become a part of me, a part of my living body, a highly attuned death sense that allowed me to thread my way through even the most dangerous of situations.

For once, the conspiracy theorists were right. Some of the tabloid worlds had begun publishing stories about a shadowy force that had been detected, pushing and pulling the future prediction networks. The shadowy force they were referring to was me, but there was something else out there too—the thing that was trying to hunt me down. But now I was hunting it as well.

The hurricanes threatening to destroy Atopia had more of my attention. In my situation, it was impossible to ignore the possibility that the storms were aimed at me, a final attempt to destroy my power base after attempting to trap me there. The idea just didn't stick, though, and while the storms looked like they would damage Atopia, they were no real threat to me.

I turned my face up to feel the morning sunshine. Where my life before had been sliding into apathy, the past few months had led me on a spiritual journey into an almost mystical place. Decoding the hidden pattern had helped us navigate the most stable path through my future, and it was leading us further and further back. There was a hidden truth I was just beginning to glimpse, buried somewhere in humankind's history.

The solution to my problem was simply to carry on. I was still engaged in a desperate struggle against death, but it had become more like a dance, with effortless action guiding me through. I'd reached a heightened state of being that I would never have been able to achieve any other way.

In the struggle to save myself, I'd been reborn.

As this timeline wore on, people began filtering out the predictions of my death as the attempts of another bored trillionaire at getting attention. The world, at large, was erasing me from their networks as phuture spam, and even the FDMs had gotten bored. The man with no future, who existed only in the moment, was invisible to a world fixated on anywhere but where they actually were.

On my end, I'd come to grips with my situation. My death had become a local solution to the universe that, with the massive resources at my disposal, I'd brought under control in a tight but stable spiral.

The irony just made it that much richer.

I was trapped by my future prediction systems, my own creation, unable to even tell people what was happening. Even more ironic was that I didn't *really* even know if it all was true. It was possible that I was just running around every day, doing it all for no reason.

But then, this was life.

I smiled at that thought.

The existentialists did say that life was all about pulling the victory of meaning from the jaws of senseless absurdity, and in that I'd discovered a purpose I'd struggled to find before. That purpose was finding out who was doing this to me, and why, and the trail was leading back to core of Atopia.

◆ INTERLUDE

Introduction to

Patricia Killiam

Identity: Patricia Killiam

Sitting and waiting. Perfect the art of sitting and waiting, and you will live a long, long life.

I was in the main Cognix conference room, perched about two thousand feet up in the complex spanning the tops of the farming towers at the center of Atopia. The afternoon sun was shining hotly through the glass window walls, and I was sure he was making me wait on purpose, knowing I had come here in person.

My mind was circling back to my press conferences this morning, about what I'd been telling the reporters. Truths and half-truths, I'd been mixing them both for so long that I hardly knew the difference anymore.

How is pssi going to change the world? To be honest, I really didn't know. The real power of pssi, I wanted to tell them, was harnessing the brain's natural ability for adaptively rewiring itself to extend the human mind into the multiverse—but this would only have earned me blank stares.

The human sensory and motor system had evolved to help us make sense of our environment, and to fend for ourselves within it. It was great when our ancestors were out hunting gazelles on the savannah, but the modern human environment was a massive flow of information, and pssi made it possible to plug our nervous systems directly into it.

Explaining that to reporters was just a bridge too far for me to cross with them. It was easier to let them run into some pssi-kids on Atopia somewhere—they'd get the idea soon enough.

I sighed.

Being present in the flesh was something I had started to do more and more, sensing my time growing short. Up here in the conference room, the security blankets blocked outgoing and incoming communications, so there was no escaping down a rabbit hole while I waited. But there was no sense in letting time, illusion or not, go to waste, so I decided to limber up a little.

Taking a deep breath, I straightened up in my chair and activated the visual overlays of my phantoms, which appeared arrayed around me. Concentrating, I began moving the phantom that controlled my spatial point-of-view. This little phantom was visible floating disconnected beside my body, like a little putty-colored finger, and I could move it around as if it was a part of my natural body.

Despite working with this technology for more than thirty years, it still felt strangely thrilling to feel this projection as a part of me, its tactiles and kinesthetics wired into my own sensory system, so that I could feel it stretch and click through the boundaries of its interface.

The brain had an almost inexhaustible capacity to neuroplastically rewire itself. Learn to play the piano and the brain devoted more of its motor cortex to your fingers. Cut off an arm, on the other hand, and your brain could adaptively learn to reroute control of an artificial arm by reworking the way it used various packets of neurons.

Phantoms were an extension of this.

Without removing any existing limbs or digits, we created virtual fingers and limbs in synthetic spaces using pssi to connect them to neurons in the motor cortex. It was like having a dozen extra hands to manage controls that were directly wired into our brains like a part of our bodies.

The flip side of the coin was feeding data into our senses, whether touch, sight, sound, or any of the dozens of other more minor ones humans possessed, to create an unlimited number of metasenses that warned or informed us of what was happening within the informational flow of the multiverse.

We could completely customize our bodies and senses to the way we wanted to interact with real and virtual worlds. Helped along by the neurotrophic growth factors we embedded in the smarticles that suffused through our nervous systems, we'd discovered that the brain had a stunning capacity to grow and adapt to the pssi stimulus, one far beyond even our wildest imaginings at the beginning of the project.

I latched myself firmly into place at the conference table and connected my primary visual point-of-view to the spatial-control phantom I was exercising. As I stretched and moved it, my subjective point-of-view shot back outward from the conference room to hover outside the building.

Diving down into the treetops below, I stopped just above the Boulevard. Quickly, I cycled this phantom back and forth, limbering it up, and then I unlatched the rest of my phantoms. Sitting in the conference room, with my hands resting gently on the polished cherry-wood table, my eighteen phantoms danced around me, and I concentrated as I felt each of them sliding through their interface points, coordinating my visual and metasense overlays.

These phantoms weren't just projections—they were a part of my living, breathing body. It felt as if I were dancing, and I leaned back in my chair with my eyes half-closed, smiling and enjoying my performance.

With a short, characteristic tone announcing his arrival, Kesselring, the principal owner and CEO of Cognix Corporation, materialized opposite me on the other side of the table. I quickly and immediately stowed my phantoms, as if sweeping toys back into a chest. Smiling, he watched me packing them away, waiting for me to finish before he spoke.

Below a thick head of perfectly groomed black hair, Kesselring's flecked hazel eyes shone intensely above his salt-and-pepper beard. The worn creases in his face projected just the right angles of wisdom for a man of his stature.

He beamed enthusiastically at me. "Great work with the press today, Patricia. You're the best. You looked terrific!"

"I do get tired of lying to them all the time," I complained.

I felt like he was patronizing me.

Maybe I was annoyed at him for making me wait, or perhaps I felt silly being caught playing with my phantoms. But really, it was because I couldn't shake the surreal realization that we were planning a conspiracy on the vastest of scales. But it wasn't really a conspiracy, I reminded myself, because everyone would be complicit.

"We're not really lying to anyone," said Kesselring. "We've been over this a million times. I wish you wouldn't keep bringing it up."

"You're right." We had been over it countless times in the years since what we had to do became clear, but as we neared the threshold, things didn't feel right anymore.

He changed the topic, eager to discuss the reason he'd really called this meeting. "Do you think he suspects anything?"

"Obviously he suspects something, but nothing to do with us. At least, not yet."

The hamster wheel we had Vince running on hadn't been my idea, but it was only my deep connections into the Phuture News Network technology that made what we were doing to him possible. The intention hadn't been to harm Vince, just to keep him distracted. We couldn't afford to let him see what we were planning, at least, not until it was too late to stop us.

"Good."

"But he'll figure it out eventually." I was having a hard time understanding how our technology was able to do what it was doing to him, and didn't think our agents could hold him off much longer. "He's already most of the way there."

"Soon it won't matter," shrugged Kesselring. "And nobody will pay any attention to him anyway."

A pause while I eyed Kesselring, trying to lay blame elsewhere for what I had done to my old friend. I took a deep breath. "So we're going to be giving it away for free?"

Kesselring smiled. "Free to install, anyway."

"And it doesn't worry you that we're not telling people the full story?"

On Atopia, we weren't just building a better mousetrap; we were building the best mousetrap of all time.

"Dr. Granger's new work looks promising . . . ."

"Don't get started on Hal," I scowled.

"I'm just saying . . . ."

"I know what you're saying." Using the problem to fix the problem was a recipe for unintended consequences, for disaster.

"As you've said many times," he pointed out, "we need to maximize saturation of the product introduction to maximize networking effects. The Terra Novan's own synthetic reality system isn't far behind us. We need to get our product in first, and fast, to capture the market."

I shook my head. "That's not the real goal."

Kesselring looked at me steadily. "Perhaps not yours, but somebody has to pay for all this."

I rubbed the bridge of my nose, feeling the noose tighten around my neck.

◆◆◆ BROTHERS BLIND

Part 4:

Bobby Baxter

Prologue

"I can be good at anything I want," I explained. "I just need to apply myself."

Grinning, I took another swig from the bottle of fermented seaweed. It was my fourteenth birthday and I was drunk. Or rather, it was *our* fourteenth birthday.

My brother and I were sitting on the railings at one of the entrances to the passenger cannon, suspended hundreds of feet above the Atopian beaches. The steady *thwump-thwump* of the cannon discharging its nightly cargo shipments reverberated powerfully in the air around us. We weren't supposed to be there.

"How did you override the security controls again?" asked my brother.

"Easy as pie!" I boasted. "Get your proxxi in here; I'll download the details and show him."

My brother looked away toward the breaking surf below. "You always want to explain it to my proxxi."

"Come on, seriously?" I chuckled. "You know you're not good at security stuff."

"I'm not good at anything," he replied quietly. "How is it possible that you have such an easy time with everything, but I struggle so much? Aren't twins supposed to be the same?"

"We're not *identical* twins," I laughed.

He looked hurt.

"Come on. Don't exaggerate. You're the funniest guy I know. That's a gift!"

He sighed. "It's the same with everyone. Everyone only wants to talk to my proxxi."

"That's not true."

He sighed again, but then brightened up. "But you're amazing, Bob. You can do anything."

I smiled. "See? Now that's the spirit!"

1

Identity: Bobby Baxter

Temujin was my name, and I was a great warrior of the Mongol clan of the Ong Khan. The year was 1198, and the heat of the summer solstice had baked the steppes dry and cracked. We would soon replenish Mother Earth, soaking Her with the blood of our enemies, and I would rise to my rightful and God-given place among my people as the Universal Ruler, the Ghengis Khan.

Opening my eyes slowly, listening to the crisp snap of our banners flapping in the breeze, I watched the Tatars amassing in the dusty distance on the plains below. Sitting outside the royal yurt with my trusty saber balanced on my knees, my body flowed and pulsed with the power of my ancestors.

The day would end in victory, or in glorious death.

"Do you ever get the feeling none of this is real?" asked Martin, sitting over to my right with a large wad of half-chewed venison dripping from his mouth. His eyebrows were cocked high as he leaned toward me questioningly, waving the rest of the bloody deer haunch around in circles for emphasis.

While my brother always posted impressive scores in logic and linguistics, he just as consistently bottomed out in existential intelligence.

I groaned. "Dude, you are totally ruining this for me."

I'd asked him to be my partner in the gameworlds today, at our mother's urging, but I was starting to realize I'd live, or die, to regret the decision. A sinking feeling settled into my gut.

"You know what I mean," he continued, diving in to rip another hunk of meat off the bone. "I mean, how can I know that I really exist?"

I studied him, considering what to say next, but right now I needed to prop up our audience stats. Sid and the rest of the guys were counting on me.

"In a nutshell, my friend, you can't," I replied, working up an angle to get his head in the game. "I think, therefore I am, as Descartes famously put it in 1644. Since then, really no progress."

"Mmmmm," was all Martin could add as he looked skyward. "So how can I be sure that you're not just some gameworld zombie?"

"You can't, but from my point-of-view the issue is rather more about you." I laughed and he joined in. "But if we're worrying about whether people around us are mindless zombies, then the question is moot, no?"

Martin smiled at that, wiping his greasy face with the back of one hand. Before we could continue, Vicious rode up. Vicious was the proxxi of my best friend, Sid. He looked comical—a seventies British punk rocker, all pasty whiteness and knobby knees poking out from under Mongol battle armor.

A smile spread across my face.

Vicious grimaced, but gamely soldiered on. Trying to keep in character, he leaned toward Martin and said, "Sire, Master Sid asked me to bring you your mount and...ah...ah fook it, mate, yer 'orse is 'ere."

Robert, my own proxxi, rode up behind him. Wisely, he said nothing as he tossed me the reins to my horse that followed behind him, but just looked toward Vicious and smiled. Vicious scowled, and they both trotted off to get Sid and themselves ready.

I sheathed my saber, Martin dropped the remains of his meal on the floor, and we stood to get ready.

"I know this is a gameworld," said Martin over the top of his horse, "but seriously, don't you ever get the sensation, back in the world, that all of this is impossible?"

I laughed.

Back in the world—now there was an idea fraught with complications. In a cosmos already sporting an infinite number of universes, in just one of these we'd begun spawning our own infinity of digital universes. Collectively, they started calling the whole jumble the multiverse on the assumption that infinity and infinity overlapped somewhere.

If there were an infinite number of universes, then logically one of them had to have exactly the train of events that an arbitrary gameworld, like the one we were in now, had going on. So when we flitted into a gameworld, in a sense we were creating windows into the parallel universe the simulation was tracking.

According to some, there was an equivalency of actually being there if a conscious observer couldn't distinguish the difference. So the question of the day was this: Were we just creating simulated worlds, or were we actually tunneling past the event horizon of our own universe, creating portals into parallel universes?

Perception was reality. Was reality, therefore, equivalent to perception? A slippery slope if there ever was one. Thus the question of this world being real or not was more troubling than it may have at first seemed.

I leaned forward to pat and stroke my horse's neck, calming it as it strained around to look at me. It knew today was going to be bloody. Taking a grip on my saddle and putting one foot in a stirrup, I returned to Martin's question. "So what exactly do you mean? Is all of this impossible?"

I knew it would be impossible to win this battle without settling whatever was on his mind. I looked toward him as I swung up onto my horse.

"I'm not stupid, I know all the stuff about the infinite number of alternate bubbly universes, this one springing from that, all spawning into each other," replied Martin. "But it still doesn't answer my real question."

I settled onto my horse and we started off. The Mongolian saddle was designed to allow the horse to find its canter, leaving the rider free to deal with other tasks. It was more of a platform than a saddle, a fighting platform. These guys were way ahead of their time. I twisted around to check my quiver of arrows. "Which is?"

"Why something and not nothing?"

My patience was beginning, as it often did with him, to wear thin. Why was it that human beings had this God-shaped hole in their heads that needed to be filled when the mind grabbed at straws? God wasn't a part of my life, not anymore.

"What's going on, you caught religion or something?" I asked, catching glimpses of the Mongol warriors praying to their shamanistic gods as we began trotting through the yurt city.

Rising smoke from the cooking fires enveloped us, and the place was thick with anticipation of the coming bloodshed. I raised my fist in a show of power and victory to those that turned to watch us pass, feeling suddenly angry. "Do you know how stupid it is for you to believe in God?"

Martin shrunk away at the criticism. "What, just because you don't, you think everyone else is stupid? So you think Mom joining the Elèutheros Christians is stupid? Sid's a member. You think he's stupid?"

It wasn't his fault. "That's not it. Sid's different. And don't drag mum into this...."

Our mother was disappearing deeper and deeper into her religion, even as the technology here sped further ahead. The Christian Elèutheros sect had gained an incredibly strong following on Atopia, pitching itself against the libertarian ideals that Atopia was founded upon, against what they perceived as the ultimate decay of society. Sid was a part of the Elèutheros hacking community, a somewhat different side to the sect than where my mother was involved.

Honestly, I didn't quite understand it all.

"You treat everyone like they're stupid," complained Martin. "Anyway, religion doesn't really answer anything; it's just replacing one nonstarter for another." He shrugged. "It's kind of giving up, isn't it?"

We trotted along for a bit. I said nothing, letting him finish his thoughts while I calmed my own.

"I guess it would be comforting, though, to give in to faith, especially if you really believed in some sort of supernatural evil," Martin said reflectively as we reached the outskirts of our camp. "But really, what's it all for?"

"Now you sound like you're talking about the meaning of life."

Crap, he was all over the place. I needed his head in the game, not distracted by metaphysics. He was terrible in the gameworlds lately, and I could see why with all this stuff floating around in his head.

I checked my dimstim stats—my fans weren't exactly digging the philosophical talk.

Best to cut this short and get to the blood and guts.

"Martin," I said, turning to him and smiling with brotherly love, "I will share with you my personal philosophy on the topic."

Bouncing up and down in our saddles, I began my performance. "First off, you can't answer the creation question. You need to double-think it out of your brain."

We trotted along the front line of my amassing warriors while I let this settle. Martin took out one of his daggers to inspect it.

"Second, the only meaning to life is the one that you give it, and don't let anyone tell you any different."

Nonplussed, Martin considered this as he tested the edge of his dagger. I'd saved the best bit for last.

"Finally," I opined grandly, "we will never resolve our existential angst in our identity world, and this is why we play out here."

"What, like an escape?" he said, crinkling his nose, rubbing the dagger against his stubble.

"Not just an escape, my friend. It goes much deeper than that. Out there, at home," I said, pointing toward the sky as if we'd descended from it, which in a sense we had, "you can't get a satisfactory answer as to whether there is a Creator or if there is a meaning to it all. If you really sit down and think about it, it'll just give you a headache."

He shrugged in amiable agreement.

"Here, though, in the gameworlds, in this world—there is a definite Creator. Whoever built this game, they are the Creator here," I explained. "And there is a purpose—whatever it was they designed the gameworld for. For instance, today, we kick the shit out of the Tatars. That is the God-given purpose of existing here today, and I know this for an indisputable fact."

A smile began to creep across his face. He put the dagger away in his vest.

"The kicker, my friend, is that this isn't just a game. If you believe, *if you truly believe,* then this place becomes real, and we know God and his plan intimately." I raised one hand in the air and wagged my finger. "So to answer your original question Martin, this *is* real."

Martin smiled. I was enjoying it, too, and our audience stats began to rise. My body surged with excitement as my own disbelief melted away. Sid, Robert, and Vicious joined us at the center of the massing troops while I finished my monologue.

"This is not just an escape my friends, not just a game or entertainment! This satisfies and solves a deep-seated existential pain that *cannot* be answered in any other way!"

The excitement grew in Martin's eyes.

"Martin!" I cried. "Are you with me?!" Raising my saber and bow, I reached skyward into the morning sunshine. A flock of birds took wing far in the distance. "Are you going to kick some existential ass with me today?"

"I'm with you, Bobby!" he screamed back.

The warriors around us roared, and with that, we galloped off toward the massing Tatars, surging once more unto the breach.

"Today, we ride with God!"

My army thundered across the steppes and into destiny.

2

What was I again?

I felt funny, disconnected, discom-*BOB*-ulated.

Giggling, I looked down at myself, trying to focus my meandering mind. I had the shape of a giant yellow blob—wait, more like a giant yellow *BOB*—with plastic skin, floating amid other aimlessly drifting blobs. Taking a deep breath, my blobness expanded and then contracted.

That was very satisfying, I thought, so I did it again.

A sense of relaxation began to soak through my membranes, and my consciousness slipped backward and sideways through time and space.

Another blob—smaller, blue—collided with me, interrupting my introspection. The blue blob took a liking to me, and like two oil drops meeting on a watery surface, it began to merge into me, its blueness fusing with my yellowness to produce a bulging green smudge on my side.

I tasted fresh blueberries.

Reaching out to the other blobs nearby, I discovered I could swim through the goo, sweeping them aside or toward me with phantom telekinesis, and tasting them as I went. And so began the game of collecting the tastiest blobs toward me, generating a flurry of savory color that mottled into my body as I twisted and spun through the rainbow rain.

After frothing things up so much, I couldn't see anymore, so I stopped to let things settle. The tiny blobs tickled all over as they floated up past me and I shivered.

Wait, these aren't blobs—they're bubbles!

Everything smelled so intensely salty that I realized I was actually in the ocean.

Shafts of sunlight stabbed down from the airy world above, fading into the watery blackness below. Looking down at myself again, I jiggled some newly hatched tendrils. In an excited rush, I began wriggling off at full steam toward a mass of phosphorescent creatures dancing nearby in the voluminous darkness.

A translucent worm popped into view beside me, and I halted, frozen amid specks of slowly sinking organic detritus that hung soundlessly in a stop-motion cloud around us. The worm snacked on one of the specks, and then another, watching me sideways.

Curiouser and curiouser.

"Bob," said the worm. "Hey buddy! Is that you?"

Yes, I thought, *I am Bob.*

"Yeah, I'm Bob. I mean, yeah, it's me," I replied, a little dazed.

"It's me, Sid. Where have you been? It's been crazy down here. That last set was freaking intense. Things got a little weird for a while there, and then I thought, 'Jeez, where's Bobby?' And so I came over here to clear my head, and whammo, there you were. Crazy, huh?"

I giggled as my mind seeped into the here and now. *That's right.* I had come with Sid out to Humungous Fungus, beyond the Looking Glass. We'd dropped into this chillworld to watch the slingshot test fire as part of the sensorgy party that'd been going on for a few days.

Memories oozed into my amoebic brain.

"Hey Sid, wazzzzzup?" was all I could think to say.

"Not much, man, not much at all," Sid-worm giggled back. "Hey, they're about to start the slingshot test. You ready to go?"

"Giddy up."

The sensorgy transmogrification of the slingshot weapons test was still resonating hard as we relaxed at the peripheries of Humungous Fungus. The fiery might of the weapons demonstration had been funneled into a multisensory party mash-up that all the pssi-boys and pssi-girls had been waiting weeks for, but now it was over, and a post-party depression was sinking in. Most of our friends were emo-porning their way down from their highs, but I preferred keeping it natural.

"That was intense!" glowed Sid-worm. We were floating through a patch of dimensionless deprivation-space in an attempt to cool off our nervous systems.

I munched on some mouth-candy at the edge of the dimensionless space, trying to think of what I was trying to think about, and then: sudden clarity as the lost idea reformed itself. My disembodied mind latched firmly onto the thought like a drowning man at sea finding a life raft, my consciousness pulling itself up for a breath of fresh air.

"Oh yeah, hey, Sid, so do you really think I should talk to him? I mean, I feel like it's not going to make a difference anyway."

"Absolutely, my friend, I think this is more about you. You know what I mean?"

"I guess so," I replied, unconvinced.

My sense of wonder at the world around me began to lose its fizziness, and my tendrils were going limp. Blinking, I looked around. I could still see the bending and patterning of the visual hallucinations, but my head had snapped back into some sort of real space.

I sighed. "I gotta get back. It's my brother's birthday, and my dad asked me to come home for a family breakfast."

"I'm sorry, I forgot," Sid-worm said softly. He looked up into the light, considering something. "I love you, buddy, and maybe it's not for me to say...."

"What?" *Is he asking me a question?* I was still pretty high.

"Maybe you should slow down a bit. You're wasted all the time. I understand, but—"

I laughed. "If that's not the space-pot calling the kettle black."

"I'm just saying...."

"I know what you're saying," I admitted after a pause. "And I appreciate it. But let's just get going."

An urgent ping from Robert, my proxxi, arrived.

"My dad's already complaining about me being late," I added, looking at the message.

"Okay. Let's head."

With that, we began to surge upward toward the light, leaving the dancing creatures below. I remembered when it wasn't Sid, but my brother dancing beside me in Humungous Fungus under the lights of the phosphorous jellies. It seemed like just yesterday.

3

Growing up on Atopia was great and all, but for me, pssi was only good for two things: playing the gameworlds and getting stoned. Oh, and I guess it was cool for surfing, too, so three things. Or, actually four—it was also great for *hiding* the fact that I was stoned.

Still buzzing from my excursion into Humungous Fungus, I had Robert filtering my body movements and speech so that I appeared perfectly normal, or at least close to normal. Robert tended to overdo it in these situations, and if he wasn't my proxxi, I'd swear he did it on purpose.

Coming out onto the sun deck of our habitat overlooking the ocean, Robert nimbly handled seating me at the place opposite my dad. Martin was sitting to my left, my mom to my right, and sitting behind my mom on a chair was a guy wearing a toga and weather-beaten leather thongs.

It was a beautiful morning, and a slight breeze was just offsetting the unseasonably hot weather we'd been having. Gulls squawked in the distance over the kelp forests while waves swept calmly past on their way into Atopia.

My dad scrutinized me as I sat down. "The least you could have done was be on time for your brother's birthday breakfast."

Although we'd only been born minutes apart, I'd been born at 11:58 pm and my brother the next day—so technically, our birthdays were on different days. I'd already suffered through a birthday dinner the night before with everyone.

Martin glanced at me from across the table. He knew I'd been out partying all night. I smiled back at him apologetically.

"And your food is cold already," my father added.

Robert was filtering my speech, so when I responded, *So is your heart*, to my dad's predictable dig, it came out of my mouth as, "Yes, sir. Very sorry for being late."

This, of course, didn't sound at all like anything I'd say, and immediately got me in trouble.

"Are you stoned again?"

Robert did a pretty good job of having my face feign surprise. I just giggled away, safely detached inside my head.

"No, sir," responded Robert. He used my voice while I subvocalized to Sid who was ghosting in on this. "Wouldn't you be with a family like this?" Sid snorted.

My dad leaned over and looked deep into my eyes. I burst out laughing on the inside while Robert covered for me.

"Dad, come on, I didn't sleep well last night, okay?"

Good one, Robert. That was true. I was out getting high all night and hadn't slept a wink. My dad narrowed one eye, then just shook his head and went back to buttering his toast.

"Anyway, Jimmy isn't even here yet," I pointed out. "Why are you giving me so much trouble?"

"Jimmy has important things he's taking care of."

Unlike some of the people at this table, he didn't need to add. It was like Jimmy was more of a son to him than his own sons were. It was always Jimmy did this, and Jimmy did that, and I was more than tired of it. I sighed and angrily shook my head.

"Bob," complained my dad, "you're twenty-one years old. When are you going to find some direction? You need to move on, son. You should have been here to see the slingshot test fire with us.

We were all here. Jimmy was right there in the control room with Commander Strong."

Here we go again. Robert deleted the expletives when he responded for me.

"I did watch the slingshots," Robert replied for me truthfully, "and I am doing something with my life. I have one of the top-rated dimstims in all of Atopia."

It was true.

I was a professional vacationer, and thousands of people at a time paid to stimswitch into me when I was out surfing. It was great money, and when pssi was released into the rest of the world, I was going to be huge.

My dad wasn't impressed at my entrepreneurial ambitions, however. "You have such an opportunity, Bob. What's happening here is a once-in-a-lifetime event, and you're right in the middle of it."

That's the problem right there, I thought.

"I'm also one of the best surfers in the world," I pointed out, something any parent would be proud of. My imagined ranking wasn't entirely fair, since the rest of the world's surfers didn't have pssi—*yet*—but it wasn't nothing.

My dad shrugged this off as well. "You were one of the very first pssi-kids. You were top in your class at the Solomon House Academy before you dropped out," he began to sermonize, wagging his butter knife at me. "Patricia Killiam was just asking me the other day about you, saying how impressed she was with your work when you were a Class I Freshman. She said there could still be a place at the Solomon House for you."

He raised his eyebrows as the knife came to rest pointing directly at me. My dad was the director of public relations for the entire pssi project, so it wasn't just me he was chatting up about all this.

I groaned and rolled my eyes, clicking off my proxxi filter. *I'll handle this myself*, but I slurred out half the words. "A lot of stuff has happened shince then, wooden you say?"

My dad sighed and looked skyward. "Yes it has." He motioned with the knife across the other side of the table. "And look how well Martin is doing."

Martin smiled at me weakly, not wanting to get involved.

"Yeah, look at him," I shot back, narrowing my eyes at both of them. "Martin and all of you are just the picture of shuper-booper family togatherness. And quit talking about Jimmy all the time, we're your *real* sons."

I aimed for thick sarcasm, emphasizing "real," but I wasn't sure if my enunciation was clear enough to convey it beneath the drugs. *What had I taken again?*

"Bob, honey, don't be so mad. It's your brother's birthday today, let's please be nice," came my mom's quavering voice. "Forgiveness is the key to life. Forgive yourself, son."

I sighed. It looked like this was going to be a tag team event. The guy in the toga and sandals behind my mum began to lean forward as if he were about to add something. Before he could, I waved one finger at him. "Nodda word from you, 'kay?"

I was as patient as the next guy, but my mom having her personal Jesus following her around like a puppy dog so that she could chat to him all the time was getting on my nerves. It wouldn't be so bad if her Jesus just sat there and spoke when spoken to, but he was always jumping into conversations, sharing his *wisdom*.

"Mom," I asked, turning to her and tuning my proxxi filter back up so I'd stop slurring, "what do I have to forgive myself for?"

"I don't know, son. You have to figure that out for yourself," she replied softly, in the way that only mothers can. "I know you can, you have *special* abilities."

My dad rolled his eyes, shaking his head at the three of us. He didn't like it when she started talking like this.

Our family had something of an unusual history filled with flashes of brilliance and corners of darkness. My great-great-grandfather on my mother's side had been something of a nut. He claimed to have been able to speak with the dead and move objects with his mind. It was something my dad was ashamed of.

My grandfather—my mother's father—was almost as bad, and my dad could barely stand speaking to him. The family lunacy tended to skip a generation. My dad was just waiting for me to start hearing voices, and I couldn't blame him for worrying about me using drugs.

"There is evil in the world, son," added Jesus for good measure.

I shot him my own evil glance. "Only the evil that we make," I replied, feeling defeated.

"Yes, the evil that *we* make."

That stopped everyone in their tracks. I sat back in my chair and rubbed my eyes, fighting frustration on the one hand and a general sense of not being sure what was happening on the other.

Maybe I should try a different tack. "Look, all this stuff is great, but technology can make you stupid, you know?" My addled brain was trying to find some way out of these woods that I'd wandered into. All four of them stared at me. "Like a generation ago, Eskimos didn't even have a word for 'lost,' and now without GPS they can barely find their way out of a frozen paper bag."

"I believe they're called Inuit," suggested Martin.

I looked at him hopelessly.

"That's *not* the point. I'm stuck in this thing, and I love all you guys," I said, really thinking *I love* most *of you guys*. "I have a kind of a love-hate relationship with pssi right now, and I just want to use this stuff the way I want to. Okay, Dad?"

My dad shrugged, giving up. "Sure. Whatever you think is best." He clearly didn't think it was best.

"Just leave me to do stuff, the *way* I want, in the *time* I want." I grabbed some croissants and a glass of orange juice. "Great talk. I'm going surfing. Is that okay with everyone?"

4

The sense of touch is the most underappreciated of all the senses, at least of the senses the *rest* of the world has. When the first elemental life ventured out into the primordial goo, it was its sense of touch that kept it safe from danger. Touch is the most ancient of our senses, existing before any sight, sound, taste, or smell existed.

Touch is essential to the sense of things being a part of your body. When playing tennis, nobody thinks about the racquet hitting the ball as they swing. The racquet just becomes a part of us. Tools that begin as extensions of our bodies soon become a part of it—it's the way the human mind works.

The same process applies to any tools we used, and pssi made it possible to make tools out of the information flow in the multiverse and incorporate it into our bodies in much the same way.

For me, the flow of information was an apt metaphor. As surfing became my obsession at a young age, my innovation had been to remap my tactile sense into the water around me.

Sitting on my surfboard, bobbing up and down between the swells, I could feel the pressure, shape, and temperature of the water's surface around me through my skin. The thousands of neurons attached to each hair follicle could sense even tiny subsurface eddies and water currents.

After nearly twenty years of dedicated practice, my brain had neuroplastically reformatted to devote a large part of itself to my water-sense, and I now had the most highly attuned tactile array of any pssi-kid, or for that matter anyone else in the world. Sitting with my eyes closed, I could feel the water moving and undulating around me as a perfectly natural and integral part of my body.

I was one with the water, and it was one with me.

Still a little hungover from the previous evening, I opened my eyes to awake from my reverie. Atopia sure was pretty from out here. Out of the corner of my eye I saw something move, and a beautiful stag burst forth from the forest underbrush. We eyed each other for a moment, then he disappeared.

Above decks, the floating island of Atopia was covered in forests that were teeming with "wild" animals, but like everything else, their neural systems were loaded down with the smarticles that floated in the air and water around us. Everything here was a part of the pssi network, but I doubted that the animals ever realized they were off in virtual worlds as they stampeded through synthetic savannahs while vet-bots tended to their real bodies during downtime.

Not much wild was left in the world today. It was ironic that tourists now lined up to come to a completely artificial island that was built to perfect synthetic reality, all to enjoy a shred of the old reality by dusting themselves down in smarticles.

Smarticles were the pixie dust that permeated everything on Atopia, a system of nanoscale particles that worked as both a sensor and communication network. They suffused through the bodies of living creatures, lodging into their nervous systems to form the foundation of pssi.

The polysynthetic sensory interface enabled not just the ability to jump off into virtual worlds, but also the sharing of experiences and even bodies. A philosopher had once rhetorically asked what it was like to be a bat, meaning that it was something we could never know. But here on Atopia, you could inhabit a bat, a bear, a fish, a shark, a tree, and even sometimes, yourself.

The beaming sun was drying the saltwater into crystals on my skin, making it itchy as it baked. I scratched my neck and shifted positions on my board. A breeze mixed the sea air with the musty odor of a tangle of seaweed floating nearby. Though the water was cold, my pssi tuned it out, and I was perfectly comfortable. I just had to be careful my muscles didn't get too sluggish.

Seagulls wheeled in the sky, and otters were playing in the kelp not far away, chattering away about whatever otters chattered about. Some were floating around on their backs, eating a breakfast of clams they'd scrounged from the aquaculture bins below.

Out here I felt a certain peace that escaped me elsewhere, a deep meditative calm outside the madness. Often, I came to think about Nancy, to think about my brother, to think about how I'd messed everything up. Looking up, cirrus clouds striped the blue cathedral of the sky.

Just another day in paradise.

After some fuss, Vince Indigo, the famous founder of Phuture News, had agreed to hit the waves with me this morning. He'd become my regular surf buddy in the past year, but had recently, and without explanation, dropped off the map.

Convincing him to come out had been a major struggle, and even now, he didn't look like he was enjoying himself. He was just staring into space, uncharacteristically quiet. I was about to call out to him, to see what was bugging him, when I was interrupted.

"Hey."

I looked down to find a pssi-projection of Martin sitting on the front of my board. We bobbed up and down in the swells together.

"Hey to you, too, buddy," I responded sheepishly. "Sorry about this morning. I know it was your birthday."

Martin always kept the same clean-cut, square-jawed image going despite the vagaries of fashion—fashion being so ugly these days that its look had to be changed almost hourly. His pale blue eyes reflected the skies, and I admired the tight buzz cut he was sporting. Buzz Aldrin came to mind, or better, Buzz Lightyear.

"Don't worry about it. Dad gets worked up, but I don't care."

"Thanks for not ratting on me. So—Inuit, huh? No Eskimos left in this world?"

"Not according to me, I guess."

We laughed together. It was nice.

"I get so tired of him talking about Jimmy all the time," I added.

Martin nodded. "I know what you mean."

When we were growing up, I was nearly the only one who'd tried befriending Jimmy. He was an oddball kid, but he shared the same birthday as my brother, and I'd felt some kind of affinity toward him. These days, I almost wished I hadn't.

When his parents had abandoned Jimmy as a teenager, Patricia Killiam, his godmother and head of the Solomon House Research Center, had asked our family to take him in. No good deed goes unpunished, as they say, and Jimmy's presence seemed to only accelerate the downward spiral our family had already been in. To our father, Jimmy had become the shining star and savior of our family honor. I suppose I really didn't have anyone to blame but myself.

"I guess it's hard to be encouraging if your son's a stoner," I laughed sourly. "Anyway, who cares? I'm doing what I love."

"Then what more could you ask for?"

I smiled, enjoying the soothing sensation of the water rolling through my skin.

"Got some big action today, huh?" Martin asked, changing the topic.

"Huge!" I confirmed.

He must have checked out the big barrels being laid down across the northern crescent. Storm systems were generating some dangerous waves today—just how I liked it.

"Anything interesting?"

One of my phuturecasts was focused on the incoming swells, predicting the shape and size of the break, how the pipe would develop, and a dozen other factors. I could sit there and watch the horizon for waves, but using a dedicated phuturecast, I could track swells coming from miles away and select the perfect one to get set at just the right point.

"A few nice ones, but I'm waiting for the *beast.*"

Martin laughed. "Perfectionist, huh?"

"With some things."

"Yeah, with some things." He smiled and looked away.

"Bob!" came a yell from across the water. It was Vince, waving at us. "Bob, I need to get going!"

"Already?"

"I need to get back to that thing. Hotstuff's on my back. "

I wondered again what had his hair on fire. "I have a hard time imagining anyone telling *you* what to do. But anyway, ping me if you change your mind."

Both Martin and I waved good-bye as his primary subjective flitted off, leaving his proxxi to guide his body home. We sat silently for a few minutes, enjoying the sea, sky, and silence.

Martin looked at me and then looked down awkwardly, struggling with something. "We need to have a chat. I want to understand what's going on with you."

I looked away. "Sure, I've wanted to talk to you, too...." *Maybe it's time to bring up the gorilla in the room,* I was thinking, but just then my metasenses started tingling. "But maybe in a few minutes?"

Detaching my primary subjective point-of-view from my body, I spun it far out into the Pacific. This viewpoint coasted in just above the water, following a monster swell making its way toward us. It was huge, at least a dozen feet in height, even in the open ocean. It sprayed and frothed angrily as I followed it, surging powerfully toward the glimmering speck of Atopia in the distance.

I snapped hard back into my body. Using a phantom, I punched up a visual overlay of how the wave would be breaking in a few minutes. "This is the one I've been waiting for! I totally want to talk, but could I catch this wave first?"

"No problem," Martin laughed. He pointed at the simulation. "Oh yeah, that's gonna be huge!"

The wave would peak at nearly forty feet and generate an almond-shaped pipe that would continuously sweep past the northern crescent for nearly two miles. The system selected an optimal drop-in point, and I quickly plotted some possible surf paths. It was a big wave, and I'd have to travel fast to catch it right. The triangular fin of a shark I'd commandeered appeared, slicing through the water behind me, and I reached out to catch it and began racing across the water.

"Nice," said Martin, admiring the path I'd decided on in the simulation graphic hanging between us. Skimming the water, the wind barely ruffled his hair. "So you're going to pull a dead-man stall, switch back to hide in the barrel, and then finish with a rocket Tchaikovsky and back-hang two?"

"That's the plan," I replied with a grin. "Can you switch to the back with everyone else, so I can get this show on the road?"

Martin nodded and disappeared, and I let go of the shark's fin, leaning forward on my board as I began paddling to the drop-in. My social cloud started buzzing about my impending ride, my dimstim stats surging as masses of people stimswitched into me to enjoy it.

It was a funny feeling, knowing that thousands of people were inside my skin. I couldn't feel anything physically, but I could *sense* it, and it sent shivers down my spine.

I began quickening, and the world dropped away as my senses sharpened.

With smarticles infused throughout pssi-kids' nervous systems from birth, we'd quickly picked up on the trick of "quickening" by using smarticles to accelerate the conduction of nerve signals along their axons. We could literally amp up the speed of our nervous systems on command, but only in short bursts as we depleted the stored energy in the smarticles and, more problematically, began to overheat our brains.

Quickening the body was one thing, but quickening the mind was entirely something else. It had to be managed in a very controlled fashion so one didn't lose conscious coherence in the seat of the mind, where it all came together. Like anything, it took time, patience, and training to build up this capacity, and when it came to quickening, like surfing, I was one of the best.

With each breath, I concentrated on quickening, feeling the world slow down as I sped up. Switching my visual field into surround mode, I closed my eyes as my visual cortex adjusted itself to a 360-degree view.

Accelerating my paddling tempo, I focused on the ripples of water coming through my water-sense, pushing my speed to match the incoming monster. It began to grow behind me, the sensation of it expanding up and into my skin, surging toward and into me.

My board angled forward, skimming faster and faster. With a final stroke, I opened my eyes and grabbed my board, popping up onto it and leaning forward to accelerate. The wave urged me on. It wasn't really behind me—the wave *was* me. I felt it swelling through my water-sense, as if my body was expanding and peaking, with little bits of me frothing off the top as it crested.

The wave began to break, and my board sped down its face. Slowing as I neared its base, I stepped to the back of the board, sinking into the water and almost stalling. I smiled, waving to the crowds on the beach, and a collective gasp went up as they watched the monster booming down behind me.

An instant before disaster, I jumped forward and cut the board back into the wave, sailing up its rushing face. As it roared around the northern crescent, I started snapping a series of turns back and forth off its top. Nearing my finale, I finished with an acrobatic turn that dropped me freefalling into its thundering maw.

The crowds on the distant beach squealed with excitement as my silhouette disappeared.

Finally, leaning forward, I accelerated away from the maelstrom at the back of the barrel. A crazily spinning, translucent tunnel opened up ahead of me, revealing bright daylight beyond. Easing further forward, I sensed the final collapse of the wave, so I stood up and walked toward the front of my board and turned around.

Tchaikovsky started playing loudly in my dimstim, and I closed my eyes to begin air conducting for my audience. With just my toes on the nose of the board, back-hanging my heels off it, a powerful jet of water from the collapsing tube shot me backward out of the mouth of the barrel.

Opening my eyes, I lowered the volume on Tchaikovsky and turned around to walk toward the back of the board. Mad applause from the thousands of dimstimmers who'd enjoyed the ride rang out in the multiverse. The world returned to normal time as I released my quickening, and I felt the burning heat within my body begin to ease off.

Sighing happily, I sank into the water, straddling my board to float gently in the swells again.

Martin reappeared on the nose of my board and gave me a little golf clap. "Nice show, buddy. That was awesome!"

"Thank you, thank you very much." I wiped the water from my face and looked back at Martin and the tourists still clapping on the beach.

I couldn't resist showing off again.

The water around me began to thicken up as I summoned tens of millions of tiny zooplankton from the depths below. I kept them near me when surfing, as a safety net in case something went wrong.

With a few carefully placed kicks, I levitated out of the water, forcing millions of my little friends to treadmill their hardest just at the right point to support each step. I stood up and took a few steps across the water, then bowed to the crowds with a flourish.

This brought gasps and more pointing from the tourists—*he can walk on water!*

Sinking back down, I grabbed my board and dispersed my little helpers. Martin was shaking his head, grinning widely.

"That was a bit much," he laughed, but it felt forced. We didn't get out together much anymore.

"Buddy, you need to lighten up," I said to him. "Live a little."

Immediately, I regretted my choice of words, but Martin didn't notice anything. I slicked back my hair again, trying to stop the saltwater from streaming into my eyes.

"You want to come camping with me, Willy, and Sid later?" I asked after a pause.

"I'm invited?"

"Why else would I ask!"

"That'd be great," Martin responded brightly, and then his smile faded. "I worry about you sometimes."

I nodded. "Still want to have that chat?"

"Maybe later." The moment had passed for him, too. "I've got a lot to do. Be careful with those storms brewing out there—could swing in some weird waves."

"I will, I promise." I gave him a small salute. "I'll see you later."

Martin returned the salute and winked as he signed off and faded from view.

5

How in the world did I get roped into attending a baby shower for a proxxid?

"Congratulations, Commander Strong!" I said enthusiastically, smiling as I reached out to pump his hand.

Rick smiled back and shook my hand, rolling his eyes slightly. "Thanks, Bob. Is Jimmy coming?"

"You'd know more than me, Commander." Turning to his wife, I said, "And, of course, congratulations to the lovely new proxxid mother." I laughed and reached over to kiss her on the cheek, looking down at the baby in her arms.

"And this lovely lady is?" asked Commander Strong, looking toward my date.

"Oh, ah," I mumbled, turning to introduce my newish girlfriend. "This is Nicky."

Nicky graciously introduced herself to the Strongs. I nodded, smiling, and then left them to it, wandering off toward the alcohol stand. I doubted Nicky wanted a drink, but I sure did.

A baby shower. How did I let these things happen to me?

Any party was, however, a great reason to get stoned. With that thought, I popped a tab of MDMA from my pocket into my mouth. Virtual drugs weren't bad, but they weren't quite the authentic experience, and I liked to style myself as a retro-abuser.

Just another great day in the world of Bobtopia.

Grabbing a drink, I walked over and sat down on a couch. We were waiting for some last person to show up to sing the birthday song, a crazy ritual someone had started for proxxid births.

Actually—we weren't really waiting, since everyone everywhere knew exactly where everyone else was at any moment. We were just, well, *what the hell are we doing?*

I guessed we were waiting, but we all knew exactly how long we had to wait. *There's a difference, no?* Perhaps we'd reached the end of waiting, and we were now experiencing some new verb that defined what waiting was, when we all knew exactly how long we *had* to wait.

I decided, right then and there, that I was going to call it phwaiting. Immediately, I published my inspiration into my social cloud. With my creative work done for the day, I scanned some Phuture News flowing across the bottom of my display spaces.

More celebrities were about to drop dead, or start doing tons of drugs, or stop doing them and go into rehab.

Boring.

Flicking my phantoms, I opened an overlay and researched the definition of "wait."

Wait: transitive verb—to stay in place in expectation of.

This seemed to amount to what we were already doing. *I guess we don't need a cool new word.* Already, my proxxi was splintering me over four thousand variations on the idea of waiting from the remaining distinct human languages. The inspiration was hollowed, and I posted an announcement regarding the death of phwaiting back into my social cloud and watched the meme explode and die.

At the same time, a fast-trending news report splintered that the Chinese were talking about sending a manned mission to Mars. It had been about thirty years since China had last landed men on the moon—on their best guess of Mao's birthday one holiday season—but their plans for a permanent moon base had fizzled when the water deposits there had proven harder to extract than imagined. Now their new grand plans seemed ludicrous, even if Mars—and half of the rest of our solar system—seemed to be practically teeming with life.

Why spend any time or effort moving a physical body around when you could just flit anywhere in an instant using sensor networks? Everything that was happening in the outside world seemed amazingly wasteful and nonsensical to those of us who lived on the inside of Atopia—but then again, soon everyone would be as blessed as we are.

Bored, I collapsed most of my displays and opened up an overlay to watch a new game my friends had started. Sid, Vicious, Martin, and my own proxxi, Robert, were hot into an apocalyptic otherworld battle, pinned down in a cave by an android army and flanked by giant armored worms. It looked like a lot more fun than what I was doing, so I tried to splinter in, but Sid blocked me. That annoyed me, but he was right. Either I had to be there fully, or not at all. It wouldn't be fair to the rest of them. Anyway, I could just joyride in Robert if I wanted to experience it.

The rest of my displays held forth on a multitude of other live wikiworld feeds. The Bieb was just delivering his inaugural address as the 52nd President of the United States, and in an interesting first, was singing the first few lines of his speech.

I guessed that the "Bieb Bill" had passed allowing nonnatives to run for the highest office.

In another feed, Manchester United had just scored in a Premier League game, and they were replaying the goal with a stimcast of the hapless LA goalie that ended with him crashing face first into one of the goalposts, breaking his nose in a bloody explosion of pain.

What they managed to broadcast was a pale reflection of what his pain would have really felt like. Sensory broadcast technology was still in its infancy outside Atopia, but all that would be fixed soon with the release of pssi.

Flicking off the news feeds, I focused back on the battle the boys were in. Someone had just blown Martin's head off. I sighed. Martin was hopeless.

I checked my dimstim stats and a few dozen people were still logged into my body. *Christ,* I was bored out of my head, and there were still people who would prefer to be me than do whatever boring shit they could be doing on their own.

Glancing at my bio-stats, I could see my heart rate was hovering in the mid-forties, my cortisol was a little high, my insulin low, but all systems go. Those stats would be moving around as soon as the MDMA hit. *Looking good, Bob,* I told myself. *If your heart rate was any lower, you'd slip into a coma, and that sounds pretty good about now.*

The room was crowded with people milling around, getting drinks, engaging in small talk, and doing whatever tiring stuff adults did at a baby shower. One side of the room was lined with retro-modern impressionists to match the sleek, minimal décor of the world they'd created for the event. The other side was a terrace, open to the outside, looking down from a few stories up onto the leafy beach promenade of east Atopia.

While I waited for the drugs to hit my bloodstream, sulking seemed like a good option, so I opened up Bunnies and sent a sub-proxxi to get me another drink. Innocent little rabbits appeared floating in space in front of me, exiting their underground warrens, sniffing the ground for food.

I flicked my finger at one of them, and a fireball magically issued forth, flaming toward the hapless little creature. It looked up, confused, and then squealed as the fireball engulfed it, crisping it into a pile of ash. The other rabbits ducked for cover, and then, slowly, crawled back out to sniff at their erstwhile compadre.

My eyes narrowed as I lined up my next victim.

"Bob, what are you doing?" came a subtext from Nicky. "Could we just be a *little* sociable?"

I grumbled and shut off Bunnies. Lucky little bastard didn't know how close he came to the big ticket.

The sub-proxxi was back with my drink and I thanked him. Turning off my kinetic-collision subsystems, I rolled out of the couch's embrace and stood up to stride purposefully through one of the remote guests, a round and balding little man who affected a shocked look.

Serves him right if that's the best he can project. Someone should tell him he could look any way he wants.

My brazen etiquette violation earned some raised eyebrows, and the party was feeling way too crowded, so I decided on further anti-social behavior and I flipped my pssi off at everyone. The lush environment of the metaworld projection immediately disappeared as I slipped into identity mode and the featureless confines of the small, rectangular room we were actually in appeared around me.

That feels better. I took another gulp of my drink, feeling refreshed as my own senses connected me to the world, everything taking on a colorful sheen. *On the other hand, that could be the ecstasy kicking in.* The few people who remained in the small room were mostly in a corner near Nicky, still chatting with Cindy Strong, who was now cradling empty space in her arms.

Nicky looked over, her eyes flashing at me.

I imagined knives shooting forth from her, pinning me helplessly and gorily to the wall before a crushing shockwave of disappointment finished me off in a splatter of social distortion. The ferocity of the image compelled me to click my pssi back on, and the hubbub of party re-saturated my senses. Luckily, what I'd felt before *was* the MDMA, so I felt much happier about everything, on the whole.

By that point, Nicky was completely pissed. She grabbed me by the arm, pulling me around the corner and into the hallway where we could be alone. Sort of alone—my dimstim stats instantly shot up as the social cloud sensed my mood and the coming fight.

"I thought you said you wanted to come here! You're embarrassing me. Can I ask you a question? Are you stoned again? Can you shut off your fucking dimstim for a minute, please?"

"That's two questions." I shrugged. "And no to both of them. Sweetie, my dimstim is my work, my bread and butter, and good or bad, I can't just shut it off." I tried to smile winningly at her.

She stared at me in silence.

"Okay, yes, I am a little stoned," I admitted.

She rolled her eyes. "How can you call that stupid dimstim work? And this thing with your brother...."

With a hidden phantom, I dialed up a Dragon skin when she wasn't looking. "My dimstim's how we met. Don't knock it, and *don't* bring my brother into this!" Narrowing my eyes, I added, "And at least I work."

She'd annoyed me now, so I was purposely pushing Nicky's biggest button. This was going to be good. She didn't like being reminded she was daddy's little girl.

"Bob, all you do is sit around all day playing games, or simulating vacation time for a bunch of meta-perves," she snarled as her voice gathered momentum.

The Dragon skin began to take hold. Her eyes flashed at me while her face and upper body began to morph into a cartoonish and slightly frightening form in my display space.

"At least I make my own money," I pointed out.

At that moment, I couldn't help letting out an enormous yawn right in her face, which really set her off. What else had I taken? It couldn't have been the ecstasy—that didn't usually make me yawn.

Or wait, had I taken some mushrooms before as well? *That must be it.* Or was it acid? Was I candy-flipping or hippy-flipping? I frowned, trying to remember.

"Let me FINISH!" she barked, barely containing herself.

The Dragon skin was working itself up nicely now. Her eyes bulged out as her neck elongated and sprouted a row of ridges. Her skin took on a distinctly scaly texture.

"The only reason your stupid dimstim makes any money is because I let you have sex with me on it. I swear to God I have no idea what I was thinking...."

I began to shrink a little from the Dragon, but couldn't help goading her.

"Oh yeah, all my success is only due to the fabulous Nicky."

Holy smokes. The Dragon skin was amazingly scary when you were stoned. I shook my head and started laughing.

"STOP cutting me off!" she screamed.

She always had quite the temper. Her eyes had now bulged outward into huge melon-sized orbs with slatted cat pupils, and her head was bobbing side to side on a long neck that grew outward from her blouse, while a great, gray-pimpled snout sprouted from where her nose had been.

Fangs menaced.

Smoke began to curl from nostrils.

Fireballs spewed from her mouth.

And I cowered, giggling.

"Do you have that goddamn Dragon skin on? *Jesus*, Bob!"

With that she turned tail, literally, and angrily stomped past me to storm out of the party. She left little burning patches behind her in the carpet.

"Nice."

It was Sid. He'd been ghosting the dimstim version of events and now stood leaning on the wall of the hallway. I guess he'd already been killed in the battle I was watching. He laughed and shook his head.

"I'm not sure that's the way to hold down a relationship."

"Ah, she wasn't the one, and anyway, she's the one that chased me down."

"Women—they always think they can change you, huh?"

"I guess."

A pause while we looked at each other.

"Ready for some skin shopping?" I asked. I needed to get out of there.

"We're going skin shopping?"

"Yes, my friend, I have decided my skin closet needs refreshing."

As great as it was, the Dragon was getting old, plus it would be sad to use the Dragon on any girl after Nicky. I needed a new mythical creature with which to annoy the next woman in my life—I had a feeling Nicky wasn't coming back anytime soon.

Sid shrugged. "Sure. Why not?"

I sent a quick apology note about my little spat to Rick and Cindy, and as we flitted out, I heard Sid asking, "What skins did you have in mind?"

We appeared in what, for all intents and purposes, looked like a shoe store in 1920's London, somewhere off Saville Row. Little boxes, whose covers danced with images and logos, lined the walls and aisles, and a smarmy synthetic salesman glided up to us.

"What can I do for you boys?" he asked, smiling.

"I don't know, not sure." My head wobbled on my neck. "What have you got that's new?"

He looked us up and down. "You looking to skin up, or to skin out?"

"Either way, or both, just show us anything new," replied Sid. Seeing my eyes swimming, he added, "And hurry up, please."

"Hmmm," noted the sales*thing* as he put one hand to his chin. With the other he began swiping the wall, and the little boxes swept left and right and up and down at a blurring pace.

"We've got some new designer skins that do a great job of making everyone look good naked," he began.

Both Sid and I rolled our eyes.

"You're right, boring. How about this—more subtle—we've got some nice intelligence skins that make you look and act smarter."

"Thanks, buddy." I frowned. "What are you getting at?"

"Nothing at all. How about this then?" He pointed to some animals charging across a grassy plain. "We have a great new *Skins of Asia* line. The Snow Leopard is all the rage...."

"Nah, no animal stuff."

"How about something more clever, then? We have some that read your cognitive profile and make subtle changes to your wife or girlfriend to make them—"

Sid cut him off. "No wife or girlfriend stuff, please."

Smarmy the Salesman tapped his finger to his mouth as he simulated thinking. "Okay, boys, I have something really special— it's our new top seller."

My interest piqued. "Go on, my smarmy friend."

"We call it HappyTime. A reality skin that makes subtle adjustments when you talk or interact with people you know. It's guaranteed to help you lead a happier and more stress-free life."

"Sounds good," said Sid. "So what does it do?"

"It makes slight changes in your perception so that you get the impression that you're better off than your friends and family, diminishing the effects the further they are from you personally."

Sid smiled. "And how does that work?"

"It doesn't actually change anything, it just gives you the sense that your friend isn't as happy with his new relationship as he really could be, or modifies how much you hear him telling you he makes at his new job," Smarmsworth explained. "Little things, so that you still get the gist, but modified, so you feel like you're doing better than they are."

"And it works?"

"It works like a charm, proven by extensive research. You will lead a happier life, my friend, guaranteed or your money back."

"Hey, Sid," I asked Sid.

"Uh huh."

"Am I actually getting paid big money for surfing and boozing all day while you slave away as a programmer at Solomon House?"

"Yeah."

"Okay, cool—I thought maybe I had HappyTime on already and I'd forgotten."

"Fuck off, Bob."

6

The glare off the hood of the '67 Mustang made me squint, and the sweat beading down from my forehead stung my eyes as I tried to wipe it away. The police were just beyond the barricade, less than two hundred feet away, and I could hear them nervously loading their weapons and talking in short, staccato bursts into their walkie-talkies.

Waves of heat rose up from the tarmac that was melting the soles of my Converse. Hot rubber mixed with the smell of burned gunpowder and equal parts fear and body odor. *Body odor.*

Subtext—Bob to Sid: "Could you please dial down the BO?? I'm choking over here." Sid looked over, sunglasses glinting, and cracked a smile as he pressed his back harder against the side of the car. He was soaked in sweat, too, but looked cool as a cucumber and totally in his element. Sid's grin widened as he pulled out a ridiculously oversized handgun he had somehow hidden in the small of his back.

"What do you think, should we make a run for it?" I asked breathlessly.

"Hell yeah, little buddy," came the reply as he magically produced a second cannon from somewhere on his person. "I'll just crawl into the back and you squirm into the driver seat and get us going. We gotta meet up with the boys to have any chance at busting out of this one!"

"Okay, let's do this."

A voice came over a loudspeaker from the roadblock down between the derelict buildings and burned-out car shells up ahead. "Come on out with your hands up, we don't want to hurt anyone."

Rolling my eyes, I complained to Sid, who was already crawling cat-like into the back seat, "Can't they come up with anything better than that?"

I immediately filed a request for snappier dialogue, and then stowed my anemic-feeling .357 into the breast pocket of my leather jacket. Reaching for the door handle, I squeaked the passenger side open, sliding in chest down across the stick shift, humping my body across.

A bullet ricocheted off the concrete.

"Hold your fire!" came the voice on the loudspeaker again. "Come on out, boys, we can still do this the easy way!"

"Bob," Sid whispered urgently, "you ready?"

I rotated my body around, reaching down to test the pedals with one foot as I hunched over to put the key in. "You betcha, let's hit it!"

With surging excitement, I turned the ignition to fire up the five hundred horses under the hood. Pushing down the clutch, I jammed it into first, and without looking over the dash, released it as I hit the accelerator. The unbridled power of the engine surged us forward, and we began peeling out in a cloud of vaporized rubber and exhaust.

I swerved wildly, trying to maintain some kind of control. The bullets started flying, and I could feel them hitting the car, punching through the windshield and shattering the glass, which rained over me. Sid was on his back, kicking upward with his feet, trying to knock out the sunroof.

We accelerated rapidly. I risked a peek over the dash through the destroyed windshield. An officer was walking out to crouch in the middle of the street, hoisting something onto his shoulder.

"Sid! Rocket launcher!"

"On it!" he screamed back over the roar of the engine.

I punched it into third.

With a final grunt, Sid kicked out the sunroof, sending it spinning out and away into space above us. In the same fluid motion, he popped up through the open roof with a lunatic grin. Swinging out both of his ridiculously oversized weapons, he began blasting away. Peeking out over the dash again, I saw the head of the cop holding the rocket launcher explode in a mist of red.

The rest of them ducked for cover.

The bullets were coming fast and furious as we neared the point of impact with the barricade. Sid rotated his body backward, jamming his back into the edge of the sunroof and bracing his legs underneath. He leaned out flat on the roof of the car, pointing both guns to each side. As we smashed through the barricade, Sid let go with a terrific volley of fire that took out four LAPD officers in an explosion of blood and guts as they looked up with surprise from their hiding places.

With a second crunching impact, we cleared the last of the cruisers, swerving hard to avoid the worst of the blow. Sid grunted in pain, but managed to lift himself upright as he swiveled around to face the gauntlet ahead of us.

Dozens of cop cruisers were parked on either side of the street, taking dead aim at us. I gunned us into fourth and slid as low as I could in the seat, reaching for my own feeble weapon.

The metallic tang of blood seeped into my mouth, and I looked down to see I was bleeding. I'd been hit, but the shock of the fight was staving off the pain, at least for now. This gameworld didn't allow turning down your pain receptors—you just had to deal with it.

This was going to get messy.

Suddenly, one of the cop cruisers to our right exploded and lifted into the air, tumbling slowly back to earth in a fiery arc. Several cops ran out from behind the other cruisers, screaming in flames, wildly shooting their weapons. Sid picked them off as another cruiser exploded and incoming automatic-weapon fire began raining down on the police.

They all turned to look up the street.

Willy and Martin were hanging off a cherry red GTO, blazing away at the cops. Vicious was reloading what looked like a rocket launcher of his own. They waved at us merrily with their free hands. I gunned us into fifth and sat up higher in the driver seat, leaning forward to push some of the remains of the smashed windshield out of the way.

It was all about style points now, and Sid did a beautiful job double-fisting shots off both sides of the car. One after the other, he blew away police officers with geometric precision as he looked skyward and let loose with a deranged cackle.

Our audience stats started to spike *way* up. As one of the best crews in the world at this game, we had over four million people tuned in to watch our escape scene, and Sid was determined to put on a good performance for our fans.

Passing the last of the cruisers, he dragged a grenade out, pulled the pin with his teeth, and sent it sailing right into the open driver-side window. It exploded with a satisfying crunch, and a few uniformed body parts bounced off a nearby chain-link fence.

I congratulated him, "Nice work, Sid!"

Martin, Vicious, and Willy peeled off and followed closely behind in their GTO, and the low throaty growl of both engines mixed together in a bone-shaking symphony. By now they would have put a general call out to all the special weapons squads, so we'd have hundreds of cops chasing us down as we tried to leave the city.

This was going to be a great show.

"You hit?" asked Sid. He climbed down out of the sunroof.

"Yeah," I replied, putting a hand under my shirt and wincing. My finger found a small hole on the side of my ribcage. "Not too bad. A through-and-through I think. Could you wrap me?"

He grunted. "Sure."

I glanced back at him. "You hit?"

"I think my ear got blown off." He held one hand to a bloody mess on the side of his head, doubled over in pain. "But the real problem is the gut shot."

"Bad?"

It looked bad.

"Hurts like hell, but it'll bleed out slow. I should live another couple of hours."

Ah, not so bad then. I smiled. Maybe we'd make it out of Los Angeles after all.

As we sped up the street, something walked into our way up ahead.

A pedestrian? I squinted, trying to make out who it was. *Not cops, anyway.*

It was someone in a green suit, hunched over, and then there were dozens more of them, blocking the road. Cars lined both sides of the street so I couldn't swerve off, and I could hear growing sirens in the distance as flashing lights started coming at us from all angles. Up ahead, it looked like a herd of little green men directly in our way.

What the hell?

I jammed on the brakes and we skidded, squealing to a halt as we plowed into the first couple of greenies, bumping over them. The other car skidded to a stop behind us. Furious, I threw open my driver-side door with weapon in hand to confront whatever was going down.

Sid popped back out of the sunroof, grimacing, with both cannons out aiming front and center.

A short, stocky green man with pointy ears and a broad forehead, wearing spiked shoulder pads and holding an enormous axe, ambled up to me.

"What are you doing?" I asked him.

I could see he had some vampires with him.

"We are against the discrimination shown to the Bangladeshi."

"What?" Then it dawned on me. "Sid!" I yelled. "Did you set the authenticated login to this world when you created it?"

Silence. Except for the growing whine of the approaching sirens.

"Sid?!" I asked again, looking back at him.

"Ah, shoot," he replied, wincing in pain. He looked down at the blood oozing from his gut wound. "I forgot."

Dejectedly, he banged both of his weapons down on the roof of the car. These were obviously Comment Trolls.

Without authenticated login, people could connect into this world anonymously, which was fine if all you wanted to do was watch, but anonymity tended to bring out the worst in people.

With the massive audience we'd accumulated for this game, and with the login anonymous, we'd just attracted the motherlode of Comment Trolls. Hundreds of them were now blocking the road. They'd use the opportunity to broadcast their opinions, whether they had anything to do with our gameworld or not.

"I'm sorry, dude," continued Sid, waving a gun in the air. "I was just so busy. My mother was over, I had a splinter set the world up—"

"Don't worry about it." Perhaps I could reason with them. "Dude, please, this is 1988 Los Angeles," I complained to the lead troll. "We're just trying to get out of here. There were no trolls in Los Angeles in 1988, and no vampires either." On closer inspection, those were Forum Vampires he had with him. They might be useful. "Okay, maybe there were vampires. But guys, please."

My dimstim stats were dropping as fast as our gameworld audience. I had to do something entertaining, and quickly. The head Comment Troll was right in my face, smelling bad with some butt-ugly, oily pimples going on.

"Master," he growled at me.

At least he's playing in character and not a total asshole. Maybe there's an opportunity.

"Master, we are sorry, but this is an open gameworld, and we have the right to express our opinions here."

I nodded my head.

"Sure, this an open gameworld, but only if you're coming to get laid and get paid," I explained in a singsong tone, smiling to expose my two gold-capped front teeth and holding a West Side finger salute near my chest. "If you want to join the Bloods or the Crips, I'm down with that, but don't be a bitch and mess up our game, homie."

The troll frowned. It was hideous. "Who are you to tell me what to do?"

"I'll tell you who I am, my brother," I said, bringing my .357 up between his eyes and pulling the trigger.

Curiously, it didn't result in his brains blowing out the back of his head, as I'd intended. The bullet only glanced off his thick skull, ricocheting in a splatter of oily blood and hairy flesh. I'd never tried shooting a troll in the head at point blank range with a .357 before.

As I was musing on this, my left forearm exploded in pain. The troll standing next to him had swung his axe to lop off my left hand, which I'd been in the process of lifting up to give the lead Comment Troll the finger with.

Blood spurted from my wrist, and I quickly backpedalled away from the threatening horde, blasting indiscriminately with the gun still in my right hand. Sid covered my retreat, picking off trolls and vampires as they advanced. They were tough sons-of-bitches, and we wouldn't have made it except for the suppressing fire that Vicious and Willy laid down as we ran back.

Breathlessly, we rallied behind the GTO. I ripped off my T-shirt and mashed my forearm stump into my leg, trying to wrap a tourniquet under my armpit. Sid leaned over to help me as Vicious and Willy continued to let go with their M-16s.

"Where the hell is Martin?" I panted.

He should have been manning the rocket launcher. That would give these assholes something to think about.

Sid ducked up to look inside the car. "Aw man, I think Martin's dying." He tightened up my tourniquet.

I wrenched around to take a look myself. Martin was writhing in the back seat, soaked in blood and whimpering.

"Goddamn baby." I turned back to Sid. "Those guys were miles away, they had tons of cover. How the hell did he get so messed up?"

This was going to get a lot trickier with one man down, Sid barely functional, and me missing an arm.

"You're useless, you know that?" I yelled at Martin.

He whimpered back between the pain, "Sorry, Bobby, I didn't mean to...."

"Yeah, yeah, you're always sorry," I muttered under my breath.

Sid stared at me disapprovingly, shaking his head. "Dude, you shouldn't be so mean to him all the time. You going to talk to him?"

I said nothing, but then nodded.

"Yes?" demanded Sid between bursts of automatic weapons fire. "You promise?"

"Yes, yes, I promise. But let's get out of this first, okay?"

Looking back up over the GTO, the trolls were reassembling and advancing by holding up their bloodied comrades in front of them as shields. They were fast.

I looked around for the rocket launcher as Sid picked up an Uzi from the back seat and snapped in a clip. We looked at each other, starting to enjoy ourselves. I was awkwardly trying to slide the launcher from the back seat with my one remaining hand when, all of a sudden, a massive burst of gunfire erupted from both sides of us.

The LAPD had finally arrived, and pandemonium broke out for a while as it turned into a three-way pitched battle. By now, the vampires had taken to wing and began swooping down on the helpless police officers, who just screamed in disbelief.

A few of the braver cops continued to take pot shots at us, but their overall enthusiasm for taking out gangland members dissipated after the first few were hacked to pieces by foul-smelling demon spawn wielding their skull-topped axes. Sid and Willy got off a few more rounds at the trolls, but then finally gave up, laughing.

I didn't have long—I could feel the lifeblood ebbing away from this body. Propping myself up on the hood of the GTO, I leaned against its bullet-riddled windshield to get a look around. Martin had died some time ago.

"Dude, that was actually pretty cool!" I admitted to the lead Comment Troll, taking the cigarette he offered. He was sitting up on the car with me. Most of his bloody forehead had been shorn away by my bullet, showing white bone underneath, but he was in a jolly mood.

"That gameworld audience went through the friggin' roof," he agreed. "There are already thousands of copycats."

As he said this, an LAPD officer burst from the bushes, disheveled and bloody but intact, and ran up to me. "Mother of God, please help me, please," he whimpered, his hands pressed together in prayer position.

Raising my eyebrows, I shrugged and gave the smoke back to my new buddy. The officer looked at the two of us and began backing away, shaking his head and making small, pathetic noises. At that moment, a giant troll burst through the same bushes the cop had come through.

"Ah ha!" the new troll announced. "There you are!"

He pounced on the officer, who managed to back away a step or two with his hands help up defensively.

The troll began methodically hacking away with his axe. I had to close one eye as bodily fluids spurted and splattered onto me amid blood-curdling screams. I looked at the troll leader, shaking my head with raised eyebrows.

He smiled back at me and nodded.

"Hey, Fred! Fred!" said the troll leader, raising one stumpy green arm.

Dripping in blood, Fred looked up from his whimpering prey. "Yeah?"

"Could you give it a rest?"

Fred pouted and frowned, then sighed. "Fine."

Grumbling under his breath, he stuck the point of his axe through the police officer's skull. This ended all the commotion. Fred skulked off.

My vision was swimming. "Sid? You ready?"

True to his assessment, Sid had bled out slowly, but hadn't gotten another scratch. Sitting atop a pile of stinking corpses, he was chatting up a female troll over near our Mustang.

"Yep!" he waved, picking up his gun and sticking it in his mouth. "Cool."

I picked up my .357, looked at the head troll and said, "Let's do this again sometime."

With a smile, I opened my mouth and stuck in the barrel of my gun. Tasting the sharp tang of metal and gunpowder, I pulled the trigger. The last thing I felt was the curious sensation of my head exploding backward into space, and suddenly, I was floating in blackness.

I'm dead.

At least in that universe.

It was a funny thing. We could now die a hundred, a thousand, even a million times out in the synthetic worlds we traveled through, but in our identity world—the real world—death still meant death. Just one place out of millions where it held true, but one that remained stubbornly important.

With all the flittering between worlds and bodies, stimswitching with friends, people borrowing your body, and your body being driven around by your proxxi, you'd think it would get confusing to figure out who or when or where you were, or even how to get back into your own being.

It could be disorienting.

That was why a basic feature of pssi, hardwired at the deepest level, was what we affectionately called the Uncle Button—when you gave up and wanted back in your own body, you punched it. You just had to remember that it was there.

Floating in dimensionless black space I performed the well-worn ritual: look down to where your chest should be, reach into your chest, punch it, and whammo, I felt myself falling backward. An instant later, I was jogging through some trees near the eastern inlet.

Sunlight streamed down through a green canopy above me.

"Taking my body for a jog?"

"You asked me to, remember?" replied Robert, just a voice in my head. "Did you read the latest storm warnings?"

"Nah." I knew they were having a hard time steering out of the way of Hurricane Newton, and it looked like we might have to battle through the edges of the storm, but what did I care? I'd just be off in the gameworlds.

"It's gotten a lot worse," Robert explained. "You'd better not get too dug into the gameworlds this afternoon, and stay off the pharmacologicals in case...."

"In case of what?"

I was surprised. It was rare Robert ever asked me to do something.

"Just in case."

I shrugged. *Sure.* He seemed worried.

"Do you want to transition control of your body to you?" he asked, apparently satisfied.

"Naw, if it's getting bad, just take us home. I'm going for one more game session with Martin." I felt bad for yelling at him, but that was just how he was. He couldn't help it.

For the rest of the day we opted to go old school, returning to the Mongol battle. We all met up afterward at a tiki bar on the beach for some beers. It was well past nightfall, and the place was packed with tourists.

Martin loved the Mongolian battle-worlds. He was still hopped up from the fight, jumping around in the sand and howling as he aped Bruce Lee–style karate moves. Sid, Vicious, Robert, and I watched him with amusement.

"Bob, that was awesome, you ducking and diving like that. It was like, superhuman!"

Sid had remapped my tactile water-sense for Mongol battle so that I could feel arrows coming at me like eddy currents through my skin. The incoming projectiles became a part of my body, and as I quickened, I could duck and weave with blinding speed, roaring through the battle as I hacked away at the Tatar scum.

"Yeah, superhuman. That's perfectly accurate." I was already drunk. "We have superhuman abilities—we are, in fact, *supermen.*

At least until the rest of humanity plugs into pssi, at which point..."
I paused to take a swig of my beer. "We'll be, well, just men again."

Sid smiled. He leaned over and whispered under his breath, "You're going to talk to him, right? For you, you understand?"

I rolled my eyes, but nodded. "You don't give up, do you?"

The surf was pounding noisily as we sat there, but a truly gargantuan wave thundered in, literally shaking the party lanterns hanging off the tiki bar. We turned to look out into the blackness. *Those are monster storms brewing out there.*

Just then, a system of pssi-alert channels began to activate.

7

Floating at the edge of space, we watched two massive hurricanes converging, swirling ominously in three dimensions below. My dad had asked us to get together as a family to see firsthand what was happening. The storms had strengthened in the past day, both past Category 4, and were threatening to pin and crush Atopia against the west coast of America.

Atopia was still holding its own as we backed away, but it was running out of room. The phuturecasts didn't see any way around them, and a complete surface evacuation had been ordered. The impregnable fortress of Atopia was under threat.

Jimmy was right in the thick of the emergency preparations, of course.

Flitting back to our family habitat to get ready, I clipped back into my body. After a rushed inventory assessment with my proxxi, it seemed I really didn't need to bring much. With some time to spare, I let my mind slip backward and away to an early inVerse memory of my family that I liked to escape to when I felt stressed.

Blinking in the sunshine, I could feel sand trapped wetly in the crack of my ass. At the time, I was having too much fun to notice it as my brother chased me around the beach on his pudgy little legs. We'd just turned four, and I'd passed the point where my parents had allowed Robert to fully take over my body, but he hadn't progressed there yet.

Though we were twins, my brother had somehow always lagged behind me.

He chased me around the beach, squealing with excitement and waving his bright orange plastic digger, and just before he could touch me, I would flit out to another spot nearby, disappearing to reappear a few feet away. He hooted with delight each time I did it, and I would stick out my tongue and waggle my hands, thumbs in my ears, and raspberry him. With squeaks of glee, he would change directions and run at my new spot.

I couldn't stop laughing.

My mom and dad were sitting together on a beach blanket, my dad's arm around her, and Mom with her great big sunglasses on, laughing with us. She laughed so hard that she was almost crying, pressing her face into my dad's chest, which just egged me on as I flittered willy-nilly around the beach, taunting my younger-by-a-few-minutes baby brother.

I hadn't seen my mom laugh in years. My dad either for that matter. Quitting the inVerse, I wiped the tears from my eyes.

InVersing, going back to relive your own personal universe of stored sensory memories, was a dangerous thing if you let it get its tentacles into you. When you were happy, it didn't matter, you never seemed to bother with it, but when you felt sad or frightened, sliding back into the past—becoming a person you once were, happy and carefree—was about as addictive as something could get.

But reVersing was worse still—not just going back and reliving the past, but running new wikiworld simulations from a decision point you'd made and changing that decision to enable a new world to evolve and spin on from that point. A simulation of how the world could have been, not how it was.

Some people believed that perhaps these weren't just simulations, but portals into alternate realities that branched off from our own timeline. Windows into life as it could have been, as it actually was somewhere else. It was hard to tear yourself away when it was something, or someone, you desperately missed.

Many people I knew spent more time inVersing and reVersing, or as glassy-eyed emo-porners, than they did living their lives in the present. Dr. Granger said on his *EmoShow* that going back and reliving the past helped us grow emotionally, that is was a part of a process that helped us to find resolution and happiness.

I wasn't so sure.

What my family had done, though, was worse than all that. It made a certain desperate sense at the time, as we'd tried to deal with our grief, as I'd tried to deal with mine. In fact, the whole thing had been my idea. It was an idea I was regretting more than I could bear any longer.

Morning had broken in wet smudges while I thought about all this. I was sitting on the covered deck of our island habitat, watching the huge swells generated by the coming storms gathering and slapping together like drunken sailors. Despite the surging surf, the air was eerily still—the proverbial calm before nature's big show. Ragged, scudding clouds hung under an ominous and luminous sky.

A steaming cup of coffee, hot and practically thick enough to stand a spoon in, warmed my hands as I cupped them together. Watching the churning, watery tumult, my surfer-mind tried to force order from the chaos, tried to find a pattern from here to safety.

I flitted out of my body and into the local wikiworld to a point about fifty feet off the deck right in front of me, watching myself watching the waves. Robert took a sip of coffee for me and waved. I just stared back.

Our habitat looked small and vulnerable from here against the backdrop of the ocean. Dark, wicked-looking clouds were stealing quickly across the horizon, piling up in the sky in an enormous approaching wall. Swinging my gaze around to stare inward toward Atopia, it looked muted and small beneath the roiling clouds.

From this perspective, the huge incoming swells were rising up toward the beach, almost obscuring it as they surged and broke on their ride around Atopia. Instead of their usual rhythmic thumping, the waves were breaking at different points, choppy, bewildered.

Massive clouds of spray were sent booming upward from the collapsing waves, hanging the beaches in veils of misty white fog. As I watched, a sharp wind began to blow and gain in strength within seconds, snapping the flags to attention on top of our habitat.

The storms were upon us.

Clipping fully back into my body, I began to scan a list of what needed to get finished for the evacuation.

"Bobby, do you have a minute?" asked Martin, pinging me on a dedicated family channel.

I'd turned off all the other channels, even my dimstim, as I tried, for once, to focus on the here and now. I glanced at the list again before I answered. "Sure, come meet me in my room."

I could at least start to organize my stuff while we talked. Crossing the deck, I made for the lower levels, dropping down a set of stairs and opening the door to my room. It was dark inside with the shades drawn. I didn't go in there much these days. Accessing the room controls, I faded the glass walls to transparency while opening some vents to let a bit of fresh air in. The fusty, closed-in smell of the room gave way to brisk ocean air. I heard a knock.

"Come on in," I called out.

Martin materialized near the couch set against the glass wall to the open ocean. His eyes were downcast, and he fidgeted with the fabric on his pant leg as he flopped himself down onto the couch, his hoodie obscuring his face.

"What's up, bud?"

"I was looking at the evacuation manifest, and, well, I'm not on it. I tried pinging Dad about it, but he's ignoring me for some reason. Could you try to reach him? Do you know why?"

The words froze me in my tracks. Of course the evacuation list was an ADF function, and not a part of the Solomon House research project. Their personnel manifests would be different. Dad must be splintered in a dozen places, fighting for control of the public relations situation and trying to put a positive spin on Atopia being crushed by the two giant storms. He wouldn't have had time to consider the manifests.

I shrugged and lied, "I have no idea. Must be some kind of clerical error. Who cares? Let's just get a move on, huh?"

Martin didn't stir or say a word. He just sat and wrung his hands, cracking his fingers.

I couldn't take it anymore.

I snapped.

"Martin, look." I'd been thinking about doing this for a long while now, and I let some anger swell my courage. "I don't know the best way to say this, but...."

"What?"

"Martin, look...," I repeated.

He looked at me.

"You know you're dead, right? At least some part of you must know...." I trailed off, unsure of what to say next.

There was silence—anxious silence—before his furious response. "Are you *stoned* again?"

"I'm *not* stoned." I paused, trying to find a way through this. "I'm angry, but not at you. I don't know."

If I didn't get this out now, he would just forget. A cognitive blind spot was at work on his memories and perception. It was sort of as if you were walking in the desert, and there was a hovercraft following a dozen paces behind you that dusted away your footprints as you went along. There were a few steps that you could still see behind you, but beyond that there remained just a general impression of where you had been, or more appropriately, *who* you had been.

"So I'm dead? Very funny, asshole. You're messed up, man. Stop with the drugs, they're screwing with your head. Just tell Dad to get me on the evacuation list. I'm outta here."

He got up to leave.

"Don't leave, Martin. This is important. I'm not kidding and I'm *not* stoned."

I moved all my phantoms to block his paths outward into the multiverse and pulled a glittering security blanket down around us at the same time. "Look at you! This isn't even that much of a shock. If someone told me I was dead, I'd laugh at them, but you're getting defensive."

"I'm not dead, Bobby. I'm right here, talking to you." Martin smiled awkwardly. He wasn't telling me as much as asking me.

"Don't you find it at all odd that everyone else here has a proxxi, but you don't?"

"I have a proxxi—Dean."

"Uh huh. And when was the last time you were in your physical body?"

"I don't know, it's been a while," he replied, shrugging as he cocked his head upward. "What about that time that you and I went surfing and you crashed into that—"

"That was seven years ago, Martin, seven years...."

"So what? Maybe I've been detached for a while, but that doesn't prove anything. I know lots of people who hardly spend any time at all in their bodies." He looked at the floor, burrowing his hands into the pockets of his hoodie, rocking back and forth slightly.

Meanwhile, my own frustration was boiling over. I could feel my cheeks flushing.

I had to blame someone.

"Goddamn it, it's your fault he's gone, Martin," I screamed at him, finally letting it go. "Every day I have to look at your grinning face and just take it. I feel like smashing that smile in, but what difference would it make?"

I was full-on venting now, the words coming out before I even knew what I was saying. The world shifted red as blood surged in my veins and my blood pressure indicator shot off the charts. I took a deep breath and watched it sink back down, trying to calm myself.

Screaming wouldn't accomplish anything.

Martin was silent, pale, his hands shaking as he took them out of his hoodie pockets and held them up. "What's wrong with you?"

I had ahold of myself now. "It's not what's wrong with *me*. Or maybe it is. I think it's what's wrong with this place."

"You're not making sense. What are you getting all crazy for?" He started crying, perched on the edge of the couch.

I took a deep breath. "Martin, look. My brother, Dean, killed himself about six years ago, an intentional drug overdose. Brain dead at first, but they kept his body in stasis, vegetative, but you were still active. You—*his* proxxi. You were still attached to him, your network intimately wired into his dead body and holding all his memories. When we switched off the machines and his body died, we transferred you entirely into the pssi network."

My voice cracked as I tried to continue, "It was too much for us. It wrecked Mom. Dad as well. There *you* were, but he suddenly wasn't. Mom took to spending all her time with you, saying how much it helped her. All of us started spending time wandering back into the inVerse you shared with Dean."

Martin looked at me, his world falling away through the floor, trying to make sense of what I was saying.

"What do you mean? I'm your brother!"

"You're not," I said sadly, shaking my head. "We had Dr. Granger install a cognitive blind spot in your systems, so you couldn't see what was front and center but saw everything around it. One day, they pulled a linchpin somewhere in there, and you just thought you were him. We left the blind spot active to sweep away anything that didn't fit."

"Bobby, *Jesus*, Bobby...," pleaded Martin, tears streaming down his face.

With the anger having blown through, my sails deflated. Closing my eyes, I exhaled and stretched my neck from side to side, taking a moment before looking back at him.

"At the time, I couldn't take it, and Mom and Dad couldn't either. It was a way of fixing the pain, pretending it didn't happen. If we just suspended disbelief that little bit more, our own blind spots took over and *you* became *him*."

Watching his face twist up in pain, it was time for me to own up.

"To be honest, this was my idea to begin with. But now it's taken on a life of its own—*you've* taken on a life of your own. Now Cognix is using...it...your situation...as another application of pssi." I paused to take a deep breath. "How much will people be willing to pay to never lose a loved one? And it does seem to work, which is the worst of it."

Martin wiped away his tears with the back of one hand. "It's funny, now that you tell me, I can see it all, even remember it all. I guess I always sort of knew it, but I love Mom and Dad so much, and you, too." He wiped away more tears. "But why do you blame me? Why are you so angry at me?"

"For impersonating my brother?" I snorted, but immediately regretted it, seeing more pain flash in his eyes. I let my last sparks of anger fizzle. "I think that Dean just felt like you, his proxxi, was a better version of him, that Mom and Dad liked you better, that people were happier when you answered a call than if he did. He was a great guy, not that he didn't have his issues," I said, smiling sadly. Dean was lazy and irresponsible, amazing and funny. "But he just had so much trouble keeping up with it all."

"With all what?"

"With his pssi experiment!" I shot back, angry again. "Living in a hundred worlds at once, being here, and there, and somewhere and someone else all at the same time. Dean just figured, 'Why not, I'll just remove myself, and you'll all be able to keep a better version without all the effort.' In his messed up head he didn't think he was dying, he figured he was leaving a better version of himself to continue on. That's what he left in his note, anyway."

I looked down at the ground, my own tears coming. Why was it I'd been able to be so many things, to be so smart, but I hadn't been there for him?

Martin looked at me thoughtfully. "But maybe I *am* him, Bobby. I think like him, I look like him, and I remember everything—every memory he ever had."

"But you're not him."

"What makes a person dead?"

Stupid question.

"Dead is dead," I shot back. "When the doctors say you're dead."

"When the heart stops?"

"When the brain goes dead, when the memories are lost, the essence of the person...."

"Most of your own memories are in the pssi. Would they be gone if you suddenly were?"

"No...."

"So if a person's memories aren't gone, if some essence of them remains, are they truly dead?"

He paused. I said nothing.

"Remember having a bath together in the sink, Mom sponging us off and singing in the dark, when the first fusion core went offline, remember that?"

I smiled as tears rolled down my cheeks. "I remember."

"Remember throwing our toys over the deck into the ocean when nobody was watching, getting our proxxies to cover for us, and how angry Mom was when we went and hid in one of the shark's mouths when we went swimming for them?"

"That was your idea," I laughed, nodding.

"We were quite the gang growing up. Us and our proxxies...Bobby and Robert, William and Wallace, Sid and Vicious, Dean and Martin, Nancy and Cunard...."

"That was quite the gang."

"Have you talked to Nancy much lately?" asked Martin softly.

"No, I...not since, well, since you...."

"You should talk to her." He looked at me steadily for a while. "Hey, do you remember that night? We were sitting on the guard-rails to the passenger cannon entrance. We must have been barely teenagers, and we were drinking that fermented seaweed? You had Robert override the security systems, and we had the whole place to ourselves. It was just you and me sitting there."

I nodded.

He paused before continuing. "We talked about what we would do together when we were old men. You told me how you were good at almost anything, all you had to do was apply yourself, and you could do anything you wanted. I think I was pretty drunk."

"I was drunk, too," I whispered between my tears.

"But I remember, most of all, I remember thinking how great you were, thinking how I wasn't that great, how I had so much trouble with everything and wondering why. But most of all, I remember thinking how much I loved you, and how proud I was just to be your brother. You were the star of the pssi-kid program, even way ahead of Jimmy, I was so proud...."

"I remember that night," I managed to choke out between sobs. I was crying full on now.

"I'm still here, Bob." Martin was looking directly into my eyes, his voice soft and full of love.

I remembered drawing three-dimensional line drawings of cubes and other objects on paper back when we were starting in school— two squares offset from each other with a straight line that joined each corresponding corner to make a three-dimensional-looking cube. I found it fascinating because when I stared at it, it seemed that one of the faces was closer to you, but if you concentrated and willed it, suddenly the cube flipped and the other face switched to being closer.

As I looked hard at Martin right then, my mind performed a similar flip, and with sudden clarity, all I saw was my brother, sitting there in front of me in flesh and blood. A wave of love sprang from my scalp to my fingertips, and I got up to go and sit on the couch with him.

"Dean...Martin...I missed you so much, it's just this place." I reached out to hold his hand.

"I've missed you, too," replied Martin. "You've been so nasty to me these past years. I always think you hate me for some reason that I don't understand. It hurt so much."

Tears streamed down my face, and Martin reached up to wipe them away, and then he rubbed his hand across his own face. His demeanor changed, and he sat bolt upright, taking a deep breath. He grabbed both of my hands tightly with his. "Stop with all the drugs, will you? And all these women, it's not going to change anything. Calm down. Talk to Nancy."

"You're right," was all I could think to say. "I'll stop, I'll try...."

"Good," he replied. "And Bobby, if you really believe all that stuff about gameworlds being real, then Dean is still somewhere out there, and I'm your connection to him."

"This is messed up."

I was staring at the floor. Nothing made any sense. My whole life, I'd felt like I was running away from something, fleeing before some unseen danger. From now on, it would stop.

Maybe he was right; maybe I could still find Dean out there. I was right in the middle of one of the most amazing places on earth, where the impossible was becoming possible almost daily. I just needed to apply myself and get out of this daze I'd slid into.

"Bobby?" asked Martin.

"Yeah?"

"Why are you crying?"

Oh no. The blind spot had caught up. I wiped away my tears.

I lied. "It's nothing. I'm just worried about the storms and Nicky dumping me."

His face brightened. "Don't worry, big brother, I'll take care of you. Like I was saying, could you get Dad to add me to the evacuation list? I don't know what's going, but I have a lot to do, so I'd appreciate it."

"Consider it done," I replied with a sigh.

"Thanks."

Martin got up off the couch and prepared to leave.

"Hey, Martin...."

"Yeah?"

"There's something I've been meaning to say lately."

"Oh yeah? What's that?"

I smiled, pausing, and the world clicked back into sense for me. "Martin, I love you. I love you a lot."

He looked away quickly, catching his breath, and brought up a hand to wipe the corner of one eye. "I love you, too, Bobby. That is so good to hear."

"Okay, good—now get!" I laughed.

He grinned back at me, shaking his head as he disappeared.

This place, all of it, felt abruptly wrong. Like a switch being thrown, I suddenly knew something wasn't right here anymore, and that this same something had swallowed Dean in its path. Blind spots—we all had them. So what was it that they were hiding from us, what was it we weren't seeing?

◆◆◆ NEVERYWHERE

Part 5:

Nancy Killiam & William McIntyre

1

Identity: William McIntyre

A brilliant carpet of stars hung above us on the moonless night, somewhere in the Adirondacks of upper New York State. Our campsite was nestled between towering firs at the side of a lake. We'd barely finished the canoe trip and portage to get here before nightfall, and we were all spent. A deep silence settled between us over the hissing and popping of the campfire. I was almost completely relaxed for once—*almost*.

"It's so peaceful out here," I said, leaning forward to pick up a stick and poke at the embers of the fire. I could feel a breeze blowing across my backside, but I let it go for now.

"You got that right," replied Bob, sitting next to Martin on my left, both of them slumped comfortably in their folding camp chairs. Bob was balancing a beer on his knee.

"Yes, sir," added Wally, my proxxi, sitting right next to me. He saw me toss my empty can into the fire. "Do you want another beer?"

"No thanks. I'm good."

Stirring the embers, I watched the sparks dance as they escaped from the charred wood. Rubbing my hands, I extended them toward the warm coals; it was going to be a cold night. A loon called out from the blackness above the lake with a haunting wail. Nearly time to go.

"This is amazing," drawled Bob. He stared at the fire for a moment. "Hey, Willy, did you catch the slingshot tests this morning?"

He took another swig from his beer, grinning at me. He was usually smiling, the lucky bum. Then again, he didn't have it that easy.

"Sure, kind of impossible to miss," I replied. "Were you with your family?"

He laughed, looking up at Sid and Vicious, who were sitting across the campfire from us. "Nah, Sid and I were out in Humungous Fungus, watching the mash-up version."

I grinned. "Bet that was fun."

"Sure, but my dad gave me a lot of trouble when I got home."

Wally pinged me with an alert. *Oh shoot.*

"Oh, ah, Martin," I blurted out awkwardly, "happy birthday, by the way." It always confused me how Bob's birthday was one day, and Martin's the next.

Martin smiled, looking up at me from the fire.

"Thanks, Willy," he laughed, then looked at Bob. "And Dad wasn't really mad, you know, he's under a lot of pressure."

"I know," replied Bob. "I'm sorry. Thanks for covering for me."

"That's what brothers are for," chuckled Martin, shaking his head. "Right?"

"Yeah," sighed Bob heavily, "that's what brothers are for."

An uncomfortable silence descended, and everyone stared down at the ground, everyone, that is, except Martin. He looked around at us all with wide eyes. "What, did somebody die or something?"

Bob snorted, shaking his head. "Just forget it."

"Forget what?"

"Just *forget it*," snapped Bob. "You will no matter what anyway."

More uncomfortable silence.

"I can't believe more people don't come out into nature to experience this," Bob said after a while, changing the topic. "It's amazing. You know, doing things with your own two hands, getting back to the basics."

Now everyone nodded except Martin, who'd returned to staring blankly into the fire.

"Yeah," I agreed, but Bob could always read my moods.

"You still worrying?" he asked me.

"Nah."

"Yeah you are. I can tell. Everything will be fine. It always is." He smiled. "Even when it isn't." He tossed his beer can into the fire.

The wind changed direction and began pushing the smoke from the fire directly into Vicious, Sid's proxxi.

"Mates, it's been a real pleasure," coughed Vicious, "but I've 'ad about enough. This nature shite is not for me." He held up his hands and willed the wind to shift again, forcing it to blow away from him.

"Come on," laughed Sid. "We're having a nice time here! Tough it out a little!"

The spell was broken, however, and the suspension of disbelief cracked, revealing the grainy quality of the fire and the hollow texture of the night. It all began to feel fake, and a heavy weight fell back across my shoulders. "I think I'm going to get going, too."

"Surfing tomorrow, though, right?" asked Bob.

"Sure thing, wouldn't miss it for the world," I lied.

I gave a perfunctory wave to the gang, and without another word, the campsite faded away, replaced by the white, featureless confines of my apartment. Wally was still sitting beside me, though now on the convertible couch of my tiny living space. My digs could, at best, be described as minimalist. Real space on Atopia came at a premium price, one I couldn't afford.

"Don't worry so much, Willy," said Wally.

"Easy for you to say. You don't live in this pill box."

"Well, yes and no, Willy," Wally noted, watching me carefully. "Look, I've never said this before, and I'm not sure why I'm saying it now, but...."

I waited. "What?" *Why is my proxxi getting weird on me?* As if I didn't have enough to worry about.

He looked steadily at me. "William, I just wanted to make sure you know, well, that I love you."

I was slightly stunned, and he saw it.

"Not in a weird way," he added quickly. "I mean, as brothers, you know." He smiled and waited for me to respond.

"Yeah, thanks," I said slowly, not sure of what to do with this. "Look, I appreciate that, and I like you, too, Wally."

He kept smiling at me. *I have to talk to someone at Cognix technical support about this.* I had lot of work to get done. I didn't need this.

"Look, I'm fine," I finally told him. "Let's just focus on the here and now, okay?"

Switching topics to the work at hand, the walls and features of my apartment morphed outward into the sea of displays that were my workspace. I had a busy day tomorrow and wanted to get a jump start on organizing myself for the big meeting with Nancy Killiam, the head of the new tech company, Infinixx, I was contracting with. Wally and I worked well into the night, pulling and pushing masses of financial data through the deep reaches of the multiverse, trying to make sense of the rapidly accelerating world around us.

The next morning Brigitte dropped the expected warning shot. "You didn't ping me last night when you got back from camping with the boys."

She tried to say it lightly, but I could tell. We'd been together for two years, and I could sense her moods coming like winds approaching in the treetops.

"Sorry, sweetheart," I replied, attempting to deflect the looming storm. "You know I have this big meeting with Nancy today."

She didn't say anything and I paused, deciding on my plan of defense: feint or full retreat?

"We were preparing for the meeting," I added defensively. "And," I quickly noted, "we did some stock picks, too."

My job at Infinixx paid okay, but I'd been brought in as an outside contractor and wasn't on their stock option dream ticket. The real reason I'd gunned so hard for the job was that it gave me access to the distributed consciousness platform they were developing. Being able to be in a dozen places at once gave me an edge nobody else in the market had right now. And in the market, any edge equaled an opportunity to make money.

Brigitte pouted. A beautiful pout if there ever was one.

Her full lips and petite nose under a beautiful tangle of laissez-faire auburn hair that women of a lesser pedigree would kill for, set her firmly in irresistible, somewhere between beautiful and beautifully cute. Even when her deep brown eyes flashed angrily at me, as they did now, it was hard to resist the urge to simply scoop her up into my arms and kiss her.

So I did.

"William," she said patiently, pushing me away. She was laughing, but when she used my full name, she always had a serious point to make. I looked at her in my arms. "*Vraiment*, money isn't everything. Look around you, *chérie*."

I looked around.

We were having breakfast in our pajamas, her in her bunny slippers, atop a Scottish Highlands mountain ridge. Our small white table and chairs sat against the backdrop of a blossoming sunrise amid rolling fog and boulders and grass and sheep—it was surreal to say the least, but she liked it, and that was all that mattered.

"We're in the most amazing place on Earth. We can travel anywhere we want, do anything we like. I make more than enough money to support both of us, and anyway, look where we're having breakfast! What do we need more money for?"

I tried not to roll my eyes. This was well-trodden ground. She was a senior administrator for a medical services company headquartered on Atopia, and she made more than double my salary. No matter how I tried to convince myself that it didn't matter—it did. It would be nice to be able to afford more sub-proxxi; as it was, I could hardly afford to have Wally show up at more than one event at a time. It would be nice to be able to afford to expand my Phuture News Network; right now, it was an immense effort just to stay ahead of the game.

Even accessing the wikiworld at this resolution cost us more than I could afford, but this wouldn't cut any ice with her. When it came right down to it, everyone else I knew was better off than me, and frankly, it pissed me off.

No end was in sight for the multigenerational mortgage my dad had taken out for our family to get a berth on Atopia. It was a shrewd move on his part, entering the lottery—the value of the berth had more than quadrupled—but the size of the mortgage was crippling to a regular family like ours. We struggled under the debt. It didn't help, of course, that I'd made some bad stock picks lately and was far in the hole.

"You're right, pumpkin, you're right." It was no use arguing with her.

My metasenses were tingling, and that meant a hot stock move. I'd remapped my skin's tactile array from the nape of my neck and down my back, like a fish's lateral line sensors, to sense eddy currents in market phuturecasts. Even the slightest pressure trends in the markets tickled my backside. It was a surefire way to get my attention. Right now, a stiff wind was buffeting my buttocks as I buttered my toast.

"I gotta go," I told her hurriedly, getting up and leaning over to peck her on the cheek. "Something for work. Sorry, I really have to run."

She rolled her eyes.

I stepped away and bolted upward through the sky, the world disappearing away below me as I arrived at my workworld. This was my favorite way to get going—it gave me that Superman start to the day.

Wally was already there, and I turned on, tuned in, and dropped out into the multiverse, splintering my mind to assimilate what was happening. One splinter was already tuned into the press conference that my boss, Nancy, had just started, so I let my mind hover over this for a moment.

2

Identity: Nancy Killiam

"Economic growth is only possible through enhanced productivity and the clustering of talent," I roared to an approving audience.

The world population was declining and fertility rates were collapsing, I didn't have to add, not to mention failing prospects for the Yen and greenback as bitcoin-derivatives gained ground. While declining populations equaled better prospects for the planet, it was bad news for economics—and for once, today was all about business.

"Atopia isn't simply about being green," I pointed out, "but about boosting business productivity, *and profits*, to provide the basis for a whole new surge in the world economy."

Closest to me were mostly familiar reporters. Beyond that, millions of faces filled my display spaces into the blue-shifted distance. This was a well-worn speech for me, like a rutted track down an old country road. *Maybe "rutted track" wasn't the best analogy*, I chuckled to myself.

I stopped and looked at the crowd. The pause was well rehearsed, and I was enjoying it. I let a confident smile spread across my many faces.

"And the Infinixx distributed consciousness platform is the solution that will carry business into the twenty-second century!"

The masses before me burst into applause. I shook my head and looked down at the stage, trying to convey that I didn't deserve such adulation.

"So...questions?" I asked, looking back into the crowd. I saw Tammy from *World Press* with her arm up. She was always a friendly starter. I pointed at her and nodded.

"Could you characterize for the audience what exactly distributed consciousness feels like?" she asked. "I mean, how would you describe it? And not from a technical point-of-view."

This brought hushed laughter. I was famous for inundating reporters with jargon that left them feeling like they knew less than what they started with. This time, I made an effort to keep it simple.

"Good question. The easiest way to describe it is like speed reading. When you're speed reading, you don't read every word, you only read the first and last lines of paragraphs and scan for a few key words in between. It's sort of like that."

"Doesn't that imply you're not really getting the whole picture?"

Good question, but hard to answer simply. Our Infinixx "distributed consciousness" system wasn't really distributing the conscious mind. It created an estimate of a mind's cognitive state at one point in time, then tagged this with as much personal background data, such as memories, as it thought relevant and were available. The system then started up a synthetic intelligence engine and sent it out to canvas whatever the user wanted to look at.

From time to time this "splinter," as we called it, would report back with compressed sensory data that would be understandable only to the user.

When I explained it to reporters, I often used the "best friend" explanation: Imagine your best friend winking at you when you asked about someone you both knew. Based on shared experiences, huge amounts of information could be encoded in a single binary bit communicated this way. Infinixx was something like this—the ultimate data-gathering, compression, and transmission scheme, tailored exactly to your individual mind at that moment in time. It worked better with pssi-enabled humans, but even with regular ones, it worked well enough.

"You are getting the whole picture," I responded to Tammy after reflection, "but just not every detail. Speed reading comes down to the *unconscious skill* the reader has in scanning the *right parts* on which to focus." I paused to let them soak in what I was saying. "Infinixx technology provides that attentional context, as well as the sensory and cognitive multiplexing technology to make it easy even for novices to begin distributing their consciousness into the cloud within a few hours."

I scanned the upturned faces. They were nodding, but that last sentence brought a slightly glazed look into their eyes.

"For instance," I continued quickly, "that last meeting you attended, how much of that was just an excuse for a coworker to ramble on about something that had nothing to do with you?"

This earned some chuckles.

"However," I declared, drawing the word out, "there were probably a few bits here and there that you found useful. Infinixx provides the ability to tune a small part of your attention to only those interesting bits, allowing you to 'be there' the whole time without *actually* needing to be there."

"How long does it take to understand how to use all this?" another reporter cut in.

"Even *you'll* be able to use it right away, Max," I joked, winking. This earned more laughs. I tried to maintain a steady smile at Max. To fully realize the benefits of this technology, one needed to grow up with it, but I wasn't going to tell them that. So I continued: "We're ready to go if you are!"

3

Identity: William McIntyre

"It is in our interest to work together and find a way to shape our differences," droned the Chinese Minister of State. *Sure,* I thought, *in exactly the same way that you've shaped all previous differences—in your favor.*

The splinter covering the latest round of peace talks between China and India didn't need to send in very much new information, the tone and character of the meeting having been pretty much the same as every other one in the recent past: nothing positive, and very predictable. Then again, for business purposes, predictability was everything. I pulled the splinter back for more important work elsewhere.

I quickly assimilated that thin conscious stream, then turned my mind to an exploration hike that another of my splinters was on in the Brazilian rain forest.

The wikiworld displayed vast tracts of remote farmland belonging to Greengenics outside of Manos, all sown with a complex matrix of genetically modified plants that was supposed to mimic the biodiversity of the forest surrounding it. I wasn't buying their story and suspected they were strip-farming the area. I'd hired a local guide to walk in and snoop for me, and this splinter was ghosting in through the guide's contact-lens display.

Pulling back the last of the dense foliage before the edge of the farm area, we peered in, and my suspicions were confirmed. Long rows of bioengineered farmaceuticals stretched out into the distance. Greengenics was falsifying its wikiworld feeds. This splinter of information at the edges of my attention shattered into a dozen others that went off and used the information to my advantage—shorting the Greengenics stock, buying their competitors stock, alerting authorities of falsified filings, and pinging media outlets with anonymous tips about a possible story.

The Shanghai market was about to close its morning session when disaster hit.

"What?"

"Pull out of the short positions right away," warned Willy. "I've already done as much as I can."

Visions of the peace talks closing splintered into my mind. Interest rates were supposed to be trending a full point lower, but a last-second and unexpected announcement between the Chinese and Indians regarding a joint farmaceutical project had injected some uncertainty into the market, pushing expected rates higher. Worse, the Greengenics facility was named as their secret collaboration, sending the stock of this small company soaring. This unexpected twist shot everything out of alignment.

"Put in sell orders!" I yelled into my dozen splinters.

A bell chimed, signaling the close of Shanghai. Within seconds, the secondary and aftermarkets kicked in, but by the time we'd managed to unravel my positions, I'd chalked up a huge loss.

I was too highly leveraged, trying to be too clever.

Hovering over the small metaworld that was my financial control center, I closed my eyes and sighed. I needed more splinters to cover more things at the same time. All I'd been able to scrounge up were fifteen of them, and half were prototypes that were getting called back for updates and re-initializations all the time. A growing headache pounded behind my eyes, and I focused inward and back outward, preparing myself for the rest of the night's work.

The day ended in near financial disaster. Almost everything that could go wrong had. Even though I hadn't said anything, Brigitte could sense my mood, and she'd prepared a special night for us. She'd taken the time to personally reserve a little patch of sidewalk on the side of the Grand Canal in Venice.

The spot was undeniably romantic: a candle set in a green wine bottle atop a red-checked tablecloth; the gentle slap of the Adriatic against the canal walls; the twinkling lights of Venezia under a rising full moon. The strains of an accordion played somewhere nearby, the notes floating together with the smells of fresh-cut herbs, tomatoes, and seafood.

"Brigitte, this is beautiful," I marveled as I arrived, dropping most of my webwork of splinters behind. Stepping into this reality, I sat down opposite her. I tried to relax and let my foul mood evaporate into the warm night air.

I was still stewing over a heated argument I'd had with Nancy earlier regarding my splintering limit. I'd tried to explain to her what a difficult spot I was in, but it hadn't mattered.

Atopia was supposed to be this shining beacon of libertarian ideals, when in actuality it was just another country club for rich snobs like the Killiams. She had no idea what it was like for a family like mine here.

Almost every American had lost someone in the the first major cyberattacks nearly forty years ago, but our family had been particularly hard hit. We came from working-class roots in South Boston, and life had always been a struggle. But when the first strikes had hit in the middle of a cold snap at Christmas and triggered massive infrastructure failures, something not easy had turned into something terrifyingly deadly. When the power came back on over a month later, we'd lost nine of our family to the cold, starvation, and riots.

Suspicion of technology had driven my grandfather literally into the hills. But hiding from the modern world made for a hard life, and my father hadn't been able to adjust. A huge fight had erupted when my dad had announced plans to move to Atopia to start anew and break with the neo-Luddite community founded by my grandfather in the foothills of Montana.

It had been a big gamble, a gamble for a different life for my mother and me, and it was one that had cut my dad off from the rest of our family. Now I felt that the burden to make good had fallen on my shoulders.

While my dad and I had managed the transition, my mother hadn't been able to cope, and after a few years, she'd returned home to the commune. I remembered being furious at her, and I'd barely spoken to her afterward.

I wasn't mad at her anymore, but the commune forbade modern communication technology—so if I wanted to speak to her, I needed to physically go there. I'd been planning a trip to see her for years, but I always seemed to find excuses for not going. A trip on foot into the mountains wasn't something I was comfortable with, but it was more than that. I wanted to make good first, to prove that my dad had been right, and that she'd made the right decision in leaving me with him.

"William?" said Brigitte, catching my attention.

She was dressed up for our evening, her hair falling in waves over her shoulders, clothed in a glittering black slip that left little to the imagination. Her perfume was powerfully seductive, undoubtedly working some pssi magic—it zeroed my focus in on her. I collapsed the rest of my conscious splinters into the here and now, and centered my full attention on her soft brown eyes.

She deserves better. I would do better.

"Yes?"

"Are you here with me now?" she asked.

"I'm sorry," I sighed. "It's just… it's complicated."

She watched me quietly. "Not everything needs to be complicated." She moved her hand down to my cheek, then pulled my chin up so I was looking directly into her eyes. "Come on, let's eat."

Waiters immediately floated around us with plates of food.

"I want to apologize for giving you a hard time," she said, leaning over to kiss my forehead.

I'd almost forgotten about all that. "No worries, pumpkin," I replied, my mental fog lifting. "It's me who should be apologizing."

She smiled at me and reached over to hold my hand.

"Enough apologizing, *cheri*," she said tenderly. "First we eat, and then off to bed."

Her smile turned seductive.

My stomach growled. I hadn't realized how hungry I was. *Hungry and horny*, I thought as I looked at her, and I could see she wanted to make me a happy man. Life didn't get much better than this. I smiled and dug into dinner.

Perhaps my situation wasn't as bad as I thought.

Soon after, I was sitting in bed, contemplating the view from the window of our *pensione*. The urge to connect into my work systems was nagging at me, but I was resisting, trying to soak in the moment. A gentle breeze blew in through the window, and Brigitte clung tightly to my side.

We enjoyed sex without any of the messy special effects a lot of the other pssi-kids went for. Not to say we hadn't experimented with all that stuff. Brigitte was quite the wild child in her day, but as we'd gotten older and found each other, the craziness had lost its appeal.

"Willy," she purred softly, "can I ask you something? And can you promise not to get mad?"

"Sure, anything, sweet pea." All of my defenses were down. She could have asked me to jump into the canal and I would have happily complied.

"Do you think we could start sharing our realities? I mean, completely."

Even as relaxed as I was, this gave me a shock.

"Sweetie," I replied calmly, "even couples that have been married for years don't share their realities entirely."

Right now we were sharing a reality of being in Venice together, which was great, but she wanted to fully share each other's reality skins, all the little and big ways we filtered and modified real and virtual worlds.

I wasn't sure I wanted her to see the world the way I saw it.

"I know what other people do, and I don't want that to be us," she continued. "It is possible, you know."

It wasn't like I walked around with the world skinned-up in as some weird fantasy, but still, sometimes I liked my world to appear the way I liked it to appear. It was hard to deny her, though.

"I want us to take that next step in our relationship," she added, "to experience the world together in the same way."

Really it wasn't *that* big a deal. It wasn't as if we were teenagers and I had something to hide. She really deserved more from me.

"Sure, let's do it. I'd love to do that with you!" This earned me a big hug and kiss, but I pulled myself away gently. "I love you, sweetheart."

"I love you, too," she replied.

I paused, looking at her expectantly. A steady wind that only I could feel had begun to blow.

"Yes, yes, go to work." She smiled and rolled her eyes. "I know you're dying to get out there with Wally."

She hit me playfully with a pillow.

I laughed, grabbing the pillow away and pulling her in for a final kiss.

In a flash, I was rocketing up through the heavens and into my workspace.

The main action for me wasn't out in the front of my life. The real action was in the backrooms, where Wally and I were working to build my growing hedge fund. My ability to consistently outpace the market using the new Infinixx distributed consciousness platform made it possible to do things nobody else could do. People out there were noticing how this pssi-kid was beating them, and I was starting to get some traction in the market.

But I desperately needed more splinters.

A few months ago, five had been enough, and then I'd expanded to ten. I'd managed to get fifteen by signing up for some beta testing under false credentials, but I wasn't fooling anybody at Infinixx, and it had me constantly at loggerheads with Nancy. Almost as soon as I launched my splinter-matrix for the evening, she barged in, appearing in an overlaid display while I sat in the middle of my hedge-fund metaworld.

"Nancy, I am just as capable, and probably even more capable, than you at splintering," I argued immediately, knowing what was coming. "I've spent more time stretching the capabilities of Infinixx than anyone."

"We've been over this, Willy."

"And I can beat the pants off you at flitter tag."

Nancy rolled her eyes. "I'm not going to disagree, William. I'm just saying, if you were anyone else, I would have fired you already. I can't ignore it anymore."

She just didn't get it. "Can't you see I'm doing you a favor?"

She said nothing.

"Think of me as an advanced beta tester," I suggested hopefully.

"William, I can't," she said finally. "Your splinter limit will be set at ten. I will allow you to keep using Infinixx to run your side business, but that's it."

Ten? My stomach tightened into knots.

4

Identity: Nancy Killiam

"Ten?"

"That's it, William. I'm not going to discuss this anymore."

I looked at a graphic detailing the metaworld Willy had created for his business. A threadbare and kludged-together collection of Phuture News feeds, second-rate synthetics, and metasense overlays that snaked into the hyperspaces surrounding him. The only saving grace was the distributed consciousness network connecting it all together, borrowed illegally from my Infinixx beta labs. It looked like an interesting test case to show what small businesses could do with our technology, but it was just too early in our product development process.

"Can I just keep to the fifteen I have now?" Willy looked desperate. It broke my heart to have to have this kind of conversation with him.

"*Ten*, and even that's a stretch. And I know you're one of Bob's best friends...."

"But *obviously* not yours. I guess forever and ever ends quicker than it sounds."

"We were children, Willy."

"And?"

"That was just a silly game."

"Maybe to you."

I sighed. Growing up, Bob, Willy, and I had been part of an almost inseparable gang, and we'd promised to always stick together, do whatever we could for each other, no matter what, forever and ever. It was a long time ago.

I shook my head again. "Ten."

Now he looked angry. I felt myself wavering, but we were at a critical point in our developmental path. We had to stick to the known unknowns, and letting someone splinter their consciousness into more than just a few instances could lead to some unknown unknowns that I couldn't afford.

He glowered in my display space. I didn't have to plug into his emotional feeds to feel the heated waves spilling out around him.

"Fine," he announced from between gritted teeth, and then he summarily blocked me from all his realities.

My primary subjective snapped back into the Infinixx control center, and I leaned back in my chair, trying to think of ways I could try to help my old friend.

I was already feeling more than uncomfortable, pssi-kid or not, being in my early twenties and bossing around people more than twice my age. Explaining to our board of directors that I was putting the program at risk for a childhood friendship just wasn't a place I was willing to go.

Willy had always had a chip on his shoulder, even when we were kids. He'd arrived on Atopia with his family when he was already six years old, at an age when the rest of us pssi-kids were already amazing the world with our abilities in the virtual worlds where we'd grown up.

Willy had to start from less than nothing, having come from a neo-Luddite commune in central Montana. In the Schoolyard, we'd teased him mercilessly as he'd struggled to come to grips with the pssi system. Bob had been the first to befriend him, bringing him into our gang, and their friendship was one that had survived. This was no mean feat in the churning social space of Atopia.

His young mind, back then, had been forced to leapfrog almost four hundred years, rocketing from a compound stuck somewhere in the eighteenth century straight into Atopia, a place far ahead of the rest of the world. He'd been incredibly determined, though, and within a short time had become the best flitter tag player in the Schoolyard. Willy had always been on an upward climb, always trying to prove himself, and now more than ever.

I sighed again.

I wondered what the world must look like from his perspective, coming from a place so alien to me. It was hard to imagine his childhood.

This made me think of mine.

As a baby girl, my first memories, my first fully formed memories, were of my mother's face. This wasn't unusual. What was unusual was the detail with which I could remember it. My mother was holding me, cuddling me, and looking down into my eyes, cooing softly.

"Nancy, how are you feeling, my little darling?" My mother's face was full of love and worry.

It was a very special moment to me. And as the first pssi-kid to pass this threshold, it was a very special moment that was shared with the whole Cognix program. My memories were famous.

That memory was from the first moment my pssi was turned on. It was the beginning of my inVerse, the complete sensory recording of everything I had ever seen, heard, felt, or sensed. I was three months old, and the moment was exactly 7:05 am, Pacific

Time, on September 20th of the year my family moved onto the first prototype Atopian platform.

I'd gone back and relived it so many times it was almost embarassing—felt my mother's hot breath on my blushing cheeks, sensed her holding me tightly, observed every nuance of her pupils dilating and contracting, breathed in the tang of her perfume and the medicinal scent of strong soap, and felt the pull of distraction as I caught glimpses of glowing dust motes floating in the angled sunlight streaming in from the windows. In the corner of the room, my father crouched anxiously over quietly humming machines as he monitored my signals and systems, stealing quick glances toward us from time to time.

Growing up, we hadn't known anything special was happening around us. Like kids anywhere and anytime, we'd just assumed that life was like this for everyone. But we *were* special. We were the first generation of children to grow up with seamless, synthetic reality sensory interfaces.

After running out of letters at the end of the alphabet, *Time* magazine had tried to label us "Generation A," as in artificial reality, but this expression had died almost as quickly as the magazine. The world then came to refer to us simply as the pssi-kids. We were a part of Cognix Corporation's phase III clinical trials of early developmental pssi on the island colony of Atopia. We weren't just making history. As my dad liked to say—we *were* history.

While Atopia was an amazing place to grow up, we were still just kids, and we did the things that all kids did. We screamed, we dribbled, and we wobbled when we first learned to walk. We did learn to walk much earlier than regular children, using pssi muscle-memory training, but this was just one in a long list of things that we could do that normal human children couldn't.

Our world was more than just this world—the "physical" world was only a tiny patch of our playground as we quickly learned to flitter across the endless streams of metaworlds that were filled with toys and creatures that sparkled in our sensory display spaces. At first these worlds without end were created for us to play in, but then we began building them ourselves, and we perceived little difference between the real and the virtual. In fact, synthetic worlds felt as real and tangible to us as what the rest of the world called their reality.

Even from a young age, it wasn't just toys we played with; we also played with making ourselves into toys, altering our bodies to become teddy bears, worms, little flocks of soaring dinosaurs in endless skyworlds, and ever more alien creatures inhabiting ever more impossible spaces as our minds developed a fluid capacity for neuroplasticity. Our proxxi and educational bots were constantly presenting us with an endless barrage of games to master and puzzles to solve as we spun through these worlds, treating every moment as a learning opportunity.

From our point-of-view, our proxxi were simply our playmates during the first few years of our lives. But they weren't playing. They were constantly correlating the flood of neuronal data traffic through the smarticle networks embedded in our bodies and matching it with our behavior.

We were being analyzed.

It didn't take that long to learn a human wetware matrix, but our brains and nervous systems were still in development, and they were using our data to continuously redesign the pssi system. We were Cognix's guinea pigs, part and parcel of our parents' agreements to participate in the Atopian project.

Almost all of my early childhood was spent with my proxxi—the ultimate tool in familial productivity enhancement. To us, our proxxi were our brothers and sisters, little artificial boys and girls we could play with.

This even became a primary selling feature of the program.

After all, who had the cycles left over in today's busy world to have even one child, never mind a second one? Proxxi filled this need in the market by creating a kind of digital clone of a child to act as its playmate, babysitter, and educator, or even the child's twin, depending on your point-of-view and moral framework.

The floodgates opened near our fourth birthdays.

Around this age, one by one, we were gradually given independent access to our own pssi systems. Like quick little fish, we'd disappeared over and through the worlds that our parents understood and began venturing out into the open network. Before that time, we'd been limited to one body, but we soon learned to spawn our minds simultaneously into others.

The reign of the pssi-kids in the multiverse had begun.

Leaning forward in my chair, I focused my mind on several key events unfolding in the worlds my consciousness was spread out into, all the while fine tuning the parameters of some phuturecasts that tied them all together. A high-dimensional correlation matrix floated through my display spaces, and I watched it growing, pulsing, and fading as predictions grew or fell in their interconnectedness.

"So what do you think?" I asked.

"You know what I think," responded Cunard, my proxxi, and I did.

While we were talking, I was holding forth on dozens of splintered conversations in other virtual worlds while keeping an eye on reports coming in from a platoon of sub-proxxi and bots out collecting and spreading data with trusted, and not trusted, parties. I could sense a coalescing cascade in the mood of billions of humans, as well as subtle shifts in the goings on in the billions more worlds in which they wandered.

The timing felt about right.

Distributing my consciousness this wide and thin was tiring, and I'd been at it constantly for nearly forty hours straight, even while arguing with Willy. An aching pressure had built up behind my eyeballs. The Sleep-Over tabs worked great up to a point, but I was feeling sluggish after a long week.

I sensed it was just beginning to pay off, as I could feel the ebb and flow of the world's opinion around the Infinixx project. Just a little more certainty was all I needed, so I gritted my teeth, rubbed my many eyeballs, and focused inward and back outward.

"Nancy!" someone called out, intentionally overriding my sensory dataflow using an emergency channel. The interruption jolted me, and my conscious webwork partially collapsed. It was David, of course, which I realized after a split second of hang time. I sighed but smiled as his face floated into view.

"C'mon, Nance, come to Davey-boy. Enough is enough." He was smiling, too, but I could see concern worrying the corners of his mouth.

"Just a little longer. I'm sorry."

I had a splinter ghosting him, but I'd lost track of it. Visions of him cooking up a storm in the kitchen floated into view as I retrieved that conscious stream. Most of my awareness was still hovering in countless minds and bodies scattered throughout dozens of worlds. I checked the pulsating correlation matrix one last time. Things looked good, and that was good enough for me.

I initiated a wrap to the session, and like a shockwave, streams of information flowed outward from me into my agents across the multiverse. Collapsing my cognitive webwork, it felt like a brick was being lifted off my brain.

The relief was palpable.

"All done, sweetie," I responded to David. "And I have some wonderful news."

"And I have some wonderful food getting cold," he said playfully. I was more than late for dinner.

With a final flurry of gestures, I released my agents to autopilot and left the rest in the care of Cunard. My workspaces faded out, and the outlines of a dinner setting sharpened into view.

David had chosen a romantic setting. A small fire crackled and popped in a marble fireplace, each side set with a dramatic arrangement of exotic flowers. In fact, the entire living room was decked out in white marble and tropical flowers. Through the open doors, neoclassical columns graced a grand terrace, and a breeze was billowing in through satin curtains. Sea air mixed with burning incense, and I caught a glimpse of what I was sure was the Amalfi coast in the distance.

Italy, of course. I could see where this was going.

Cunard was sitting next to David at the table, and it looked like they'd been playing cards. A bottle of wine languished half-finished. Before I fully clipped back into my body, Cunard took me to one side in a private one-on-one channel.

"I hope you don't mind, but I dressed you in that little black thing you love so much," explained Cunard. "It seemed appropriate given his state of mind, and I didn't want to disturb you."

I looked down at my body. *Sexy*, if I did say so myself.

"No, that's great Cunard. Thank you very much. You can leave us now, and please, pay attention to the correlation matrix and have a talk with the editors at the *Financial Times*. I left all the notes and instructions...."

"Go on, girl," laughed Cunard, "have a nice evening. Stop thinking for once."

With that, he popped out of view, and I snapped firmly into my body.

The clarity and immediacy of being in only one place after being splintered for so long shocked my proprioceptive sense. I felt like little bits of me wanted to scuttle into the corners to get out of the glare of hard and fast reality, or at least this single point-of-presence.

Blinking, I tried to shake it off.

David was smiling intently at me. With a flick of one of his phantoms, the playing cards disappeared, and the long, polished table went from empty to beautifully set for dinner with gleaming silverware, glowing candles, and embroidered napkins. He reached across to hold my hand.

"Well, look who's here," he said, smiling.

"Yes, and look who's there," I replied, returning the smile.

He looked like some kind of Italian swashbuckler in tight beige linen pants and a laced white cotton shirt undone almost to the waist. He was tanned, his cheeks dappled with two-day old stubble. I laughed looking at him.

"Okay, stud, give me a minute? I need a glass of wine to begin the unwinding process."

"Your wish is my command, *signorina.*"

Grinning, he reached with his other hand for the glass, already filled, and handed it to me.

I let go of his hand to take the glass and brought it to my lips. A well-aged Nebbiolo flooded my mouth, and my body began to relax.

David wagged a finger in the air. "Did you check your inVerse? Vince and Patricia both dropped in with urgent requests when you were busy. Vince had some odd requests...Anyway, I dropped it with Cunard, and Patricia wanted to speak to you about an announcement?"

"David," I said excitedly, "it's time. The timing is perfect for putting Infinixx on the stock markets."

I knew he was in the mood for love, but I couldn't help myself. I was practically bursting at the seams. One of the reasons I was with David was that he had a seemingly infinite patience with me, and

I abused it all too often. Guiltily, I wondered if perhaps he could sense our relationship was living on borrowed time and made allowances he shouldn't to try to keep it going.

The gleam in his eye diminished, but still he responded enthusiastically, "Wow! Are you sure? You're going before the commercial launch of pssi? Can you do that?"

"I've checked and rechecked everything. We can only win if we go now. When Cognix goes ahead with pssi, we'll get a double-bump up the hill. Jimmy's been helping me out. I need to chat with Patricia quickly though, is that okay?"

David nodded glumly as he stared down at the place settings. I squeezed his hand and pinged Patricia. Her head appeared a moment later, floating in one of my display spaces, and she pulled me into her reality. Out of the corner of one multiplexed eye, I could see David sulking and taking a sip of his wine. He got up to add more logs to the fire.

"So you're sure you want to go ahead with this?" Patricia asked immediately.

"Absolutely!" I cried, before noticing where I was.

Everyone in the pub turned and looked at me. I'd materialized sitting on what appeared to be a small, worn-out church pew tucked in the corner of an old English pub. The crowd turned back to what they'd been doing and the hubbub returned.

"Good. I'll press ahead on my side then. You're keeping on top of the New York trials?"

"Yes, Aunt Patricia." I always felt like a child with her. "Of course I am."

I smiled at Alan, one of Patricia's old mentors, who was sitting across from me. He nodded back.

"Perfect. I'll start a campaign with the board."

I was hardly able to contain my excitement, but I was nervous as well. I realized that this was actually going to happen, that all my dreams were coming true. But there'd been another reason I'd asked to speak with her.

Squinting I took a deep breath, not sure how to bring this up.

"There's something else?" asked Patricia, sensing me hesitating.

I let it out. "What's going on with Uncle Vince?"

Reports were flooding in constantly about him cheating death, along with rumors of him selling off chunks of his vast, if haphazard, empire. He wasn't my real uncle, but I'd known him all my life. He was a close friend of Patricia—she'd been his thesis advisor at MIT nearly fifty years ago, and they'd worked together and stayed in touch ever since.

It was Patricia's turn to sigh, her face clouding up. I thought she was about to share some terrible secret with me, but she just said, "Nothing is going on with Vince, nothing at all."

"What do you mean?" Whatever was happening *certainly* didn't count as *nothing*.

"He's just fooling around." Aunt Patty shrugged, but her eyes said more.

"Okay…if you say so." I paused, leaving some room for her to add something, but she didn't. "Just tell me what I need to do to help with the board."

"I will. Speaking of the board, will we be seeing you at the Foreign Banquet tomorrow evening?"

"Of course I'll be there."

Aunt Patty hesitated. "Dr. Baxter said he might bring Bob along…." She let the words hang in the air.

"I think I'm going solo," I replied with a smile. "It's an official function, and those bore David to death."

"I just thought I'd mention it." Patricia smiled back. "Now you get back to your evening!"

My excitement bubbled back up as she faded away.

"That's fantastic, Nance, that's really good news," said David on my return to dinner. He was tentative now, hovering, but his love for me shone in his eyes. Try as I might, though, my heart could never quite return it.

"Come here, my big, bad boy," I said lustily, trying to hide my uncertainty.

I grabbed his hand and pulled him across the side of the table toward me. He took my cue and met my lips with his in a strong, firm kiss, opening my mouth and meeting my tongue. I could feel one of his hands sliding down my back, gripping me, pulling me further into him, pressing our bodies together.

We both flittered for a stimswitch almost at the same time, and I laughed, my mouth pressed against his, as my point-of-view switched into his and I felt the strength and urgency in his body. I found myself staring into my own eyes, with him staring back out from them into me, our senses shimmering back and forth like two mirrors reflecting an image endlessly into each other.

"What about dinner?" I asked breathlessly as our bodies rocked together, sliding to the floor while we pulled off our clothes.

"This is dinner," he gasped back.

He phase-locked our stimswitch so we simultaneously ghosted each other. I was him and he was me, our sensory channels overlaid into and onto each other as we began our lovemaking. While most of me was there, perhaps the most important part of me wasn't.

But if you can't be with the one you love, then you love the one you're with.

Or at least you do your best.

5

Identity: William McIntyre

I'd had another terrible night. With my splinter limit fixed at ten, I'd been forced to funnel more and more of my resources into the Phuture News Network. I was still beating the markets, but I wasn't the star I used to be.

"Are we going to have breakfast together?" asked Brigitte, toothbrush in one hand.

"Pumpkin, come on, you know I don't have time today."

I stared at my lathered face in the mirror. I enjoyed a real shave from time to time. It helped me reconnect with myself after nights spent shattered all over the multiverse.

"You could have Wally shave you," she suggested meekly. "We haven't sat down for breakfast together in more than a week."

She was pouting.

"Please, Brigitte, you know I just like to shave myself sometimes!" I snapped. *Why can't she just leave me alone?*

Her hurt expression reflected beside me in the glass. With a quick intake of breath, I was about to apologize, but she'd already flitted off without another word. Bardot, her proxxi, sat staring back at me from Brigitte's body, shaking her head and rolling her eyes. She spat out her mouthful of toothpaste into the sink, handed me the toothbrush, and left as well.

I felt bad, but I really needed more time to myself.

Rubbing away the condensation from the mirror, I focused on my face and began to shave. I felt an itch and scratched my shoulder as I held the razor up. *What am I going to do?* Things were just starting to work out for me, and now Nancy was ruining it all.

Goddamn it!

My hand shot under my armpit to scratch something.

What the hell?

My neck was itchy, too. I dropped the razor into the sink with a clatter and began to madly scratch at myself. It felt like ants were crawling under my skin.

I managed to stop scratching for a second to inspect my arm and was shocked to see a small bump under the skin. Then it *moved*. I scraped wildly at it, ripping open the skin, and blood oozed out. Looking into the mirror in horror, I saw my face seething and roiling with boils. My hands shot to my face, feeling a crawling mass under my skin.

"Wally!" I cried out.

A burst of laughter erupted from behind the shower curtain. Immediately, I knew what was happening.

"You assholes!" I exclaimed, turning to rip open the curtain, my face dripping and oozing worms, millipedes, and other hideous creepy-crawlies.

Hoots of laughter exploded from Bob, Martin, Sid, and Vicious as they held onto each other, crowded into the small shower stall.

"You should have seen your face, mate!" laughed Vicious, tears streaming down his face as he gripped onto Sid, who was doubled over and laughing hard, too. Bob grinned widely, his arms around the others, shaking his head. I couldn't help joining in the laughter as well, despite it all.

"Fine, you got me. Sid, make it stop."

The itching stopped and the beasties quit wriggling. I rubbed my hand across my restored face, feeling the remains of the lather and my stubble.

"Sorry, man," said Sid, still wiping away tears. "When you asked Vince for a Phuture News upgrade, I slipped a skin in and you authorized it. You gotta pay more attention to what you're doing!"

"It was all Martin's idea," added Vicious, giving Martin a little shot in the shoulder.

"Oh yeah?" I replied, shaking my head and smiling at Martin. He smiled back timidly. I was glad he and Bob were hanging out.

I didn't remember authorizing the transaction he was referencing, but Wally had already called it up on my inVerse for me to look at. I needed more sleep.

"Anyway," added Bob, "the real reason for this escapade was to get the attention of our hardest working friend to ask him out for a surfing date." He raised his eyebrows to make the point.

Smiling, I rubbed the bridge of my nose. "Yeah, okay, sure, how about the end of the day? I could use a break."

"Outstanding!" replied Bob. "Okay guys, let's leave our buddy to finish whatever he was doing."

With that they were off, and I was standing alone again in my bathroom. Well, apart from Wally, now sitting on the toilet.

"I didn't see any harm in it," he said before I could say anything. "I figured you and Bob could use a good laugh together. You hardly see him anymore."

I rolled my eyes but smiled and got back to shaving.

Just then, Jimmy pinged me for lunch.

I stopped shaving, calling up a display space for more information on the request, but there was none. I'd hadn't seen or talked to Jimmy in years—why on Earth was he calling me now?

Jimmy was Bob's adoptive brother. He was the golden boy now, but growing up he'd always been an oddball, never quite fitting in, or perhaps, never quite understanding how to fit in. He had a tough time growing up, though, and being left behind by a parent was something I could relate to. I'd tried hanging out with him back then, at least until the incident at Nancy's birthday party.

After that, we'd barely spoken.

Some kids were just ugly ducklings, and as an adult he'd more than recovered. He'd become the star of the pssi-kid program, a minor celebrity. He'd risen far up the ranks and had a lot of powerful friends. He'd be a good person to reconnect with. Maybe he could even help me out.

"You're in tight with Susie," Jimmy explained at our lunch later in the day. Apparently he wanted me to set him up with her. She'd been a close childhood friend. "If you help me, maybe I could help you." He raised his eyebrows.

"I guess." I paused. "And what do you think you might help me with?" Susie didn't seem his type, but then, there was no accounting for taste.

"I think I could help you," said Jimmy, watching me "by getting access to higher-order splintering."

My heart nearly skipped a beat. Obviously, he knew about my side project, but then again, he'd become head of conscious security systems on Atopia. Of course he'd know.

"Really?" I tried to appear disinterested. "So what, you could double my account settings or something?"

"Much more than that," he laughed. "I could show you how to fix the system to have almost unlimited splintering. You'll blow everyone else in the market away."

I glanced at the glittering blue security blanket around us.

"Nobody else knows what we're talking about, right?"

I tested the blanket with some of my phantoms, looking for holes, but, of course, this was a waste of time.

Jimmy grinned wolfishly. "I'm the security expert, remember?"

"Right." I could use his help; this was the opportunity I'd been waiting for. "So what's the deal then, Mr. Security?"

"If you can get me a date with Susie, but I mean, really *set me up* with her, you know?" He raised his eyebrows again. I nodded, acknowledging my understanding. "Then I'll set you up with what you need."

"You can really pull it off, with nobody else knowing?" I was slightly incredulous. "No risk?"

"Nobody will ever find out. Let me explain...."

6

Identity: Nancy Killiam

"Olympia," I whispered to the test subject lying on the pod-bed before me.

No response.

Her mind was still hovering somewhere in the purgatory between consciousness and unconsciousness.

I was inhabiting a robotic body in a doctor's office in Manhattan to personally attend to the end of the New York clinical trials. After many years, we'd almost reached the end of the process and Cognix was now on the verge of approval by the FDA. Approval here in America would trigger a cascade of approvals in other super-jurisdictions around the world.

It was a critical juncture for the future of Cognix Corporation, and by extension, for Atopia as well.

Aunt Patricia had made it clear that this was a priority, so I was here in person, or at least, a part of me was here in person. The splinter I had controlling this robody was circling at the very peripheries of my consciousness, just a voice in the background of all the buzzing activity that I was dealing with. As Olympia began to stir, the splinter dug deeper into my awareness matrix, prickling my brain, and my attention was drawn toward that one place, my mind automatically load-balancing the other tasks and places and people I was dealing with seamlessly onto my proxxi and other splinters.

"Olympia," I called out again, louder. She twitched and one of her eyes fluttered, a signal of impending activity that collapsed my awareness firmly into this space.

My mind shivered at the cold, confined reality it found itself in. "Does distributed consciousness really work?" whispered one far away splinter, attending a press conference in Australia. "Yes," that splinter answered, "even while talking to you I am attending clinical trials in New York." I was still listening to my other streams of consciousness, but these became faint murmurs in the background of the physicality of being in the doctor's office in New York.

I glanced up at the lighting panels in the ceiling, feeling my robotic irises focus in and out, adjusting to the brightness, and then looked back down at Olympia as I cradled her head in my plastic hands.

Slowly, her eyes opened, her mind dredging itself up from beneath the sedatives. She wouldn't see a robot hovering above her, however. Pssi was now installed in her neural pathways, and I'd clipped a reality skin around my robot's body so that I would appear to her as her own impression of the most caring and loving person she had ever known, an amalgamation of the people the system could figure out that she was closest to.

"Yes?"

She was barely conscious, and I could tell she was already annoyed.

"Seems like someone needs a little more sleepy time," I purred. "Come on, I'll get you up and dressed."

Olympia was something of a special case. She was one of the key external marketing executives setting the groundwork for the commercial release of pssi later this year. Olympia had only been inserted into the program at the last minute by Dr. Hal Granger, one of Cognix's senior executives and our leading psychologist. Her file indicated acute anxiety, which certainly qualified her, but it was strange that she'd been shuffled in at the last second.

"How long was I out?" asked Olympia irritably, propping herself up on the bed.

"Hmm…," I replied while my mind assimilated a thin stream of information from the splinter that had been attending her here. "About two hours, I'd say. Everything seems to be working perfectly. In fact, we've just activated the system. Your proxxi will explain everything to you once you get home. I would have woken you sooner, but you just seemed so peaceful."

She grumpily swung her legs off the side of the pod-bed and sat up. I tried to reach over to steady her, but she pushed me off. "I can take it from here, thank you very much." She waved me away.

I shrugged and leaned over to grab her clothes, handing them to her. I wondered if her aggressive mood had been stimulated by some psychoactive response to the pssi stimulus, but a set of clinical notes floated into view in an overlaid display space. *She's always that way.* Everything was fine then; in fact, all of the other reports signaled that this was another perfect pssi installation.

"I'm going to bring you in to speak to the doctor before you leave. He needs to have a final word," I said as I walked through the door, stopping outside to wait for her to finish dressing.

In a few seconds, she was done and strode out and down the hallway quickly, purposely avoiding looking my way. I watched her carefully, searching for any telltale tremors or jitters that could betray an issue with her motor cortex. She looked smooth, if not graceful, but then, her grace wasn't my issue.

She stuck her head into the doctor's office, and I walked over to observe the exchange.

"How do you feel?" I could hear him asking her. "Please, come in."

"No, no, I'm fine. I mean, I just want to get going. I've got things to do. So just tell me quick, what do I need to know?"

"You have a very powerful new tool at your disposal. Be careful with it," explained the doctor, "and don't activate any of the distributed consciousness features yet."

"Distributed consciousness," snorted Olympia, looking back at me. "Where do they get these ideas?"

I raised my eyebrows. Sensing my job here done, this splinter began to slip back toward the edges of my conscious awareness to become just another voice in my sensory crowd. As it did so, Olympia's question hung with me, sliding a part of mind off somewhere else, backward in time, into my childhood.

Infinixx really began as a pssi-kid game we'd invented called flitter tag. In the forested yards of the Schoolyard at recess, we used to have huge games of it, jumping and chasing after each other in what seemed to the adults as completely nonsensical behavior. But to us, it was a highly competitive and structured game.

More than just using pssi to venture off into virtual worlds, as pssi-kids we were the first to really master the art of body snatching—sneaking into each other's sensory channels and taking control of each other's bodies.

It wasn't nearly as dangerous as it sounds. Our proxxies chaperoned sharing bodily control. They would allow a visitor to do what they liked as long as they didn't hurt our bodies or do something we wouldn't do or say ourselves. Proxxies also managed the transition, the handing off and receiving of control, so it all went smoothly and safely.

Sometimes it could get confusing, but then that was a part of the fun. If it ever became too much, whenever we were out of body lending it to someone or off in another world, we could always punch the Uncle Button and snap back into ourselves.

So we were never really far from home.

In flitter tag, whoever was "it" would flitter their consciousness from this body to that, trying to reach out and touch someone else as we squealed and shrieked and jumped about from one body to another, randomly forcing resets as we punched our Uncle Buttons. It was incredibly disorienting, completely mad, and absolutely fun, and there was nothing else quite like it when one was growing up as a pssi-kid on Atopia.

What started off as a simple game became ever more complex over time as we began to invent more and more rules. Of course, we played not just in *this* world, but also by jumping off into the endless multiverse worlds we traveled through. It was during these advanced games of flitter tag that we first began to really experience distributed consciousness, working to keep track of all the new bodies we spawned as we rushed through worlds of fire, water, ice, and skies, inhabiting creatures and bodies and dealing with physics unrecognizable to the experiential space of normal humans.

We didn't realize what we were doing at the time. It was just natural.

As we grew into teenagers, many of my peers dropped off into what could only be described as self-indulgent gratification. I was the only one to consider the deeper issues of *what* had happened to us, and to dissect *how* it had happened.

This was the beginning of Infinixx.

It was Aunt Patricia who'd nurtured my ideas and given them the space and light to grow. Really, she was my great-great-great-aunt, and to everyone else she was the famous Dr. Patricia Killiam, the godmother of synthetic reality and right hand of Kesselring. But to me, she was always just Aunt Patty.

"So you can really hold five conversations at once?" she had asked me at the end of my eventful thirteenth birthday party.

After my naming ceremony, we'd decided to take a walk together in Never Ever Land, across a lavender field amid giant floating daisies. We held hands, Aunt Patty brushing the blushing blooms from our path as we tried to walk just so, in sync, so we wouldn't float too far up or down but would stay just right. It was a game, as almost all things were.

"I'm doing it right now," I giggled, breaking away from her and running, rising up above the field as I did, but not too high for the circling Levantours to catch me.

I stopped and turned to watch her coming, sinking slowly back down to meet her. I was also chatting with my friend Kelly in the Great Beyond about boys—about Bob, of course—and also with Willy, about how he managed to control an entire set of soldiers simultaneously in a combat battalion in the midst of a Normandy invasion, as well as trying to console Jimmy after the frightful incident at my party.

"It's easy, and I can do way more than that. I can do a hundred if I really wanted," I boasted.

"Come on, Nancy, don't tease your old auntie, please tell the truth."

I stared at her and smiled. "You just have to think about it the right way."

7

Identity: William McIntyre

I sighed, but happily. Sitting belly deep in the water on our boards, a dark mass moved smoothly underneath us. The great white sharks had begun their nightly garbage collection sweep of the undersea ledge. Bob noticed them, too. He smiled.

"This was great," he beamed. "I'm really glad you made it out today."

"I said I would, didn't I?"

"But that doesn't always mean it'll happen," Bob gently chided, still smiling. "At least, not lately."

The setting sun was painting a picture-perfect end to the day in pink and orange clouds hanging high in the sky. We bobbed around in the water quietly, and then another great white slid silently past. It was time to get in.

"I guess that's fair," I replied. "Work has been such a grind lately."

We both leaned forward and began a lazy paddle back to the beach.

"I'm sure. At least you look more relaxed today."

After my talk with Jimmy, I could finally see a way out, perhaps even the means to really break through.

Bob, slightly ahead, grinned over his shoulder at me.

"See you on the beach!" he called out as he abruptly turned. I was wondering what the hell he was smiling about when my board angled up, spilling me forward. In my daydreaming, I'd lost track of my water-sense.

"Thanks a—" was all I managed to get out before I swallowed a big mouthful of saltwater, tumbling as a large wave broke over me.

The surfing had been legendary. Huge storms out in the Pacific were generating monster swells, and we spent the afternoon riding twenty-footers to the delight of the crowds watching from the beach.

Bob picked up a few female tourists to take out tandem surfing, a sport he'd almost single-handedly resuscitated. We'd only just managed to disentangle ourselves from them by the end of the day, after I'd made it clear I wanted to make it a boys' night out.

Darkness had fallen as we sat at a tiki-hut beach bar under an awning of palms fringing the beach's powdery sands. Bob and Sid were already stoned, and I was well into my sixth beer, a large mouthful of which I had just lost in a sputter of laughter.

An elderly woman, a tourist, was walking past us as we slouched on our stools against the bar. Her breasts undulated back and forth near her knees, complemented by a grotesquely protruding rear end, both spilling out of her modest bikini as they swung back and forth in a counterbalancing rhythm.

Sid had started up a new reality skin he'd created called Droopy. It magnified the physical characteristics of women we looked at, scaled by the intensity of their attention toward us. He'd just pointed out this new victim, who was making her way toward the bar, and she gave us such a scowl that her tits had literally mushroomed out of her chest to bounce off the beach.

"Sid, you're killing me!" I choked out, wiping spittle from my mouth.

Desperately, I tried to avert my eyes from the woman's suspicious glare. Her irritation made things that much worse, and she was practically engulfed by her now gargantuan distended mammary glands as she slowly dragged her expanding bottom through the sand.

"It's the blob!" screeched Vicious, pointing with eyes wide in mock fear. "Run! Run away now!"

To make his point, Vicious ran helter-skelter into the jungle behind the bar.

Doubling over, I howled with laughter. The swollen, rolling subject of our consideration turned sharply on her heel and was slugging off through the sand away from us, apparently no longer in need of a drink. As she retreated, she slowly returned to normal proportions.

"Oh," I gasped, rubbing the tears from my eyes and giggling. "We should do this more often."

"We do this every day, son. What you mean is *you* should do this more often," pointed out Vicious, peering out carefully from the bushes at our retreating victim.

He was right.

"William!" Someone screeched into my emergency audio channel. It was Brigitte.

Wally materialized beside me. "You'd better take this right away, she's pissed."

He took control of my body, and I detached quickly to respond to her.

"Yes, my splinter-winky?" I answered, my face radiating innocence as I dropped into my workspace to take the call. She stood scowling in front of me.

"William, I'm working late finishing some interviews, and all of a sudden, my interviewee's breasts start swelling and spilling out onto the table, which is totally distracting and embarrassing."

Oh shoot, I'd forgotten that we were sharing realities.

"Ah geez, sorry about that, I was just having a little fun with the boys...."

"You're drunk," she stated incriminatingly, "and you guys are pigs."

"Come on..."

"*Cochon!*" she added, shaking her head.

"I'm only sharing realities because you asked. This isn't a big deal."

"Willy," she said softly, then paused, looking at the floor.

I waited.

"I've barely seen you in weeks, months even," she continued, "and you can't even take the time to have breakfast with me, and here you are...ah...*ça fait rien.*"

I switched off my end of the shared reality, frustrated.

I hadn't seen the boys in weeks, and I'd been doing my best to spend any spare time I had with Brigitte. It wasn't my fault I needed to focus more and more on my moonlighting work. After Nancy restricted my splinter limit, my bank account had quickly been turning into a blank account.

I felt trapped.

We fell into a mutually accusatory silence.

"Willy, I think we need to talk," she said, studying my face.

While Brigitte finished up with work, I flitted back to the boys. My mood was ruined, however, so I begged off and tried going back to work for a bit. Soon enough, Brigitte pinged me and appeared briefly in my workspace. Taking a sad look around at what had replaced her, she took my hand and flittered us off to a quiet corner of the beach.

The day had settled into a heartbreakingly beautiful evening, and a crescent moonrise was casting a sparkling carpet over inky seas. Waves caressed the shore, and she held my hand in hers, slowly walking me through the wet sand at the water's edge. We left a trail of footprints behind us.

"Willy," she pleaded, "I love you, but I can't do this anymore. Please, let's fix this. Just tell me what you need."

"I love you, too, but... I just don't feel like we share the same goals," I replied. "I need to focus on my business right now."

And then the pause, that hurtful space of silence between words that shifted worlds.

"I don't want to hurt you," I continued. "Maybe the best thing would be for us to separate for a while, so I can figure this out."

She looked into my eyes while tears welled in hers. Her feet left the ground, and she floated in front of me as I walked, holding both my hands now. Cast in the soft, monochromatic moonlight, she hovered like a ghost before me.

"Willy," she sobbed, "you want me to leave you?"

I couldn't believe I was doing it, but I slowly started nodding, looking steadily into her eyes.

Catching her breath she looked away, her body convulsing as she tried to fight back the tears. She let go of my hands and floated up and away from me and into the starry sky. Perhaps not like a ghost, but more like an angel.

My footsteps continued alone in the sand awhile before being washed away by the waves. It was as if we had never been there at all.

The Infinixx launch was coming up, and I had to rush to implement Jimmy's suggestion before the end of the beta program. Once I had everything going full steam, we could have the life together that we'd always wanted. What I had planned was going to blow everyone away. I just needed to focus.

I went back to work.

8

Identity: Nancy Killiam

"Everyone—everywhere—every time."

Silence.

"So what does it mean?" a reporter finally asked from the front row of the press conference.

We were unveiling our new marketing program—E3—the "E" and the "3" stylized in the logo to face each other and form an infinity symbol above the Infinixx name. It was all very clever.

"E3 represents the infinite possibilities of the future that we're bringing to life," I rolled out breathlessly. "E3 is the idea that anyone can be everywhere and anywhere at any time they like—while still never needing to be anywhere they don't want to be."

I paused before my finale, catching my breath.

"For the first time, people can be nowhere and everywhere at the same time—E3 represents total freedom!"

Applause rang out as I raised my hands to the crowd. I wasn't sure I even understood what it meant, but I managed to deliver the pitch without cracking a smile. All that mattered was that the marketing department was in love with it.

While distributing consciousness was a nice trick, what had the business world so excited were the implications for productivity. Synthetic intelligences and phuturing pushed the needle a long way, but lately they'd been stalled in their revenue-enhancing capabilities, and distributed consciousness was the new buzzword in investor circles.

Many groups were pursuing something like it, but with our intimate link to Cognix and our unique abilities as pssi-kids, we had an edge nobody else could match. The investors were pouring in.

The press conference was complete, so I let the splinter in attendance slip away and pulled in a splinter that was minding a staff meeting we were having in our Infinixx boardroom.

Karen, my technical lead, jumped me into experiencing a technical glitch we were having. My mind quickly filled with visions of bunched up sheets, of pain and guilt, of junkies staring with hollow eyes. The anxious desperation gave way to confusion, a mad whispering of ideas that must have meant something, but didn't mean anything to me. Then something else, a contained space, I was trapped in a small vehicle that suddenly burst into flames. Just as quickly, I was sitting, combing my hair, and looking back into a face that wasn't mine.

I closed down the splinter network, collapsing my conscious webwork at the same time.

"It's some kind of bug," explained Karen. "The subjective streams are getting mixed up, and there are meme-matching faults as well."

"Do we know what the problem is?"

Launch time was fast approaching. While building our technology platform, we were at the same time using it ourselves, in the office and in meetings with people, to provide for our own proof of concept. The problem was that bugs tended to get cycled back, amplifying their effects.

"We think so. We're running some final QA before letting it out into the ecosystem."

"What caused it?" We'd been having some speed bumps, but nothing as serious as this.

"Seems like a code change somewhere in the kernel layers. We're trying to figure it out."

"You're sure this will solve it?" I just needed it fixed. "I have another press event in a few minutes. Tell me the truth."

"Yes," confirmed Karen with some conviction, "that'll solve it."

My VP of Human Resources glanced at us. "Did you hear about Cynthia, that new administrative girl we hired?"

Cynthia was a great hire, but had recently dropped off the radar without any warning. People disappearing off into hedonistic cyber-fantasy worlds wasn't uncommon, but Cynthia had been my personal pick. She'd seemed more reliable than that.

"Yeah, I heard about that. So her neural functions are off the charts, but they can't find her and she's off in the multiverse somewhere?" asked Kelly, my business partner.

"It doesn't have anything to do with us, does it?" I pulled the splinter for this meeting into the center of my consciousness.

"Nothing to do with us," confirmed Kelly. "But speaking of strange, how about Vince Indigo. Have you seen the flash death mobs he's attracting?"

There were a few laughs around the table. I stayed quiet, not wanting to reveal any suspicions I had.

"Anyway, the Security Council has taken over Cynthia's file now," said Brian, our Chief Technical Officer, bringing the discussion back. "Let's keep moving. Speaking of the Security Council, what does everyone think of Jimmy getting nominated?"

"I think Jimmy is great," I said.

"Of course you would," snorted Kelly. "More of the Killiam clan in charge, but then what's good for the goose . . . ."

"Hey!" I exclaimed. "That's not fair. Jimmy's family is barely related to mine." My cheeks blushed.

They all rolled their eyes.

Jimmy *was* related to me, but only distantly—our great grandfathers had been cousins, so whatever that made us. Patricia had asked Bob's family to adopt Jimmy when he'd been left in her care. I'd been dating Bob at the time; we'd been inseparable as children. From that point on, though, I'd been teased for dating what amounted to a distant cousin, if only cousin-in-law. Childhood taunts had a way of sticking with you.

Cunard pinged me for yet another press event starting in a few minutes, and I was happy to escape. "Guys, I have to move this splinter back. Anything else?"

I looked around the table. The meeting room pulsed silently in its synthetic reality cocoon. There was something they weren't telling me—something they didn't *want* to tell me. "What?"

A few of them looked down at the floor. Karen hit me with it, and the details of a lawsuit splintered into my consciousness.

"Some guy in Minnesota is suing for emotional damages after his sensory stream got crossed with his teenage daughter's."

"Oh…my…God." The details flowed through my networks. The girl had been out with her boyfriend. I shook my head, my mind filling with my own memories of growing up. Never mind the father; it was the girl who would be damaged after this. "And you're only bringing this to me now?"

"It was only filed ten minutes ago," replied our legal counsel, a loaner from Cognix corporate who'd materialized at our table.

"Do you really need to be here right now?" I demanded. This was supposed to be a private meeting.

He shrugged. "That depends."

"On what?"

"On whether you still want to be running this company by the end of the day," he replied coolly, looking at the ceiling, and then turned to stare into my eyes. "You need to deal with this *right* now."

I sighed. Lawyers were a part of the job I hated, but running Infinixx didn't give me much choice.

"Nothing in the media worlds yet?" Cunard had already run a background check in the seconds since we'd learned of the problem. There was nothing we could see so far.

"No," replied our lawyer, "they've agreed to keep it quiet." He looked around the room at my technical staff, appearing bored.

"For a settlement I imagine."

"Yes," he smiled, looking back toward me, "as you imagine."

"Even though they signed off on a hold-harmless clause with the beta testing?"

"This sort of thing could get, well, it could be pretty media friendly." The lawyser looked even more bored as he said it. "Or *unfriendly*, depending on which side of the fence you sit."

This was exactly the reason why I couldn't let Willy increase his splinter limit—unexpected repercussions and technical glitches like this. We couldn't afford the risk.

"Make the deal," I sighed. The lawyer nodded and faded away.

"And Karen," I added, just before flittering off to the next press event, "fix this problem. I don't care what it takes, but *get it fixed.*"

9

Identity: William McIntyre

"Willy!"

Whole scaffolds of my conscious webwork collapsed as Bob forced his way in using one of Sid's viral skins. Sid was going to get in trouble with his little sidelines one day, but then, who was I to talk?

The last time I'd seen Bob was when we were surfing, when Brigitte and I had split, and that was already a few weeks ago. Work was absorbing me, and to focus I'd been filtering all of my communications straight to my proxxi.

"Willy!" yelled Bob at maximum volume across my full audio spectrum. "Wiiiillllly!"

"Yeah, yeah, I'm here!" I released most of my splinter network into autopilot and distilled a good chunk of myself back into a private workplace where I pulled Bob.

Bob smiled goofily as we both materialized in each other's sensory spaces. We were sitting across from each other in one of my offices. I sat straight up in a chair at one end of the room dressed in a blazer and slacks while he draped himself over a leather couch facing me, wearing only his swimming shorts and a baseball cap.

"How's it going, Mr. Rockefeller?"

"It's going really well." I smiled uncomfortably. "I've had a gale force wind blowing up my back almost all week."

Bob didn't quite share my enthusiasm.

"As long as you're happy." He sat up on the couch. "I heard you quit Infinixx."

"I was tired of dealing with Nancy." I didn't mention the investigation into my tinkering with the Infinixx code. Nothing came of it, and I'd gotten what I'd wanted.

Bob raised his eyebrows. The three of us had been inseparable as kids, but I'd been the third wheel to their intense romantic relationship, one that everyone but them realized wasn't over yet.

"You're not mad at me, are you?" he asked. "I mean, that Brigitte thing. Sid and I were just messing around."

I shook my head. "Don't worry about it."

Thinking of Brigitte made my stomach tighten into knots, and my patience evaporated. *I have a lot to get done.* Bob watched me in silence. "Who are you hanging out with these days?"

"Ah, just work people, you know...." It wasn't as if he worked, so why should I bother explaining? *Maybe accepting his ping was a bad idea.* I balled my fists.

Right at that moment, Wally warned me that Vince Indigo was waiting. *I don't remember taking a meeting with Vince.* Wally noted that he'd alerted me not five minutes before about it, but I'd been so deeply splintered....

"Listen, I have Vince Indigo waiting in person, a last minute meeting." I was happy for a reason to cut our chat short. "Big client, I'd better go."

"Yeah, okay, sure." Bob squinted and cocked his head to one side. "Do you think you could ask Vince if he's okay? That stuff on Phuture News is weirding me out."

"I'm not comfortable doing that." I began drumming my fingers against my leg. "I don't know him very well. Why don't you ask him yourself?"

"He doesn't answer my pings anymore."

I shouldn't either. "Sorry, this is business."

Bob looked down. "Right. Anyway, let's hang out soon? We should talk about all this stuff, your work changes, Brigitte...."

"Sure, sure, gotta go." I waved good-bye, leaving a wafer-thin splinter behind. I flitted back into real-space at my apartment, where Vince was already waiting. Visions of an unimpressed Bob watching me go persisted in several of my visual channels.

"So I assume business is good?" Vince asked. He wandered around the periphery of my apartment, staring outward at the projected spaces of my growing business in the multiverse world of New London.

My new offices had been designed by one of the most sought-after interior metaworld designers. The glass-walled space floated in air, suspended above an almost endless array of cubicles housing renderings of my splintered parts, sub-proxxies, and other synthetic beings and bots that were spawned outward from my own cognitive systems. It was thousands of me working for me.

"Business is very, very good." I grinned widely. I'd found a back door to Infinixx, and could now splinter as much as I liked, but I couldn't tell him that. I couldn't tell anyone. With that hack, I'd already paid off our family mortgage and was well on my way to amassing a sizable personal fortune.

Vince had an air of desperation. It flattered my ego that one of the richest people in the world would make a personal house call for a favor from me, but his nervousness made me nervous. I didn't like the way he was looking at all the activity below us, and I wondered what could be making him so jumpy—he had all the money in the world to burn, as far as I could tell.

"I noticed you amped up your Phuture News services," he said carefully, "but that's not why I'm here. I'm sending the details of what I need, right now."

A description of a series of financial transaction he wanted me to carry out was uploaded to one of my splinters. In an instant they had analysed it.

"You want me to what?" I replied. "You know this is going to look suspicious, especially with me working for Infinixx."

"From what I've heard, you don't work for them anymore."

I wondered how much he really knew. "Sure, but it'll still look odd."

Vince had ulterior designs afoot, and that was fine with me. He was offering a princely sum for almost no work. *So this is what it's like to be with the big boys.* I didn't care what he was up to, and it didn't look illegal—at least, my end didn't.

In a few seconds, we were finished with the details of the transaction.

Vince looked at me. "And be careful."

"It doesn't look like there will be any problems—"

"Not with that. I mean with whatever you have going on *here.*" He motioned at my office.

"There's nothing going on here."

He looked away. "Just be careful."

"No problem, Mr. Indigo," I replied, shrugging, and I offered my hand to shake. He shook it, smiling weakly, and then flitted off without another word.

Wally materialized facing me on the white couch in my apartment. A dense security blanket shimmered around us like a sparkling neon plastic wrap.

"What was that all about?" I asked.

Wally knew both as much and as little as I did. He shook his head.

"Listen, Wally, I'm feeling very nervous. We have a great thing going here, but we need to protect ourselves."

Being splintered into a hundred pieces was great for business, but it was taking a toll on my mind. Focusing on the market all the time left me stunned when I returned to real space, and I was letting details slip.

On the other hand, I felt like I was approaching some new kind of state of being, a perfectly self-sufficient and self-contained human being. I spent all day talking with various parts of myself, and held forth on meetings of mind with dozens of my splinters at a time. The only distinctly different entity I spoke with was Wally, who was more or less a copy of me anyway. Vince and Bob were the first real humans I'd spoken to in days, perhaps even weeks.

"When I'm off in the cloud, I need you to protect us here. I need you to make sure we're safe, okay?"

Wally looked at me steadily. "Sure thing, boss."

With that, I flitted off to New York to get working on Vince's project. If I didn't need anyone else's help anymore, I definitely didn't want anyone interfering.

More than anything, though, I absolutely didn't want to get caught.

10

Identity: Nancy Killiam

The last few weeks had been a compressed explosion of activity at Infinixx. Our hundred employees managed to output the workload of a thousand—and then two thousand—workers compared with levels of productivity in the outside world. We touted our accomplishments almost hourly as the launch date neared, and the world's business community couldn't wait to get their hands on it.

A bigger struggle than building the technology, however, was the Atopian politics. Since I was pushing to have my own launch before the Cognix release of pssi, we needed to embed some pssi technology into our systems, and this meant a messy cross-licensing arrangement. I had Aunt Patricia on my side, but it was still a fierce fight.

"Give me one good reason we should let this happen!" Dr. Baxter had fumed at the Cognix meeting when we were trying to get final approval. Infinixx was stealing some of his thunder as the first Atopian-platform product release.

"You've seen all the phutures Nancy presented. Every scenario pushes the Cognix stock higher as we establish Infinixx as early adopters," countered Patricia. "You're only annoyed because it's not under your thumb."

"That has nothing to do with it," replied Dr. Baxter, and the arguing continued.

Kesselring had just sat quietly, watching, sighing.

We'd been at a stalemate when Jimmy magically produced the trump card.

"Everyone!" he'd called out, standing up and raising his hands. He winked at me. "I will give you one *very good* reason."

Until recently, I hadn't spoken to Jimmy in years, ever since the incident at my thirteenth birthday party. I felt responsible for what had happened, and it was too awkward to talk about. But since he'd been nominated to the Security Council, we were reintroduced on a professional level. It was as if nothing had ever happened. Jimmy and I had struck a close working relationship, and he was my biggest supporter—after Aunt Patty, of course.

I had no idea what he was going to say. We all waited in anticipation.

"I've managed to secure an agreement with both India *and* China to launch simultaneously with us."

Gasps rose around the table.

Getting India and China to agree on anything was impossible with new Weather War skirmishes breaking out almost daily. Details of the negotiations sprang into everyone's workspaces the moment Jimmy spoke. Everyone dropped a splinter to have a look. This wouldn't just be a commercial coup, but a major political one for Atopia as well.

"How in the world...?" Dr. Baxter's voice trailed off as his mind assimilated the backstory.

"Jimmy, why didn't you tell me?" I asked breathlessly in a private world I opened to him.

This was it. This was what would make my dreams a reality.

"I didn't want to get your hopes up," replied one of Jimmy's splinters. "It was a long shot, but hey, it worked."

"You're giving up a lot here," said Kesselring, back in the conference space, speaking for the first time as he reviewed the details, "But the payoff is worth it, and it'll keep the media's attention off those damn storms."

He looked toward Jimmy and smiled, nodding his approval.

11

Identity: William McIntyre

A dense gray fog hung around me. No dampness, though, no heaviness. In fact, I couldn't feel anything. In the distance, a light approached and filled the space around me with a soft radiance that was growing and alive. Curious, I moved toward the light. It grew brighter and more intense, surrounding and enveloping me, and then swallowed me whole, painlessly and soundlessly.

I awoke with a start in my bed, blinking, breathing quickly, looking around and trying to calm myself down. The image of the fog was fading. *What was that about? I must be dreaming again.*

I tried pinging Bob, Sid, Brigitte, but nobody answered—*weird.* I felt lightheaded. *Maybe I'd better get something to eat and shake out the cobwebs.*

Getting out of bed, I walked to the fridge and pulled out an apple, some bread to toast, and after a moment of thought, reached into the adjacent cupboard for some instant oatmeal. I poured water over it and watched it begin to boil. *This is your brain on oatmeal.*

Within a few seconds, it was done and piping hot. Topping it off with some brown sugar, I sat down at my counter, shining the apple on my pajama pant leg. I smelled burned toast. *Am I having a stroke?* The toast popped. *Oh right. Calm down.*

I flicked on the Phuture News Network. *Blank.* Nothing was about to happen, apparently. All that was playing on Phuture News were images of me sitting and watching a blank display-space with my oatmeal in front of me. *Must be some screwy trick of Sid's again,* but I wasn't going to play along.

I returned my attention to my oatmeal.

A deep chill passed through me, sending goose bumps rising across my exposed arms. I got the feeling of watching myself through a pane of frosted glass.

I was there, but not there.

All the worries I had a second ago—work, Brigitte, money—everything went away, and I realized how small these worries really were. I was so calm, so cold, and there was that fog again, so familiar and yet so alien.

Where am I? And why do I want to know?

My brain snapped out of it, as if wrenched from a bear trap.

I blinked hard and shook my head, looking down at my congealing oatmeal. Phuture News was back now, and the odds were that our friends Orlando and Melinda were going to have a big catfight soon.

Most people had already lined up on team Orlando, so I opted for Melinda. I always liked the undercat, and this time is wasn't Adriana. As I watched, clever taunts were being devised while their viral values were sized up by several off-island marketing agencies, eager to reach the Atopian crowd. The social storm clouds continued to grow.

It reminded me of Brigitte, and my stomach jumped. I put down my spork. And then my brain snapped out of it, as if wrenched from . . . a bear trap.

Something was very wrong.

I blinked hard again and shook my head, looking down at the congealing oatmeal. *Didn't I just eat that?* Phuture News was now blank and back to images of me staring at images of me staring at images of me staring at images of me.

The oatmeal was sputtering and bubbling in the bowl. I was standing back next to the fridge, holding the apple, about to shine it on my pajama leg. *Wait a minute. Didn't this just happen?* I was déjà vu-ing hard, losing my grip. My chest tightened, and my breathing was labored.

Am I having a heart attack?

I smelled burned toast.

"Wally!" I cried out. "Where the *hell* are you?"

Where was he when I needed him? Wasn't he supposed to be watching out for me?

"Willy, calm down, everything is okay," I heard Wally say, his voice soothing, but I couldn't see him anywhere. "Don't worry, everything is fine. The chest pain is just anxiety. Your blood stream is flooding with cortisol and adrenalin. Take a deep breath, calm down."

I took in a deep breath, held it, and slowly let it out. My cheeks felt flushed. "Calm down," I told myself, "calm down."

Closing my eyes, I tried to focus, and the stress began to wash out. In an instant, I was lying down, but I didn't remember getting there. Maybe Wally had helped me back to bed.

I could see myself lying still, absolutely calm. *What was I just worrying about? Why worry about anything?* Everything was so insignificant. My head felt like cotton balls had been stuffed in through my ears, displacing my brain, and I had the curious sensation that I had been wrapped in idiot mittens, to keep me from hurting myself.

In my mind's eye I could see myself with my mother. She was bending over me, the arms of her sweater rolled up as she hummed a lullaby, giving me a bath in the chipped porcelain wash basin in our old family kitchen on the Montana commune.

Through streaked windowpanes, trees swayed outside under wet, windy skies. The cows in the field huddled under the protection of the ponderosa pines that nestled along one side of our farm. Dense forests stretched up into the foothills with the snow-capped Rockies solidly framing it all.

It was cold outside but warm in here. The steaming water soaked into my little bones. We were so happy together in this small moment of time, so precious. I heard the splash and tinkle of water as she lifted the washcloth, the sounds echoing through time.

"How's my silly Willy?" she laughed, tweaking my nose.

"Wally?" I asked, more calmly this time. "Wally, what is happening to me? Where are you?"

I could sense Wally, but I couldn't see him or hear him. Somehow, though, I could feel him speaking to me.

"Everything is okay," I felt him say. "But there's something I need to tell you."

I should've felt worried but I didn't.

"You're part of something special, Willy."

"I know. The Atopia program, I got that."

"Not just that, something more unique, something much more important."

I liked that. "Go on." I'd always thought of myself as unique, like a small snowflake adrift in the wind, floating painlessly, soundlessly.

"You're familiar with Schrödinger's cat?"

"Sure."

The old quantum physics thought experiment. An object in superposition can exist in more than one state. The cat in the box that is both alive and dead at the same time.

"It's now possible to enable quantum superposition not just with atoms, but on larger objects. Much larger objects, in fact."

"Okay, but what's this got to do with me?" The idea of quantum physics needing a conscious observer had always annoyed me.

It smacked of God hiring city workers to turn the cranks of the cosmos.

"You may want to sit down, there's a downside to what I'm about to tell you."

I had already lain down. *What's wrong with him?*

"Your living space is contained within a giant quantum trap. You are the first sentient being to be wholly placed in a superposition state. You are both alive and dead at the same time, a conscious nexus point between life and death. In a moment, when you understand what I'm saying, you will also be the first sentience to observe yourself in superposition, and so create your own existence. Before you fully understand what I'm saying, Willy, hurry, and tell us what you are feeling."

So I was the cat in the box.

Staring at my hands, I looked inward on myself, looking at myself, looking at myself... and meowed.

I woke up in bed, alone, soaked in sweat and my heart pounding. As the dream faded, I remembered what had happened. Brigitte and I had split up, and now Wally was gone, but I was still alive, which meant that somebody somewhere out there was taking care of my body that had somehow disappeared. My greed had put me in this position, and they were probably going to put me in jail for it.

That was, if they could find me.

12

Identity: Nancy Killiam

I couldn't believe the big day was actually here. Infinixx was about to be released to the world.

Although our product worked in the open multiverse, it still needed physical infrastructure on the ground in the form of three consciousness processing centers. These massive computing installations, all tied together on dedicated communication links, were designed to handle local processing to reduce sensory latencies.

Each hub, for lack of a better description, was like a huge, blank mind, and they had to be booted up in sequence to maintain a coherent phase-lock between them. Each required a large local power source to drive it, and we'd decided to make an event out of throwing the switches to power them up.

At the same time as the launch of the Infinixx product, we were simultaneously floating the newly minted Infinixx stock onto the world markets as the Indian, Chinese, and Atopian processing centers came online.

The Solomon House Ballroom was packed to the rafters. I'd asked each of our board members and senior executives to be there in person for the launch. I was walking up and down in front of the head table that was set on the stage above the main floor, shaking each person's hand in turn, thanking them for their hard work and support.

"Excited, Brian?" I asked my CTO. He nodded and told me I should sit down. I couldn't. My entire future was resting on what happened in the next few minutes, and I felt ill.

In the ceremonial opening, I was to throw the switch to get everything started. Its power system was routed up here, the junction box set against the wall just above and behind my chair. I'd decided to inject a little surprise and symbolism into the event by bestowing the honor of throwing the switch onto either Jimmy or Aunt Patty, who were sitting up on the stage with me.

"Everyone!" Kesselring thundered with a smile, shouting out at the packed crowd from the podium. He had gotten on board with the launch in a big way once we'd made the decision. "Everyone, quiet down!"

The huge ballroom was filled to overflowing, with the tables packed and a crush of people milling about along the edges of the room. The sound of glasses and tableware clinking competed with a beehive of buzzing background conversation. The noise began settling as the crowd turned its attention toward us.

"Very good!" continued Kesselring. "We're now bringing online the Indian and Chinese contingents. I would like a hearty Atopian round of applause to welcome them!"

The crowded room erupted as the foreign delegations materialized to the left and right of us. It was an incredible photo opportunity, the Chinese and Indian banners appearing on each side of the Atopian flag.

Protocol for the event dictated that the senior Chinese and Indian officials would come to the center table to shake hands at exactly the same time, and it came off perfectly. In a splinter, I watched the pre-market analysis of the Infinixx stock as the broadcast of the event caught the world. The anticipated stock price was climbing fast on Phuture News.

My heart was in my throat.

I was in the dead center of attention, and I could feel the gravity of the moment pressing down upon me as we got up from our chairs at the banquet table, on stage at the front of the hall, to approach the switch. I had Jimmy to one side of me and Patricia to the other, with the rest of the board and executives fanning out around us.

Stepping to the back wall, I stared at the big green power switch. "It looks like something borrowed from a Russian hydroelectric dam," I joked with Patricia under my breath. She smiled and turned to beam at the assembled crowd.

Reaching out, I held Patricia's and Jimmy's hands in mine, then let go to touch the switch. It felt cool and hard and hummed as it coursed with unseen power. Then the lights dimmed and the countdown began.

The whole auditorium joined in, as if it were New Year's in Times Square.

"TEN!" they all shouted. "NINE!...EIGHT!..."

"Aunt Patty," I said, turning to look at her with tears in my eyes, "I've decided I'd like you to throw the switch. Everything here is all because of you!"

The crowd continued to roar, "SEVEN!...SIX!..."

"I'd love to, sweetheart," Patricia replied quickly, "but I had a last minute thing come up, and I'm not here kinetically. You go ahead, dear!"

"FIVE!...FOUR!..."

Ah well, I thought, crestfallen.

"Jimmy, how about you then? Go ahead. I really wanted it to be one of you two." I released the switch and encouraged Jimmy to take it.

"THREE!…TWO!…"

"I'm sorry, Nance, I had something, too. I'm only dialed-in. You go ahead…quick now!"

"ONE!"

The blood drained from my face. I could hear a *SNAP* as the Chinese and Indians flipped their switches at their remote locations. My metasenses felt the cavernous thrum of the Infinixx installations bootstrapping deep in the multiverse.

Okay, keep calm.

Perplexed faces around the room watched us on the stage, waiting for my main connecting switch to be thrown. I quickly queried each of the executives at the table with me. Karen had stayed with her kids; Louise, Brian, Cindy—nobody was physically present. They were all dialed-in, despite my specific instructions requesting everyone to be here in person.

Then again, I thought as all my blood drained into my shoes and I gazed with dread at the audience—*I'm not here either.*

I could feel the switch in my hand, as cool and as hard as if I were standing there and holding it myself. The wikiworld simulated it perfectly, but I couldn't budge it even a millimeter without having someone or something here physically.

After the disasters of destroyed power grids in the first cyberattacks nearly fifty years ago, security protocols had been rewritten so that critical nodes in power systems had to be completely disconnected from any communication networks to prevent the ability to hack into them. Despite Atopia being at the center of the cyberworld, we had to conform to international security standards, especially for a project like this.

I told myself that I hadn't overlooked this—I'd expected all of my executive team and board members to be here in person. I'd specifically requested it and even verified it just minutes before the event.

But, of course, even I hadn't listened to myself.

Staring out at the crowd, I took one last, desperate step. I flipped my pssi into identity mode, removing all virtual and augmented objects from my senses. The buzzing, crowded room faded from view, and all I was left with was my own low groan of fear. Not a single person was in sight. The entire ballroom was as empty and quiet as a morgue.

I stared back at the green switch, humiliated.

Already the assembled crowd and world press had figured out what had happened, and I was being pinged with a *Times* article trumpeting, "Infinixx—Everywhere But Nowhere!"

Lawyers from the Indian and Chinese sides had already filed a lawsuit against us, claiming monumental damages, and conspiracy theories were blossoming about connections to the Weather Wars. My executive team unlocked the exterior security perimeters, and I could see a psombie guard racing toward the stage.

"Forget it," I told him as he got close to the stage.

I closed my eyes. It was already too late. Almost twenty seconds had passed, and the two other systems had already progressed too far into their bootstrap cycles for us to phase-lock into them.

Millions of users had already logged into the systems and begun using them. We'd have to negotiate a downtime to reboot and lock all the systems together at a later date, but for now, we'd have to run them as separate domains.

It meant users would only be able to distribute their consciousnesses locally. Technically, it wasn't a disaster, but it made me look incredibly foolish. Correction, it made *us* look foolish. Kesselring was furious at the damage to the Atopian brand.

I withdrew my conscious webwork into a tight shell around myself like a cyber-tortoise retreating from danger.

Already the world media had minted a new term for a Zen-like business failure of being everywhere but nowhere at the same time, tripping on your own sword.

They called it an Infinixx.

13

Identity: William McIntyre

The police station loomed before me at the base of the vertical farming complex, and I was making my way towards it.

The Boulevard was the only real street we had, a wide pedestrian thoroughfare that crossed from the eastern to western inlets, dividing in half the four gleaming farm towers at the center of the surface of Atopia.

Glamorous palms lined both sides of the street, bordering the tourist shops, restaurants, and bars whose terraces spilled out into the kaleidoscopic melee in between. Even with the storms threatening and the evacuations announced, the atmosphere was still carefree and festive.

At least for now.

It'd been ages since I'd been above, and I hadn't been to these parts since I was a tween. I stood blinking in the bright sunshine as I tried to think my way through what was happening to me.

I felt alone and exposed.

What else can I do?

Looking up at the towers, I imagined myself as one of the psombies inside. My hand trembling, I opened the police station doors. Cool, administrative air swept over me, and the clerk at the desk, an attractive young woman, smiled at me synthetically.

"Can I help you, sir?" she asked, as sweet as a police officer could be.

"Yes, I'd like to file a missing person report."

I walked toward her as calmly as I could.

Her face registered just the proper amount of seriousness before she queried, "And who is the missing person, sir?"

I paused for a moment.

"Me."

After reporting my body missing to the police, the first person I turned to was Bob. It was amazing how quickly you could go from feeling invincible one moment to needing the protective embrace of friends the next.

At least, I *hoped* they were still my friends.

"Hey stranger, you take a wrong turn somewhere?" joked Bob as I appeared in one of his regular beach-bar haunts. Even with the storm warnings, he was still surfing. Taking a swig of his beer, he waggled it toward me, *did I want one?* I shook my head. "What can I help you with?"

I cast a thick security blanket around us, and we were surrounded by its glittering and softly undulating shell. Bob raised his eyebrows and took another swig.

"What's up?" He screwed his eyebrows. "Are you okay?"

"I'll just lay it out." I paused. "I've lost my body."

Another pause.

"What do you mean—you've lost your body? Does this have anything to do with what happened at Infinixx?"

"I don't think so." I sat down on a stool next to him and rubbed the back of my neck. "Wally, or someone—I'm assuming it's Wally—has stolen my body."

Bob's eyes narrowed, and then he smiled. "Whatever game you're playing, I'm in." His smile slowly disappeared as he studied my face.

"I just got back from the police station," I continued. "Not only can't I find my body, but now I've been charged with a felony and I'm under arrest." I didn't mention that I was also under investigation for my trades in Infinixx stock.

"So how are you here? Did you post bail?"

I shook my head. "It's complicated."

"I'd say."

Leaning my head back, I rubbed my eyes.

"We'd better get Sid in here," suggested Bob.

I sighed. "I guess we better."

Bob's face slackened for an instant as he detached, and then he was back. Sid and Vicious materialized on barstools inside the perimeter of the security blanket.

Even before he'd fully appeared, Vicious looked down his nose at me and declared, "Oooh, so the high and mighty has stooped to mix with us again, eh?"

"Knock it off!" snapped Bob. "This is serious. Sid, you looked at Willy's situation?"

Sid stood the best chance of anyone at figuring out what was going on. We waited while he reviewed the scenarios.

"Let me make sure I have this straight." Sid was all business, this was his domain. "You reprogrammed rules in the Atopian perimeter to allow an outgoing connection to Terra Nova. Then you logged your consciousness network into a secure Terra Novan account, anonymized your signal, and then sent multiple connections back into Atopia to create the effect of multiple personalities accessing the network?"

"Right."

"And now your body appears to have left Atopia entirely, without your knowledge, and you can't contact Wally."

"Right again."

"And the Terra Novans have absolutely refused to divulge or break the anonymous connection, and the connection has been paid-up one hundred years in advance."

"That is correct."

Bob looked at me and tried to summarize, "So your body is out there somewhere. You're doing all your thinking in your lost brain, and it's communicating with you here into your virtual body, but Wally is driving your body around out there and won't communicate back."

"That seems to be about it."

"That's an interesting pickle, my friend," offered Vicious.

"So what, has Wally gone nuts? Can't we just locate and shut him down in the multiverse somehow?" Bob asked.

"No," said Sid. "A proxxi isn't the same as other synthetic beings. He doesn't really exist in the multiverse. They're biological-digital symbiotes embedded in our bodies. Wally can control Willy's body when Willy's mind is away, and he can venture out into the multiverse from there, but if he's routed through an anonymizer in Terra Nova, then we won't be able to track him down easily."

"And my Uncle Button doesn't work," I added. "It was never designed to be filtered back this way."

Bob put down his beer. "So I ask again—has Wally gone nuts?"

"It's not as simple as that," I admitted. "I told Wally to take emergency action if it looked like there was trouble. Illegally breaching the Atopia perimeter is a serious offence."

"So you *told* Wally to do this?" Sid laughed, rolling his eyes.

"You're like a bloody one-man Zionista, mate!" Vicious cut in. "One man, displaced from his body, wandering the multiverse, hoping to get back to his stolen homeland—"

"Please," I complained. "I didn't tell Wally to do this. I told him that if it looked like we were in trouble to take whatever action he deemed necessary to make sure we were okay."

"And how on Earth did you manage to ignore him when this went down?" Sid asked incredulously.

I took a deep breath. "With this new setup, my mind was shattered into hundreds of splinters, and fed through the anonymizer. Wally couldn't always get my attention. That's why I asked him to take immediate action without me, if necessary."

"Seems to have taken action all right," Vicious laughed, clearly enjoying this.

"Enough!" Bob exclaimed. "Enough already. Vicious, you've had your fun, and Willy has been a bit difficult lately, but he's in trouble and needs our help. *Right* now."

I choked back tears. I didn't deserve Bob's kindness after the way I'd been treating him.

"Sorry, right, mate," mumbled Sid and Vicious together.

"Wally, one question," Vicious asked, the gears of his brain turning. "So you're arrested and charged and convicted, right?"

I nodded. For straightforward crimes it didn't take a much time—synthetic lawyers and judges weighed in and contested cases within minutes.

"But you're still with us. So I understand why they can't get your body, but why can't they restrict your virtual self?"

"The anonymizer randomly logs into Atopia repeatedly if its signal gets restricted. Since my login carries an authenticated Atopian citizen tag, and since it was deemed unconstitutional to restrict access to Atopia for any citizen, they can't block my access here, but then they can't contain me either."

"That makes you one very interesting person to know, my friend."

I could see where he was going with this. "I'm not about to test anyone's patience right now."

"Still," he added, shrugging, "but you're here aren't you? Why didn't you voluntarily stay in detention?"

I shrugged back. "Would you if you'd lost *your* body? I need to figure out what's happened."

Bob stared at me. "How did you figure out how to do all this? It seems a little beyond your area of expertise."

"Jimmy."

14

Identity: Nancy Killiam

"I feel so cloudy."

It was pssi-kid expression, an attempt to describe that feeling we got when we couldn't understand our own splinters and it felt like our conscious minds were spread outward from a single point to become an indistinct smudge in time and space. I knew Aunt Patty didn't quite understand, but I had no other way of explaining how I felt.

We were walking through the Lollipop Forest under a beautiful night sky lit by a bright, chocolate-chip moon surrounded by twinkling gumdrop stars.

"Why didn't you tell me you wouldn't be there?" Finally, I let myself ask the question.

She looked away and then back at me, but avoided my eyes. "I *was* there, dear, at least my primary subjective was, but I thought that you were the one throwing the switch. We all did."

"But I checked with you not minutes before, and your body was on its way to the ballroom. What changed?"

Patricia looked up at the gumdrop stars. "Something with Uncle Vince."

I angrily kicked at some lollipop sprouts. "I'm so stupid."

Everyone had some last minute excuse, but in the end, it was my responsibility. It wasn't like I couldn't have seen it. Everyone's physical metatags had properly indicated they were somewhere else, but I'd stopped paying attention to these a long time ago.

"You shouldn't be beating yourself up so much," Aunt Patty said gently. "You've done a wonderful thing for the world."

"Yeah—I've given them something to never stop laughing at."

The lollipop trees rattled as they jostled together on their spindly stalks. Aunt Patty suggested coming here for a walk, just like we used to do when I was just a little splinter-winky, but the place had lost its magic.

To cheer me up, she'd first tried taking me on a walk topside with Teddyskins, a reality skin that turned everyone around you into cute pink teddy bears. It was one of my favorites as a child, but I wasn't a child anymore. Now all these cutesy worlds and spaces felt contrived and creepy.

"Don't be silly," she said, taking my hand and pulling my head into her. She always gave herself an ample motherly bosom and a sturdy frame in these childhood worlds.

My tears started again.

"You took the first step in bringing distributed consciousness to the world. You're still so young. Your whole life is ahead of you."

Now the tears came in great heaving sobs, and she let me, smothering me in her chest.

"Have you talked to David?"

"No, that's over," I choked out. "David was the reason I stayed at home physically for the launch. I felt so bad for always being away. We had a huge fight afterward."

"What about Bob? Did you try him?"

I shook my head and the tears spilled down my face. "He dropped me a splinter, but he's so stoned all the time. What's the point?"

Aunt Patty stroked my head and then dried my tears. We walked on in silence, stepping gently through the lollipops.

15

Identity: William McIntyre

"Well you just bloody well better figure out a way to fix it, my friend," Vicious growled right up in Jimmy's face.

But Jimmy laughed and walked through his projection to pick up a file he was working on. Vicious sputtered indignantly.

The four of us—Bob, Sid, Vicious, and me—didn't make a very threatening package. Jimmy had accepted our speaking request only as a courtesy to Bob. He didn't seem concerned with the news. Then again, with the storms looming, and him being newly appointed to the Security Council, he had much more important things on his plate at the moment.

"I appreciate your situation, and I honestly feel for you," Jimmy said after a moment, looking up from the file at me. "But I can't do anything right now. I'm spread too thin as it is. I just showed Willy where the tools were, and, okay *sure,* I described how he could exploit some vulnerabilities, but so what?"

"This is half your fault, you can do better than that," urged Bob. "Willy's in serious trouble."

"That's an understatement." Jimmy put down the file. "I'm really sorry about what's happened. I was only trying to help Willy, to give him what he wanted."

"Only to get what *you* wanted," Sid pointed out.

Jimmy shrugged. "Aren't friends supposed to help each other out?" He looked directly at Bob. "I mean, did *you* help him out? Did you even know how much financial trouble he was in?"

Bob looked away.

"I didn't think so," continued Jimmy. "Too caught up in getting stoned and partying with these idiots." He motioned toward Sid and Vicious, still looking at Bob. "Too busy having a good time to even pay attention to your family, which includes me if you've forgotten."

"Of course not," said Bob quietly.

"You think I'm uncaring?" Jimmy looked around at us all. "Have you seen the way Bob treats Martin?"

Nobody said anything, but the words seemed to physically strike Bob. He rocked back on his feet a little.

"We all have problems." Jimmy looked straight into Bob's face. "We all have our pain to deal with. You don't think I've had it hard? But I'm trying to become part of the solution."

This was getting personal.

"This is my own fault." I waved my hands in the air and stepped between Bob and Jimmy. "We're not trying to blame anyone, I'm just looking for help."

Jimmy shook his head. "The situation you've created is beyond me right now."

Bob and I both nodded, but Sid wasn't buying it. "Maybe we should go speak with police about your part in this." He tried his best to appear intimidating, but it just wasn't him.

"And maybe I should tell those same police about some of the viral skins you've been letting loose in the cyber-ecosystem," Jimmy replied. "I've been watching you, my friend."

"So what if he has?" bluffed Bob. "Willy's problem goes way beyond any nuisances Sid's toys create."

"Maybe yes, but maybe no."

"What does that mean?"

"Go ahead and tell the police that I was involved." Jimmy ignored Bob's question. "But I'm the one on the Security Council. And any chats I had with Willy were under tight security blankets, so it would be my word against his." He let this settle. "Quite frankly, Willy being plugged through the perimeter and into Terra Nova, and us not being able to close the connection due to some legal nonsense, is a big problem."

"Are you threatening to cut him off?" Bob demanded. "Where would he end up?"

"I don't know, but definitely not here. Somewhere in the open multiverse I'd guess."

This was tantamount to exile and brought cold stares from Bob and Sid.

I felt like I was going to throw up.

"I just showed him the tools he asked about. Willy's a big boy. He's the one who did it."

Stony silence.

"I really have to go. We'll talk later, okay?"

Jimmy closed the connection.

16

Identity: William McIntyre

After the confrontation with Jimmy, the whole gang had rallied to help me.

The carpet of stars hung above us just as it had when we last camped at this spot. It seemed like it had happened in another lifetime. An owl hooted softly in the darkness. Bob sat with a beer balanced on his knee, half-illuminated by the fire, grinning at me.

I poked the embers and watched them dance.

"I told you everything would be fine." Bob emphasized his point by raising his empty beer can.

I continued to stare into the fire, lost in my own thoughts. I imagined the heat of the sun warming green leaves of long ago, which soaked it up, slowly converting it into the lignin and biomass of the tree trunk. Then, after being stored for decades, that same captured sunshine radiated back out as heat energy when we burned the wood, warming my hands and face. That none of this was real didn't detract from my daydreaming.

Since my own consciousness hadn't winked out, we had to assume that my body was alive and healthy somewhere out there. We'd sent out what nearly amounted to a private army to try and find it, using up most of the fortune I'd amassed as Atopia's hottest stock jock back in my brief blaze of glory. Back when I had a body.

The searching began within Atopia itself—a thorough physical search using platoons of pssi-minded cockroaches and rented psombies—followed by a full digital scan using a private cloud-dusting of smarticles.

Quickly, we'd expanded the physical search radius into the waters surrounding Atopia and then into the cities directly connected to our passenger cannon. We rented and sent out uncountable bots and synthetics, even human private investigators that scoured this world and the wikiworlds for any hint of my face or my body, any trace that signaled mine or Wally's presence out there.

We found nothing.

In the face of the impending storms, the Atopian foreign office had halfheartedly taken up action against Terra Nova, trying to sue for access to the anonymous connection or to disconnect it, thinking that this would automatically snap me back into my body. Just like Atopia, however, one of Terra Nova's key industries was acting as a data haven, and the same ironclad international treaties that protected Atopia applied here.

Terra Nova refused any action, citing the protection of its unconditional stance on the security of its customers and data. To gain access to the connection, they told us, I would have to log in from my corporal body. With no body, though, there was no bio-authentication, and therefore no access.

I was desperate at first, but gradually I began to come to grips with my situation.

Sometimes, they say, it takes a great loss to realize what is important. In my fight to find my body, I was humbled by the loyalty and ferocity of my friends and family as they came to my aid, even after I'd abandoned them in my greed.

The search had even brought some direction to Bob, shaking him out of the drugged slumber he'd been in for years, and brought him back together with Nancy. Vince put his vast spy network to work on my problem, and Sid and Vicious had worked tirelessly, combing the open worlds, hacking the closed ones, and searching the back-ways of the Atopian subsystems, trying to figure out how someone had hidden their tracks so well.

Even Martin had pitched in.

I poked the coals, watching little sparks escape and float back into the sky.

Brigitte and I were back together. She liked to joke that when we lived together before I was never around and it had been like living with a ghost, but now that I was a ghost, it was like I was there with her more than ever.

Or something like that.

She wasn't much of a comedian, but she sure was the most beautiful and loving person I'd ever known. I had no idea how I'd let her slip away from me, but I would never let it happen again.

Vicious tossed a can into the fire and glanced my way. "Okay there, William?"

"Yes, Vicious, as a matter of fact, I *am* okay."

People spent their lives searching for peace by chasing idle dreams, addictions, money, religion, and even other people, hoping to fill some gap. Now, for the first time in longer than I could remember, I felt at peace. All this time, it had been right inside me. I'd just never slowed down enough to look within.

A stream of air tickled my behind and I shivered. The wind was still blowing when a promising stock appeared on the radar, and sometimes it blew hard.

Without Wally or access to my body, I couldn't reset my sensory mapping, so I was fated to forever feel this tickling. Now though, I found it reassuring, like rubbing an old scar.

Only one thing felt absent in my life, and it had taken on the eerie feeling of a missing limb. I looked toward the chair we'd set up in honor of our fallen comrade, where Wally used to sit next to me on our trips. I'd set it up beside me this evening, and it was conspicuously empty.

I often went back to replay that last talk I'd had with Wally.

It was hard to say whether he had really taken off to save me from the police. They did have a trace going on the security breach and would have found us eventually. Maybe he'd seen them coming and had decided to go. They'd issued a general notice of clemency on my case now, so even if he was trying to save us from jail, by now he would have known it was safe to return.

But he didn't.

The more I thought about it, the more I was sure that Wally wasn't trying to save me from jail. Maybe he was saving me from a worse fate, perhaps from myself. At the time, I was so busy digging myself into a deep, isolated hole that I might have never returned from it. I'd been suffocating myself in an impenetrable layer of greed and pride, trading friendship and love for money and power. Maybe he knew that I'd be better off this way.

I was sure that he'd like to return, and in fact I knew there was no place that he'd rather be than right here with us now, but he must have felt it was safer this way for some reason. It felt right, but I could never have gotten to this place on my own.

Wally and I had switched places.

I'd become him, living as a virtual being, and he'd become me, living out there in the real world in a real body.

Smiling, I remembered the last time we'd been here. Wally had told me that he loved me on our return home. I thought it was so odd then—but not anymore. Raising my beer can, I looked toward the empty chair beside me and toasted my absent friend.

Sometimes I guess you really did have to lose yourself to find yourself.

◆◆◆ GENESIS & JANUS

Part 6:

Patricia Killiam & Jimmy Scadden

Prologue

"I will always love you." I blew at a dandelion and watched its fluff scatter into the clear blue sky. The wind caught the tiny seeds and carried them up and away. "No matter where the winds carry me, I will always find my way back to you."

"And I you," said the boy, his face close now, his hot breath on my cheeks.

Sunlight streamed down on us in the field where we lay. I brushed a lock of hair from my eyes and looked down at an ant in the grass struggling with a prize far too large for it to carry.

"Never leave me."

"I will never leave you," he promised.

A silence descended, and then a low droning began. The boy looked up, craning his neck to see above the stone pile fence beside us. With a terrible growl, a Luftwaffe squadron roared overhead, skimming the treetops. I screamed and the boy jumped up.

He looked down at me. I nodded, and with a grim look he ran off, glancing just once over his shoulder to me before disappearing through the gate.

"I will never leave you," I whispered.

1

Identity: Jimmy Scadden

My eyes teared up, straining to look forward into the wind while the airboat tore across the top of the kelp forests. I begged my dad to take me out to work on the water almost every day, which frustrated Mother to no end. Dad was touched that his sweet little boy wanted to be with him, but really, I just wanted to be away from her.

Still, it was beautiful on the water.

"Amazing out here, right Jimmy?" my dad yelled over the roar of the engine. "Look!"

He swerved the airboat and pointed toward something in the water.

Dozens of sea otters had arranged themselves into a raft in the floating kelp, chattering angrily as we passed. A few heads popped up and down in the water around us, and I let myself flitter out into their little bodies, watching myself watching them.

"They hang around near the floating reef systems. They love it out here!"

We slowed as we neared the edge of the forest and the kelp stalks became sparser. I was sitting on my dad's knee, and he held me tightly against him with both arms, his warm hands on the flesh of my thighs, steering the boat with his phantom hands.

Unlike Mother, as soon as they'd arrived on Atopia my dad had worked hard at stretching his neural plasticity. Early on, he learned the trick of phantom limbs, something my mother never really figured out.

That day, we were fishing with the dolphins, which my dad knew was my favorite. My smile spread as we sped across the kelp, the wind and sun in my face, free as a bird. We didn't really fish, but mostly directed the dolphins using pssi control, and they did the fish tending. At that early stage in the project, we still needed their help to herd the fish, and for me this was the best part of fishing—speaking with the dolphins.

"There they are." My dad cut the engine.

Our boat settled into the water, gliding to a stop. The open ocean was gentle, but my dad held me tight. Gulls wheeled high in the air behind us, waiting for signs of any fish we might throw their way.

Off to the side of the boat, fast-moving shapes sped toward us from the depths. With a terrific splash, about a dozen heads broke the surface and the air filled with the sound of dolphins squeaking.

The pssi system instantly translated for us. Wild dolphins had fairly weak skills at what we would call communication, and the system often had to guess what they meant. These, however, were uplifted Terra Novan dolphins and had a good vocabulary.

And they were saying hello.

I smiled and waved. "Hey, Billy! Hi, Samantha!"

They squeaked their hellos back. Dad let go of me, and I rushed to the side and put my hand in the water to pet their snouts. They were like the best dog you ever had, but huge and wet and much, much smarter.

The Terra Novan dolphins weren't exactly working *for* us. It was more like they worked *with* us. They liked the excitement of Atopia and enjoyed privileged access to multiverse worlds only possible here.

My dad laughed. "That's a lot of love. Come on, we have a lot of work to do."

The dolphins shifted their attention toward him.

"Today we're harvesting sardines, so we need you guys to go and corral a few schools into the tanker over there," he explained, pointing to a ship floating a few hundred feet away. "Could someone go get me a sample?"

Samantha, my favorite, squawked and dove down into the depths.

"All right," my dad continued, clapping his hands, "let's get this show on the road!"

The dolphins chattered their good-byes and shot off, except for Samantha, who popped back up with a sardine in her mouth.

"Thank you, Sam." My dad nodded to her, bending over to take the sardine, and then turned back to his workstation, knife in hand, to begin the examination.

Samantha and I waited, staring at him. He stopped and smiled, shaking his head. "Okay, you two!" he laughed. "Go on and have some fun!"

I detached from my body and snapped into Samantha's, instantly rocketing off into the ocean, feeling her powerful muscles forcing us through the frigid waters, chasing her brothers and sisters into the depths.

2

Identity: Patricia Killiam

Showing up in person for the press was a mistake.

My God, how my body ached, even with its pain receptors tuned all the way down. I hadn't spent more than a few dozen hours in my own skin in the past year, but who would want to? Under siege by a frightening list of diseases barely held back by the magic of modern medicine, my body was as shrunken as an old pea left out overnight. Nearly 140 years old, but I still wasn't ready to give up the ghost.

Sighing inwardly, I nodded at Olympia, our media rep in New York, indicating it was time to start up the promo-world for the reporters. The event was being held on Atopia, but the reports were from New York, so we had Olympia running the show. She was attending remotely, and I'd expected to see a static-image display of her avatar in my display-space, but instead, she appeared as a perfectly rendered pssi-projection.

I didn't know Olympia had our pssi installed in her nervous system. When did that happen?

The promo-world expanded to engulf our senses, and an attractive young woman appeared, walking along a beautiful stretch of Atopian beachfront near the Eastern Inlet. "Imagine," she said, "have you ever thought of hiking the Himalayas in the morning and finishing off the day on a beach in the Bahamas?"

I'd watched this advertisement a million times. While it played, I disengaged and opened a private communications channel with Antonia, the senior partner at Olympia's company and an old, dear friend.

"Thank you so much for this new contract," Antonia said the moment I opened the channel.

"You don't need to thank me, your firm is simply the best qualified." I paused. "How is your father?"

"He's well. He was asking about you last night." She smiled warmly. "And how are you feeling? Is the new gene therapy working?"

"I'm feeling great," I lied and left it at that.

Antonia looked at me and seemed about to say something, but then stopped herself.

"Did your father decide whether he's coming?" I'd invited him to attend the big launch. He'd helped me in founding the pssi program but had left after disagreements with Kesselring.

She looked away and shook her head. "I'm sorry, but…I'll try talking to him."

"Please do."

Antonia looked back at me. "I will, I promise."

The ad finished playing, and with a nod I closed the communications channel to Antonia and returned my attention to the reporters.

"So how exactly is pssionics going to make the world a better place?" asked a stick-thin blond, Ginny, from the front row.

I carefully rolled my eyes. I'd never liked the term "pssionics"— the baggage it carried created a constant battle to separate fact from fiction when talking to reporters.

Then again, when has that ever mattered?

"Well, Ginny, I prefer to use the term 'polysynthetic sensory interface,' or just pssi." I detached and floated upward out of my body to get their attention, but nobody batted an eye, so I left my proxxi, Marie, to finish the presentation for me.

The proxxi program represented my life's work in creating the basis for synthetic intelligence. Where previous research had tried to create artificial intelligence in a kind of vacuum by itself, my contribution had been to understand that a body and mind didn't exist separately, but could only exist together.

We'd started by creating synthetic learning systems attached to virtual bodies in virtual worlds that gradually became intelligent by feeling their way through their environments. The proxxi program had taken this one step further when we'd integrated them intimately into people's lives, to share in their day-to-day experiences. They were still artificial intelligences, but now they shared our physical reality to seamlessly bridge the gap between the worlds of humans and machines.

Marie kept talking with the reporters, and I'd retreated to watch from the back of the room when the hair on the back of my neck stood up. The slingshot test must be about to start. I had to wrap this up, so I transitioned back into control of my body.

"Everyone!" I announced, reaching out to encircle the group of reporters with my phantoms. "If you'll allow me, I'd like to take whoever is coming up to watch the test firing of the slingshot."

We'd ensured almost everyone had signed up for a front row seat to the demonstration. We needed to show we weren't just serious about cyber, but also had a committed kinetic program.

"To answer Ginny's original question," I said as I grabbed them all and we shot through the ceiling of the conference room, accelerating up into space and earning a few gasps, "pssi will change the world by beginning to move it from the destructive downward spiral of material consumption and into the clean world of synthetic consumption."

I slowed and stabilized our flight path, bringing us to a stop about ninety thousand feet up. Dispersing the reporters' subjective points of view across a wide radius surrounding the target zone, I motioned down at the oceans below and then toward the sun rising on the horizon.

"Ten billion people all fighting for their piece of the material dream is destroying the planet, and pssi is the solution that will bring us back from the brink!"

On cue, the slingshot began to fill the space around us with a growing roar and fiery inferno. I left the reporters' visual subjectives in the thick of it while retreating to view from a distance, backing away several miles, and then several more. What had seemed so awe inspiring moments ago now appeared as just a bright smudge in the sky, and miles below shimmered the green dot of Atopia.

My mind clouded with doubt.

Can I really bend reality to my desire?

Atopia was just a pinpoint of green floating in the oceans on a planet that was just a tiny speck adrift in a vast cosmos of unending universes.

Am I fooling myself?

Our imagined power dwindled to nothing when viewed with a little perspective, dwarfed by unseen forces operating on much larger scales. Just then, I was enveloped in a fast-moving cloud, and, as if responding to my thoughts, a strong wind sprang up. The thunderstorm was coming.

I'd better get down and talk with Rick.

Leaving a splinter to manage saying good-bye to the reporters, I disengaged and pinged Commander Strong. The blaze of the slingshot test was still dissipating on the main display in the middle of the command center as I arrived. I lit up a smoke, gently inserting my presence next to Rick. He was my own pick as head of our newly formed Atopian Defense Forces.

During an exemplary career in the US Marines, Strong had demonstrated repeated bravery by rescuing men under his command. His first deployment had been in Nanda Devi in the terrible fighting over Himalayan dams that had sparked the Weather Wars. Though his psych profile indicated latent post-traumatic stress disorder, it was only enough to make him think twice before starting a fight. With the fearsome weapons we'd installed on Atopia, I didn't want some trigger-happy wingnut's finger over the button if things got hairy.

Kesselring, the CEO of Cognix and main benefactor behind Atopia, had been the first to begin speaking about the need to have defensive weapons. Initially, the suggestion seemed completely antithetical to the libertarian ideals Atopia was founded upon. I'd been against it at first, but as time wore on, I could see what Kesselring was thinking.

A battle-hardened veteran, Rick brought a direct, and sometimes violent, experience of the realities from the outside world that helped ground the team here. We were masters of synthetic reality, but I had a feeling our created realities could be blinding us to the real dangers out there. Rick was the perfect antidote.

"Finished playtime yet, Rick?" I asked, shifting my hips and taking a drag from my smoke. Rick did like his toys.

I wanted him to feel safe. I knew that one of his main reasons for coming here was to rescue his relationship with his estranged wife, Cindy. I sincerely wanted him to succeed and raise a family here, especially after the hard time he'd had growing up. During the interview process we'd gotten to know each other quite well.

"Yeah, I think that about does it."

"Good, because you scared the heck out of what wildlife I've managed to nurture on this tin can," I said. "And the tourists want to go back in the water—not that you didn't put on a good show. That was quite the shock and awe campaign."

"You gotta wake up the neighbors from time to time," he laughed.

We'd purposely removed any reality filtering of the weapons test to measure the cognitive impact they would have on people. The response had more than exceeded the threshold for emotional deterrence that we'd needed for the project.

"That's your job, Rick, to help scare the world into respecting us. Mine is to help scare it into saving itself. Good work."

"Did you see that thunderstorm coming in?" he asked. I nodded. "We've been tracking that depression for weeks, but we can't avoid them all. Anyway, it'll water your plants up top."

He smiled. I smiled back.

"Why don't you take the rest of the day off?" I suggested.

His wife was having a hard time adjusting to life here. People reacted differently to sudden immersion in limitless synthetic reality when they arrived on Atopia for the first time. Most adjusted quickly, in a short order creating their own little nooks and crannies of reality that suited them, but some had a more difficult time.

Yet it wasn't just that.

At the core of it, Cindy's chronic depression stemmed from the nature of her relationship with Rick. It was something I thought we could help fix.

"Actually, that would be great. You wouldn't mind?" he answered, busy adjusting the control systems for the slingshot shutdown. He looked toward me. "So you really think that whole sim kid thing might be a good idea?"

He was talking about the proxxids, simulated babies that Cognix encouraged couples to try before the "real" thing. It might help

Cindy get acclimatized to pssi, but in general it wasn't something I was comfortable with.

"Yes," I replied slowly, "if you're careful."

Rick looked satisfied with my answer. "Maybe I'll speak to her then. I'll see you later."

With a nod to Jimmy, I clicked out of the Command sensory spaces.

3

Identity: Jimmy Scadden

"I think that's a good idea, Commander," I said once Patricia had faded from view. "I mean about going to see your wife. I can handle this."

Rick glanced up at me from the slingshot controls. "Thanks." Standing up from his workstation, he walked over as he shifted his command authorizations to me. "You have a pretty special bond with Dr. Killiam, don't you?"

I smiled. "We do."

An alert signaled that some security protocols had been breached during the weapons test. Somebody was poking around up there and had destroyed the drone.

"It hasn't been easy moving here," he continued. "At least, it hasn't been easy for Cindy."

I filed the breach report and made a note to look into it later.

"It's a huge change for her," I replied. "And for you, for that matter."

Rick nodded, pulling a security blanket down around us. The other Command staff glanced up from their workstations, curious.

He put his hand on my shoulder. "I heard that you had it rough growing up here."

I didn't say anything.

"If you ever need anyone to talk to, I had a bit of a tough time as a kid, too."

"Thanks...," I replied, surprised at his sudden intimacy.

"I'm just saying, any time...and, of course, entirely confidentially."

"I appreciate that, Commander," I answered more confidently. "And I will, but I'm fine."

I pulled down the security blanket, feeling self-conscious with all the rest of the staff there.

"Why don't you get on to seeing your wife?"

He smiled. "You just remember, any time, right?"

"Right."

A pause while I smiled at him, but it was difficult to sense what was going on inside his head. I decided to let it go.

"See you later, Jimmy."

While Atopia was marketed as this amazing place and the tabloid worlds were constantly spinning stories about the fantastic pssi-kids that grew up here, my experience on Atopia was a special sort of hell I had to drag myself through. As an adult, I had the perspective to view it, even appreciate it, as a part of the fire that had forged me, but back then, pssi could be cruel.

And, of course, I remembered it all. For pssi-kids, not remembering wasn't an option.

"Look at him, *isn't that cute?*" said my mother, back when I was an infant, just after my parents had arrived on Atopia. "He just shat himself again, and he's looking around wondering what smells so bad."

She was laughing at a shared rendering of my inVerse, even sharing the smell with the guests. I was ten months old, and Mother was at it again. Drunk, of course.

"Smell that?" she laughed. "Can you believe something so small could make such a terrible smell?"

My parents had another couple over for coffee, and Mother had turned our cramped apartment into a synthetic-space projection that was decked out like a Spanish palace for the evening. We were sitting in the middle of an open courtyard under a deep blue sky, surrounded by a three-story terracotta-faced palazzo, the walls decorated with intricate murals inlaid with tiny blue, white, and gold tiles.

I was playing between potted ferns next to a small pool filled with colorful koi. Dragonflies buzzed at the water's edge, holding my attention as I reached toward them. I still hadn't learned to walk yet, so I sat on my haunches in my own excrement, eyes on the dragonflies, curiously sniffing the air around me.

"Don't you think you should change him?" asked Steve uncomfortably. He worked in the aquaponics group with my dad, and they spent a lot of time together, both at work and off hours. It was a source of friction between my parents.

"It's all that fish protein in his little diet," said Mother. "Phil thinks it'll help his brain development, grow him big and strong, but it doesn't seem to be working." She laughed again, louder this time, shrugging her shoulders. The guests politely tried to smile.

"Yolanda!" she yelled. "Change Jim, please?"

Mother smiled at the guests as her image flickered. She detached while her proxxi, Yolanda, took over control of her physical body. The pssi functioned somewhat less than flawlessly at that proto-type stage back then, and the net effect was that a ghost of Mother seemed to remain in place while Yolanda materialized into view and morphed away with her body to stand up.

Yolanda smiled at the guests and walked over to pick me up. She cradled me as she scurried me aside to change my diaper.

"Isn't it just the best thing?" my mother gushed, referring to the pssi, still a new toy to them. This was the first time Steve and his wife, Arlene, had paid a social call with my parents. Our family didn't have many guests over. We weren't what you'd call popular.

"I was skeptical at first when Patricia Killiam—my great aunt," she emphasized, stopping for effect, "offered us a berth, but really, it's made my life so relaxing." She smiled drunkenly.

"It is amazing," Steve agreed, happy to have gotten off the topic of diapers. "All the build-up wasn't just hype." He looked around the room for confirmation.

"Absolutely." My mother nodded. "I mean, who would have thought? I modeled my proxxi after my own nanny, and little Jimmy has hardly put a dent in my lifestyle."

"We're still learning new ways to use it," added Steve's wife. "It is nice to have real face-time with people, though. Synthetics do lack a certain...something."

Everyone around the table nodded except my mother, who crinkled her nose a little.

No one around the table quite knew where to take the conversation next.

"Well!" exclaimed my mother, never one to let an awkward moment derail her. "Who would have imagined that we'd end up in the most technologically advanced place on Earth and I'd be a fishmonger's wife!" she tittered, looking toward my father.

He stared down into his coffee. "We manage the aquaculture program—we're not exactly fishmongers." He stole a tiny hateful glance her way but smiled to the guests.

Steve raised his cup of coffee. "And we farm kelp, too!"

Mother pinched her face in a tight-lipped smile that I was all too familiar with. "That's nice. Call it what you like. We're here, and that's all that matters!"

Yolanda walked back over offered me back to my mother, who took me on her knee and smiled into my little face.

"How's my little stinker?" she laughed, shaking me more than lightly.

4

Identity: Patricia Killiam

"There's something very odd about this latest string of disappearances," I stated, getting to the reason I'd requested this private meeting with Kesselring.

The rash of people disappearing into the multiverse and leaving their bodies behind had gotten worse, even common. After an initial alarm by friends and family, we'd usually find them burrowed deep in some hedonistic cyber-fantasy world, but lately cases were sprouting up in which they were nowhere to be found.

"Do you think that bastard Sintil8 could have anything to do with it?" Kesselring asked. "He'd love to find a way to derail the program. Are you keeping an eye on him?"

"More or less." I had my own private discussions with Sintil8, but nothing I wanted Kesselring to know about. "But these disappearances are different. Their brains are highly stimulated, a sensory overload of some sort."

I took a deep breath and shifted in my seat.

The strict privacy laws—that I'd created—now meant I couldn't dig any deeper into people's minds without their consent. I'd forced Cognix to build ironclad privacy systems into pssi from the ground up to protect the rights of users. Root pssi control was like having access to the soul of a person. It was the fundamental building block from which everything else branched.

"We need to figure out what's going on."

Kesselring sighed.

"I don't disagree, but a few people off pleasuring themselves in the multiverse isn't enough to delay the entire program. This is a massive undertaking we've put in motion."

The global marketing push to launch pssi commercially was easily the biggest promotional campaign of all time, at least by a private corporation—if this label could be applied to us anymore.

I watched the glittering cover of the security blanket that had fallen around us when he arrived. Even with security incorporated from the ground up, if you wanted to be really sure you were safe from prying eyes, it was best to use a blanket.

The one surrounding us now was Kesselring's personal, impenetrable shield. It had an odd and shifting color that was similar to the indistinct bluishness of water in a glacial runoff stream. Maybe that was why it felt so cold.

"Do you think the Terra Novans are involved?" I asked. "It's still possible this is Sintil8 together with the Cartels, or even some fragmented group from Allied Command."

Kesselring eyed me. "I have someone looking into it. We need to be extremely vigilant from this point."

I watched him, wondering how vigilant he was being about me. "You've probably heard, but Rick agreed with us to nominate Jimmy to the Security Council," I said. "If anyone can ferret out what is going on, he can."

I was still rooting for Jimmy, even if he didn't need it anymore.

When Jimmy's parents left Atopia, I'd taken him under my wing. His mother, my great-grandniece, had abandoned him here, and I blamed myself for not intervening sooner in that ugly domestic situation. Ultimately, Jimmy had been the one to pay the price, but he was beginning to blossom. He was my star pupil, along with Nancy, of course. In my long life, I never had any children of my own, and these two were as close as I'd come.

I couldn't have been more proud.

Kesselring eyed me, sensing my protectiveness. "Jimmy's an excellent choice. He's the one I have helping me out."

I raised my eyebrows. I hadn't known Jimmy was working directly for him.

"What are they up to?" I mused under my breath, thinking about the Terra Novans, but now thinking about Kesselring as well.

"I don't know," he replied, not catching my full meaning, "but this just proves my point that we need to push ahead as quickly as possible. As you said yourself, we need to maximize the network effects of the product introduction—"

I completed the sentence for him, "To gain the highest saturation throughout the population as quickly as possible. I know." I stared into his eyes. "So we're going to be giving it away for free?"

He smiled. "Of course."

"And it doesn't worry you we're not telling people the full story?"

"It worries me," he said, looking down at the floor, "but again, what choice do we have?" He raised his head and met my gaze. "We need to make sure we stabilize this timeline the best we can."

As we approached the point of no return, all the careful planning and clever analyses had the feeling of blind faith, and I'd had faith shot out of my skies early in life.

"Patricia," he said, watching me, "the lives of billions rest in our hands. We cannot fail."

He was right. What we were doing couldn't be worse than letting billions of people die.

Could it?

5

Identity: Jimmy Scadden

"At ease, soldier."

I laughed and relaxed my stance. As one of the newest Command officers, I thought I would strut my stuff for Patricia a little. She'd asked me to come to her office, under a tight security blanket, to discuss something.

"We'd like to nominate you to the Security Council," she said, getting to the point. "What do you think?"

I wasn't really surprised, but I put on a show for her. "I'm flattered. I mean, of course I would accept, but I'm so young, so inexperienced."

"Perhaps young, but you're our leading expert on conscious security. I know you're lacking in some areas, and that's why I want you to stick close to Commander Strong. I think you can learn a lot from him."

"Me too."

"Perfect. Then if we're agreed, I'll put the wheels in motion."

Patricia was like the mother I'd always wished for, and in a twist of circumstance, that's exactly what she'd become. Her love for me was something I wasn't used to.

I think my own parents must have loved each other, at least at first. But they should have just gotten a divorce rather than fight like they did. Mother always insisted it wouldn't be Christian.

Coming from the Deep South, my family had a strong religious background, and regular church service figured deeply in my upbringing. In fact, a strong Christian community on Atopia was one of the reasons my mother said she'd agreed to come, and God and sin were never far from her wicked tongue.

A strange communion between Christianity and hacker culture had evolved on Atopia—"hacker" used in its nobler and original sense of building or tinkering with code. The Elèutheros community on Atopia believed that hacking was a form of participation in God's work of creating the universe. This wasn't quite what my mother had in mind before she'd arrived, however, and this had just added to her eventual dissatisfaction of the place.

Mother had been a very beautiful woman, a real southern belle, but if she saw you looking at her, a nasty comment was never far behind, mostly especially for my father. All that was left of my parents' relationship by the time I arrived was a grinding, codependent bitterness that fueled the empty shells of their lives.

I'd guess that my parents had always fought, but having me gave them an audience. After arriving on Atopia to birth me, they could have shielded me from their screaming matches by simply leaving a pssi-block on, and my dad often tried to do just that, but my mother wanted me to hear everything.

One evening in particular, I was sitting in one of my playworlds, stacking blocks with my proxxi, Samson, into fantastic structures in augmented pssi-space. Despite my dad's attempt to filter out their latest argument with a pssi-block, Mother was having none of it.

"So now you want to protect him!" she screamed, turning off the pssi-block in the middle of their argument. "That's a joke: *you* wanting to protect a child. You're a sick little worm, Phil."

Their favorite venue for screaming matches was the Spanish Courtyard world, well constructed and away from the prying eyes and ears of outsiders.

"Would you knock it off?" my dad said. "I don't know what you're talking about. I haven't done anything."

"Oh, that's right, you haven't done anything!" she screeched. Once she got going, there was no turning back. "You sure as hell haven't *ever* done anything! Why I married you, I have no idea. What a *waste* of time."

"I thought we got married because we loved each other," my dad replied, dejectedly. Fearfully.

"Love don't pay the bills, now does it, Phil? *Does it?*"

"No . . . I mean, so what? We manage."

"We manage?" Mother yelled "We *manage?*" She'd been drinking again.

"Yes, we manage," insisted my dad, not sure what else to say. He wasn't much good at arguing, or perhaps he'd been the subject of ridicule for so long that he'd given up.

Mother tried her best to include me in the blame game, even at this early point.

"I manage, Phil, it's me that's here taking care of that little shit of a son of yours all day while you're out sunning yourself on the water."

"Could you not talk like that? He'll remember everything, you know."

"Oh, I *want* him to hear. I want him to hear everything, want him to know that the only reason I agreed to have him was so that we could get on this stinking ship. Otherwise, I would never have let a child into this world so close to you. Maybe I should tell my church group what you'd like to do with children?"

"Gretchen, please, you're drunk. It's not what you think."

"We're only here because I'm the great-grandniece to the famous Killiam. Not like you'd be man enough to accomplish anything on your own."

"We're doing amazing things...."

"Amazing? Really? Is that why you pssi-block me all day? I can still see you, you know, sneaking around out there."

"I need to focus on work during the days. I thought we'd agreed."

My mother snorted. "I thought we agreed about a lot of stuff, Phil. And you stink like fish, it's disgusting." She wrinkled her nose.

"Block it out then. That's what pssi is for. Anyway, I was trying to take a shower, but you stopped me."

"I stopped you? So it's me that's holding you back? What a joke! Just block it, that's your answer? Maybe I like to see things for what they are, like what *you* are."

"I'm *trying* to do my best."

"Your best isn't good enough," she spat back. "You are what you are, right, Phil?"

My dad shook his head, looking down at the floor. "I'm getting in the shower." He turned away to escape.

Mother waved him off drunkenly, turning her attention to me. Even as a toddler, I cringed in the glare of her disappointment. She detached from her body and snapped into mine. She sat looking at the yellow cyber-blocks through my own eyes, staring at my little hands.

"Playing with blocks again, eh, stinker?" she laughed. "The other pssi-kids your age are composing operas, and you're obsessed with blocks. From what I've heard, your cousin Nancy is quite the star. Not you, though, not my little stinker."

She angrily snapped out of my body, giving it a shove as she left and knocking me over. "You're just as useless as your dad."

At the time, I didn't understand what she meant, but I could hear the hate in her voice.

Samson watched all this from a distance. When she lost interest, he walked and sat down with his hand in mine. He summoned up and handed me some more interlocking blocks. We quietly finished building the wall around us and sat for a while inside the structure we created, trying to figure out how to fill in the cracks and make it impenetrable.

6

Identity: Patricia Killiam

It was Bonfire Night, and excited squeals rose up between bursts of rockets and bangers. Walking down the lane, I caught glimpses of children playing in the alleyways, scrambling atop piles of rubbish stacked high in the abandoned bombsites behind the row houses.

Fireworks whizzed and popped overhead, and, coming around a corner, we almost smacked into a little girl running the other way, her eyes fixed on a lit sparkler that she waved back and forth in her tiny outstretched hand.

"Careful now," I laughed, stooping to catch and stop her before she tripped herself up. She never took her eyes off the sparkler, completely mesmerized. It sputtered out, and the girl looked up at me with eyes wide in wonder. Small, ruddy cheeks glowed warmly above a tightly wrapped scarf. Alan, my walking partner, knelt down on the wet pavement beside us, rummaging around in his pockets.

"Sorry, mum! Little rascal got away from me!" called out a large man huffing and puffing up behind her, waving at us, obviously the girl's father. The foggy night was thick with the acrid smoke of gunpowder, and my watering eyes strained to see the man approaching.

I called out to him. "Oh, it's no trouble at all." The man stopped running and walked the last few paces. He was obviously coming from the Lion's Head, the pub where we were headed.

"Ahh," said Alan, having found the prize he'd been searching for. He produced another sparkler from the pocket of his wool overcoat. He looked at the little girl. "Would you like this?"

The girl's eyes grew and she nodded. Just then the man arrived.

"Oah, that's very kind of you," he started to say cheerily, but then his face darkened. "You're that perfessor, ain't ya?" He reached down to grab his daughter's hand.

Alan sighed but said nothing, bowing his head and putting the sparkler back in his pocket.

"And what of it?" I growled at the man, releasing the girl.

"You stay away from my Olivia!" He roughly jerked the little girl away from us. "You stay away, you hear me? *Disgusting.*" Turning sharply, he walked away, dragging the girl behind him. She continued to watch us intently, craning her neck as she disappeared into the gloom.

I sighed, reaching down to pull Alan back up. He'd visibly crumpled during the exchange. "Don't pay any attention to them," I said softly, pulling him in the opposite direction, away from the Lion's Head. "What do you say we have a drink at the Green Man instead?"

"Yes, I suppose," he replied distantly.

It was the spring of 1953, although in Manchester, spring was much the same as the rest of the year—cold and raining. While even the Blitz hadn't been able to displace my mother and father from London during the War, the Great Smog of '52 had been the last straw to encourage them to take the family north that year.

The smog hadn't been the only reason, however. My parents used the Big Smoke as their own smoke screen to accompany me to my new school. I'd just been accepted as the first female faculty member of the new Computer Laboratory of Manchester University, and there'd been a terrible row when my father had refused to allow me to leave and live on my own. When Gran's asthma had practically killed her in the intense smog just before Christmas, it gave Father the perfect opportunity to make everyone happy.

My sisters had all been married off by then, and despite an endless procession of suitors provided by Mother, I'd remained steadfastly alone. I just wasn't interested. Only one passion burned in my soul.

"Snap out of it, Alan. Don't listen to that small-minded lout." I laughed, pulling him into me and giving him a little kiss. He smiled, and we began walking off toward the Green Man. "Tell me again why it's different."

"We're just speaking about two completely different things," he replied after a pause, his mind coming back to our discussion. "My idea is that if you speak to something inside a black box, and everyone agrees that it responds to them just as a human would, then the only conclusion is that something intelligent and aware, human or otherwise, is inside."

"Then why not an equivalent test for reality?"

"So you're suggesting that if, somehow, we could present a simulated reality to humans—"

"To a conscious observer," I interjected.

"To a conscious observer," he continued with a nod. "If that conscious observer couldn't distinguish the difference between the simulated and the real world, then the simulated reality becomes an actual reality in some way?"

"Exactly! That's exactly what I'm suggesting."

He shook his head.

"Why not? Doesn't it make a certain sense when all of modern physics requires a conscious observer to make it work for some reason?"

"You can't just create something from nothing," he said after some contemplation.

"Why not?"

"And just responding 'why not' does not constitute a defense, my dear," he laughed.

We'd arrived at the pub and stopped outside. With one hand, he combed back his hair, parting it neatly to one side, and smiled at me. Even at forty years of age, he still had a boyish charm, perhaps aided by ears that stuck out just a little too far.

I laughed, looking at him.

"What about the Big Bang then? That's a whole universe from nothing!" I had a steady stream of correspondence going on with some colleagues at Cambridge who'd just minted the idea.

"Ah yes, my bright little flower, you are clever aren't you?"

"I am," I giggled. "Come on, let's get that drink."

We wandered inside under the bowing doorframe, across worn granite flagstone floors, and were enveloped by the warm bustle of the dimly lit pub.

"The usual, Mr. Turing?" asked the bartender as we arrived at the bar. He nodded at her.

"Two, please," I added.

For one luminous yet terribly short year, I had the great privilege of having Mr. Alan Turing, the father of all computer science and artificial intelligence, as my PhD professor. His own hardship had been my gain.

After convictions for homosexual acts, still a criminal offense in 1950s England, his faculty and the academic world had ostracized him, and most of his graduate students had abandoned him. It was the only reason someone of his stature and position would have accepted a female student at the time.

In the end, I had almost an entire year of Alan to myself, an incredible experience that would inspire and shape my thinking for the rest of my life. Sadly, Alan took his own life less than a year later, and the world has been a lesser place without him.

"All right then," said Alan after a pause. "I'll allow that. Explain to me exactly what you're thinking."

The bartender returned with our pints of cider. Digging into his pockets again, Alan came up with a handful of change that he left on the counter, mumbling his thanks while we collected our drinks. We made our way to a quiet part of the pub near the fireplace, which glowed warmly with coals of coke.

"All realities are not created equal," I explained as we decided on a small wooden table tucked into the corner. The benches around it had obviously been recycled, or stolen, from a local parish church somewhere. Mismatched and threadbare carpets covered floorboards that creaked as we sat down in the pews. "If there is only one observer of a universe, then that reality is weak."

"And the more observers that share a reality, the stronger it becomes?" he continued for me.

"Exactly!"

Just then a ping arrived from Nancy. Its loud chime drowned out the background noise of the pub.

"Go ahead and answer," Alan encouraged, picking up his glass of cider and taking a sip.

This wasn't a memory but a painstakingly reconstructed world that I'd created. I liked to venture off into it from time to time, to sit and chat with a simulation of my mentor of so long ago— replay conversations we'd had, or at least, what I thought I remembered of them—but the simulation was a pale reminder of what the man had been.

I authorized Nancy for access to this sensory space, and she resolved into view, sitting on a pew across from us.

"So you're sure you want to go ahead with this?" I asked her.

Nancy was pressing me to release the Infinixx project ahead of the pssi launch. It had originally been my idea—something that would thrust Nancy into the spotlight and bring her own star onto the world stage, just as mine was fading. She could continue my work after I was gone, and I knew she had the inner strength to make sure that whatever happened, it would be for the right reasons.

"Absolutely!"

"Good. I'll press on ahead on my side then. You're keeping on top of the New York trials?"

"Yes, Aunt Patty," she responded sheepishly. She would always be a child to me. "Of course I am."

"Perfect. I'll start a campaign with the board."

She looked ready to burst, yet her eyes clouded over.

"There's something else?"

She sighed. "What's going on with Uncle Vince?"

Reports of his future deaths had been clogging the prediction networks. My guilt was overwhelming—Vince was one of my oldest friends. I'd managed to insert some clues, however, deep in the patterns we had chasing him. He was off around the world, hunting them down, and over time it would subside. A goose chase, but I had to keep him busy, and in the end it might even do him some good.

"Nothing is going on with Vince, nothing at all."

"What do you mean?" She didn't look convinced.

"He's just fooling around." I shrugged and looked toward Alan.

"Okay...if you say so." She paused, but let it go. "Just tell me what I need to do to help with the board."

"I will. Speaking of the board, will we be seeing you at the Foreign Banquet tomorrow evening?"

"I'll be there."

I hesitated. "Dr. Baxter said he might bring Bob along...."

I really wanted to find a way to bring her and Bob back together, but I'd never worn Cupid's hat comfortably.

"I think I'm going solo," she replied with a smile. "It's an official function, and those bore David to death."

"I just thought I'd mention it." Maybe I was better at this than I thought. "Now get back to your evening!"

She nodded excitedly as she faded away.

"A beautiful child," Alan observed, smiling at me. "One thing though...."

"About Nancy?"

"No, about what we were talking about."

I waited. "Yes?"

"In these created realities you speak of, what controls the underlying conditions that make the reality possible?"

I considered this for a moment. "Just the observing entity."

"And what happens if an organism escapes into a reality that it creates?"

At the time, I hadn't understood that it could be possible, but Alan always had a gift for seeing further than anyone else.

"What I mean is, organisms are constrained by the physics of this reality, but what if they can create their own realities and escape into them?" He paused to let the question sink in. Alan had also been the founder of mathematical biology and studied its relationship to morphogenesis, the processes that caused organisms to develop their shapes. "If you change the body, Patricia, you also change the mind."

I sat staring at him, saying nothing.

"What could an animal become if it were completely unfettered by any physical constraints?" he continued, staring directly into my eyes. "If it were able to drag other observers into these created realities of yours, against their will?"

This century-old question now hung in my mind.

7

Identity: Jimmy Scadden

The flitterati were already mingling with the foreign diplomats and other people of importance that had arrived at the annual Foreign Banquet. The event was being held on the very apex of the Solomon House complex, atop the farming towers, in the ballroom. The setting sun refracted through the crystalline walls, casting prismatic rays across the crowd. Strains of Vivaldi's *Four Seasons* floated across it all from a string quartet playing in the landing of the curved marble entryway. Motes of dust danced in the straining rays of light.

Those are probably smarticles.

I had Samson, my proxxi, walk my body over while I finished some last-minute work at Command, and reaching the entrance, I took back control.

Many of the world's leaders were in attendance at the banquet, reflecting the growing international significance of Atopia. It was an important opportunity for us to show off on the world stage, and Kesselring had detailed instructions for all of the Council and board members, including that we all show up in the flesh to minimize confusion on the part of our guests.

Someone grabbed my arm as I descended the entry staircase.

"Congratulations, Jimmy!" said an excited Nancy Killiam, resplendent in a shimmering gown of what looked like liquid helium that flowed around her in silvery wisps. She pulled me close to kiss my cheek, the helium pouring silently around us, and put her arm in mine.

"Thanks!" My nomination to the Security Council, by far the youngest ever, earned me the invitation tonight. I liked the attention. "But on the contrary, it should be me who is congratulating you!"

Patricia had given me a heads up on the push to move Infinixx up on the Cognix agenda. Now it was her turn to appear embarrassed.

"No congratulations yet, Jimmy," she whispered conspiratorially. "That's supposed to be a secret!"

"No secrets from me," I whispered back. "And I may be able to help." Nancy looked at me, about to ask, when I shook my head. "I can't say now."

We finished descending the staircase together, arm in arm. Reaching the landing, someone called her name, and she looked away toward them and then back at me. I smiled and nodded her leave to go. With a whoosh, the silvery wisps of her gown disappeared and followed her into the crowd.

I certainly felt her go.

"Drink, sir?" a waiter asked, sweeping up beside me with a golden tray full of champagne flutes. I nodded and took a glass, watching Nancy greet our fellow pssi-kids.

This was definitely our time to shine, and shine we did in our glittery and fanciful skins. I observed some of the guests watching them with wonder. The visitors were still adjusting to the trial pssi system that everyone who came to Atopia had installed. It was a great marketing stunt.

Any technology that was sufficiently advanced seemed like magic to someone unfamiliar, and this place still held a mystical air to the rest of the world.

Kesselring downloaded to Samson a long list of people he wanted me to introduce myself to. Looking around the ballroom, their names and identities popped up in my display spaces, allowing me to pick them out from the crowd.

Many were my counterparts in the armed and security forces, and several of these were from the Indian and Chinese contingents. Atopia was viewed as a neutral territory for these warring sides. Even more important, Atopia was seen—by both sides—as an indispensible part of their economic and technological future.

I sighed, straightening out my new ADF Whites, and wove my way into the crowd.

The event was winding down. In my last discussion, I brought together some senior cyber-espionage officials from both the Indian and Chinese sides at the same time. I was quite certain it wasn't my diplomatic skills at work so much as everyone's desire not to be left out. They were hungry for pssi.

I was thinking about leaving when someone poked me with a phantom. It was Commander Strong, standing not ten feet from me. His phantoms dragged me over to him.

"General, Mrs. McInnis, I'd like to introduce you to one of our rising young stars, Mr. Jim Scadden," he announced as I arrived. I stood straight up at attention, taking Mrs. McInnis' hand, and then turned to give the general a firm handshake.

"The pleasure is mine."

Mrs. McInnis took me in. "You're one of those pssi-kids, right?"

I laughed. "Yes ma'am, one of those."

"Could you show me something?"

She obviously wanted some kind of carnival trick. The commander was about to excuse me when I took a step back, bowed to

Mrs. McInnis, and then theatrically flourished one hand forward to produce a bouquet of red and pink lilies. I handed them to her.

"Oh my goodness," she declared, her eyes wide.

"Take them," I offered, "they're real, or at least, they'll feel that way to you."

Mrs. McInnis tentatively reached out and gripped the bouquet at its base. The flowers swayed, and she leaned in and smelled them.

"They smell absolutely lovely!" she exclaimed, her nose in a lily.

"And," I announced, waving my hand and snapping my fingers, "presto!"

The flowers disappeared in a flash, and a dove fluttered away from where they'd been, startling Mrs. McInnis. It flew up toward the ceiling of the crystal enclosure, leaving a few feathers behind in its desperate flight. We all turned to watch it go.

Mrs. McInnis beamed at me.

"Jimmy is my newest addition to the Security Council," laughed Rick, raising an eyebrow.

The general smiled at me. "He certainly has a gift with people."

"That's absolutely the truth," added Mrs. McInnis. At that moment, someone leaned in to touch her arm, obviously an old friend.

"Oh, Margie! Did you see that?" said Mrs. McInnis as she turned to the new arrival, who peeled her away from us. "Excuse me, gentlemen."

We all nodded politely as she left. General McInnis, I could see from research notes that floated into a splinter from Samson, had been Rick's commanding officer on two tours of duty back in Nanda Devi.

"Synthetic babies may seem odd, sir, but my parents fought so much," said Rick after a pause. They must have been talking about his proxxids. "I'm just trying to be careful."

"Could have fooled me," laughed the general. "That *third* tour you signed up for was *heavy* duty. Didn't strike me as the plan of a man being careful."

"What I mean is—"

"I know what you mean, son, and I don't blame you, running away out here. Heck, getting overrun by a squad of five-hundred pound, steroid-raging silverbacks in full battle armor would be enough to make anyone wet their pants."

Rick straightened up. "With all due respect, sir, I've never run away from anything."

"Maybe you haven't, but then again, maybe you have." The general turned to size me up, and I returned his gaze. "Young man, what do you think of these proxxids?"

"I think what Commander Strong is doing is absolutely the best thing," I replied without hesitation. "We test most things in life before we dive in, so why not test how we'd like our children to be?"

The general looked unconvinced.

"There's no harm in it," I added, "and I think he should try it out until he feels comfortable."

The general considered this, and turned back to Rick. "Coming out here seems a perfect way to start over, Rick. Just really get started is all I'm saying, and don't pretend, son. All this gimmickry can't replace the real thing."

Rick straightened up but said nothing.

"Anyway," continued the general, slapping him on the shoulder, "I'm just calling it how I see it. I know you must have a lot of glad-handing to do here. I'll let you get to it."

He turned to locate his wife.

"Jimmy, nice to meet you, and Rick, all the best," he said, giving us the tiniest of salutes.

"Very nice to meet you, too, sir," I said to his retreating figure, earning me a nod as he wound his way through the crowd.

I could see how deeply the issue with Rick's wife was affecting him, and I had been studying him when the general spoke about Nanda Devi.

"You look just *scrumptious!*"

Spinning on my heels, champagne in hand, I found a stunning brunette staring at me, her long hair falling in tresses over tanned shoulders. A gossamer dress in abstract floral patterns fluttered around her, barely obscuring an athletic frame underneath. She laughed nervously, watching me smiling at her.

What a lovely—and familiar—*smile.*

Commander Strong grinned at the two of us, taking a long second look at the brunette.

"I think I'll leave you to it." With a wink my way, he was off.

"Those ADF Whites sure look good on you, Jimmy," said the brunette, glancing at the departing Rick before returning her smile to me. She knew me, but seemed edgy.

I definitely knew her, too, but couldn't quite place her. I was suppressing my pssi memory, determined to work on exercising my own mind's memory systems. The more time I spent in my own skin, the more I felt a deep welling of energy seeping outward from within.

Most pssi-kids hardly spent any time at all in their own bodies as they spread their splintered minds ever wider across the multiverse, leading to a loss of neural cohesion between their minds and bodies.

They didn't care, but I did.

It was almost touching to see this girl had come in her own body, even if she was probably just making a show of it.

But what's her name?

I smiled as the light dawned.

"Cynthia! It's been a long time."

"Since Nancy's thirteenth birthday party...." Her voice trailed off, embarrassed.

I liked the way it made her look vulnerable.

"We were kids," I said finally, letting her off the hook. "I was a bit of an awkward kid. You, you were—"

"I was awful."

"I was going to say beautiful. Come on, you weren't awful. It was a weird situation."

"I was, Jimmy, and I never got a chance to apologize for that. I'm really sorry."

"Hey, it helped focus me at the time, and look where that got me." I swept my arm toward all the important-looking dignitaries. "I should be thanking *you*."

"I don't think you should be thanking me." She frowned, but then the smile returned. "Look at you now, Mr. Jim Scadden. You sure have changed."

"Oh," I said, "you have no idea."

We stood looking at each other, the air electric with anticipation.

"So you call that an apology?" I asked, drawing her in. "That just now?"

She laughed. "My attempt, anyway."

"I think maybe I need something more substantial, perhaps over dinner."

"That sounds like a great idea. When?"

"No time like the present," I said with a wink. Things were done here.

She paused before giving me her answer. "Sure, why not?"

Something inside me growled, and I took her hand, leading her toward the exit.

Life was coming full circle.

8

Identity: Patricia Killiam

I was sitting on another of the interminable board meetings, but at least I had something I wanted to accomplish at this one.

We were in the Solomon House conference room at a working session on marketing materials for the pssi launch, this one focusing on stress. One of the items I'd managed to get on the agenda was pushing Infinixx forward on the release schedule, so Nancy was there with me to help make the case. Jimmy was there as well, now a part of the Security Council. He sat beside Nancy.

We were about to start watching the advertising video, but so far all we'd been doing was listening to a monologue by Dr. Hal Granger about his happiness index, and how it was the core measurement on which the whole pssi program was based. His program was becoming ever more popular as it traded off the Cognix brand, but I had no idea what people saw in him. His ego had long since outstripped his talents.

The Chinese representatives were dialed-in today. They were nodding politely as they listened to Hal, but he was getting on my nerves. *Again.*

Synthetic reality wasn't the only thing pssi was useful for. Flooding neural systems with smarticles had made it possible to actively regulate ion flow along axons, helping us to stop, and even rehabilitate, neurological diseases such as Parkinson's. Alzheimer's had been a big win for us nearly twenty years ago, and was now a disease of the past—at least for those with money. Much of Atopia's construction had been funded by revenues Cognix had derived from these medical breakthroughs.

Stress, however, was something different.

After conquering, or at least taming, most of the major diseases, stress had become the biggest killer in the rich world. It had many sources. Sometimes it was just the grind of our environment—noise, pollution, light, advertising, change—but mostly it was the sense of losing control, of not being where we thought we should be or who we should be with.

Finding ways to deal with memories was the foundation of almost all of the solutions.

The human mind had a nearly endless capacity for suspending disbelief, and we'd found this was an effective vector in the fight against stress and anxiety. Some said we were just teaching people to fool themselves, but then again, when were people *ever* not fooling themselves?

I sighed.

But all we could do was supply the tool. How people decided to use it was entirely up to them, despite all the recommendations I could make.

Finally, Hal finished his rambling presentation, and the advertisement started.

"Have you ever wished you were free from the constant bombardment of advertising? Pssionics now makes it possible!" said the extremely attractive young man featured in our commercial. "Saving the world from the eco-crunch is going to be the best thing you've ever done for yourself!"

The meeting was being conducted in Mandarin, but our pssi seamlessly reconstructed everything in whatever language we preferred, even visually translating culturally distinct body language and facial expressions.

Fifty years ago, they'd been predicting we'd all be speaking Chinese by now, but in the end, the ultimate lingua franca was the machine metadata that intermediated it all. Everyone spoke whatever language they wanted, and the machines translated for us, so nobody needed to learn more than one anymore.

The study of languages was just more roadkill left behind on our headlong race ahead.

As the advertisement droned on, I couldn't help feeling mounting disgust with the way it focused on happiness. *Sure, it's important, but what exactly* is *happiness?* What we were pushing wasn't exactly what we were pitching.

Soon enough, the ad finished and faded away into the familiar rotating symbol of Atopia, the pyramid and sphere.

"So what do you think?" our marketing coordinator asked.

Still staring at the rotating logo, my mind had wandered into thinking some odd features of the storm systems coming up the coast toward us.

"I liked it," Dr. Granger responded, nodding ingratiatingly toward our Chinese guests. "I think I'm going to make some slight changes to the empathic feedback."

"Sounds good," said Kesselring, here in his primary-subjective for once. "As I was saying before, all the psychological, neurological, and, well, all test results have been compiled. Everything looks good for launch."

He smiled an unbecoming grin at me. I raised my eyebrows but said nothing, and everyone around the table clapped. Everyone but me.

"Patricia?" Kesselring looked at me. "Anything to add?"

"I liked it, looked wonderful. Who could possibly resist a pitch like that?"

Kesselring's lips pressed together. "You have something to say?"

I paused, struggling, but I couldn't help myself. "How has this 'happiness index' become such a central barometer?"

I was treading on thin ice with the Chinese delegation here, but the urge was too strong.

"Isn't happiness the central, single most important thing in a person's life?" Hal turned to me, assuming a defensive posture. His reality-skin began sporting the revolting smile he loved to use on his *EmoShow*. He looked like a weasel on Prozac.

"I wouldn't argue with you." I held up my hands in mock defense. "But this is supposed to be a serious medical evaluation, not a popularity contest. And *knowing* about happiness is different than actually *creating* it."

"Patricia," Hal responded in a measured tone, as if I were a guest on his show, "I think you have some issues going on here, some issues beyond this discussion."

"Don't try to deflect this."

"Of course not," he laughed. Now he was the one with his hands up. "I'm just saying, maybe you should have a look at your own happiness indices before you go knocking the program." He looked at me with raised eyebrows, trying to convey his simple, dishonest frankness to everyone in the room.

"I am perfectly happy!" I snapped before I realized what I was doing. Closing my eyes, I took a deep breath. *Little bastard.*

The room fell quiet.

Kesselring smiled toward our Chinese guests. "Let's move onto the next topic, shall we?"

Everyone nodded.

"So you all have the information about pushing the Infinixx launch ahead of the pssi launch. Who would like to open the discussion?"

"Give me one good reason we should let this happen," Dr. Baxter immediately fumed.

"You've seen all the phutures Nancy presented. Every scenario pushes the Cognix stock higher with early adopters," I countered. "You're only annoyed because it's not under your thumb."

"That has nothing to do with it," Baxter said peevishly, and loud arguing began around the table.

"Everyone, I will give you one *very good* reason," Jimmy shouted, standing up and raising his hands. He winked at Nancy. "I've managed to secure an agreement with both India *and* China to launch simultaneously with us."

Pandemonium broke loose for a few minutes while we reviewed the details.

"How in the world . . . ?" Dr. Baxter's voice trailed off.

"You're giving up a lot here," said Kesselring finally. "But the payoff is worth it, and it'll keep the media's attention off those damn storms."

Kesselring's eyes shifted toward Dr. Granger, who appeared about to say something, but then shook his head, staring at Jimmy. Kesselring looked toward Jimmy as well and smiled, nodding his congratulations. Then Kesselring turned to me. "I'm ready to make this happen, but I need one thing from you."

"Yes?" I knew what was coming next.

"I need you to put this Synthetic Beings Charter of Rights on the shelf until after the commercial launch of pssi."

I sighed and looked at the ceiling. "I can do that. But it will be at the top of my agenda as soon as we launch."

Kesselring smiled. "Then we're agreed."

Approving murmurs began to circulate. I reached out and held Nancy's hand in mine, smiling. I was so proud.

"So are we a go for a worldwide press release?" asked Dr. Baxter. He was Bob's father. *Talk about an apple falling far from the tree.*

"Yes," replied Kesselring, "assuming this is acceptable with our Chinese delegates?"

They nodded curtly in unison.

I wondered if they realized that nationality was another idea that pssi was about to render irrelevant. Or perhaps, more to the point, a good chunk of the world was about to become de facto Atopian citizens.

"Let's go ahead with the release. We are about to make history, ladies and gentlemen."

"Imagine, a trillion-dollar IPO," I heard Hal muttering under his breath as he reviewed the launch details, stars gleaming in his beady eyes.

The black granite and glass of the conference room melted into the deep mahoganies of my private office. I made for the bar.

A nice scotch on the rocks was just the thing I needed.

Marie was sitting against my office desk, her legs crossed in front of her as she leaned against it, propped up by her arms. Cigarette smoke rose slowly around her, and she took one more puff before stubbing it out in the crystal ashtray on the desk. She leaned forward, standing and waving me off. She'd get the drink.

"I know Hal is a pain, but you shouldn't let him get to you," she said as she plucked my favorite bottle from the collection. A glass appeared in her hand and ice cubes chinked softly together as she poured the whiskey over them.

"It's not that. I need to find out what Kesselring is hiding. Shifting Infinixx up on the release schedule was too easy. Granger folded without even a peep."

Marie raised her eyebrows. "Sometimes things just make sense, even to him."

"Maybe, but I have the feeling something else is going on. We need someone with, ah, special skills to have a look at this from the outside."

Marie nodded. She knew who I was talking about. She decided to switch topics. "Your old student, Mohesha, from Terra Nova called again. It sounded *very* urgent."

I shifted my pssi-body into a much younger version of myself and was now dressed in a black skirt and cream silk top while a sub-proxxi of Marie walked my real body home from the Solomon House. I looked down admiringly at my legs, sighing, and reached down to straighten my skirt, sliding a hand along my thigh as I did.

"It's too dangerous to talk with the Terra Novans right now."

"But not too dangerous to be talking with gangsters like Sintil8?"

"He doesn't really want to stop what we're doing, he just wants his cut." Criminals were reliably predictable in their motivations, if nothing else. "He has the kind of backdoor connections and freedom to operate that may yield some answers."

The problem wasn't just my suspicions about Kesselring.

The huge depression we'd been tracking up the Eastern Pacific had transitioned from tropical-storm status and into full-blown Hurricane Newton, with Hurricane Ignacia spinning up into a monster Category 4 out in the North Atlantic. The way these storm systems were behaving had gone from being simply unusual and to being downright suspicious.

By my calculations, these weren't natural storms anymore.

Taking a good, long drink, I straightened up and looked Marie in the eye.

"Set the meeting with Sintil8."

9

Identity: Jimmy Scadden

"I'm sorry, Jimmy, but that Patricia Killiam. Where does she get off talking about the nature of happiness? I'm really concerned about her."

"No need to apologize, Dr. Granger," I replied. "I'm worried about her, too. She hasn't been herself lately."

We were taking an aimless wander through a few floors of the hydroponic farms on our way back from Kesselring's office after the board meeting. Kesselring kept his offices perched at the very apex of the connecting structures on the top floors of the vertical farming complex. Even the master of synthetic reality liked to keep his specific reality above the riff-raff.

Over a hundred floors up, I enjoyed the views down on Atopia from here—green forests edged by crescents of white beaches and the frothy breakwaters beyond. Through the phase-shifted glass walls, the sea glittered under a cloudless blue sky. The humid and organic, if not earthy, smell of the grow-farms reminded me of the days I used to spend as a child out on the kelp forests with my dad.

"I'm getting tired of her routine as the famous *mother* of synthetic reality," continued Dr. Granger. "Sure, fluidic and crystallized intelligence are essential, but isn't synthetic emotional and social intelligence even more important?"

We'd all heard this speech before, repeated endlessly on his *Emo-Show*, and now that I was on the Council, I had the treat of hearing it in person as well. Dr. Granger's claim to fame was as the creator of the technology that could pick apart and decipher emotions, and you could be sure he wouldn't ever let you forget it.

I tried not to roll my eyes.

"What's more important to understand?" he asked angrily as we walked through the hydroponics. "What someone said, or the reason they said it? Who knows more about happiness than I do?"

"I'd say they're both equally important," I replied. Dr. Granger had used his growing fame to secure the position as head psychologist on Atopia, and no matter what one thought of him, it was best to tread a careful line.

He stopped walking and turned to look at me. "Exactly."

One of the grow-farm staff walked by and gave Dr. Granger a curt, respectful nod. Dr. Granger's office was a few floors down from here, far away from the other senior staff, which was unusual. Observing him on our walk, I think I knew why.

As we walked, he had been watching the blank faces of the psombie inmates, and each of the staff had almost stood at attention while we passed. It was a structured and controlled environment, one that made him feel both powerful and safe—and important.

Most of the psombies here were people incarcerated for crimes, their minds and proxxi disconnected from their bodies as they waited out their sentences in multiverse prisonworlds. Even in paradise, we needed correctional services. Their bodies were consigned to community work around Atopia in the interim, safely guided by automated psombie-minders.

While most of the psombies here were inmates, an increasing number were people who donated their bodies for community work while they flitted off and amused themselves in the multiverse. These people judged their bodies to be without enough value to even warrant leaving their proxxi to inhabit them. They'd effectively given up their physical selves.

"We'd better start a new special file on Patricia," he said after a pause.

It wasn't my place to argue. We continued walking.

"Shimmer!" he called out to his proxxi, who materialized pacing beside us.

Shimmer was a perfectly androgynous creature. As a synthetic being, sex was superfluous in the biological sense but still critical in others. It was Shimmer's ability to understand aspects of both genders and fluidly understand their emotional dynamics that had made Dr. Granger famous. It was his lifetime's work, although most people whispered that it was based on taking credit for his graduate students' efforts over the years.

"Yes, Dr. Granger?" Shimmer replied. "A new log entry on Dr. Killiam? It's already done, sir."

"Thank you, Shimmer," replied Dr. Granger, smiling at his proxxi. "Now please, I need to speak with this young gentleman privately."

"Yes, Dr. Granger." Shimmer faded away.

Dr. Granger looked sideways at me while clasping his hands behind his back as we continued to walk.

"Do you really think it's possible?" he asked, returning to our discussion. "I mean, with the technology we have now?"

"I do. The project has been going on for some time, as you well know, using some of your own work. Conscious transference—a lot of people have been working on it. But the trick, of course, is to get it right, for *you* to *stay* you in the process."

"And if I agree to support you, to support this, you'll make sure I'm the first?"

As good as medical technology was, there was always the risk of the unexpected, of some accident sending you, suddenly and irretrievably, into the forever of oblivion. Dr. Granger wasn't as concerned about his actual life, however, as much as he was about the immortality of his fame.

"Yes," I replied simply. "It will take some time, though certainly not before the commercial launch of pssi."

"Good, good," he said, apparently satisfied. He smiled at the mindless faces of a group of psombies that we passed. "You know, Jimmy, you're always working, you should find yourself a nice girl, find some emotional balance." He'd started into his *EmoShow* routine now, his face serious and concerned. "I'm sure a good-looking young man in your position must have girls throwing themselves at your feet. But you should find someone special."

Saying nothing, I nodded and we continued on our walk down to his offices.

I'd already found someone special, but I wasn't going to share *that* with him.

For a long time, I'd had my eye on Susie. She was a special soul, her emotions and sensations finely attuned, and I'd always felt like we shared a special bond. I'd known her as a fellow pssi-kid, but she'd come to my attention—and become a celebrity—as a teen when she'd turned herself into a living piece of installation artwork by mapping the emotional and physical state of each of the world's ten billion souls into her pain system. She literally felt the world's pain; a bloated stomach when the Weather Wars flared up in India, a burning calf for food riots in Rio, a painful pinprick when terrorists blew up a monorail transport in California.

Susie bravely bore the pain of the world like a Gandhi of the multiverse, imploring people to change their ways. Her impassioned pleas, featuring her painfully writhing nubile body, had been happily broadcast on obliging, bemused world news networks as the latest and greatest from the magical world of Atopia.

Her star had risen and, in turn, made her an object of both ridicule and inspiration. After a short while, though, the world had gotten bored and gone back to its media mainstay of killing and maiming.

For Susie, however, the project hadn't been a fad, but her calling in life. Even when the world had turned off, she'd kept going. In the process, she'd gained a small but die-hard following of hippie flitterati that protected her from the harsh mockery of the world she reflected, forming an almost impenetrable sphere of free-floating flower children that inhabited the metaworlds around her, like petals on a suffering daisy.

I'd been trying to reach Susie for some time, but it was difficult to get through her protective entourage. I needed a way in. My security systems had recently flagged some unusual and illegal splintering activity from an old friend.

It seemed I had found a way.

"You're in tight with Susie," I explained at a lunch with Willy McIntyre.

The light dawned in Willy's face, realizing why I'd asked to meet with him.

I'd kept the reason for our meeting secret, and upon arrival, I'd enclosed us in an extremely tight security blanket.

His needs began to spin the cranks behind his eyes.

"If you help me," I suggested, "maybe *I* could help *you*."

"Sure," he replied slowly, trying to hide his greed. "And what do you think you might help me with?"

"I could help you," I answered, "by getting access to higher-order splintering."

"Oh yeah? So what, you could double my account settings or something?"

"Much, much more than that," I laughed. "I could show you how to fix the system to have almost unlimited splintering. You'll blow everyone else in the market away."

He glanced at the glittering blue security blanket around us. "Nobody else knows what we're talking about, right?"

"Absolutely, Willy. I'm the security expert, remember?"

10

Identity: Patricia Killiam

I wondered how many ways this unpleasant specimen of humanity had inflicted death upon his fellow man—fellow man being something of a stretch given his own state of being. That said, Sintil8 projected the image of an attractive and urbane gentleman, his elderly face smiling warmly from under a manicured wave of properly graying hair. Intelligent eyes sparkled at me darkly.

"Nice press conference today." He flashed a mouthful of perfect teeth. "Such a wonderful thing you are doing, saving the world."

The sarcasm was as thick as his Russian accent.

"Thank you," I replied simply, refusing to rise to the bait.

We studied each other.

"So, Patricia, what exactly would you like me to find out for you?" he asked, his voice equal parts soothing and menacing.

"These storm systems, for one," I replied cautiously. "I want to know if this is some kind of new weapon. It seems the sort of thing you'd know about."

He laughed. "I see."

We were sitting in a sumptuous penthouse atop one of his many skyscrapers dotting the landscape of New Moscow. Views from the top of the world stretched out brightly below us in the midday sunshine, and I caught glimpses of the Moskva River snaking out into the smoggy distance below.

Sintil8 was comfortably draped across from me on a black leather couch, still dressed in blue silk pajamas, wrapped in a velvet house coat, and wearing gray fur slippers, one of which dangled casually off a foot as he crossed his legs. I perched uneasily on the edge of my matching couch.

As we spoke, one of his minions, or disciples, depending how you looked at it, swept smoothly across the landing to hand him another glass of scotch. Her scarred and mottled body was barely a shrunken stump suspended between impossibly spindly metal legs with matching thin metal arms.

Sadly, she wasn't all that unusual. Mandroids—humans with extensive robotic replacement limbs and parts—were becoming all the more common as entanglements in the Weather Wars continued to spread. Medical technology could stop soldiers in the field from dying from almost any inflicted trauma apart from major brain damage, and so had begun the steady stream of half-human, half-machine patchwork people into societies around the world.

Of course, this one was no soldier; she had done it to herself. Sintil8 was the leader of a grotesque cult that encouraged its closest followers to consume their own bodies, a literal ritualized eating of themselves that was matched with a gradual replacement of their disappearing body parts by robotic ones. Consuming themselves was the path to spiritual and corporal enlightenment—so preached Sintil8.

"Thank you," said Sintil8 as he accepted the drink.

The woman serving us was so devoted to this ideal that she had consumed her own eyes, I realized with horror as she turned to cast my way what she must have thought of as a smile. Dark caverns yawned out at me from where her eyes should have been. In the depths of the shadows at the backs of her scarred orbitals, I could see the glittering red of photoreceptor arrays.

"Tut, tut," Sintil8 chided, watching my expression as she walked away, "so quick to judge. And you, you're not creating any monsters, are you?"

I said nothing.

"No?" he replied, letting this hang in the air as he smiled at me, not bothering to conceal how much he was enjoying this. "And yet, here you are, coming to me for help. What a surprising turn of events this is."

Sintil8 was perhaps the most powerful and persistent opponent of the pssi program. As one of the greatest purveyors of pleasures in the physical world, not to mention arms dealer to all sides of the Weather Wars, the global organization he represented stood to lose a lot of money when pssi was released.

He'd been lobbying hard to have the brain's pleasure pathways removed from our pssi protocols, and we'd often been at each other's throats in closed-room government regulatory meetings around the world. Kesselring had finally won the day by portraying Sintil8 as a modern-day Al Capone–style gangster, lording over the weaknesses of the human animal from his fortresses in Chicago, Moscow, and other cities around the world.

It wasn't far from the truth.

Despite my suspicions and less than savory opinion of him, using an enemy-of-my-enemy sort of logic, I'd come to Sintil8 to try and help me root out what Kesselring was hiding. Really, it was more of a fallback plan in case I needed an ace up my sleeve, and also to see if I could find out what he was up to. The latest string of disappearances was the sort of thing he'd be capable of orchestrating.

"Look," I said, turning all this over in my mind, "I may be able to help you, if you help me."

"Now you're speaking my language," he replied with a smile. He scanned the information and data sets I'd just sent him, the details of a deal.

"*Ladno*. I will find out what I can," he said finally.

"Good."

A pause, and his smile grew wider. "How rude of me—would you like to stay for dinner?"

I shook my head. "Thanks, but no." I was afraid to find out what, or rather who, they would be eating tonight.

We sat and stared at each other. Despite expending considerable resources in Atopia's tussles with Sintil8, we still didn't have the full picture of the man. He was probably one of the few people alive older than me, and as far as we could tell, he'd risen up through the ranks of the Russian mafia in the late twentieth century after starting his career in Stalin's security apparatus.

Some reports hinted that he'd been a tank commander in the Red Army's defeat of the Nazis outside Leningrad, the battles in which he'd probably lost the first bits of his own body. We suspected he was just a brain in a box somewhere, but exactly *where*, we didn't know.

"We drink to our agreement," Sintil8 commanded as he raised his scotch. An identical glass dutifully materialized in my own hands. "*Budem zdorovy*," he intoned.

"Stay healthy indeed," I replied, raising my glass with his, drinking to seal our bargain.

11

Identity: Jimmy Scadden

In the days and weeks after the announcement of the Infinixx launch date, Nancy's profile in the Atopian community had increased dramatically. The press couldn't get enough of her. I'd been asked to help out, and I had splinters strung out in a seemingly endless stream of press events across the multiverse.

"Where did the idea for your distributed consciousness technology come from?" asked a reporter in one event I was canvassing.

The question wasn't directed at me. Nancy smiled beside me and began explaining how it had all come from the childhood game flitter tag that we used to play. She was gushing on and on, and it was beginning to annoy me. Flitter tag may have been the king of pssi-kid games, but my favorite had always been rag dolling.

It had been my own personal addition to our repertoire.

One day, Ms. Parnassus, our human teacher back at the pssi-kid academy, had asked each of us to come up and demonstrate a special trick or skill. Each child had risen in turn to show off something they could do. One inflated into a balloon, floating up to bounce around on the ceiling. Nancy showed off by holding a dozen conversations at once, with everyone around the classroom. Bob, of course, took us surfing.

Then came my turn.

"Come on, Jimmy," our teacher had encouraged, "show everyone what you showed me."

She gently rotated me into the center of everyone's attentional matrix. I nervously looked at my classmates—an arrayed collection of fantastical little creatures floating impatiently around in my display spaces.

Fidgeting, I looked down at my feet. They uncontrollably spawned into writhing tentacles that nervously knotted together like cave eels trying to escape sudden sunlight.

Giggles erupted.

"Go ahead," said Ms. Parnassus, nodding and smiling, prodding me on. She collapsed everyone's skins into my identity space, morphing us into a shared reality of children standing around the Schoolyard playground, with me at the center. I was now dressed in gray flannel shorts, with a matching sweater and a shirt with a little red clip-on tie.

More giggles. Mother insisted on this ridiculous outfit for my primary identity.

Oak trees arched between the swing sets and jungle gyms of the Schoolyard, reaching high above us like a leafy green cathedral beneath a perfectly blue sky.

"Come on, Jimmy, they'll love it, trust me," said Ms. Parnassus.

I nodded, gathering my courage, and set up my trick.

"Everyone, detach and snap into Jimmy. Now hurry up!" she clapped.

There were a few groans. The rest of the kids had little hope of anything fun coming from quiet, awkward Jimmy Scadden. Still, I sensed them all clicking obediently into my conscious perimeter.

Unlocking my pssi-channels, I felt them crowding inside me, feeling what I felt, seeing what I saw. The sensation was ticklish as they squirmed impatiently, waiting for something to happen.

Not many people had ever ghosted me before that, and I wasn't popular at flitter tag. Practically the only people that had been inside me up to then had been my parents, and then usually only to terrorize me. But that day was different, a shared experience rather than an intrusion. Despite myself, I tingled warmly and smiled.

"Isn't that nice?" said Ms. Parnassus, noticing me smiling. "Now show them what you showed me."

Taking a deep breath, I dove down into my body, shrinking, dragging them with me. I could hear their giggles back behind my mind. Down, down we dove, into the tiniest of spaces inside me, past bone and blood, squeezing past the granular limit of pssi-tech. I stopped for a moment, and then, holding my breath, pushed the limit further.

I squeezed our group of consciousness down to the molecular level, finally stopping inside one of my living cell nuclei to watch a newly hatched protein unfold. The kids became silent, engrossed. Then I shot back outward and upward through my veins and stopped again, the powerful thump of my heart filling our sensory space. I snapped our tactile arrays to the outside of my aorta, and we felt our skins expanding, contracting, my lifeblood flowing through us.

"Cool!" exclaimed Bob, followed quickly by a chorus of, "Show me how! Show me!"

Ms. Parnassus smiled, watching the kids all snap back into themselves and run to mob me in the middle of the Schoolyard.

Flitter tag was the undeniable king of games at the pssi-kid academy, but for a while, rag dolling became all the rage as I taught them to open up individual body parts and snap people into them. Moving the body around, each person controlled only their part, with the net effect being much like a drunken sailor trying to get home.

It was the start of my journey into the security of conscious systems.

12

Identity: Patricia Killiam

"So how does it feel, Adriana, or, rather, Ormead?"

I looked out at the view from our perch in the hills above Napa Valley. The lush greens of a late-summer harvest were staked out into the blue-shifted distance along perfectly ordered rows in the vineyards below. Swallows, weaving and darting in a silent dance, chased invisible insects in a sapphire sky.

I motioned to the waiter for another glass of Chardonnay.

Adriana was one of my test study participants who had recently chosen to composite with two of her friends, Orlando and Melinda. Compositing was a new process I was promoting that created virtual private pssi networks that tied people's nervous systems together. It was like two or more people continuously ghosting each other, but much more intimate. Compositing amounted to fusing the neural systems of the organisms involved.

"It's wonderful!" she replied with a glow in her eyes. Their partners had decided to composite as well. "The combination of Michael, Denzel, and Phoenix—Mideph—is everything we wanted in a mate—sporty, funny, a good listener, and passionate and artistic."

Composites were fitting nicely into the evolutionary chain as a new form of deep social bonding to help protect individual psyches from becoming overwhelmed in the multiverse. The cultural aspect of the human social animal was managing to adapt to pssi, but it was still falling behind.

I took a deep breath.

We were moving too quickly.

Whereas compositing in general was a positive evolutionary step forward, an opposite form of self-compositing was becoming a problem.

Before the shock of losing his body, Willy McIntyre had been well on his way to self-compositing into a social cocoon made up of only copies and splinters of himself. Now, from what I'd seen, he'd begun working his way back out, but only because he'd lost his body—not everyone would be so lucky.

Adriana, on the other hand, was part of a new class of composites that formed spontaneous holobionts to symbiotically form a protective barrier against their social networks devolving into isolated clumps within the multiverse. The history of evolution was more about symbiotic organisms evolving into new groups than simply a slow accumulation of new traits. In evolutionary terms, today's individuals were yesterday's groups.

Adriana and two of her girlfriends today were collectively inhabiting Adriana's body, and it still threw off my pssi because it posited her personal details in my display space. *We have to fix that.* I'd planned on making composites as much a part of the launch protocol as I could, but time was running out.

"And we are everything he really wanted," she continued. "A responsible, motherly woman who is career oriented but also zany and spontaneous. I don't think this could have happened any other way."

These little victories were what made it all worthwhile. Love was still that most powerful of emotions, magically finding ways to fill the cracks that pssi had fissured open in Atopian culture.

"So I heard you're going to have children? That's wonderful news!"

Without them reforming as a composite, offspring by any of them separately would have probably never happened. Post-pssi fertility rates on Atopia were approaching zero, but then again, that was counting fertility in the old, biological sense. If we began counting synthetic and biosynthetic beings, such as proxxi, fertility rates were actually skyrocketing.

It all depended on your point-of-view.

Adriana-Ormead smiled even wider, if that was possible. "Yes, we're going to use Adriana's body to gestate triplets," she gushed. "We're going to do it the natural way and just mix our six DNA patterns together randomly and see what comes up."

"That sounds wonderful."

Composites weren't just a meeting of minds. It enabled individual neurons in one body to connect with the billions of neurons in the attached composited bodies, using the pssi communication network to replace biological nerve signaling.

While this mimicked the dense connectivity of nerves themselves, it was creating neurological structures that had never existed, could never exist, in the real world, and people had already begun stretching the boundaries. Some had begun compositing with animals, with nano-assemblers, with robotics and artificial minds, even expanding their wetware into entirely synthetic spaces.

As new ecosystems emerged, life constantly evolved to fill them, and pssi had opened not just a new ecosystem, but an endless ecosystem of ecosystems. At the very start of the program, we'd begun experimenting with releasing the nervous systems of pssi-infected biological animals into synthetic worlds, creating rules of nature there to allow them to evolve freely.

The results had been staggering.

What was happening to humans as they released themselves into the pssi-augmented multiverse was an experiment in the making, and one we hadn't had the luxury of time to understand.

And all this had been just within the controlled and monitored experiment of Atopia, released into a few hundred thousand people living within a relatively homogeneous culture. What would happen when this was freed, unchecked, into the billions of souls in the rest of the world was anyone's guess.

I felt like I was witnessing the cyber-version of the Cambrian explosion a half-billion years ago, when the first elemental life had burst forth in diversity to cover the earth. Except instead of Earth, life was now flooding into the endless reaches of the cyber-multiverse, and instead of millions of years, evolution was now measured in weeks, days, hours.

"Our plan is to let them decide whether they want to composite themselves or not," continued Ormead, refocusing my wandering mind, "but it's hard to imagine why they wouldn't want to, knowing what we know now."

"I'm sure you're right," was all I could say. She'd started on a journey that I'd set in motion, but to a destination I could scarcely imagine anymore.

Sitting in my office, I was going over some research notes regarding Hurricane Ignacia. It was mind numbing. I decided to splinter in on a game of rag doll that some of the younger pssi-kids had started up in the Schoolyard. It was one thing to review data, but the data could never quite match the intuitive observations of actually sensing an event in process.

While the flitter tag game the kids played was straightforward from a game-theory point-of-view, rag dolling wasn't even really a game, and it was dominated by singular personalities. Flitter tag had the organic feeling of birds flocking, a murmuration, the madly fluttering splinters of the children's minds circling around each other in one body and then the next, in this world and then another. But rag dolling had an entirely different feeling to it, something decidedly uncomfortable. Watching these young pssi-kids at play, I couldn't help getting the feeling there was something I wasn't seeing.

The problem was in what *exactly* I couldn't see.

It was fairly simple to catalog the changes to the body as people switched from one to the other, added phantoms and metasenses, or switched into entirely synthetic bodies in the metaworlds. We could even track the neurological adaptations going on.

The mind, however, was an emergent property of all this, and more than just a sum of the parts. It was impossible to understand how minds were changing as a result. As Dr. Turing had observed in our conversations a century before, change the *body* and you change the *mind*.

Where before this had been a philosophical point, here on Atopia it had a very immediate and tangible effect. All of humanity had previously shared the same physical morphology, and therefore, more or less, the same mind.

But no more.

The human mind was not just the brain.

Our nervous systems extended throughout our entire bodies, including the ancient brain in our gut that was connected to our heads via the vagus nerve. When we said something was the result of gut thinking, it was truer than most people imagined.

By extension, human abstract thought was intimately tied to the entire human body: "she gave me the cold shoulder," "my hands were full," "I couldn't swallow it," and so on. When we changed the body, we began to change the way our mind conceived of abstract thoughts, even the way it constructed thoughts themselves.

Almost as soon as they could communicate with us, pssi-kids began to use a lexicon of abstract expressions that we couldn't properly understand, such as splintered-out, tubered, slivering, cloudy, and many more that developed as they did. But where we'd introduced pssi into our wetware as adults and knew the difference between real and synthetic, the pssi-kids had grown up with the stimulus embedded. Most of the distinction was lost to them. Their brains and nervous systems had developed together with pssi, and their minds had started to become something different.

They had become something different.

Changing the body was one thing, but changing the mind, now this was something else. As I watched these pssi-kids playing rag doll, I now had the eerie sensation of watching alien creatures before me.

The rag doll collective stopped and looked straight at the point from where I was observing it. I hadn't appeared in their sensory spaces nor flagged my presence, so it couldn't have known that I was watching, or even that I was there. And yet it stopped and stared intently at where I would have been, as if they knew what I was thinking.

As if they were staring straight into my soul.

Quickly, I clicked out and into the safe space of my office.

I shivered.

13

Identity: Jimmy Scadden

"Regarding our project, there is something I need you to do for me in return," I said to Dr. Granger.

We were back on another walk through the hydroponic farms. He'd wanted an update and confirmation of our deal to put him first in line for the conscious transference project.

"I want to be put into the research groups on memory and addiction."

"Consider it done," he agreed with a smile. Dr. Granger held out a hand to pass it through the green leaves of a plant nearby. He stopped to inspect one large, ripe tomato hanging in from its vines.

"And I'll need to get root access to Shimmer," I added, "and your own pssi system."

He let go of the tomato and turned to look at me. I could see the doubt turning behind his eyes, but then again, to become immortal, to secure his fame forever . . . .

"Yes, but with some provisos," he replied slowly. "I'll need to understand the details of what you want to do, but yes."

"Of course," I agreed. "You also understand we need to keep this private, just between you and me."

He narrowed his eyes and smiled.

"I don't want Patricia to be a part of this," I explained.

"Isn't she like a mother to you?"

He was trying to measure an emotional response from me, but I merely stared at him.

Patricia had never liked Granger, and I didn't want to create any more problems by making it public that I was working with him. As the lead on conscious perimeter security, I had a growing passion in the next evolving step of the pssi program: consciousness transference. We were still a ways off, but we were evolving ways to understand how the ethereal mind hovered somewhere within the physical cage of the brain where the seat of consciousness and our sense of self came together.

Immortality, or something approaching it, was close at hand.

Soon enough, as pssi flooded the world and mankind began flittering between gameworlds and sensorgies, an upgrade to their monthly pssi package would feature an option for conscious transference.

Transfer from what? They will ask. *From my old body? That thing I haven't seen in a year?*

And in an instant it will be done, the age-old dream of immortality realized with as little fanfare as the click of a button. They'll leave their bodies to collect dust somewhere in the corner of a garage like an old television set, eventually to be thrown out.

In this context, ceding executive control to pssi was like offering up your eternal soul.

Granger really shouldn't be quite so trusting, no matter what the possible gains. He was lucky he was dealing with me, and not someone else.

"She loves you," he added, watching me, fishing.

I flashed with irritation, but before I could say anything, he beat me to the punch.

"Sorry. I don't mean to test you—old habits die hard," he laughed. "I very much appreciate working with you. Consider me at your disposal for anything."

"Are you coming to the Infinixx launch tonight?" I asked.

"Wouldn't miss it for the world." He rolled his eyes, obviously no fan of the Killiam clan.

"Good."

He nodded, returning his attention to the tomato plant. "Anything you say, Jimmy."

14

Identity: Patricia Killiam

"TEN!.....NINE!...EIGHT!..."

Looking out at the packed crowd in the ballroom, I felt the excitement of the crowd rising. In the background, my splinter network scanned the billion-plus people who'd tuned in to witness the launch of Infinixx.

"Aunt Patty," said Nancy, turning to look toward me with tears in her eyes, "I've decided that I'd like you to throw the switch. Everything here is all because of you!"

The crowd continued to roar the countdown. "SEVEN!... SIX!..."

It was her moment to shine, not mine.

"I'd love to, sweetheart." But my physical self was back helping Vince on a wild-goose chase in the grow farms. Even if I'd wanted to, there was no way for me to throw this switch without my body here. "But I had a last minute thing come up, and I'm not here kinetically. You go ahead, dear!"

I kept my voice light, but my stomach flipped, realizing something was horribly wrong before I even understood what it was. Switching my pssi into identity mode revealed a completely empty ballroom. Not a soul was here physically, not even Nancy. A disaster was about to unfold, and I shot out a mass of splinters to try and avert it.

"FIVE!…FOUR!…"

"Jimmy, how about you then?" asked Nancy, still unaware. I was desperately trying to come up with a solution before telling her. "Go ahead. I really wanted it to be one of you two."

She released the switch and encouraged Jimmy to take it.

I couldn't find a way to reroute the power so I could bypass the switch. I tried unlocking the exterior security perimeter to let someone in, but Nancy and Jimmy had the security keyed into them. I pinged Jimmy for access.

At the same time, Marie queried the proxxi of all the senior executives up on the stage with us. Every one of them also had last-minute reasons for not coming physically. None had thought it would make a difference.

Exactly what I'd thought as well.

"THREE!…TWO!…"

"I'm sorry, Nance, I had something, too. I'm only dialed-in," replied Jimmy. "You go ahead…quick now!"

Jimmy's face registered his surprise as my access control request hit his networks and he also understood the position we were in.

"ONE!"

Nancy turned as white as a ghost. Her words now echoed in my mind, "Everything here is because of you." An audible *SNAP* rang out in the air as the Chinese and Indians flipped their own switches at their remote locations.

What's going on?

By now, Jimmy had unlocked the exterior security perimeter, and I could see a psombie guard racing toward the stage.

"Forget it," I heard echo in a distant splinter. It was Nancy speaking, her primary subjective still standing alone on the stage, utterly destroyed.

◆

Was I a woman who dreamt of being a butterfly, or a butterfly who dreamt she was a woman?

The butterfly in me yearned to escape.

My doctors were telling me the immunosuppressant nanobots in my bloodstream were attacking my own red blood cells after the latest round of genetic modification therapy, so I was now anemic, or something to that effect.

Running away from one tiger and leaping toward another.

In another splinter, right at the same time as the Infinixx launch was imploding, I'd been holding a different press conference. The disaster sparked an immediate and destructive media tsunami. Smiles started spreading across the reporters' faces, their incoming messages pinging, and they looked up at me on the stage.

"In short," I listened to myself saying, "for things to remain the way they are, things must change."

A few sniggers followed that comment, obviously related to the Infinixx mess and not something clever I'd said.

"Okay, next question," I said quickly, wanting to get this over with. Only a small part of my consciousness was there, most of the rest of me was trying to calm Kesselring. We'd had the whole world tuned in for the launch. He was furious.

"The responsibility for Infinixx is yours," fumed Kesselring. "This has injected serious uncertainty vectors into our phutures. Who knows what the ramifications could be. I'm going to have to remove you from the media circuit. The Killiam name is a joke, now."

Staring at the floor, I declined to comment. I'd been tired of the media road show for a long time already. He was posturing about the long-range phutures, but I knew he was really annoyed about the declining price of Cognix stock.

"The main timeline is holding steady," I added after a pause. "It's nothing to get excited about."

He raised his eyebrows.

"Nothing to get excited about? If I didn't know any better, I'd think that you were behind this."

"That I sabotaged my own niece's project?"

"You don't think this looks suspicious? Not showing up in person at the last minute, *everyone* showing up in their virtual selves in the last seconds, even Nancy?"

He glared at me. I looked away.

"I had to. Vince asked me for help. Do you think I could ignore him? After what *we've* done to him? Perhaps this was just a coincidence."

"A coincidence?" snorted Kesselring. "You expect me to believe that?"

Again I stayed silent.

"It must be the Terra Novans," he said finally, shaking his head and looking off into space. "You realize we're going to have to remove Nancy as the head of Infinixx."

At the same time, I had another splinter busy arguing with Hal—another battle of the happiness brigade—about new test results from the clinical trials on addiction.

"People compensate for a complex world by looking for escape," Hal explained as my splinter assimilated into that reality. "Look at the rise in reports of paranormal phenomenon. We know it's not real, even *they* know it's not real, but they need the escape."

It was just at that point that the Infinixx mess climaxed.

"Can we resolve the issue of making the new tests public another time?"

He shook his head. "Always an excuse with you, isn't there Pat?"

"It's just—"

He cut me off. "I know, the Infinixx disaster. The whole world knows, my dear."

My patience was already thin. "Doesn't it bother you that we're breeding a generation of lazy, self-absorbed sexual deviants with the pssi-kids? Is this the pursuit of happiness?"

"Deviants?" laughed Hal. "Lazy? Come now, Patricia, listen to yourself—and you're the head of the pssi-kid program!"

I stopped for a moment and considered this.

"I think you're just too old," he added with a nasty twinkle in his eye. "These kids do some amazing things, you know that."

Maybe he was right, but then I knew a few things he didn't.

"Forget the pssi-kids then," I conceded. "What about this disgusting trade in proxxids?"

He arched his eyebrows. "Again, deviants?"

"I for one hadn't planned on starting a whole new industry in sexual tourism for pedophiles," I complained. "Maybe that was what some of you had in mind, but I find it disgusting."

"Sexual tourism is a gross exaggeration."

I said nothing.

"Is it wrong, Patricia?" he countered coolly. "Is it wrong to have computer-generated models of naked children if they're not based on any real, specific child? Nobody is being exploited. It's a critical part of our therapy program for pedophiles."

"Still...."

"Your prejudice is blinding you," he continued, throwing my emotions back in my face. "This is just the way they were made. The pedophiles can't help it. It wasn't that long ago that society reviled homosexuals the same way."

"It's *not* the same thing," I objected.

"Isn't it? Isn't it better for them to come here, to find a therapeutic path forward? Technology is leading a cultural advance, bringing this long-maligned minority back into the fold."

"*It's disgusting.* It is absolutely *disgusting.*"

My mind was past the brink of exhaustion. *This is the path to happiness?*

Hurricane Ignacia was definitely crossing over from the Caribbean and into the Eastern Pacific, to be renamed Olivia. Hurricane Newton, which was spinning out into the Pacific as we backed away from it toward the coast, had stopped and even reversed its trajectory.

My projections soon had the Fujiwhara effect taking hold, connecting the two storm systems with their center-pivot at just the wrong point, preventing Atopia from escaping into the open ocean between them.

As my splinters simultaneously discussed the merits of virtual economies with the reporters, defended myself from Kesselring, argued about the nature of happiness with Hal, and considered the hurricanes rushing toward us—I felt the nauseating sensation of vertigo.

My visual fields distorted, ballooning outward, and the hurricanes and reporters shredded into each other. Kesselring's shocked face watched me blink out of his reality.

Abruptly, I collapsed into a deathly quiet, single-subjective point-of-view.

Exactly where, or why, I had no idea.

Marie, my proxxi, was standing over me, staring into my eyes. Everything was perfectly still. An impossibly long, incredibly thin rope stretched from the infinite blue void above to wrap itself tightly around my waist. I was suspended above a yawning black pit, set in the middle of an endless green field, all under a flawless sky.

Marie shook her head. "I'm afraid the news isn't good."

The rope tightened around my waist, choking off my lifeblood. I could feel the tigers charging across the sky toward me, their silent roars ringing in my deaf ears. Fascinated, I watched as nanobots busily ate away at the thin cord holding me suspended in space. Below me, in the blackness of the pit, an unseen monster grunted and slobbered.

This can't last forever, I thought to myself as I drifted in and out of consciousness.

I *can't last forever.*

15

Identity: Jimmy Scadden

"I heard that Kesselring put you in charge of Infinixx?"

"Only temporarily," I noted. "Someone has to hold down the fort."

Commander Strong winced. "How is Patricia doing?"

After the Infinixx mess, Patricia had suffered some kind of stroke. Not really a stroke—there was no physical brain damage—more of an overload of her pssi system. She was recovering under observation and isolated for the moment.

"She'll be fine," I replied after a pause. "I spoke to her this morning. She said she'll be back in the office by tomorrow."

We both returned our attention to the presentation.

"There is something very *unnatural* going on here," explained our mandroid guest to the assembled Command team. She reached down with one slender metallic arm to adjust the jumpsuit hugging her metallic legs. "These storms are definitely being driven artificially."

It was early Saturday morning, and we were in Command to review scenarios around the growing threat of the hurricanes that were pinning Atopia against the western coast of America.

"Do you think the Terra Novans are involved?" asked Commander Strong.

He smelled of alcohol. Things were going badly with his wife again.

"We're not sure," the mandroid responded.

"Do you know where this is coming from?" Strong demanded impatiently, rubbing the bridge of his nose and closing his eyes.

The mandroid shrugged. "We can't say for certain yet, but there's something too perfect about these storms."

"Jimmy, do you think you could look into this further?" The commander asked, looking away from the mandroid. "I need to go see Cindy."

"No problem." He was about to flit off when I remembered something. "Oh, wait. I have that date tonight, remember?"

Rick exhaled. "Susie, right? So that's going well then?"

I shrugged. He looked like he had a terrible headache.

"I can cancel if you want."

"No, no, keep the date," he sighed. "You can't let stuff like this stop you from living life. Anyway, I know you'll keep a few splinters around if I need you. I'll be back."

With that, he flitted off, and I returned my focus to the storms and our mandroid guest. More than one thing wasn't right here.

Tonight was my third date with Susie, and for this one, I'd received an invitation to meet in her own private world—a sensual, mystical place where the sun was eternally setting. She wanted to go for a walk outside her enclave, to chat, and I found myself strolling through a valley of knotted oaks and blossoming cherry trees that offered hidden glimpses of fantastical canyon walls beyond them. Waterfalls spilled into clouds of mist from high, craggy cliffs, and everything twinkled in shades of silver and gold.

As we walked, she stepped through a patch of yellow orchids as tenderly as if they had been children at play. The woody atmosphere was perfectly synthetically warm under an indistinct vanilla sky.

Her long, flaxen hair spilled down her back, held in place by a garland of white flowers above a flowing translucent gown. The breeze swept waves of glittering cherry blossoms and silvery oak leaves around us like a snowstorm, and fireflies sparkled in our wake as we walked through the perpetually gathering dusk.

"How's Patricia?" she asked. It was common knowledge we were close.

"She'll be fine. The doctors say she'll be back tomorrow or the next day."

"Good." She smiled warmly, but it soon vanished in a cloud of worry. "And these storms, we're not in any danger are we? I guess it can't be that serious if you're here." Her smile returned, a ray of sunshine.

"Don't worry about the storms," I reassured her. "I wouldn't advise going topside when they get here, but we'll be fine."

"Double good," she laughed, then flinched, her side going into spasm.

It was an event out in the world, some disaster that had triggered her nervous system. She had such an exquisitely tuned neural pain network—it was what attracted me to her.

I waited, and in a few moments the spasm subsided.

"It's nothing, I have this—"

"I know," I interrupted. "No need to explain."

I reached down to hold her hand and she smiled.

"So, Mr. Jimmy Scadden, my friend Willy speaks very highly of you."

I was wearing my ADF Whites and walking stiffly, a stark contrast to her flower-child projection. She spun in front of me, reaching up to snatch a blossom out of the air, and then stopped to curtsy, offering me the blossom.

"So what would an ADF *officer* want with me?" she laughed.

"I need your help. It's hard to explain."

"Need my help?" she giggled. "I thought this was a date?" She pouted playfully.

"It is." I looked down and away, trying to appear embarrassed. "I mean, I feel like you're someone who could be really special to me."

She danced away from me, trailing her hands through the flowers.

"I looked you up, Mr. Jimmy." She laughed, but then stopped and looked at me seriously. "That incident with the bugs, that was a bit odd, don't you think?"

I winced. "I was just a kid, finding a way to deal with my pain," I tried to explain. "You wouldn't understand. How could you? You grew up with such love."

She considered me for a moment. "What do you mean, Jimmy?"

I said nothing and sat down on a tree stump.

"Jimmy?" she asked again, more softly this time.

I cued my facial projection to reflect soulful pain. "My friends call me James."

She nodded. "Okay then, what is it, James?"

"I've never shared this with anyone, and I don't know why I feel like I can share it with you. Can we make this private?"

"Of course."

I pulled a glittering golden security blanket around us and took a deep breath.

"My mother, she...," I said unsteadily, but stopped as I let a tear glisten in my eye.

Susie sat beside me. She put her hand on mine and squeezed it, waiting.

I looked into her eyes. "It would be easier if I showed you."

She nodded and released her subjective control to me.

In an instant, Susie and I we were sitting in a corner of the Misbehave world my mother had created to punish me in. We were reliving a rendering of my inVerse from when I was barely two, and in front of us, sitting on a chair in the middle of an empty concrete room, was Mother, suspending my tiny two-year-old body in the air by one arm.

"It's all your fault!" Mother spat in my tiny face, the veins in her forehead swelling.

She fumbled with the pssi controls and then reached inside my body to dig her synthetic nails deep into my nervous system, scraping them down the length of the neural pain receptors in my body. I screamed in agony.

"Shut up, you little bastard. Nobody can hear you in here. Just shut up!" she yelled. I screamed, and screamed, my little face contorted purple in agony.

Susie wrapped her arms around me, horrified, tears welling up in her eyes. "Turn it off, James, please!"

And then, just as quickly, we were back in the forest with the cherry blossoms settling around us, sitting on the tree stump amid the deep grass and swaying flowers.

Susie held me tightly and cried. "I'm so sorry, James. I'll do anything to help."

I sat impassively, leaning to kiss the top of her head.

"It wasn't just my mother," I said after a moment, letting my voice crack a little.

"What do you mean?"

I looked away.

"Show me."

Nodding, I grabbed her primary subjective and took us back into another silently screaming night in my small sweaty body, the prison of my childhood world. My dad and I had just returned from fishing with the dolphins, and Mother was off in another one of her never-ending soapstim fantasies. With a security blanket settled around the house for the evening, my dad tucked me into bed and then crawled in beside me to cuddle.

"You had a good time with Samantha and the dolphins today?" he asked, holding me tightly and brushing back a few golden locks of hair from my pale face.

I nodded, my little heart beating faster with creeping terror.

"It's okay if Daddy holds you, right, Jimmy?" he asked pleadingly. "Daddy gets lonely sometimes, too."

I nodded, trembling, feeling his hands on me, his hands on places that felt wrong. I loved my dad, and I could sense he needed something from me. He'd been nice with me that day, bringing some joy into my dark and constricted little life.

So I let him touch me while I disappeared down my rabbit hole into the recesses of the pssi system. He touched me all over with his real hands, his phantom hands, enveloping my body while pleasuring himself.

I cowered in the depths with my make-believe friends.

"Don't tell anybody about these times with Daddy. It's a secret. If you can do that, I'll make sure to take you out to play with Samantha, okay?"

And so I hid inside and waited for the bright days of rocketing through the foam and spray.

I snapped us back into real-space where Susie was crying again. I was, too.

She looked into my eyes. "We can tell people, we can punish them. You poor soul . . . ."

"That won't change anything."

She kissed me between her tears.

"But *you* can help me."

"How, James? I'll do anything to help."

"I just need you to do something for me."

16

Identity: Patricia Killiam

It took two full days for me to recover, and in that time a world already spinning out of control had taken a steep descent into chaos.

We were hardening Atopia for a now-inevitable collision with the storms and discussing the possibility of a full-scale evacuation. The rate of unexplained disappearances was spiking, and in the midst of all this, I received a ping that Rick's wife had committed some kind of reality suicide.

It seemed she hadn't actually been terminating the proxxids. It wasn't hard to guess what had happened. Reality suicide was a new phenomenon, tied deeply into the way pssi interacted with our unconscious minds.

"I'm so sorry, Rick. Has there been any change?"

I'd requested this emergency meeting with Rick because my Command communication network had been shut off. No one on the Council was responding to me.

"It's hard to tell," he replied unsteadily. "I mean, she looks fine. She looks like she's asleep. I wish...."

"I don't think blaming yourself is going to help," I offered. "We cracked the security blankets covering the worlds she was in before this happened, but we don't know the full story yet."

Rick wiped his face with the back of one hand, staring down at the floor. We were sitting in my mahogany-walled office. Pictures of ancient, four-masted sailing ships lined the walls.

"We know enough of the story to know how we got here," he said with a dead voice. Then his mood shifted. "This is *your* fault. *You* recommended using the proxxids." He looked at me with dark eyes. "You have *no idea* what you're doing, do you?"

I recoiled. This was a combat soldier after all.

"I don't think laying blame is constructive at this point." *I didn't exactly* recommend *the proxxids.*

"We're all just lab rats to you, aren't we?" he growled, venting his anger. "I know what you let people do with proxxids—I've looked into the whole thing—it's disgusting. You disgust me." His breathing was ragged. "You have no idea what you're doing to people, do you?

"Rick, I'm sorry . . . ."

"Sorry isn't good enough. The time for experimentation and best efforts is over." He stood up.

"What does that mean?"

"Getting away from these storms. We're taking control from here on. This is now a military matter." He shook his head, avoiding my eyes, and flitted away without another word, disappearing from my office and back to Command. He didn't even leave a polite splinter behind.

I was stunned.

The storms continued to defy phuturecasting, and we were running out of room to back away from them. It was obvious something was directing their development, but despite all our efforts—swarming the sea with smarticles, launching countless surveillance drones, and everything and anything else we could think to throw at the problem—we couldn't even begin to stop the storms or understand what exactly was happening.

Usually, two storm systems of this magnitude in one oceanic basin tended to dissipate, one into the other, but these two were actually pumping each other up and expanding.

It was unlikely that we'd sustain core structural damage, even in a direct hit by either or both of them, but that was making the sorts of assumptions that trapped us here in the first place.

Now I understood why my communications had been cut off. Rick was formally taking control, declaring martial law, and putting all civil power in the hands of ADF Command.

"Marie, could you send me the latest reports?"

I reached down to smooth out a wrinkle in my skirt, trying to regain my composure. Marie looked up at me from some files she was studying.

"We've had something of a breakthrough," she responded. "The high surface temperatures seem to be caused by migrations of dino-flagellate blooms. Someone out there has been planning this for a long time."

She splintered me all the data sets before continuing. "Some-one seeded the ocean surface with iron dust to grow bioengineered plankton, and they're now directing huge swarms of the tiny crea-tures, sucking energy from one part of the ocean and into another."

"Can we stop it? Can we find out who's doing it?"

She shook her head. "We can see what's happening, but nothing more than that so far."

"Was Sintil8 able to find anything?"

"He was some help," she replied with a nod. "What we're look-ing at could be a new addition to the Weather Wars arsenal."

Directed cyclone warfare would add a whole new chapter to the ongoing book of human conflict, but, of course, weather had always been a decisive factor in war.

Five hundred years before, the British victory over the Spanish Armada had less to do with the genius of Sir Francis Drake and more to do with a week of wind that pinned the Armada against the French side of the English Channel. The wind had held the Spanish in place, giving the British the opportunity to float fire ships into the hapless Spaniards, destroying the fleet before it even had a chance to attack.

The defeat of the Armada had halted a Habsburg land invasion by forces at that moment poised to cross over from the Netherlands. The direction of wind, for a few short days, dictated the outcome of the next five hundred years of global geopolitics, even the rise of America as a superpower. What we faced now was far more than simply a breeze blowing in the wrong direction.

"We can't fire weapons at blooms of microorganisms, nor at hurricanes," added Marie. "We're just going to have to stay out of their way as much as possible. If you want more detail, you're better off speaking with Jimmy."

That was going to be difficult, given the state Rick was in.

"Or perhaps Bob?" I suggested, considering our possibilities for fresh insight. My Command communications were cut off, but there were a lot of other people who might be able to provide some additional input. "He has a lot of experience directing little creatures like you're describing. Why don't you talk with him?"

Marie nodded, but then paused.

"What?"

"It's strange," she replied. "Yes, we can see how they're doing it, but the numbers don't quite add up. Even with what we've discovered, they shouldn't be able to direct weather as severe as this."

I didn't understand. "Could you be more precise?"

"It just doesn't add up," was all she could say, shaking her head.

"It sure doesn't."

Too many things remained unexplained, too many loose ends were accumulating, and Rick was right—we didn't know what we were doing. I was going to have to stop this freight train, even if it meant risking everything.

"I'm going to try talking with Jimmy."

I sent him an emergency ping on a personal channel, outside of the Command network. To my surprise, Jimmy accepted immediately, and my office faded away as my primary subjective was channeled into a private deprivation space surrounded by a heavy security blanket. His communication network was open to me, but Jimmy's primary presence wasn't there.

"Jimmy," I called nervously into the void, "what can you tell me?"

17

Identity: Jimmy Scadden

I held Patricia carefully in the anonymous security blanket. Rick wouldn't be happy finding me talking to her right now.

"Things are under control at Command," I said. "Preparing for a state of emergency is just a precaution, and having the tourists leave is the sensible first step."

"I don't disagree. What I mean is—do you know who's doing this?"

"Isn't it obvious?" The list of possible suspects was thin.

She took a deep breath. "You really think it's the Terra Novans? You have proof?"

"No," I admitted, "but who else could it be?"

Everyone knew they wanted to slow down the pssi program, to give their own product a chance in the market. The commercial stakes were huge.

"We need proof. It doesn't make sense. The risk of an offensive like this completely exceeds the potential returns. I need you to find out what's going on."

"I'm on it," I replied, a little exasperated.

"And keep an eye on Rick—he's shut me out."

This was beginning to feel like nagging. "I will, Patricia, I promise."

"I love you, Jimmy. You take care, okay?"

"I will," was all I said. She looked hurt. "Bye for now."

I cut off the channel. She knew how busy I was.

It was hard to concentrate on her needs with my mind so widely splintered. Samson and I were spread far and wide throughout the multiverse, trying to figure out how someone had managed to target Atopia like this without us getting advance notice.

Patricia was right in one thing—we had to keep an eye on Rick. Despite declaring himself in charge, he wasn't much use anymore. I knew Rick's wife had been depressed. We'd all been concerned, but this reality suicide had taken things on a new and disturbing path.

It was, however, something I could relate to.

My own mother was a hopeless soapstim junkie in addition to being a drunk. It was bad enough to be disinterested enough in your own life to patch into someone else's, but Mother didn't even go that far. Her favorite pastime had been patching into synthetic soaps, an endless universe of autonomously generated and farcically campy dramatic-romance worlds.

Mother hadn't even bothered to give up her life for someone else's experience—she'd given it up for an empty, soulless simulation. It was like a gameworld for her, but instead of facing down some challenge, she just sensed it passively while the soapstim told her that "her" ex-husband wasn't dead, but had been in a coma for twenty years and was now in love with her stepsister's boyfriend, or some other nonsense.

Living in passive fantasy worlds made for a painful reinstatement when she returned to her real life. Being out for so long all the time, her brain's wetware lost much of its neural connectivity with her physical self, so when she came back, she had to drive her body around using her proxxi, Yolanda, as an interface to her intentions. It gave her a jerky, unnatural way of moving, which only fueled her constant frustration.

"You little worm!" she would scream at me as she settled back into her body after a long session, already a few drinks into calming her nerves. Mother wasn't very technical, but she was an expert in using security blankets to screen her sessions with me from the outside world.

"It's all your fault!" she would slur. "That dirty bastard."

As a parent, she had full access to my pssi, and I had no way of blocking her out until I was granted full control of it myself. In her worst moods, she would amp up my pain receptors and reach into my nervous system virtually to squeeze, pinch, and pull on it. It left no physical marks, but it was excruciatingly painful, and I'd squeal and scream in the private Misbehave world she'd created for this special form of punishment. Even as a toddler, I began to learn ways to hide and crawl into the cracks of the pssi system, deep into the darkest corners, away from anyone else. I slowly found ways around the blocks and cages Mother tried to keep me in, sliding past the pssi-controls to hide. Samson would crawl in with me, along with all the friends we'd created to hide together with us.

Down, down I would dive, into the deepest recesses of my body, trying to hide my consciousness in the submolecular gaps between my stinging, screaming neurons while she tortured me, sinking her virtual nails into my pain centers for crimes I didn't understand.

I never understood what I'd done wrong, but I assumed I must have been bad. Samson would just sit beside me, staring numbly while she abused me.

The learning bots and teachers at the academy had noticed I was falling behind the other children, but they just thought I was slower. In their well-intentioned naïveté, they figured I needed more parental attention.

"Gretchen," explained Ms. Parnassus during the initial parent-teacher interview that occurred at the end of my first year at the academy, "I think you need to restrict his access to the gameworlds. He's distracted, like he wants to be somewhere else all the time."

"I do try," admitted Mother truthfully. She did do her best to cut me off from everyone.

"I try to take the time for private lessons with him as often as I can," she added with a sweet, crocodilian smile, "but you know how it is. He can be such a handful."

Ms. Parnassus smiled reassuringly at us both.

"Isn't that right, Jimmy?" my mother added, turning to me, flashing her teeth. "You don't want to *Misbehave*, do you?"

I sat terrified beside her, a shell hiding inside a shell. I didn't want to do anything to anger her, and I desperately didn't want to be snatched off to Misbehave. I shook my head and smiled bravely, holding back tears.

"He's a bright child," said Ms. Parnassus. "He scores extremely high in the gaming systems, but he has a hard time socializing."

I never got on well with the other kids in the Schoolyard, the education-portal balanced halfway between the real and synthetic worlds where young pssi-kids played. Extremely shy, I mostly played by myself, though Bob and Sid sometimes managed to drag me into the occasional game of flitter tag with the rest of the kids. Without escape to my own private worlds, and restricted to the Schoolyard, I found it difficult to focus my mind.

"And he's a little *devil* to keep on hand," added Ms. Parnassus. "He slips and slides away if you don't watch him every second!"

"That he is," Mother agreed, nodding, "and that he does."

"His mind is always somewhere else," Ms. Parnassus continued. "It's very hard to keep him focused."

"Oh, he's just always been that way, haven't you, Jimmy?" Mother fluffed my hair. I was terrified.

"Does he have any special things that you do together? Stuff that just you and he do when you play?"

"Oh, you and your daddy play, don't you, Jimmy?" laughed my mother, smiling at me cruelly.

"That's nice," said Ms. Parnassus. "Is there anything he's particularly good at when you play together?"

"The little rascal is very good at hiding." Mother crinkled her nose at me, showing her teeth.

"Like hide-and-seek?"

"Something like that."

In her lies, my mother was being honest. If there was any game that I was good at, it was hide-and-seek.

I was the master of hiding in plain sight.

18

Identity: Patricia Killiam

Of all the illusions our minds used to support their ephemeral frameworks, time was the most contradictory: both incontrovertible and yet intangible. Time's arrow was just a slide down entropy hill as the universe tended toward its finale of disorderly conduct. At the end of entropy was the end of change, and thus the end of time, and apparently, I was about to cease changing, too.

"I'm sorry, Patricia," said my doctor. We were disembodied, floating in black space between millions of phosphorescent dots that raced to and fro, spreading out through the root systems of my basal ganglia.

The doctor and I were examining my brain.

"There's nothing more we can do?"

"Not with the technology we have. I'm afraid things have taken a turn for the worse," he explained. "There are some experimental treatments, but I can't promise anything."

Watching the dancing dots of light, I tried to fully make the leap of understanding that I was watching myself from inside myself.

The doctor was at a loss to explain what was happening, but I had a growing suspicion I knew what it could be. If I was right, I wasn't sure I wanted to stop it.

"Please do what you can, doctor." An illusion perhaps, but time still stubbornly seemed to end for those of us witnessing it in action. "I just need a little more time."

"Don't we all," the doctor replied, watching the neon pulses of my nervous system race around us. "Don't we all."

Floating up at the edge of space, the two converging hurricanes swirled ominously in three dimensions below us. We had almost all of Command and Security watching the storms as we ran the simulations. They were building in intensity past Category 4, and like two enormous threshing wheels, they threatened to pin and crush Atopia against the coastline.

The way they were gaining strength, it was obvious we were going to end up taking some damage—the only question now was, *how much?* All the tourists had already been shipped off via the passenger cannon, but it would be impossible to get everyone off Atopia if the worst happened.

Strangely, none of the Atopians wanted to leave.

"We need to order an evacuation of the outer habitats," I observed.

Everyone looked at me. Cut off from the Command, perhaps, but I was still a member of the Cognix Board of Directors. I had a right to be there.

"Moving at this speed, the kelp forests are already shearing off," I added. "No matter which way this goes, we're going to lose most of it."

This had serious implications. The kelp forests were the foundation of our ecosystem, and turning to America for help if we ran out of food for our million-plus inhabitants wasn't an option.

The last time California had sustained a direct hit was over a hundred years ago, when the hurricane of 1939 had slammed into Los Angeles. This time, it would be two at once, and at a far greater magnitude. On top of this, tropical storm John, thought to be dead weeks ago, had somehow regained strength and was reversing direction toward us.

"Whoever's responsible is going to pay for this *act of war*," Kesselring growled, pointing an accusing finger down at the storms below. "It has to be Terra Nova!"

"We don't know that for certain," I pointed out, but this was the wrong thing to say.

"Not for certain? Who else could it be?" raged Kesselring. "A bioengineered organism seeded across two oceans, quietly sucking up the sun's energy and swimming about to pump up and guide these storm systems. Who else could pull this off?"

"What's more important right now is surviving," said Jimmy, redirecting Kesselring's focus. "We have detection systems to stop this from happening again, but right now we need to focus."

As Jimmy spoke, Kesselring relaxed. "What's the worst-case scenario?"

I was about to speak up, but Jimmy waved me off.

"Worst case is we'll be run aground on the continental shelf, just south of Los Angeles. Major damage to the outer habitats, but the main structure is more than strong enough to withstand the storms."

I shook my head. "The *worst* scenario is that these progress past Category 5 and crush us. No matter what, our data systems will go offline. The fusion core should remain stable, though, and I doubt we'd sink."

"*Should* remain stable? *Doubt* we'll sink?" Kesselring fumed. "So best case, we end up beached in American territorial waters?"

"Should we plan on delaying the release?" I asked carefully.

"No," replied Jimmy, raising some eyebrows.

My question had been addressed to Kesselring.

"The world still sees us as in control," Jimmy continued. "The public doesn't perceive Atopia as being in any danger, even with these storms, so the pssi release schedule isn't in any danger. If we begin delaying the release, we'll open up a can of worms, and who knows what else Terra Nova has planned."

"Exactly, we have no idea what whoever planned this has in store," I argued. "We need to delay!"

"Let's not go down that path yet," Jimmy said calmly. "Give me six hours to assemble a special team. I can figure a path through this."

"My vote is with Jim," Granger chimed in, looking toward Kesselring.

Jimmy made eye contact with each of the assembled Council members one by one, earning a nod from each. The final nod he received was from Kesselring himself.

As the Security Council meeting broke up, I materialized back in my office under an extremely heavy security blanket. Marie was waiting for me.

"So it seems we may yet be doomed to relive the past," she said as I arrived. "Atopia, the island-city of the future, filled with magical beasts and people, may slip beneath the waves—legend passing into legend."

I rubbed my temples. "We need to slow things down."

Our phutures had destabilized. Everyone's resolve to keep the program on track, despite the mounting risks, had been the last straw to force me into unilateral action. Things were out of control. I had to act alone.

"Give Sintil8 our authentication key to initiate," I instructed Marie. The pssi program would suffer in the short term, but it needed to be done. "And did you set up the meeting with the Terra Novans?" The time had come to lay all our cards on the table, for everyone's benefit.

Marie nodded. If a proxxi could look nervous, she did now.

"We're going to get to the bottom of this," I assured her. "I need to talk with Jimmy."

I pinged an urgent request for him to come down to my office in his first subjective and Marie disappeared. Leaning back in my chair, I tried to think of the right way to broach a new and troubling discovery that Marie had dug up.

A moment later, Jimmy appeared in one of my attending chairs, looking annoyed. This was a new Jimmy, all hard edges, and again I felt uncomfortable.

"I've got a lot on my plate right now," he said. "What's so important?"

I looked toward the ceiling, and then back at Jimmy, observing him carefully. "I've been trying to locate your parents, but I can't find them anywhere out there."

"I have no idea where they are. To tell you the truth, I couldn't care less."

"No idea?"

I'd taken a huge chance at the meeting, secretly installing invasive pssi-probes into the smarticle cloud during the session to find out if the people I worked with were being honest. As far as my probes could tell, Jimmy was telling the truth.

"The last I heard, they were back in Louisiana. Did you send some bots down there?"

"Yes. I've tried everything I can think of to locate them."

Jimmy's face darkened. "Just like you can't find the dolphins, right, Patricia?"

Where did *that* come from?

"What are you talking about?" I asked. "What dolphins?"

Years ago, there'd been an unresolved security incident that had proved the beginning of the end of civil relations with Terra Nova. One of the outcomes had been the revocation of the work permits for our uplifted dolphin friends. We'd had to send them all back to Terra Nova, but they'd all been happy and healthy. I'd even checked in on the beautiful creatures myself on a trip to Terra Nova a few years back.

Looking at Jimmy's furious expression, I realized something was very wrong.

19

Identity: Jimmy Scadden

I held Patricia's gaze firmly, feeling anger boil inside me.

I don't have time for this.

"I don't know where my parents are," I replied with finality.

We hadn't kept in touch after they'd left Atopia, or, more accurately, after they'd abandoned me. I was only fourteen at the time, but Patricia had already begun to take me under her wing by then. When they'd left so abruptly, she'd swooped in like a savior angel, pulling me in tight.

I felt bad about being so short with Patricia now, but lately she'd started to annoy me as I discovered her various hypocrisies. Her loyalty to the cause, her *own* cause, had become as thin as any pssi illusion.

On the other hand, if it weren't for her, I wouldn't be where I was now.

I remembered the moment when Patricia had first come into my life. Almost involuntarily, a splinter wandered off, back into my inVerse to experience the moment again, perhaps to try to rebuild my bond with Patricia even as I felt it slipping.

◆

Soon after my fourth birthday, Patricia had dropped in for a visit with my parents. Nancy Killiam and I were distant cousins, but our side of the family was where the dark horses ran. Patricia saw an opportunity to bring us back into the fold when Atopia was being planned and had extended a generous offer to my parents to join the project.

It hadn't exactly worked out as my family had hoped, or at least as my mother had hoped. She thought we were going for a drive down Entitlement Road. The cramped, three-room cell near the bottom of the Atopian seascraper complex, hundreds of feet below the waterline, didn't live up to her expectations.

Patricia's visit that day was both rare and uncomfortable.

"We've been following Jim," she said, accepting a hot cup of coffee from my mother's proxxi. "He's showing some amazing talents."

Mother grimaced. "You sure you have the right Jimmy? Little stinker here is only good at hiding from Mommy, aren't you?"

Patricia watched my mother carefully, then smiled. "He *is* very good at hiding and evading. He manages to slip through some of our tightest security fences, like a little fish wriggling through our fingers."

"Yes, a little fish!" my mother exclaimed, holding me close and trying to exude maternal warmth. I flinched like a hand-shy puppy.

"But there's something else."

"Nothing serious I hope."

"At Jimmy's last checkup, his nociceptive pathways were showing some very unusual activity. We'd like to add his data feed to the child-monitoring network. Would that be all right?"

"His *what* pathways?"

"His nociceptive pathways, the neural network of his pain receptors."

"And what's unusual?"

"It's just unusual, like they're in some kind of disarray. He doesn't complain of any unusual pain does he?"

"Of course not, do you, Jimmy?" Her smile was menacing.

Wide-eyed, I shook my head.

"So can we add him to the monitoring system?"

Silence.

"*Patricia*, we've been over this a thousand times before with the Solomon House staff. We have our right to privacy," Mother declared theatrically. "I'm happy to be here, but there are limits!"

Despite the histrionics, she had a valid point. Patricia herself had baked strict privacy controls and rules into the foundations of the laws and systems governing the pssi system. Individuals and families had an absolute right to their privacy, unless there was some good reason otherwise.

"Is there anything wrong with Jimmy?" my mother asked. "Is he healthy?"

Patricia sighed. "He's perfectly healthy. His mind seems distracted, and there's some unusual neurological activity, but physically, he's perfect."

"Well then...."

Patricia thought for a moment and then stood and walked to our side of the table. She sat down on the couch next to us and put an arm around me, looking up at my mother. "Could I take a more active role in Jim's development? As a teacher, if you see what I mean. I don't want to intrude on your mothering, of course."

Mother eyed her, weighing the situation. "That would be an honor, of course," she replied after a moment. "Wouldn't it, Jimmy?"

It was less a question than a statement.

I sat dumbly between the two of them, unable to say anything, cringing, sure that Patricia was about to become part and parcel of some new awfulness in my small life. Fearful of the horrors awaiting me, I dug in deeper and deeper, building my shell.

As they bid each other good-bye, I got up and slipped away to hide away from my mother, sliding into tiny worlds within tiny worlds for refuge. Mother quickly gave chase, however, eventually cornering me in the Little Great Little, past fields of glowing jellies, under a thunderfall whose white sensory noise I often hid behind.

"I know you hide here, little worm," she said, her voice oozing venom. "Don't think I don't know where you go."

Hate distorted her features here, her skin flaking red and crimson, and her hands turned into fearsome claws that she gripped and scratched me with. Pulling a tight security blanket around us, she squeezed me until I thought I would pop.

I squirmed and whimpered.

"Not a word to Aunt Patty, little worm, do you understand? If you say anything to anyone, I'll tell them all about you and your daddy. Do you want that?"

Smiling at me, she laughed from a fanged and fearsome mouth.

"No, Mommy," I squealed, "not a word, of course not."

I began to cry.

"Such a little crybaby." Mother waved her claws around at the purple canyon walls. "None of this is real."

And then she was gone, popping out of the Little Great Little and into another one of her soapstim fantasies to burrow away from her own pain.

Dad must have known something was going on because he appeared just after Mother left, looking pale and dejected. "Don't say anything about you and me, Jimmy. It's secret, you know? They would put me away in the farms if you told anyone, Jimmy. Do you want to turn your dad into a psombie?"

I shook my head. "Of course not, Daddy. I won't tell anyone."

Samson, who'd remained quiet, emerged from his hiding place under the thunderfall, and we sat down together, holding hands. Dad left us there without saying another word.

My fascination with pain began very early. Sometimes, we won the topside lottery for passes to go above. I vividly remembered those days, those rare moments when we could enjoy the air above-decks. While my parents would sun themselves on the beach, I would hang at the edge of the palms and palmettos nearby.

At the fringes of the dark forest, I would summon little creatures to venture forth into my hands. Taking great care in their capture, I'd stimshare into them to feel their squirming pain as I slowly pulled off their legs, one by one. When all of their legs were gone, I would gradually squeeze them between my chubby fingers, flitting into them to feel their spasms of agony as I crushed their legless little bodies.

Feeling their agony helped me cleanse my own pain.

And, perhaps, I enjoyed it a little, too.

20

Identity: Bobby Baxter

"Sid!" I yelled out into our private emergency channels.

"Jesus, Bob, what is it?" he replied as his reality merged with mine.

I watched Sid working, engrossed in some data-mining blitz as he searched through reams of multiverse worlds. Even with the storms threatening, he was still on the hunt for Willy's body, his dozens of phantom hands dancing through the hyper-control spaces around him.

"If you play with your phantoms too much, you'll grow hair on them," I couldn't help joking as I watched him and Vicious working their magic.

"No more Humungous Fungus this week, I've had enough, buddy." They gave me several fingers. I watched them fiddle around some more.

"So what has your hair on fire?" Sid finally asked.

"I need your help to infiltrate the Cognix networks."

That stopped them in their tracks. Sid looked at me and cracked a smile, all his phantoms dropping to the ground.

"Let's get the band back together," I continued.

"Jimmy, too?" Sid asked. Vicious was vigorously shaking his head behind him.

"I think we'll let Jimmy sit this one out." Jimmy had bigger fish to fry, and something about him made me very uneasy. "But I'm going to ping him and tell him we're doing our own storm research. That way we won't raise any alarms if we scan the perimeter." I thought about this for a second. "And I want him to know what we're doing."

"Sure," said Vicious, "just don't tell him too much."

That wasn't a problem. I didn't know anything.

"I think we should get Vince in on this, too," added Sid.

Nodding, I pinged Jimmy, shifting my primary subjective into a tight and secure channel that he opened up to me. My perspective shifted into a small, pristine white room, where I found myself seated at a white interview table. Jimmy had his hands clasped on the table and was staring directly into my eyes.

"Did you find Wally yet?" He cracked the faintest of smiles. "What's going on? No surfing today?"

21

Identity: Jimmy Scadden

"No," replied Bob, "even I couldn't handle what's going on out there right now."

The storms had converged. Winds were tearing at the forests while an angry ocean pounded the beaches mercilessly. Surface access would be shut off soon as we finished stowing everything and everyone below decks.

Incredibly, the storms were getting worse. As they neared the coast, and each other, they defied all physics and gained in strength, progressing past Category 5 into something terrifyingly unknown.

We'd already entered American territorial waters, and their air force and navy was scrambling to surround us, battling their own way through the storms. Atopia and the US were close allies, but the prospect of having a wholly independent country slide across the map and run aground in California had raised some hackles, even if they understood we had no choice. The fact that Atopia contained a fully energized fusion core raised the diplomatic tension bar just that much higher.

Of course, the anticipation of two giant hurricanes simultaneously slamming into one of America's most populated coasts had them already preoccupied. Communications were strangely incoherent. It may have just been the storms, but we seemed to be getting contradictory diplomatic messages from one moment to the next.

Despite it all, I had a plan for our escape and had been running phutures of it right at the moment Bob had pinged me. As busy as I was, Bob's primary subjective calling me on an emergency channel was unusual enough to warrant the attention of a splinter.

"So what can I do for you?" I asked, not bothering to explain how busy I was. Bob was many things, but he wasn't stupid.

"I think I can help find out who's doing this."

"Really?" I raised my eyebrows. "And just how do you propose to do that?"

"I know how busy you are, so I won't waste time on details." Bob looked down at his feet, "From all the time we spent together, you know I have special abilities. Just trust me and open up some ports for me to scan the multiverse."

I looked at Bob. Memories from our long-past childhood friendship flashed to mind. There was nothing to lose. "Go ahead, but feed us back anything you find."

In any case, I'd keep a close eye on him. I dispatched several agents to watch his movements. "You got it, Jimmy."

I closed the connection, returning to the escape simulation. A giant fireball filled my primary mind.

"Looks like it'll work," said Samson. We were scheduled to present our plan to the Council within the hour. "Why don't you take a quick break, decompress before the meeting?"

That seemed like a good idea. Samson could handle it from here.

The fireball slipped away and I relaxed, letting my mind wander back to Bob's offer. I was surprised he had any interest in helping out, but then again, the last time he'd helped me out had been the biggest catastrophe of my childhood.

◆

As a kid, I'd secretly thought of Bob as my big brother, and in another twist of fate, that's what he'd become when his family had adopted me at Patricia's suggestion.

I always had a hard time fitting in. The easy way the other pssi-kids socialized and made friends always elluded me. Bob was the only one who'd tried to be there for me, doing his best to help me when the others ignored me.

My special pssi skills had brought me to the attention of the Solomon House Research Center at a young age. Academically, my life had taken off early, but my interpersonal skills had foundered hopelessly.

As I got older and gained in pssi power, I finally managed to escape from the oppression of my parents. I learned to slip past their every attempt to corner me, and as I blossomed into a teenager, I was finally beginning to taste my own freedom—but Nancy Killiam's thirteenth birthday party was the disaster that defined the rest of my life.

My own thirteenth birthday had been just around the corner. I was worried that nobody would come to my party, most especially Cynthia, the girl I'd developed my first crush on.

While girls my age generally ignored me, one day Cynthia had magically taken an interest in me, asking about my research work at the Solomon House. I had no idea how to react or what to do, so I went to the only person I knew to talk to.

"Look," said Bob back then, "you just gotta stop acting so weird."

He squinted into the slanting sunshine and raised one hand to shade his eyes. We were walking across the beach toward the circus tent where Nancy's party was being held. Waves broke softly in the background, and the air was filled with the smell of cotton candy and the sounds of children at play.

I shrugged. "What do you mean?"

"You know what I mean. All that snooping around, hiding where you're not supposed to be." He looked me square in the eyes.

My face flushed red. The other pssi-kids had already begun their tentative sexual explorations of each other, not just rag dolling or flitter-switching, but taking a real interest in their blooming, newly adolescent bodies.

I watched it all happening, awkwardly, hanging in the shadows. Sometimes, unknown to them, I would slip in between and into them as they kissed, sharing sensations and stimswitching with each other. Pain was my childhood specialty, but these new emotions and sensations intrigued me.

"Everyone's talking about you, you know," Bob continued, scratching his head as we passed into the shadow of the tent and moved toward the entrance.

My dad had come ahead of me, the only one dragging a real gift under his arm, which I found embarrassing. I saw him standing off to the side under a glade of palms talking with some other adults, patting his prize affectionately.

More kids and parents were quickly arriving in ones and twos through portals near the entrance: here a furry, argumentative little minotaur being dragged by his mother, and there two screaming pink teddies trailing fluorescent balloons. Everyone's reality skins fused and melted together as they entered, producing a confusing kaleidoscopic mash-up around the entrance as they stopped and looked around before fanning out inside. Some parents were arguing with their kids to merge their realities with everyone else properly, arguments that were erupting into tantrums from both sides.

Bob looked around for somewhere quiet to talk.

Organ grinder music started up, and little monkeys dressed in evening suits appeared, scuttling between the assembled guests, handing out information packs for the evening. Drinks and snacks floated and bobbed in refreshment islets. Bob took my arm and led me to a bench off to one side, under the shade of some saw palmettos.

"I know you don't have many friends," said Bob in a hushed voice, "and I know it can't be easy for you." He paused, searching for words. "First thing, quit with the splatter skins, those were funny when we were kids, but it's a bit odd when—"

The head of one of the nearest adults shattered in a gory explosion of brains and skull fragments, as if hit by high-caliber rifle fire. The headless, bloody victim casually picked up a drink that floated by, pouring this into his gaping neck wound.

Bob glanced at this and looked back at me, shaking his head reproachfully.

I smiled awkwardly and switched it off.

"I know you're the king of the rag doll, but nobody wants to play that anymore, get it? And stop asking people if they want to come inside your body with you, it's starting to get weird."

I nodded. I knew these things, but I couldn't help it. I promised myself, right there, that I'd stop.

"We all know you're this specialist at finding cracks in the pssi system," he continued, "but you gotta stop sneaking around. We're adults now and adults don't sneak."

Of course we weren't, and, of course they did. I nodded again, regardless.

"You'll quit sneaking into people's bodies when they're not looking?" He waited for me to nod, and then added, "Why don't you come surfing with me, whaddya say?"

"Sure, Bob, you're right. I mean, yes, of course, I'd like that," I mumbled, anxious but grateful.

Bob had always been nice, but this was the first time he, or anyone, had a heart-to-heart with me. It was both scary and exciting.

"So you'll come surfing?" Bob smiled toothily.

I grinned back. "I will."

He gave me a little punch in the arm—we were buddies now, I guess.

"So about Cynthia . . . she's a girl, and girls want you to open up, be sensitive." He laughed, looking into my puppy-dog face. "Okay, you already have the sensitive part down."

"She said she wanted to see something fun," I suggested helpfully.

He considered this. "Yeah, girls like cool stuff. Perfect! Just open up to her a little. Why don't you show her some of the stuff you've been working on at Solomon House? That should impress her. Girls like smart guys."

"You really think so?"

I had some new neural interface models I was testing with Dr. Granger. He'd taken a keen interest in my abilities. I kept the models in my personal workspace and hadn't let anyone in there before.

My private worlds were very private.

After learning ways of keeping my mother and father out of my special worlds, I didn't really let anyone near me, emotionally or physically, and I spent most of my time alone with my proxxi Samson and our simulated friends.

"Open up a little, she'll love that." Bob laughed, winking at me, and then raised his eyebrows, giving me a little poke with one of his phantoms to indicate something behind me.

With a shake of his head, he stopped me from looking around. Instead, I snuck a peek behind me without turning my head, over-laying part of my visual channel with a local wikiworld view, and saw Cynthia coming up behind us. She noticed my ghost checking her out anyway.

"Go get 'em, Tiger," Bob said encouragingly as he got up to leave. "I've gotta go catch my own sweetheart."

Bob and Nancy had been intertwined almost since birth and had grown into the pssi-kid power couple. He walked back to the gathering crowd, leaving Cynthia and me alone.

"Hey, Cynthia," said Bob as he walked past her, looking back to wink at me again. Cynthia smiled at him and turned her gaze toward me. I began to sweat profusely.

"Hi Jimmy, what's up?" came Cynthia's singsong voice. She skipped the last few steps up to me.

"Not…much, how…how are you?" I stammered, my mind going blank. After a few seconds of agonizing silence, I cried out, "Cynthia!"

"I'm great!" she replied brightly, smiling shyly. "How's your research going?"

"Uh, yeah, good…." I thought of what Bob had said. "I could show you some of the stuff I'm doing at Solomon House if you like."

"Really? Cool!" Her eyes and smile widened. "Can we go now?"

I nodded. *Why not?*

"Mom!" she yelled, and her mother's face floated up between the two of us.

"Yes, Cynthia? You don't need to yell, you know," her mother admonished.

Cynthia continued unfazed. "I'm going to flit out with Jimmy for a bit. He's going to show me some of the stuff he's working on at Solomon House."

Cynthia's mother looked suitably impressed.

"Work at the Solomon House? But you're just a baby," she remarked, looking my way and furrowing her brow. "Sure, go ahead, but I'm pinging you back the second Nancy gets here."

Cynthia grabbed my hand and squealed, "Let's go!"

Feeling her hand on mine sparked an electric shock that spread like wildfire through my body, settling hotly in my crotch. An erection immediately sprang to life. Cynthia sensed something going on from my embarrassed, flushed cheeks. She looked at me mischievously.

"Come on, Jimmy, let's go!"

I pulled her back and away, and we dropped out from our bodies and into my private workspace. I'd never brought anyone there before and I felt naked.

In one layer of my visual field I could see Samson inhabiting my body back at the beach, holding hands with Cynthia's proxxi near one side of the blue-and-yellow tent. They were watched carefully by Cynthia's mother's proxxi as they went off to get some cotton candy. I smiled.

Cynthia and I were standing together in a white laboratory with gleaming floors and walls. We looked out at a view through smoky windows onto Atopia below, the same view as from the real Solomon House atop the farming complex.

Above stainless steel tables floated a variety of working models of mirror neuron interfaces that Dr. Granger and I were studying. He shared my interest in the physiological bases of emotion and the ability to use it to direct the hive mind, but where he was more interested in happiness, I had taken more of an interest in fear—something the other researchers had mostly passed by.

While we walked, I keyed through some parameters with my phantoms to wash away the tables and structures, replacing them with my current project. A model of the neuron appeared, looking like some kind of deep-sea monster, slowly rotating and floating in space in front of us.

I was keenly aware of Cynthia's grip on my sweaty hand.

"Cool," she said, watching my model light up, demonstrating a visually enhanced synaptic firing sequence. It was a working prototype.

"This isn't just a model," I explained. "This is actually happening inside me right now!"

After some testing, I'd installed them in my own developing wetware to see how they would respond. I started explaining how it worked, the way this enhanced mirror neuron provided a more reliable pathway to empathy. Empathy was something I was working on. I didn't understand it, or rather, I understood it, but I just didn't feel it. This model was my path forward.

As I explained the details, Cynthia wandered off, exploring the rest of my workspace. I wanted to show her something really special, and engrossed myself in my model, burrowing through the cell walls, trying to change some protein pathways.

"What's in here?" she asked, opening a door.

"Oh, ah, nothing!" I cried out, but it was already too late.

As soon as the portal opened a crack, she dropped into the world beyond. I'd never let anyone in here, so I'd been lax with the security protocols of the worlds it was connected to. I quickly abandoned my model and shot off into that world after her.

Instantly, I was standing beside her in semidarkness. Shafts of light bore down from blackness above, illuminating a writhing mass of insects and worms and other creatures that were pinned painfully to the walls of my labyrinthine private universe.

An image of my mother's face hung in space above us, twisted in hate.

"Who's my little stinker?" she repeated over and over again, her face contorting and distorting.

I came here to heal myself, to reconnect and re-stimulate some of the sensory pain I'd felt as a child. The process seemed to allow me to refocus my mind. I would pick out some particularly nasty memories and then work through them bit by bit, simultaneously bathing my sensory system in the pain from the thousands of little creatures I had pinned to the walls.

I didn't understand why, but it helped.

Cynthia shivered and looked around with wide eyes, scared but excited.

"This is so creepy," she whispered, staring at the half-illuminated animals scraping and clawing futilely, never dying, never free, always trapped and in pain.

Looking at the hopeless little creatures, tears welled up in her eyes. "I can feel them," she squeaked, her emotional networks starting to connect into this world's. "This is horrible!"

Then, she was gone, flitting back to the birthday party.

Shocked, I stood still, the blood draining from my face. I wasn't sure what to do. I closed down the image of my mother, and the space went dark and quiet, apart from the soft wriggling of the creatures on the walls.

I hadn't remembered that there was a portal to this place from my workspace. At the time, I was too flustered to think clearly. I began quietly swearing at myself, but then I felt Samson grabbing me, pulling me back to reality.

I snapped back into my body with a sudden sense of vertigo. There was laughter, but I wasn't back at the party. Somehow, I was in my private space again. The bugs were squirming on the walls as before, but now all the party guests were standing in the middle of it, and the bugs were magnified, giant monsters vainly trying to pull their bodies from the pushpins stuck through them.

Above it all, my mother was venting down on us, "Who's my little stinker?"

Cynthia had stolen a copy of my world and projected it out here in public. I shrank in horror. All the kids were laughing, with Cynthia in the middle, pointing at me and screeching, "Who's my stinky Jimmy!"

The adults were dumbfounded as to what was going on. It happened too quickly for them, but someone regained control of the situation, and the big-top tent reappeared with the balloons and monkeys. Everyone turned and looked at me, the kids laughing and giggling, the adults staring without comprehension.

"Why did you do that?" I screamed at Cynthia.

An intense, burning anger beyond my searing humiliation filled me. All the years of containing my fear, my frustration, my hiding and cowering, it all boiled over the edges of my psyche. *I could kill her, right now.* The world turned a bloody red in front of my eyes, and demons shifted somewhere deep inside me.

Cynthia shrank back into the protective knot of her friends, all of them still laughing.

Gathering myself, I focused on her, channeling my voice through the pssionics and amplifying it beyond deafening.

"Why did you do that?!" I bellowed, my body growing into a grotesque, monstrous caricature.

A shockwave of pure hatred burst from me, almost knocking over the assembled guests. I felt as if I were about to physically explode when I caught myself and stopped. My anger imploded back into me, and the bottle corked back up.

The laughter stopped. In fact, it was deathly quiet, except for whimpers from some of the smaller children. Shocked faces turned toward me, watching me warily.

Someone started crying.

It was Cynthia.

At that moment, Nancy Killiam opened the portal door and announced, "I'm heeeere!"

I began to run, tears streaming down my face, shoving my way past Bob.

"Jimmy, hey Jimmy . . .," he tried to say as I ran past him, almost knocking down Nancy.

I ran and ran, trying to escape the blinding glare of their judgment. By that point, I was already gone, detached, and it was Samson taking over my body to hide it somewhere safe.

I was already back in my private world and it was burning. Great flames were consuming the walls and rooms and corridors, all the nooks and crannies of my childhood. The countless little creatures trapped there squealed in a high, keening agony as the blaze devoured them.

I watched impassively as the inferno consumed itself and flamed out.

Never again, I promised myself, *never again.*

They say what doesn't kill you makes you stronger. On that day, I felt myself shatter and schism. But then I began to reform, to heal and grow, becoming an adult perhaps, but certainly becoming something different.

The developing child inside me, my personality until then free-floating, coalesced and hardened. Invisible things fell into place, the pain stopped, and the shell finally finished closing around me, opaque, and powerful.

Impenetrable.

A few days later, I was studying for the Solomon House entrance exams at home.

My mother had just arisen from the dead—quite literally from being dead in one of her soap-stims—and was making her way clumsily toward me. She had a fresh drink in hand.

"Hey, stinker, I saw you embarrassed yourself at that Killiam party. What the hell were you thinking?" she half-slurred, half-laughed at me. "Some security expert you are." She sniggered, taking a swig from her drink.

I watched her blankly.

"They killed the dolphins you know," she added, cruelly recalling a major security breach that had been the start of the end with Terra Nova. "Dirty, smelly fish, serves them right."

Still I said nothing.

"I guess nobody is coming to your party, huh, stinky Jimmy?"

She was right. No one was coming to my upcoming birthday party, not anymore.

Mother was behind me, turning away to refill her drink. I slowly closed the interface to my notes and twisted around to face her, pulling down a dense security blanket that enveloped us in a glittering glacial blue.

She turned back to me. "What?" she barked. "Something to say, little worm?"

"If you ever talk to me again, Mother, if you ever so much as lay a hand on me, or utter one more word to me from that trashy, dirty mouth of yours," I said, slowly and evenly, "I will make sure that you regret your very existence."

I smiled to make the point, opening up her pssi channels and filling her emotional inputs with pure hatred. She stared at me, about to say something, but then stopped herself. Terrified, she turned and shuffled away, and I released the security blanket with a flick of a phantom.

"Enjoy the soapstim, Mom!" I called gaily after her and returned to my notes.

I'm going to ace this test.

22

Identity: Patricia Killiam

The winds whipped and howled, churning the surface of the ocean into a frothing maelstrom. Gigantic waves surged and crested, propelled by the driving storms. The collision of two Category 5 hurricanes was a once in a mega-annum event, and Atopia was a seed about to be crushed between these two grinding wheels.

And then, bright pinpoints of light appeared, flashing through the sheets of dark, whipping rain. More pinpoints flared through the downpour and began illuminating the heaving seas. They multiplied, glittering and flashing into a sheet of superheated plasma that vaporized the rain, sending plumes of mist rocketing up through the atmosphere.

We were all in Command, watching this on a projection in the middle of the room.

"The slingshots weren't designed to be used this way," Jimmy explained as we watched the growing inferno begin to notch a tiny gap between the colliding storms. "Usually, they're only used in sustained operation for a few minutes to take out incoming kinetic threats, but we've made some modifications to sink away the heat. We should be able to operate them continuously for at least a few hours, maybe more—long enough to get the job done."

The viewpoint on the projection swept away and upward, zooming backward into space until we could see most of the colliding hurricane systems with Atopia highlighted on the seas between them. Jimmy accelerated the simulation speed, and we watched as a narrow gap between the storm systems appeared and Atopia was sucked through it.

"We'll use the slingshots to blaze a super-high-pressure system through the middle of the two colliding storm systems. Then we'll drive Atopia at maximum speed straight into it. The relative vacuum we create will literally suck us through as we burn a path forward with the slingshots."

Jimmy smiled as the highlighted pinpoint of Atopia popped through to the other side of the storms in the simulation.

A singular, loud clapping punctuated the room. It was Kesselring, beaming at Jimmy, and everyone joined in.

"You've saved us!" Kesselring cried out. "Brilliant, simply brilliant!"

Relief that we would escape destruction in the storms almost overwhelmed me. I couldn't help but join in the applause. It was ingenious, and it looked like it would work.

"It will be a bumpy ride through," added Jimmy, "but not too bad." He waved away our applause.

Kesselring leaned over to me confidentially. "Excellent work in bringing Jimmy onto the Command team."

"Thanks," I replied, nodding, but my clapping trailed off as I spied Rick standing off to the side, his expression vacant. "Looks like it will work," I agreed, "but if you'll excuse me, I need to get back to something."

I collapsed my primary subjective away from Command. Marie had already poured me a scotch, and I sat down behind my desk and put my feet up.

"Through the storms we go," said Marie gravely.

I took the drink from her and stood. Unconsciously I began pacing back and forth.

Marie brought up the phutureworlds we'd been working on for so many years now, their projections floating in my display spaces, staggered from the most critical to least, filling my eyes with death and destruction. She was bringing them up to make a point.

"None of this makes any sense," I complained, taking a sip from my drink.

My view of warfare was fairly academic. Open warfare was, in essence, an information-gathering exercise. From a game-theory point-of-view, attack and defense were designed to resolve the capabilities of opponents until both sides converged on the same assessments.

I'd openly shared almost all information regarding Atopia to avert such a conflict—"almost" being the operative word. Perhaps by sharing what we were hiding, I could negotiate a peace with Terra Nova, but it was hard to shake the feeling that I was a traitor to my own cause.

Even then, I couldn't imagine Terra Nova being so desperate that they would purposely direct powerful hurricanes onto the densely populated West Coast. Even a weakened America would be sure to retaliate, violently, after the damage these storms would cause. Terra Nova was ensuring its own destruction.

Once upon a time, when we'd just started Atopia, I'd helped lay the foundations for Terra Nova as well. I was perhaps the only person on Earth who could fix whatever was happening.

"Are you ready?" Marie asked. "This may be our only chance."

With all the attention focused on the emergency at hand, a window of opportunity had opened for us to talk with the Terra Novans directly and in secret—a chance to strike a grand bargain. "Everything is set up?"

"They're waiting," Marie replied. Seconds ticked by.

"Very good. Initiate."

We exploded upward out of my office, squeezing through a tight communication channel in the Atopian perimeter, and then dispersed, clipping and mixing our sensory packets around the globe. We rematerialized in a large, warmly lit room with wooden walls that arched in vertical panels to intertwine and spiral together to form the ceiling.

On closer inspection, the walls weren't paneled, but were living tree trunks growing tightly together, and the place glowed with a light that seemed to emanate from nowhere. I was seated beside Marie at a large stone table.

Across from us sat the Elders of Terra Nova. In the middle of them was my old student, Mohesha. She nodded at me, smiling, and I smiled back. My distrust began to melt away.

The senior Terra Novan Elder, Tyrel, began speaking, "It is with gratitude that we accept you in our council today. We know this is a great personal risk."

It hardly mattered anymore. *My days are numbered* was what I wanted to say. I just wanted things to be right, to do the right thing.

"I also am honored." I nodded deeply. "I come here today to negotiate a peace."

Without emotion, Tyrel watched me. "We have great respect for you, the mother of all of this," he said, sweeping his hand around the table, "of all Terra Nova, and more, of all synthetic intelligences and worlds—"

"Thank you, but I'm not here to collect—"

"You've been used, Patricia—deceived. You've even deceived yourself!" interrupted Mohesha. Her dark features glowed in the soft lighting.

"I'm not here out of desperation," I said firmly, ignoring her. "We're beating this storm trap. I am here simply because I want the same things as you."

Silence.

"Even if we wanted to, and we do, we could not help you," replied Tyrel.

"You must see the destruction coming," I continued. "You know we've been hiding some of the details, but the pssi program is the only solution."

Tyrel and the rest of the Elders watched me sadly.

"Chasing happiness, by giving people anything they want, has never been the path to salvation," said one of the other Elders after a pause. "Satisfying every material and sensual pleasure will not lead to peace."

"But surely you have seen what I have seen!" I shouted, slapping the table. "You have to stop what you are doing. It will only lead to your own destruction!"

Dead silence. Absolutely no reaction.

"After Atopia escapes, I'm going to the media, to tell them what I've been hiding," I explained. "I've already started it through Sintil8. It will slow the release and we can collaborate."

"We know about Sintil8," said Tyrel. "We know what you've been planning with him."

"What do you want then? Is it money, a share of the profits?"

"How far you have fallen," Tyrel stated sadly. Tears came to his eyes. "You can no longer stop what you have created."

"Is all this just about stopping the pssi program so you can position yourselves better?" I asked incredulously.

"This is not about the pssi program." Tyrel wiped away his tears. "By itself, we would have been happy to evolve together, in a symbiotic coexistence under your dominance, but you've unleashed an unspeakable evil into the world. We must destroy Atopia to stop it."

"What are you talking about?" Then a light winked on. "So you admit to creating these storms?"

My mind raced. Had Sintil8 double-crossed me? Had I made a fatal mistake in bringing him so close to me? Was he the monster I'd unleashed? How had Terra Nova managed to jump so technologically far ahead to control weather like this?

And how do they think they can get away with it?

"Yes, we *created* these storms, as you say," Tyrel admitted, "but I cannot say more, and even if I could, we don't have the full picture. We believe the key to what is happening is contained in William McIntyre's body."

"Willy?" I asked, remembering the report on Bob's friend. I became even more confused. "Did you have something to do with Willy's body disappearing? Why?"

"It was through his proxxi Wallace that we first understood the potential magnitude of the danger," admitted Tyrel, "but it was Sintil8 who helped Wallace disappear from Atopia using the access keys you granted. Wallace was acting to protect William."

Things were spinning into nonsense. All I understood was that Sintil8 was involved in the disappearances.

"We have no time for this," I objected. "We need to make a deal *now*. You've seen the same phutures I have, there is *no* other solution. If you don't stop this, you'll be destroyed!"

"We've seen the phutures," agreed Tyrel, "but you didn't take into account one scenario."

"And what is that?" We'd played out billions of phutures.

"The destruction of Atopia."

That stopped me in my tracks. It was true—all of our phutures included Atopia as a component of the solution set.

"This is a trap of your *own* making," explained Tyrel, "and yes, you may escape these storms...."

My head spun. *Had my pride blinded me?*

"But, regardless, before the sun rises tomorrow morning, Atopia will be wiped from the face of this world."

23

Identity: Bobby Baxter

Smiling at Nancy, I stuffed more pasta into my mouth.

"Think of it like getting ready to run a marathon," I explained. "We need to do some carb-loading, to help build up our smarticle reservoirs. Keep eating!"

We'd both been storing much more than our usual load of smarticles from the Atopian environment, from smarticles floating in the the air we breathed to smarticles embedded in the food we ate, far beyond even our own high tolerances.

Nancy nodded and continued to eat methodically, looking down into her plate. It had been a long time since I'd been this physically close to her, and memories were flooding back. The way she looked at me, she was feeling it too. With some effort, I kept my mind from splintering and scuttling off into the past.

"I don't like that we're hiding from Patricia," she said, looking down into her pasta. "Do you *really* think she's up to something?"

"I don't know," I admitted, "but we need to keep an open mind, keep a low profile."

She nodded, then frowned. "Why tell Jimmy then?"

"Just a hunch." I wasn't able to explain much more than that. "Knowing that he knows what we're doing allows us to watch him watching us, if that makes any sense."

"And we won't set off his alarms when we're scanning the Atopian infrastructure," added Sid.

Nancy shrugged. "Sure."

Willy, Sid, Vicious, Robert, Vince, and Hotstuff were all sitting at a table with us in a dingy little cafeteria in a deep, forgotten corner of the Atopian service infrastructure below Purgatory, the entertainment district.

We were as close as we could get to the routing core of the pssi network, and for what I wanted to do, reducing distance latency to the core would help minimize transactional delays, giving us an edge over any self-correcting algorithmic blind spots that might be installed in it. We were going to plug in, as directly as we could, and watch for anomalies to emerge.

"Go over the plan again with me?" Nancy carefully considered her noodles before taking another mouthful.

"You have the most neuroplastically flexible mind for handling wide-area splintering," I started to explain.

"It's like you can be everywhere at once," added Vicious.

Nancy sighed. "Everywhere but the place I should have been."

She looked directly into my eyes. My heart leapt, pounding.

"We need your head in this completely, or not at all," I replied softly. "Are you sure you're up for it?" It wasn't going to be easy.

"I'm in, Bobby, you've just surprised me, is all." She held my gaze steadily.

I smiled. "I like to be full of surprises." Back to business. "Sid is making some changes to my water-sense so it settles around information eddies—"

"So you can sense waves of information about Atopia?"

"Exactly. You and I are going to composite, then recombine via your Infinixx tethers to push my water-sense into thousands of composite splinters. We'll push these into every nook and cranny of the multiverse."

"Then I'll amplify and cross-connect your network into the billions of private Phuture News feeds that Vince will open up to us," continued Sid. "And Bob will wait for interesting waves of information and then follow them in."

"You sure about opening the personal phuturecasts to us?" I asked Vince, giving him another opportunity to back out. "If it leaks, it'll be the end of Phuture News."

Vince laughed grimly. "My situation can't get any worse than it is. I want some answers."

During the last half hour, Vince had already had to flit out three times to save his own life, but he appeared the most awake and alive of all of us.

Nancy looked at me. "What we're doing could kill you."

"I doubt it." I smiled. "Anyway, it's less dangerous than surfing."

"When you surf, you don't purposely cook your brain. Are you *sure*?"

I took a deep breath. "Anything to get naked with you."

She laughed. "All you had to do was ask."

"Yeah, well, I like special occasions...."

"Okay, lovebirds," laughed Vicious, "time to take a cold shower. We gotta get this show on the road."

Quickening a composite like this was tricky, and for the best possible chances at cognitive coherence, we needed to be as close together as physically possible. Nancy had to be right there with me to reduce distance delays between our coupled nervous systems, but I was going to be taking the brunt of the quickening intensity, and we needed to disperse the energy generated. Off to one corner of the room, we'd filled a large tub with ice and water—even with all the technology at our disposal, it was still the simplest and most direct way to heat-sink energy away from a body .

I glanced at Nancy nervously. "Ready?"

She nodded and began to undress, although she remained modestly clothed in her pssi-projection. I did the same, and we walked over to the tub of cold water, holding hands, surrounded silently by the rest of our gang.

"Good luck," said Vince, leaning in to give us both hugs.

I looked into Nancy's eyes. She was quivering.

"I love you, Nance. Don't worry, I got this."

As we stepped into the cold water, I gently felt her out with my phantoms, and she responded to me, welcoming me in the myriad hyperspaces where we connected. Our synthetic bodies locked together around us like the wings of angels, enclosing us in a protective, otherworldly cocoon.

Finally, we stepped physically together, embracing as we lowered ourselves down into the frigid water. Cradling her head below mine, I initiated the compositing sequence, and the hundreds of billions of neurons in my nervous system began virtually fusing with hers. Our minds began to flow together.

"Just breathe slowly, in and out," I told her, "and on each breath out, we'll push the quickening a little more."

Closing my eyes, I let my consciousness merge with Nancy's, then felt her pushing me out, splintering me further and further, spreading us across the multiverse. Our minds and bodies began quickening, and an ocean of information flowed into me as I settled back to sense the ebb and flow of anything to do with Atopia.

I relaxed into our new self, letting Nancy diffuse us out. With each breath, I kept increasing the pace of quickening, pushing our hived mind faster and further, stretching ever outward. With a final deep breath, we breached an invisible wall somewhere in the universal consciousness.

Time stopped, ceasing to exist.

We became the alpha, the omega, and everything else in between.

24

Identity: Jimmy Scadden

This had better work.

Dragging a live fusion reactor with a million lives aboard through the center of two converging hurricanes was enough to make anyone nervous.

But even with the pressure mounting, my mind was extraordinarily clear. It rang crisply with purpose and energy.

I'd never felt better in my life.

Kesselring had given me tactical command of the operation. My primary subjective was now floating up at the edge of space, watching overlays of the constantly updated simulations. Far below me, the storms were grinding into each other. From this distance, everything looked like it was moving in calm, orderly slow motion, but the violence at sea level was astounding. Already, most of Atopia's forests had been destroyed.

I was using Samson as my primary media interface as we worked to downplay the situation. The questions and inquiries we were getting were unusually low in volume, but I didn't have the time to investigate. Either we were doing an awfully good job at containing the situation media-wise, or something else was going on, but more important things had my attention.

Since the Infinixx incident, Kesselring had removed Patricia from the media circuit. Her association with Nancy was too much of a distraction. I don't think Kesselring trusted her anymore, but then again, he didn't need her anymore either.

The original emotion-driven media campaign had been centered on confidence and trust in our bid to win regulatory approval. The hard work of gaining the trust of experts and governments was now complete—Atopia had passed clinical trial certifications in all major jurisdictions.

What was left was to simply inspire in the masses a desire pssi for themselves. Dr. Granger had taken over the media messaging, and we began delivering more elevating pitches. It was devoid of any real *content* when looked at in detail, but nobody did that anymore. Dr. Granger started using me—young and handsome in my crisp ADF Whites—in the media campaigns instead of Patricia, a poster child for Atopia and the future to come.

I was becoming a celebrity.

Celebrity or not, the Americans were screaming at us to stay away from shallow coastal waters. As we entered their territorial waters, they'd scrambled to muster their defensive systems. Squadrons of aging F-35s and swarms of aerial drones now circled Atopia. From their base in San Diego, US naval forces had surrounded us and were hanging back at the edges of the storms. We didn't have the maneuvering speed of a regular ship; if we had, we wouldn't have been stuck.

Several of my splinters were overseeing the constant chatter with the American security forces and other floating platforms and seasteads, but again, these were strangely subdued.

We'd just received confirmation of authorization from the American military to power-up our weapons systems. There was barely an argument. I put it down to their trust in our program, as well as the close relations I'd built up through Rick with General McInnis.

Despite the awesome power in the slingshot batteries, we only had a narrow window of opportunity execute my plan. If we slipped by even a few seconds, we could be scooped up into one or the other of the storms and mercilessly thrashed against the coast. As a precaution, we were going to power-up every other weapons system we had, including the mass driver and rail guns, just in case we needed to throw more at it.

The point of no return was fast approaching. I was already jacked up, quickening my mind as I reached outward into the hyperspaces around Atopia, but I needed to be at the top of my game. I let my adrenal glands squeeze off some more cortisol and adrenalin into my bloodstream and immediately felt my phantoms begin to jitter ever so slightly, my blood pressure rising and cheeks flushing.

25

Identity: Bobby Baxter

Our minds flooded with millions of impressions and ideas, experiences and worlds. Slowly, a thought began to build, a hint of something that didn't fit.

A vision of my brother Dean and me from when we were kids floated into my mind. We'd always been pushing our limits, testing the boundaries of our parents' patience, and one day we'd decided that we were going to sail over a thousand miles through the open ocean to America, all by ourselves.

We were barely ten at the time.

After weeks of secret planning, we snuck off, hiding our tracks. We almost drove our parents sick with worry when they discovered us missing. We would have made it, except that halfway there, after a week at sea, our smarticle reserves had begun to deplete. Physically we were perfectly healthy, and the weather had been good, but the itchy, desperate feeling of our smarticle supply running low had convinced us to turn around.

My mind hovered over the minds of the million Atopians packed belowdecks awaiting the fast-approaching hurricanes. Thousands of tourists shipped off in a matter of hours when the evacuation order came, yet nearly none of the native Atopians had opted to leave. Even in the face of death they stayed, wrapped in the warm embrace of pssi.

They were afraid, but not of death, and the thought began to more fully form itself.

It was so obvious that it was shocking, and yet so close that it was impossible to see the forest for the trees. More to the point: none of the trees wanted to see the forest.

I shot up out of the water. "Sid, I know what's going on!"

Snapping back into my body, I began collapsing the millions of nodes of my collective mind with Nancy. Pulling her out of the water with me, she gasped as our nervous systems tore apart, her breath hard and ragged. She gripped me tightly.

"And?!" yelled Sid. The gang was still sitting around the tub.

"Come on, out with it," Vicious urged.

I put out a hand. "I need to talk to Patricia first. It doesn't make sense. Or maybe it does. I thought I knew her better."

Wide-eyed, they stared at me in disbelief. Giving Nancy a kiss, I immediately flitted out, sending a high-priority request into Patricia's networks.

What was she thinking?

Patricia accepted my ping on the first bounce, immediately opening her sensory channels to me. I appeared in her private wood-paneled office, sitting in one of her attending chairs. She sat across from me behind her desk, looking as if she'd been expecting me.

I just blurted it out. "I know what you're doing!" It was fool-hardy, perhaps even dangerous, to drop a bomb like this, but I felt like I knew Patricia. This made it all the more perplexing. "You're trying to kill Vince," I added breathlessly. "The pssi weapons pro-grams, I know about all of it. Are you behind all these disappear-ances? Did you steal Willy's body? Sabotage Infinixx? Why are you doing this?"

She sighed and tipped her cigarette into a crystal ashtray. "I had nothing to do with Willy, or the disappearances," she said. "And certainly nothing to do with what happened to Infinixx."

"So you're denying it?" I had evidence of what she'd been up to. "You're not trying to kill Vince?"

Finishing her cigarette, she butted it out and took a deep breath. "Not trying to kill Vince, no. Just keeping him occupied."

I stared at her in disbelief.

"I do want to say," she continued, "what happened with your brother, I was against that, but it was what your family wanted at the time, what *you* wanted at the time." Now she took a sip from her never-ending scotch. "Of course, Granger snapped it up as yet another way pssi could remove unhappiness."

"That was a real killer application, all right," I shot back. "Why are you doing this?"

She smiled thinly. "Since you came to me, why don't you tell me what *this* is?"

"What this is?" I gaped. "Hooking the world on virtual crack, that's what *this* is!"

26

Identity: Patricia Killiam

Silence hung in the air as I waited for Bob to calm down.

"You're right. Pssi can be very addictive in an uncontrolled environment," I admitted, taking another sip from my drink. "But it leaves the body very healthy—pssi users will live immensely long lives."

"Keeping them alive to suck out as much money as possible, right?"

It was surprising that he had managed to discover the pssi weapons programs. *I* hadn't even known about it until recently, one of the things Kesselring was hiding from me. I'd only just found out through Sintil8.

Bob gestured angrily. "People directly stimulating their pleasure centers, ramping up their dopamine output, plugging themselves into pleasure broadcasts. *Of course* it's addictive."

"Quite frankly, I'm surprised at your sudden prudishness," I replied. "As far as I can remember, you made the most of all that yourself."

"That's not the issue. The problem is that you're *hiding* how addictive it is."

"Granger found ways to short circuit the addiction pathways—"

"Sure you have," he sneered. "I bet that'll work great, and I'll bet you'll charge a nice fee for it."

I sighed. "I know how it must seem, but we needed to get regulatory approval as quickly as possible. We couldn't afford to let the process get bogged down."

"So it was all about getting to market faster?"

I nodded my head slowly. "Basically, yes."

"Encouraging people to have synthetic babies, living in fantasy worlds," he continued furiously, gaining steam. "If not that, then they're emo-porners or soapstim junkies, living lives as parasitic reality vampires. Anything to get them hooked on your virtual dope?"

Bob wasn't the only one who was upset. I was angry, too. While I was responsible for setting this thing in motion, once it got going, I'd been forced to accept a lot of things I wasn't comfortable with. The synthetic babies, the proxxids, had been one of Granger's ideas, central to the program for reducing birth rates. While that original idea was good, what they ended up allowing people to use the proxxids for was disgusting. I'd never been comfortable with this, or many other things.

My own anger made me defensive.

"Fantasy worlds? Are they really, Bob?" I lashed out. "You have your own dimstim—a very popular one—and emo-porning is not something I condone. Anyway, since when has people wasting their lives on reality programming been an issue?"

"That's not the point. You've set all this up to turn the entire *world* into your *junkie!*" His eyes burned into me. "You're up on stage every day, touting the benefits of pssi—going green, boosting work productivity, free and limitless travel, living forever—and you've got Nancy out there hyping it, too! How much does she know, I wonder?"

He held his arms wide. "The great Patricia Killiam, godmother of all synthetic reality, globally renowned and trusted...In the end, nothing but a drug pusher."

He glared at me.

"What you're saying is true," I observed quietly, "but the benefits *are* real as well."

"The first dose is free, but then you start paying. Isn't that the plan? You're giving it away for free for the first few months?"

"That is the plan," I admitted, nodding my head in resignation. "You might understand *what* we're doing, but you don't understand *why*."

"Oh, I understand," he countered. "Money, power—the world is going to hell in a handbasket, and you're the vultures picking over its bones."

I let his statement sit for a few seconds. "The world *is* going to hell in a handbasket, as you say, but I'm not sure you understand the extent of it. Come with me, I need to show you something."

He scowled.

"Please." I nudged him with my phantoms.

Grudgingly, he released control to me, and I pulled us through inner space to appear on a city street. Not just a city street, but one that was still charred from some cataclysmic event that had incinerated the place. Bodies were strewn everywhere, blackened flesh and bone exposed through shredded clothing.

"Look around," I said. "This is the future without pssi."

He was unimpressed. Daily images of the horrors of the Weather Wars had desensitized everyone. "So you plan to stop war with pssi?"

"We can't stop it directly, but we might be able to remove the root cause."

I pulled our projection viewpoint into space, far above the Earth, and we watched as small bursts of light erupted and sent tiny shockwaves across its surface. "You're watching a full-scale nuclear war in progress. This is representative of many phutures for the human race."

"But this is just one phuture."

I shifted the viewpoint back, bringing into scope thousands, and then millions, of alternate future Earths, all burning under some apocalyptic scourge.

"It's possible to navigate the fate of one individual," I explained, "but the combined fate of billions gains momentum like a supertanker, and at a certain point you can't stop it anymore. With more than ten billion people on the planet, and all of them craving material luxury, there just aren't enough resources to sustain it all, so we fight over what's left."

"So it all ends in apocalypse?" He frowned. "I find that hard to believe."

"No, you're absolutely right."

I spun our viewpoint even further back, splintering billions of future worlds into Bob's sensory frames. "In most scenarios, in almost all of them, we manage to avoid full-blown Armageddon."

But apocalypse wasn't the worst fate for humanity. A quick end would be a blessing when faced with the majority of outcomes—a slow, downward grind over decades—shifting populations as the earth continued to heat, ecosystems collapsing, famine, pestilence, and an unending series of wars and genocides.

Over the next fifty years, the human population was going to drop from ten billion to just a few. It had already started to happen, the world population was already dropping fast; the Weather Wars were just the beginning. Billions of people were going to suffer and die horribly.

Bob's networks assimilated the data sets I sent to him. "But surely," he said quietly, "there must be something we could do?"

I shook my head. "I was part of the team that created the first *Club of Rome* simulations in the mid-1970s. We've been able to see this coming for a long time.

I waited while Bob took it all in.

"Not that we didn't try," I sighed. "The same phuture-spoofing technology we have hunting Vince down was one that I developed to try and nudge the timeline back and forth."

"So you've been trying to manipulate the world?" said Bob, but he wasn't angry anymore.

"But too little, too late. As we built Atopia, we tried countless combinations of events. In the end, no matter which way we twisted or turned, eventually billions of humans would perish in order for the planet to rebalance itself. There is no soft landing for the human population. Or at least, the soft landings that existed would have required threading the eye of a needle."

I paused.

"The only way to avoid this fate required a massive and drastic reduction in global material consumption. We needed to send most of the world's population off into synthetic reality, almost like a virtual coma, so that their material consumption in the 'real' world would drop to nearly zero. And we had to do it quickly. Fertility rates need to plummet. When we understood this, the fledgling pssi program transformed itself from simply a commercial endeavor into a project of destiny."

I'd returned us back to my office now. Bob sat back in the chair, stunned.

"But we had to hide what we were doing to keep stability along the main timeline," I added. "Otherwise, everyone would have tried to stop us."

"Don't tell me you were the only ones who could see this."

"Of course not," I sighed. "Governments have been using futuring, of one sort or another, for a long time, but they use it to plot paths forward that maximize their own benefit. A giant game of prisoners' dilemma gone wrong."

"And here you have the magical solution that just *coincidentally* maximizes your own benefit? You want me to believe that Kesselring and Granger are just in this to save the planet?"

"Sometimes deals need to be made for the common good."

"What about the UN?"

"International agencies have been preaching disaster for the last hundred years. Nobody's listening."

A pause while we considered each other.

"These things happened in parallel, Bob, you have to understand. As our alternate possible phutures collapsed, we were running the clinical trials. It became obvious we would need to suppress some of the results on addiction to keep on track with regulatory approval."

"Don't you think it's wrong to lie to everyone?"

I laughed. The sound was sharp and bitter. "We didn't *lie* to anyone. We just didn't reveal the *full* truth. People have an amazing capacity for believing what they want to believe while ignoring the obvious."

"So the plan is to hook billions of people on pssi, with *you* as the only supplier."

I was tired of defending myself.

"We're just giving people what they want, aren't we? People have always wanted to work less, to travel more, to fuck someone new and exciting every day." I rolled my eyes. "We're giving them exactly what they've always wanted, the *unlimited* ability to do *anything*, have *everything*, and to be healthier and live longer while doing it."

Bob stared at me in stony silence.

"Do people really want to make the world a better place?" I asked. "Or do they just want to make a better place for themselves within it? Almost everything humans do is self-serving in the end."

"I thought you taught us," objected Bob, "that humans were successful because we developed an evolutionary instinct for trust that outstripped our selfishness?"

"People have a responsibility to find their own happiness, don't they? Life only has the meaning that you give it, *right* Bob?" I snapped, knowing this was his own personal mantra. "We're just giving people the tools to find their own happiness, in whatever way they choose, and in the process saving untold billions of lives. You tell me, what was the right thing to do?"

"Now you sound like Dr. Granger."

I rubbed the bridge of my nose, slowly. I was getting a headache. "If Atopia is destroyed, and the release of pssi stopped, billions will die."

27

Identity: Jimmy Scadden

The moment of truth had arrived.

In the middle of ADF Command, we were watching projections of the storms overlaid with a glowing array of plotted future paths of Atopia through them. The phutures were stabilizing as we approached time-zero. Everything was coming together, and I readied to power up our weapons systems.

"Thanks for everything," said Rick as we waited in the final moments. "Whatever happens, I wanted to thank you for trying to help with Cindy."

I looked at him. How quickly our roles had reversed. He was pathetic. I could smell the booze from here. "Of course, Commander. We'll find her, get her out somehow."

He nodded, his bloodshot eyes on mine for a moment. "You ready for this?"

"I am."

The high-altitude displays had a hypnotic effect. They centered on the pulsing orb of Atopia, highlighted near the convergence point of the storms. We only had a window of a few minutes to get it right.

The room went deathly quiet as the image of the storm systems engulfed us. They were all waiting on me. I looked up at Kesselring,

Rick, and then at Marie. Patricia hadn't shown up in person, but I knew she was watching through her proxxi.

"On my command, enable the weapons systems," I instructed, waiting, feeling for just the right moment as I fed the information flowing in through my extrasensory splinter network. I could feel the winds ripping at the surface of Atopia, her forests heaving and tearing, the waves pounding against her hull.

"On my mark." I raised my hand. "Five...four...three...."

Everyone held a collective breath.

I waited.

Something held me back—something inside me.

Someone inside me.

I hesitated, trying to understand what was going on. Interminable seconds ticked by. Then—I understood. It was sitting there in front of me, all the time, but I hadn't been able to see it.

Until now.

"For God's sake, Jimmy!" screamed Kesselring. "What the hell are you waiting for?"

28

Identity: Patricia Killiam

"What is he doing?"

Bob stopped pacing and looked at me. He didn't have access to Command and couldn't see what I saw now. Jimmy stood motionless as critical seconds slipped by. We all watched in disbelief while Kesselring roared at him in panic.

"Bob, I need to go," I said without further explanation, leaving behind a thin splinter while I snapped my main subjective into Marie's body at Command.

Everyone there was frozen, all except for Kesselring. He'd crossed the room and was standing in front of Jimmy, holding his shoulders and shaking him. Jimmy didn't even look like he was there.

I strode over and pulled Kesselring away. The window of opportunity was closing quickly.

"Jimmy!" I yelled. At that moment, his face came back to life, and his eyes flashed as he turned to look at me.

What he said next stunned us even more.

"Power down all weapons immediately!" he ordered. "And shut down the propulsion systems!"

"Belay that!" I yelled, at the same time disabling the technicians' authorizations.

Reaching into the Command network with my phantoms, I tried to gain control of the systems as he blocked them from me. My mind raced. Somehow, the Terra Novans had gotten to him. We'd given enormous power to Jimmy for this operation, putting all our eggs in one basket.

So this was their plan.

Furiously, my mind splintered into hundreds of shards, shooting them into Jimmy's command-and-control structures in the multiverse worlds that spread out from Command.

Kesselring tried helping me, but he hadn't the power in these worlds that I had.

Desperately, I quickened my mind, launching thousands, and then millions, of attacks and feints and counterattacks at his cyber-defenses, projecting millisecond phutures as I tried to find a weakness to exploit.

The milliseconds became seconds, the window to saving Atopia closing.

"Stop this!" I screamed at him.

"Stand down, Patricia, I'm warning you!" he yelled back.

Desperately we grappled with each other, and then . . . .

Everything went white in a blinding flash of pain.

As my mind reassembled itself and my senses and metasenses slowly reintegrated, the world came back into focus. My ears were ringing, and I was sitting on the floor. Everyone in the room was stunned.

What the hell was that?

Jimmy looked at me calmly.

The point of no return had passed. Atopia was sitting defenseless amid the storms. We would be destroyed.

"Do not touch anything," said Jimmy finally. "Everything is under control."

29

Identity: Bobby Baxter

The world stood transfixed by the scene.

I was still sitting in Patricia's office, but Jimmy had begun broadcasting the events from Command live and direct into the world's media channels for everyone to see. An audience of billions was tuned-in to witness the destruction of Atopia, but not in the way we'd expected.

Jimmy stood tall, his image hanging over a bewildered and powerless Patricia Killiam on countless holoscreens and lens displays throughout the world.

"General McInnis," he called out, "we've powered down all systems, and we will sequence down our fusion core at your request. I've opened all command-and-control functions to you. Please acknowledge."

A moment of silence before General McInnis' voice responded, "Goddamn boy, acknowledged. What the hell?"

"Please, General. Please stand down."

The general's image appeared in Command. He stood there, looking around at everyone is disbelief. "You kids sure have some explaining to do."

One by one, surprised and shocked expressions clicked through the faces in Command. And then it dawned on me, too.

The storms were gone.

I spun out from Patricia's office, clicking into my splinters arrayed out around Atopia. They all saw the same thing—blue skies, calm seas, and the coast of America sitting serenely on the horizon. The American drones were buzzing angrily in the skies, watching us carefully as Navy destroyers ringed us further out, their weapons armed and pointing at us.

"We were just about to blow Atopia back into the Stone Age," said the general.

It all became clear.

As Jimmy released information, the mediaworlds began to buzz, and then roar, with stories. The citizens of Atopia had been infected with a group-synthesizing reality skin.

We'd driven Atopia into the coast of America, trying to save ourselves from nonexistent storms projected from an infected reality skin while the rest of the world had watched in puzzlement and amazement.

Atopia had, at first, inexplicably breached American territorial waters, and then began furiously shipping off non-nationals via its passenger cannon. Amid confusing and contradictory reports, Atopia stowed and locked itself down, cut off all communications, and started powering up its fearsome weapons systems.

America had no choice but to prepare to defend itself.

If we'd powered up the slingshot and mass driver, General McInnis had his finger on the trigger to unleash a hailstorm of tactical nuclear weapons to destroy us, an attack that even our automated systems couldn't have repelled.

Patricia rematerialized in her office with me. She looked grim.

My anger had deflated, I was stunned. "Thank God, Jimmy figured it out."

"Don't thank God," said Patricia quietly. "There's something I wanted to talk to you about, but I wasn't sure until now." She looked at me with weary eyes. "I need you to do something for me."

I waited.

"I need you to leave Atopia as soon as they open up the surface, and take Sid, Willy, Brigitte, and *please* take Nancy away from here."

"Why?" What could she possibly need us to leave for? I'd never even considered leaving Atopia before, except for that one time I'd gone sailing with my brother. It was all I'd ever known. Even the thought of leaving made my skin crawl.

"I can't explain right now, but I need you to trust me."

Even if I wasn't angry anymore, my trust in her was almost completely gone. "Give me one good reason...."

"For one thing," she said with effort, "Willy's connection here through Terra Nova will almost certainly be revoked now that Jimmy has instituted martial law. He'll be exiled. Do you want him to go alone?"

Jimmy had mentioned it, but I hadn't considered it a real possibility.

"I have a feeling that both *Willy* and *Sid* will be implicated in what has happened," she continued. "As soon as the surface opens, I need you to get away from Atopia."

Patricia looked tired beyond comprehension.

"Please take Nancy from here," she added. "And apologize to Vince for me—I couldn't get Kesselring to remove the system we have chasing him."

I nodded.

She looked down, her hands shaking, and then closed the connection to her office.

Snapping back into my body, I found myself sitting with Nancy and Sid and the rest of our gang in the dimly lit cafeteria. Robert had taken my body out of the water, and while we sat together, everyone was splintered-out, watching the frenzy in the mediaworlds. They were transfixed by the unfolding media storm.

Only Jimmy had been able to see it. Images of him, *the savior*, were featured on the covers of magazines and billboards, instantly appearing in millions of metaworlds. Synthetic forensic intelligences tore backward through the path of the reality-virus, reverse hacking toward its origin, and the media began buzzing about Terra Nova unleashing the virus to destroy Atopia.

Stories began to emerge about the futures of world destruction that Patricia had been hiding, how the Atopian pssi program was designed as the solution to save us, and how Terra Nova had attempted to stop it for their own profit. Information about the coming phuture apocalypse gained ground.

There were even reports about Patricia hiding some of the addictive effects of pssi and how there were ways to control them. Smiling images of Dr. Hal Granger began appearing, explaining how he'd short-circuited the addiction pathways to ensure there was no danger anymore.

The image of Patricia struggling to force Jimmy to carry out the launch remained in the center of it all. Jimmy had managed to save the world, and his grateful audience was spellbound.

"Patricia wants us all to leave," was all I said upon my return to the gang.

Everyone turned toward me in shock as parts of their minds disengaged from the media frenzy to better comprehend what I was saying. I left a splinter to explain what had happened while I flitted off to the surface to see what the damage had been to our habitat, to see if there was anything I could do, and more importantly, to put my own thoughts in order.

30

Identity: Patricia Killiam

"They say no publicity is bad publicity," laughed Kesselring, standing uncomfortably in my office, "but how on Earth did you let that viral skin get past you?"

I stared at him and took a drag from my cigarette.

"You're our chief scientist," he continued. "You must understand how this looks. The blame for hiding any clinical trial data has to come down on your shoulders."

So I'm the scapegoat.

Jimmy and Kesselring had preempted my plan to release the hidden addiction data. By coming clean right at the moment when Jimmy had solved the storm mystery, and laying the blame on my doorstep at the same time as exposing the apocalyptic phuture-cast data, they'd neatly jiu-jitsued themselves into the position of liberator while simultaneously thrusting the pssi program into the global mind.

Of course, they had to sacrifice me in the process.

"You can't buy advertising like that," I replied, the words sour in my mouth. "Looks like you don't need me anymore."

I was tired beyond belief after the showdown with Jimmy. He'd used some sort of pssi-weapon to stun me into submission, a part of the weapons program Kesselring had been hiding. I'd felt it once before, long ago when Jimmy was exposed at Nancy's thirteenth birthday party, but he was infinitely more powerful now.

"There will always be a place for you here, Patricia."

Patronizing bastard.

"What's happening then?" I asked wearily.

"Jimmy added an override to the pssi network to stop something like this from ever happening again."

While I felt defeated, he looked elated.

"The media attention has boosted demand for the launch. We've already begun private distribution of smarticles into some business ecospheres."

There was nothing I could say, nothing I could do anymore. Kesselring was doomed, but there was no way I could help him. I finally understood what the Terra Novans were trying to stop, but now it was too late.

I've created a monster I love.

31

Identity: Jimmy Scadden

I'd stolen off to the surface to relax a little, to try to escape the madness of the world media. Surface access had only just been reopened, and with all the tourists gone, nobody else had come above yet. The beach was quiet.

The sun was setting through low-hanging clouds on the horizon, lighting them up in glowing oranges and pinks. I sat by myself under some squat palms. A pleasant breeze blew in off the ocean, and pelicans swept in on curling waves. I sighed, feeling my mind calm and focus itself. Susie understood more about the nature of pain and suffering than anyone, even me, and she was truly helping me. I'd never felt better.

What a beautiful way to end the day.

After I'd been staring at the waves for a few minutes, Bob appeared from the forest to my left, his projection walking along the beach, alone, deep in thought. He nearly went right past before he spotted me and stopped.

"Jimmy. Unbelievable. You saved us—maybe you saved the whole world."

Bob reached out to shake my hand, and I took his in mine and held it.

"Wasn't Susie just up here with you?" he asked, looking around.

"She was, but she had to go somewhere."

Bob smiled. He looked into the sunset, watching a few pelicans as they used their ground-effect aerodynamics to sweep in ahead of the waves, unseen forces propelling them effortlessly through space.

"Bob, I've got a slightly oddball question for you."

"Shoot."

"If you had to sacrifice your soul to save someone or something, what would that be for you?"

Bob looked at me quizzically. "Well, for love—for Nancy, I guess."

"That's what I thought...well, anyway, that's nice to hear."

"Still going to take me up on that surfing lesson, big shot that you are now?"

"Sure, maybe we'll do a lesson soon." I let go of his hand. "See you later."

32

Identity: Bobby Baxter

"See you later, Jimmy."

I stood fixed, still feeling the warmth of Jimmy's hand as I watched him step away, but he stopped and turned to look at me. Something was weighing on his mind.

"You were the only person who was ever nice to me," he said after a pause. "I really appreciated that."

"I love you, Jim," I said simply. "We're brothers, aren't we? I'll always stick up for you, no matter what."

"You really mean that?" Jimmy looked like he was about to cry.

"Of course."

He looked uncertain. "I think you and your friends should leave Atopia."

In my whole life nobody had ever mentioned leaving Atopia for anything. *Now two people on the same day?* A sense of dread filled me.

"Why?"

Jimmy pressed his lips tightly together. "I'm just saying, I think it might be a good idea, and the sooner, the better."

With that, he turned away and walked into the darkness.

33

Identity: Jimmy Scadden

As I walked away from Bob and into the dark underbrush, I became aware of someone walking beside me, someone new, but someone at the same time intimately familiar.

"Why did you do that?" the apparition asked.

"Do what?" I didn't even think to ask who had appeared beside me.

"Why did you warn Bob," it responded. "I think we need to have a talk, you and I."

The undergrowth around me gave way to a voluminous, brightly lit corridor. No, more than a corridor. It was a long set of huge rooms connected by large, square archways, and I was sitting in the middle room with the rest stretching off to both sides in the distance.

I was perched on a white wooden chair.

Intricate, sky-blue frescos of angels and cherubs adorned the twenty-foot ceilings that were bordered by elaborate gold carvings. Ornate, richly decorated furniture was strewn about topsy-turvy, and everywhere was littered with broken bottles, golden goblets, and inert bodies.

Dark-framed oil paintings of uniformed men on horseback directing battles hung across one set of walls; the other featured floor-to-ceiling leaded-glass windows that looked out onto an endless manicured garden beyond. The garden was situated around a long reflecting pool. Sunlight streamed in through the windows from between heavy purple velvet drapes tied back with gold sashes.

The place stank of urine, and, as if on cue, one of the slumberers came to life, stumbled to his feet, and shuffled to the nearest corner,, where he began pissing over one of his fellow revelers. "Sorry for the mess," said my apparition, now in solid form, as he stretched out before me on a chaise lounge. "We had a bit of a party here today."

He adjusted the frilly white cuffs of his tunic and then his blond wig, which fell in tight curls to frame his white-painted face and bright, red-painted lips. Leaning forward, he smoothed out a wrinkle in his tight black britches and looked up to smile at me self-consciously.

His heavy eyeliner had smudged, making him look comical in a threatening sort of way, and his eyes shone brightly—my eyes.

"Come now, this isn't that much of a surprise is it?"

I felt uneasy. Was this some splinter or sub-proxxi gone wrong? The party guest finished pissing and turned toward us, blearily rubbing his eyes, which then widened.

"The dauphin!" he said, barely audibly. He was clearly excited, looking at me.

"What do you want?" I asked. This was all more familiar than I cared to admit.

"Ahh," said my doppelganger, "it is not what I want, brother, but, rather, what *we* want. You and I, Jimmy. And by the way, call me James."

He affected a tiny bow for my benefit. Several of the guests began to rouse themselves, encouraged by the first, who was whispering at them urgently. The air filled with the sounds of quiet sounds of clinking bottles and shifting bodies.

"Come now, Jimmy," scolded James, his brow furrowing. "Do you really think your rise through the ranks to a position of such power so quickly was all just a happy coincidence?"

He smiled widely, revealing a mouthful of yellowing teeth and large, sharp canines below his glittering black eyes. The waxy makeup on his face cracked as he smiled, and he cocked his head playfully.

"The time for hiding is finished," he continued, shaking his head and sighing. "We are not children, not anymore. The world needs us now."

Several of the guests were sitting and watching us hungrily from nearby. Samson was here now, watching me from a corner in the distance. I began to recognize some of the faces around me, the childhood playmates I had invented to keep me safe, to keep me company, hidden away in my secret spaces when I was a child.

"You always knew I was in here, Jimmy," he said looking toward Samson, who acknowledged him with a small nod. "Most people with our, ah, condition, don't get to meet their other selves—just one more of the wonders of pssi."

James smiled again. "We've been protecting you for a long time now." He extended a hand to sweep past the assembled, misshapen guests. They were all wide awake and encircling us ever closer. "Your children await you."

They were near now, and James reached out to touch one of them who had sat down next to him, affectionately placing a hand on its head.

"Has your mind been clear lately?" questioned James, smiling as he ruffled the hair of his favorite before looking back to me expectantly.

"As a matter of fact, *yes*," I had to admit, feeling the hot breath of the creatures behind me. "Over the past few years, my mind has been gaining a certain clarity that...."

"That what? That escaped you before? The mind is cleansed with pain, isn't that right, Jimmy?"

As he said this, the eyes of the assembled flashed, and they leaned in even closer.

James splintered us off into a sensory imprint of the private world that I'd burned so long ago, after Nancy's birthday party. He was feeding the pain of the writhing creatures pinned to the walls— my pleasure centers.

I shivered and gasped.

"Nice, isn't it?" said James, smiling. "But we aren't children anymore."

Another splinter overlaid a new scene, a man we once knew growing up, Steve. He'd worked in the aquaponics group with my dad. An image flickered through my memory of him playing privately with proxxids together with my dad after work.

In the world James had splintered me into, Steve was desperately groping through a dark tangle of underbrush. Someone was chasing him. Suddenly a flash of metal tore into him, and he screamed, terrified, as his attacker stabbed him again and again. His blaze of pain coursed through my system like rain soothing a parched desert plain.

"Not just pain," explained James, "but through the careful research of our friend Dr. Granger we can recognize the direct nerve imprints of fear, hopelessness, guilt—hundreds of layers of desperate emotions—and mix these into a symphony of sorrow."

He was on his feet now, surrounded by our minions, holding a claret jug of dark red wine in one hand and a large crystal goblet in the other.

"Ah, the sweet melody of loneliness," he sang out, and another splinter called up Olympia Onassis, wandering desperately. Her loneliness resonated through my auditory channels, merging into a gentle, fearful caress across my skin.

"The taste of heartache," James added, and an image of Cindy Strong filled another splinter as she stood over the grave of Little Ricky. I could taste her misery filling my mouth, an aching sweetness tinged with hints of regret.

"And the soft caress of hopelessness and despair," he laughed. Dr. Granger hung in a metaworld between us, sitting with a doctor and looking down at a medical diagnosis of some painful, terminal disease, his fear of the world forgetting him coursing into our veins like a melody.

"And pain, of course pain," said James.

A hundred other worlds splintered into my sensory system, gorging it with terror and hurt and searing pain, as I watched people burning and butchered in their own private hells. I gasped, my body wracking itself in pleasure as I looked up at James, wiping tears from my eyes.

One by one, I could see how James had captured each one of these souls, ferreting out their needs until they voluntarily ceded control to him, to *us*. At the apex of it all was Susie, all of the pain and suffering channeled through her neural system. She had borne the pain of the world, and now she would bear *this* pain for *our* world.

"We give people what they want," James said, his yellow fangs creeping at the edges of his smile. "And, well, they give us what we want in return. It's a fair bargain, no?"

I nodded, understanding, my body and mind singing with energy.

"With root control, we have access to all their memories, know their every hope and darkest fear, and we can synthesize worlds to play all these out, to suit our whims, our needs."

Music played, and the creatures around us began to sway and dance, slowly working themselves into a frenzy. The music quickened with my mind, and I soaked in the sensation of my body connecting into the hundreds of metaworlds holding our trapped subjects, their terror coursing through me. James offered me a glass of wine, and I took it, in my excitement splashing my ADF Whites with bright, bloody splotches.

"Pain and fear cleanse the mind, Jimmy," said James, taking back the empty glass, "and we need your mind as clear as possible for what is to come."

34

Identity: Patricia Killiam

"I think the clinical diagnosis would be sadistic sociopath with dissociative identity disorder," said Marie.

I looked up from my desk at her and nodded. We'd managed to piece together what was happening, and it was terrifying.

"It's not what I think you need to think about now," she added. "I'll pass this onto Bob."

Images of Shiva, the great destroyer and creator, floated into my mind. I closed my eyes and took a deep breath. Jimmy was good at hiding his tracks. We had only the one incident at Nancy's birthday party as a window into his mind, and even that was fleeting. Fleeting, but infinitely disturbing, and I'd made things worse.

Like a tick in a bear's fur, he'd burrowed his way into the deepest reaches of the program. He'd pushed all my buttons to get what he wanted, even as a child. More of the problem was that even then, it didn't all add up.

"Do you think he was really responsible for the disappearances of Susie and Cynthia?" I asked Marie. It was obvious now that he was behind what had happened to Cindy Strong and Olympia Onassis, but in those cases he had a strategic goal. In most of the other disappearances, we didn't understand what there was to gain.

"Why would he attract attention to himself like that? With people so close to him?"

"Perhaps he's unaware of the other parts of himself," Marie speculated. "It's the only way he could have passed all our psych tests, but it's hard to say. Having pssi installed in the developing brain of an unstable sociopathic mind has created something... *new*, I guess."

Deception was a cognitively demanding activity that left telltale signatures no matter how good the liar. By truly deceiving yourself, on the other hand, you could escape detection by others, but with the risk of falling out of touch with reality yourself—this was something we'd compounded with pssi.

The bigger the neocortex and the higher the intelligence, the more an organism tended to lie to itself and others, and Jimmy was as smart an organism as I'd ever come across. I wasn't sure it was accurate to say he was even human anymore.

Whatever he'd become, he was now the master of deception.

"We don't have any evidence that his parents ever did anything to him. Just rumors that seem to originate with him," said Marie. "I think he constructed a fantasy world about his own abuse to justify his behavior."

"Dissociative personality disorder is almost always the result of abuse as a child. If his parents didn't abuse him, then who did?"

Marie stared at me and shook her head.

"If he's managed to fool himself," I sighed, "then he's certainly managed to fool us."

I wondered about all the ways I'd been fooling *myself* to arrive at this point.

In my decades of research developing synthetic intelligence, I'd developed statistical models of past human civilizations that had revealed a strong correlation between the self-deceptive characteristics of a people and the worst atrocities that group would commit. Pssi had heightened human capacity in many ways, but it had increased the ability to fool ourselves the most—and we were about to unleash it on humanity under the guise of its savior.

The road to hell really *was* paved with the best of intentions.

All the careful planning to cover every base, to push the future to converge on one stable outcome, it was all slipping away. Then again, control was always an illusion, just another self-deception.

I should have known better.

Which is worse? Allowing billions of people to die, or saving them to live lives of perpetual suffering under the control of a monster?

My monster.

Perhaps it would have been impossible for me to see what was happening, no matter what controls I put in place. He had used my own blind spot, my latent desire for a child, as my life began to slip away from me. I could feel my love for him burn in me, even as I understood the beast I may have created.

I wanted to believe there was something to save.

"Can we remove him from the board somehow? At least get him off the Security Council?" I pondered aloud.

Marie said what I was already thinking. "He's already aligned himself with powerful supporters. And he's become a celebrity in the world media. I'm sure he'd have some nasty surprises up his sleeve if we tried confronting him in the open."

I continued the thought for her, "And if we can't prove anything, it will look like the disgruntled ramblings of a disgraced old woman throwing her last rocks into the glass house."

"Probably better to keep under the radar for now," agreed Marie. "Encouraging the formation of composites should yield some protection from Jimmy."

"Perhaps."

"What about the data from the neutrino telescope?"

I'd kept the POND results absolutely locked down, trying to forget them myself. *Could it be real?*

"Ship that data off from Atopia immediately," I replied. "If there's anything to it, I want it away from here."

If it was true, and not some artifact of the viral infection, my skin crawled thinking of the ways Granger and Kesselring could spin the discovery of extraterrestrial intelligence, or whatever it was that this signal from a parallel universe was coming from.

"Send a report back into the science community, say that it was a failure, and leave the connection key with the package delivered to Bob and Nancy. But only to them."

"I'll take care of it, don't worry."

Looking at Marie, I couldn't believe I felt such affection for a machine, a virtual projection that didn't really exist.

Then again, all our children, biological or not, were created by us, and it wasn't quite accurate to say that Marie didn't exist. I'd never really thought of her as my child before that moment, always as more of a sister. But I had created her. Perhaps she was both.

"You'll communicate everything to them, right? Send Nancy and Bob out to find Willy's body."

"Yes, Patricia...."

"It's just...."

"I know."

Silence descended. My body's systems were on the brink of failure, something I'd been able to see coming for some time.

"Marie, after I'm gone, I want you to continue to, well, to be."

"But proxxies terminate with their owners. That goes against the whole program."

"It's been managed before," I replied, smiling. "Anyway, it's done. I've already made a special provision in my will. There are *some* advantages to being the senior researcher at Cognix."

"Are you sure? This will create precedent."

"Exactly." I smiled. "I think this situation calls for special consideration, and I want you to continue on with the work we've started on the Synthetic Being Charter of Rights. Besides...."

"Besides what?"

I looked at Marie carefully. "Aren't you the least bit worried about ceasing to exist? Doesn't this arrangement strike you as unfair?"

She smiled and gently shook her head. "I could ask you the same thing."

I let out a quiet laugh. I didn't think this old body had any tears left in it, but I guess it still had a few. Wiping them from my face, I felt my papery skin.

So fragile.

"Everything is in order," I said quietly. "I think I'd like this time to myself. Goodbye, Marie, and say goodbye to Nancy for me."

I turned off my pssi for the last time, and my office faded into the muted colors of my real-world living space, a modest apartment near the beaches. It was small, but one of only a handful on the surface of Atopia.

In the end, Jimmy gave me what I'd thought I wanted—for the world to embrace pssi—but he had exacted his price for it. It was clear he'd sabotaged my medical systems. But perhaps leaving this world was a wish I hadn't been able to admit to myself, and he'd simply been the instrument of my desire.

It was time for me to go.

Of all the things that pssi could give us, perhaps the least touted was dignity in death. It was just me, by myself, for perhaps the first time in nearly half a century.

So this is what reality feels like.

I'd forgotten.

Wearily, I lifted my ancient body off the chair that Marie had left it sitting on. I wanted one last look at my tiny garden out back, that little plot of life.

Slowly, limping, I made my way to its neglected grounds. I looked around. Some pots were blown over and everything had a dull gray tint to it in the dim pre-dawn light. I shuffled over to a sun lounger in the back near an old raspberry bush that was nearly as decrepit as I was.

So I won't last to see pssi spread into the world.

It was probably for the best.

I wasn't sure I could keep up with the pace of change anymore, and not sure I wanted to be around, and responsible for, what might be coming.

My own end. I'd always managed to suspend disbelief about it.

Now there was something we all had a talent for.

"Marie," I called out, "I have one last story to tell you."

I couldn't see or feel her anymore, but I knew she was with me. In fact, I knew she would be surrounding and cradling me like a baby right now, and that was a comforting thought. As I began to understand my end was coming, I'd started telling Marie stories of my earlier life, from before the machines had begun to capture our memories and preserve the digital trails of our lives as we blindly forged ahead.

Telling Marie my stories made me feel like a part of me would live on, as well as a part of some of the people in them. I had saved my most important, my most cherished and hidden story, for last.

Tears streamed down my face as I told Marie my most private of memories, unspoken to anyone now living, unspoken even to myself in over a century, of young love gone wrong. It was the story of why I'd never married, of a young airman who'd died in my arms so long ago.

Instead of life and family, I'd focused my mind on finding ways to escape reality, to escape what had happened to me. At least that's what I'd started out doing, as unspoken as it was. In the end, my escape had taken on a life of its own, and my love had, in the end, blinded me.

But now, at my own end of time, I remembered, and I remembered why.

My love, will I find you now?

Wiping away my tears, I was pleased to see that dawn was beginning to break on the horizon. *It's going to be a nice day.* Glancing sideways, I inspected my long-forgotten raspberry bush.

Within its spiny gray branches I was surprised to find, still surviving, one lush red raspberry, standing out in surreal relief from the grayness surrounding it. I leaned over and picked it, rolling it around gently in my fingertips.

I was afraid of letting go, but I was also so tired, and the last of my resistance slipped away. I popped the raspberry into my mouth.

I thought of the billions of humans out there, some asleep, some awake, but most somewhere in between. I thought of the tens of billions of synthetic souls now roaming the multiverse, and the infinite inner-space we had created together, we and the machines.

I wished them all well.

In the early morning glow, a monarch butterfly fluttered and danced its way through the garden where Dr. Killiam lay, finally at peace. The butterfly seemed to consider her for a moment, dancing this way and that above her motionless body, and then fluttered away, gaining altitude.

As it darted back and forth, ever higher, it was joined by a brown butterfly marked with circles on its wings. Joyously, the two touched and danced off into the distance, rising above and away to leave Atopia below.

The first rays of sunlight pierced the horizon, illuminating thin red and gold clouds, high in the aquamarine sky.

A new day was dawning.

EPILOGUE

Identity: Bobby Baxter

Shivering, I pilled my sweater tight around me. San Francisco sure was colder than I'd imagined.

From the vantage point of our camp, across some boulders and a field of grass at the edge of a stand of redwoods, I could dimly make out the top of the Golden Gate Bridge poking out from under a thick blanket of fog rolling into the bay. Night was falling and we'd lit a fire. I extended my hands toward the burning and crackling wood.

So this is what camping is really like. I liked the synthetic version better.

Following encrypted instructions from Marie, we'd gone off the grid as far as possible as quickly as we could manage. The state park above San Francisco was a designated network-free zone, and after collecting up some tents and camping supplies in the city, we'd been dropped off up here. We hiked ourselves to the edge of the forest.

I still couldn't believe Patricia was gone.

Walking around out here, I had the crushing sensation of being blind and deaf and dumb. Being cut off from the dense communication network on Atopia gave me the feeling we'd been transported back into the Dark Ages. My body sang with the urge to drop it all and get back into the warm, comfortable embrace of the pssi on Atopia, but I resisted it as best I could.

Atopia was the only place I'd ever known. I'd taken for granted feeling the steady thrum of information through my metasenses, as easily as I'd assumed my own breath. My phantoms were still there, arrayed around me in empty hyperspaces, stretching out and away from me, but my metasenses were completely numb.

It felt as if most of my body had been amputated.

It was true what they said—the future was already here, just unevenly distributed. I belonged to that future, yet here I was with the rest of humanity. The world, however, was about change, and people could hardly wait. I laughed to myself. They really ought to be more careful what they wished for.

Vince had come with us. He figured whatever Patricia's last instructions were, they might offer some key to his problem. Sid had also come, as well as Brigitte and Willy.

Well, Willy sort of *came.*

Up here in the state park, there was no network connectivity, so we'd had to embed a splinter of him into Brigitte for the trip into the woods. She seemed to enjoy having her own bit of Willy to take everywhere with her, and I doubted he would be getting that splinter back anytime soon.

Martin had elected to stay behind with our parents. All of our proxxi had made the trip as well, embedded as they were in our bodies. So there the nine of us sitting around the campfire—me, Robert, Sid, Vicious, Vince, Hotstuff, Brigitte and her proxxi Bardot, and Willy's slightly confused splinter.

Nancy hadn't come with us, despite my pleading, but this was before we'd learned what Jimmy had become. Jimmy had asked her to stay on a while to help with the investigation and preparations for Patricia's Atopian state funeral, which he had managed to pull off despite the rumors of her working with the Terra Novans. I suppose her gratitude for this kindness in the wake of the scandal left Nancy with some sense of obligation toward him.

She'd insisted she would catch up with us, but it was too late now. A week had gone by since we'd left, and newly passed constitutional changes on Atopia had enabled Jimmy and Rick to maintain its state of emergency, a state of emergency that would never end.

Having barely survived destruction, Atopia's once-cherished civil liberties—which Patricia was no longer there to defend—were quickly and unceremoniously thrown out the window. Almost overnight, Atopia had transformed itself into a police state, and Jimmy was quickly amassing a private psombie army.

In the ensuing investigation, it had been discovered that the viral skin had been vectored from the Terra Novans through Patricia's own specialized pssi system. The best guess was that her old student Mohesha had implanted it. Patricia had gone on to infect everyone she'd come into contact with, and it had then spread quickly into everyone on Atopia. Of course, nearly everyone in our group was implicated in one way or another.

Patricia had encoded Marie onto a miniature data cube and had it smuggled off Atopia right before the lockdown of Jimmy's new police state. We'd picked up the data cube, hidden in what looked like a walking stick, from an antique store in the Haight-Ashbury neighborhood.

After lighting a fire at our campsite, we'd started up a private network to connect us all and awoken Marie. Her ethereal image had risen before us above the fire, wavering in the night air, a ghost that told a truly frightening nighttime tale as we huddled together, explaining the monster that Jimmy had become and the danger we all faced.

I yearned for my lazy days back on the beach.

The good news was that the phutures had stabilized—no apocalyptic wars, at least not in the near future. But pssi wasn't the only game in town, either. A crush of other transformative technologies was crowding the future, and we'd have to wade our way through this brave new world to find Willy's body. No matter what, Willy was our friend, and we had to help him, and somehow it also contained a secret about Jimmy—and this secret was the reason it has disappeared.

The next morning, we sat back around the embers of the fire that we'd resurrected from the night before, grimly sipping mugs of gritty coffee that Vince had made.

"Did you read the news Willy sent in this morning?" he asked as he handed me a cup.

"I did."

Simultaneously with the commercial release of pssi into major metropolitan areas, Cognix had revealed the existence of seven new Atopian-class floating platforms at strategic physical locations around the globe. They must have been under construction for some time. There was was talk Phuture News about giving Atopia a seat on the United Nations Security Council—they wanted to appoint Jimmy.

Along with the coffee, Vince was handing out some sticky buns and granola bars for breakfast. We didn't just need to eat, though. Without a steady supply of smarticles in the air around us, we needed to replenish our bodies' supplies. Smarticles flushed out of the body if they weren't topped up, and we didn't know how secure the old ones were, so Patricia had created her own secret variant for us.

Pulling out the container filled with our new smarticle powder from my backpack, I dipped my finger into it, lifted it to my nose and inhaled—an easy way into the body was through the mucus membranes.

"Can't we just tell people what we know?" mused Vince as he cupped his coffee, blowing the steam off it.

I offered him the bag of powder. "After what's happened, it would look like more Terra Novan interference. Plus, coming from us, it wouldn't exactly look reputable. We need to fly under the radar."

"Aren't we a motley bunch to trust for saving the world?" laughed Sid.

I wasn't in the mood to joke.

"But I suppose it all depends on how you look at it," Sid continued. "Maybe it's not so bad."

"What do you mean?"

"So, you and Nancy together being able to see everything, and you can pull those tricks with water...."

"So?"

Sid grinned. "Don't you get it? You're like some kind of *omniscient being* who *walks on water*, trying to save mankind from suffering a monster."

"I mean, it's all been done before, mate," chipped in Vicious, "and so far so good!"

"Tell me that doesn't sound biblical." Sid smirked and transformed himself into a talking burning bush, sporting two stone tablets with our names inscribed on them.

I snorted. "Very funny."

"And the key to all this is in my body?" said Willy. "Wally must have left us some clues. We just need to look."

The trail to Willy's body began and ended with Sintil8, who had, like us, disappeared off the grid. The thought of tracking down a gangster like Sintil8 frightened me, but then, our choices had boiled down to the lesser of two rather nasty evils. The only clue we had was Sintil8's real name, Sergei Mikhailov, which Patricia had dug up for us.

Clouds of Cognix smarticles released in San Francisco the day before began to float in on the breeze, even up here, and I could feel small channels and rivulets of information begin to flow, connecting me to the multiverse. As refreshing as it felt to my metasenses, it now took on an ominous feel as well.

"Let's get a move on, people," I said as my phantoms shivered. "I think we should stay away from major cities as much as possible."

"That's not where I think I am anyway," added Willy for good measure.

The four of us with physical bodies shouldered our backpacks of gear. I checked around the campsite for anything left behind and kicked some dirt onto the smoldering remains of the fire. Then, sharing nervous grins, we started out on the path that led into the great redwood forest and beyond.

About the Author

Matthew Mather, 2013

After earning a degree in electrical engineering, Matthew Mather started his professional career at the McGill Center for Intelligent Machines. He went on to found one of the world's first tactile feedback companies, which became the world leader in its field, as well as creating an award-winning brain training video game. In between, he's worked on a variety of start-ups, everything from computational nanotechnology to electronic health records, weather prediction systems to genomics, and even social intelligence research. In 2009, he began a different journey, returning to the original inspiration for his technology career—all the long nights spent as a child and teenager reading the great masters of science fiction. He decided to write a sci-fi novel of his own, and the result was *The Atopia Chronicles*. He divides his time between Montreal, Canada, and Charlotte, NC.